A Fate of Flames & Fury

THE OBSIDIAN BLADE SERIES

BOOK TWO

O'JUNEA BROWN

Mom and Dad... I know you refuse to not read my books.

So... the smut in this one is way worse. Let's just not talk about it please.

Love you guys!

For the girls that felt unwanted. For the girls that felt like they didn't fit in. For the girls that felt judged on every little thing they said or did. For the girls that felt less than everyone else. For the girls that didn't realize their worth until a little later in life.

This one is for you.

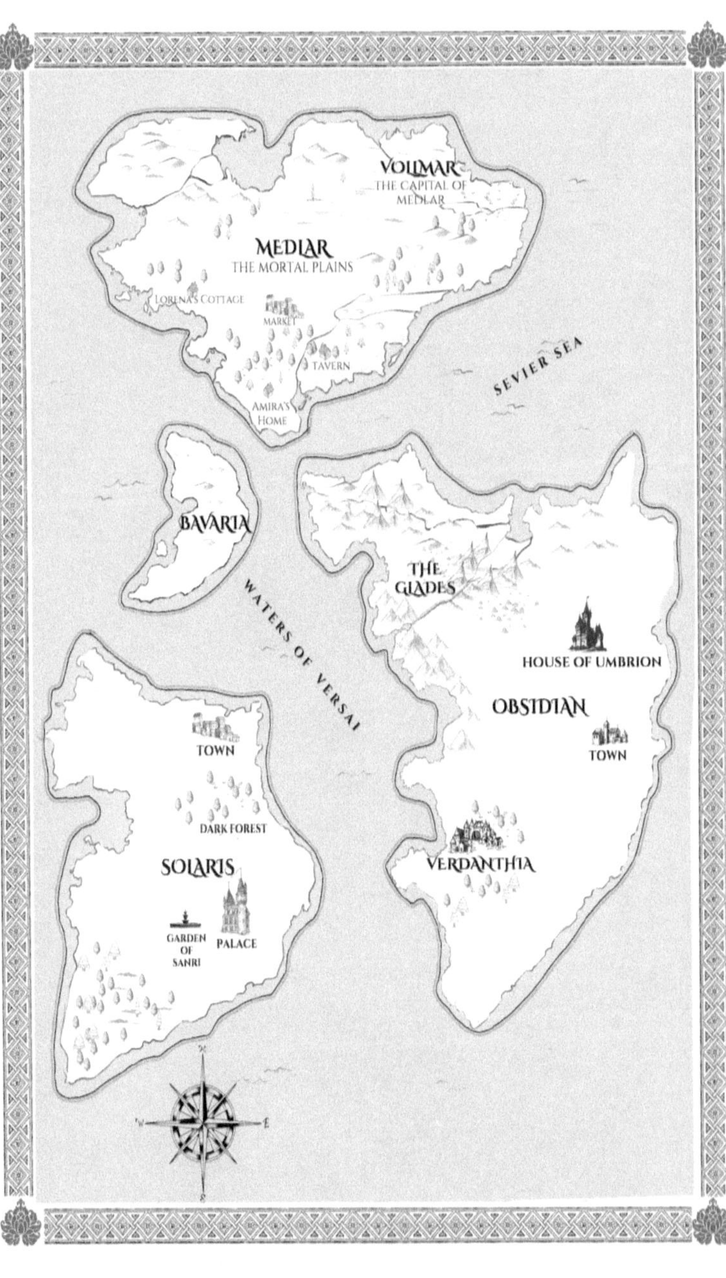

VOLLMAR
THE CAPITAL OF MEDLAR
MEDLAR
THE MORTAL PLAINS
LORENA'S COTTAGE
MARKET
TAVERN
AMIRA'S HOME
SEVIER SEA
BAVARIA
THE GLADES
HOUSE OF UMBRION
OBSIDIAN
TOWN
WATERS OF VERSAI
TOWN
DARK FOREST
SOLARIS
VERDANTHIA
GARDEN OF SANRI
PALACE

Author's Note

I stated in book one that this series would get darker with each book.

Is this as dark as it will get? Absolutely not.

I love the darkness, and there can never be enough.

Nevertheless, your mental health is always top priority. The content warnings can be found at the following link: https://ojuneabrown.carrd.co/#contentwarnings

Enjoy the darkness!

Playlist

Shatter Me – Lindsey Sterling
Hot Like Fire (Remix) – Aaliyah
Sex With Me – Rihanna
Hypnotic – Zella Day
Often – The Weeknd
Bloodline – Ariana Grande
Wolf – First Aid Kit
Bad Blood – Taylor Swift ft. Kendrick Lamar
Way down We Go – KALEO
Glory And Gore – Lorde
Another Love – Tom Odell
My Blood – Ellie Goulding
Close – Nick Jonas, Tove Lo
Don't Matter – Derik Fein
Love Lies – Khalid, Normani
Shadow – Derik Fein
Call Out My Name – The Weeknd
Howlin' for You – The Black Keys
BDE – Qveen Herby
Heads Will Roll (A-Trak Remix) – Yeah Yeah Yeahs, A-Trak

Use the QR code above to go directly to the Spotify playlist.
Enjoy!

Chapter One

Flying in the open night sky felt oddly...refreshing.

Freeing.

That is, until I took a glance down and went rigid, pressing my body even closer to Silas' chest.

For a brief moment, I felt free from the stress. The pain. The *hurt* that wouldn't escape me. And for a moment, I welcomed the thought of slipping from Silas' grasp. I envisioned myself freefalling through the clouds and stars without a care in the world, imagining the cool air wrapping around me while I tumbled through the void.

"Hey. Hey! Do not throw up on me. I'll drop you. Kidding... kind of," he said as Nova cut him a glare so vicious that I got scared for him. "Sorry. Afraid of heights?" He questioned with sympathy in his voice.

"No," I lied. "Kinda."

"Keep your eyes shut. We're almost there. I'll make sure to not make any sudden movements."

My body relaxed at his promise, and I had no idea why I trusted him so much. Although, it was probably because his demeanor and humor reminded me of my brother, Alix. Even his smile was almost identical. The image of my siblings played in my head as my eyes remained clenched shut. Not only did I miss my family, but now I was once again going to another destination that I knew nothing about.

With a group of immortals that I didn't know.

Again.

Before I could open my mouth to ask where we're going, Silas whispered, "Brace yourself. It's time to land."

Seconds went by before we dipped downward. I reflexively dug my nails into his leathers and tightened my jaw, clenching my teeth together as hard as I could to brace myself. My stomach did a flip, and for the first time, I was thankful for its emptiness.

Their large, beautiful black wings flapped lazily as we glided toward the ground below. I studied them in awe as the moonlight hit their long, black feathers, making them appear a deep purple in the light. I shut my eyes when I felt another flip of my stomach as we descended further, pressing my face into Silas' chest.

A solid thud sounded, along with others as everyone landed around us. Silas announced that we were on solid ground before gently placing me on my feet atop the stone pavement. Once I unclenched his clothing and opened my eyes, I couldn't stop myself from gawking over the people surrounding me. Their height towered over me, even towering over Raya, except for the woman. I focused on the woman they called Nova for a moment when everyone's wings disappeared except for hers. The thick, dark wings fluttered when she became aware of my stare, and I quickly looked away.

The men stared at me blankly as my eyes roamed over the outline of their muscles under their clothing. I squinted when Silas raised both of his brows, noticing where my gaze rested on each of them.

I cleared my throat, offering a smile to Silas and forcing myself out of the stupor taking over. "Thanks. Sorry about my grip..." I uttered to him as I stepped away.

"I don't think I've ever heard any woman tell me that," he said, crossing his arms over his chest, proud of his witty remark. The petite dark-haired woman smacked him on the back of the head before walking over to me. A smirk almost erupted at the sight of Silas rubbing the back of his head before I fought it away.

"You okay?" She asked with a sympathetic smile once again gracing her petite face. I wanted to tell her yes, but the moonlight was hitting her face just right, enhancing every gorgeous detail that her heart-shaped face had to offer. Her green eyes searched my face, showing every fleck of yellow sprinkled throughout. I swallowed as I admired her full lips that produced the most intricate cupid's bow I'd ever seen.

Quickly, my eyes flicked to the top of her head, and I sucked in a small breath of air. *Were those horns poking out the top of her head?* I couldn't stop myself from staring where her short, dark pixie cut showcased their shiny black tips peeking out.

The shock that portrayed in my eyes must have caught her attention, as she looked embarrassed and bowed her head while stepping away. I didn't know why, but I stretched my arm out to meet hers. "Yes. Thank you. I have no words to express my gratitude for what you all did back there. I—"

My words fell short as I turned in a circle, noting that all of them had pointy ears. Once again, Raya was the only one without them, and I had yet to see her with wings. Continuing to scan the immortals surrounding me, my eyes landed on the one they addressed as Thane, who looked less than thrilled to have me there.

"I'm sorry to be a burden," I said as I looked over, sneaking a glance at Raya still out cold in the overly muscular male's arms. His demeanor exuded strength and confidence as he held her firmly to his chest with ease. The way he looked at her made me tense, as if she was his prey and he was the predator that couldn't stop thinking about sinking his teeth into her.

"A burden you are. But my home is yours for the time being,

considering you took it upon yourself to use the crystal of Obsidian to call for our help," Thane said while placing his hands in his pockets, bringing my attention back to him. "Xavier will take your friend to our medwitch, and Nova will show you to your room."

Panic gnawed at my insides thinking about how long I would be required to stay there.

Trapped once again in a foreign place without seeing my family. *Without freedom.* My pulse quickened at the realization, and I refused to be at the mercy of immortals again. I lifted my chin and straightened my spine as I looked him in the eye.

"No."

His eyebrow raised at my answer.

"I will not be held captive again. I want to see my family. I demand to leave once Raya is awake and healed."

Thane shrugged his shoulders as he turned on his heel. "You can leave now for all I care. You're not required to stay here. My hospitality was a gift. Decline it if you wish."

My mouth popped open at his words as he walked through the wooden door at the bottom of the stairs. I stood in a stupor watching his figure retreat from my view when a heavy hand clapped down on my shoulder.

"Don't mind him. He always has something shoved up his ass when a minor inconvenience comes up," Silas winced at his own words. "Not that you're an inconvenience. But you get what I mean," he followed up as he playfully bumped his shoulder to mine and followed Thane's path down the stairs.

"Well, that was uncalled for," Nova huffed from beside me. "And I promise you I'll be having a word with him once I get you settled in."

I offered her a small smile of thanks as my gaze fell on Raya. I walked over to her in Xavier's arms and brushed the snow-white stray hairs from her forehead.

"Please give me an update on her once you take her to your..."

"Medwitch," Nova answered for me. I could only assume that was their version of a doctor here.

"Yes. Once you take her to your medwitch. Just so that I know she'll be okay."

Xavier's eyes met mine as he nodded his head in agreement before he turned to walk through a different door to the far right. And in that moment, it dawned on me just how big the platform was that we were standing on.

Are we atop a palace?

The thought startled me as I looked out past the stone border and saw nothing but bright stars and lights below. I swallowed thinking about how high up we must have been. I didn't dare walk to the ledge and look down. Nova touched my arm to bring me back to reality.

"She'll be okay," she reassured me.

"I can trust him with her right?" I asked as I watched my friend disappear in the arms of a male that I had just met less than an hour ago. A smile played across her face before she answered. "I would trust Xavier with the life of my first born. I don't have one, but I would."

I studied her face of amusement while she watched the two of them wander away into darkness. Before I could ask her why he was so trustworthy, she grasped my hand in hers and lead us toward the door Thane and Silas exited through.

"Come on. Let me get you settled into your temporary home," Nova said with one more tug of my hand before we descend the stairs.

Chapter Two

The spiraling staircase made my head spin as my eyes focused on the door at the bottom.

While Nova carelessly bounced down each step, my right hand clung to the stone wall next to me while carefully extending the other for balance. Tentatively, I took a step down toward the first narrow step and felt my foot slip. Pressing both hands firmly into the stone wall to save myself, my teeth clamped together when I felt the wounds around my wrists pull taut. Regaining my balance, I began making my way down the stairs more easily, focusing intently on each step. Nova was already at the bottom of the stairs with one foot through the open door when she peered back up at me. I released a huff when I could tell she was trying to suppress a grin.

"You do know that if you were to fall, I'm fast enough to catch you before you got hurt right?" she subtly called from the bottom. Involuntarily, I cast her a glare and slowly removed my hand from the wall as I lifted my chin. With much less grace than Nova, I made my way down the steps to meet her at the bottom.

We exchanged smirks before she held the door open for me.

My foot planted on dark marble floors before I was fully

through the door. My body remained frozen as I surveyed the ground. The sparkles held within the tiles made a starry night sky look dull. I forced my gaze upward as the surrounding walls were lit with golden sconces to provide light down the long, wide path. The smell of spices with hints of leather wrapped around me once I stepped in, letting the door close behind me. The antique vases and sculptures lining the walls snagged my attention under the golden hues of the light. Despite its darkness, where most people would be hesitant to enter, I felt nothing but invitation.

I shuffled my feet forward to follow closely behind Nova.

Pictures hung among the stone walls of males and females that were so attractive I inwardly cringed at how unappealing I must seem in this realm. I reached a picture of a woman with bright golden eyes and the most beautiful smile known to man, causing me to stop in my tracks.

Nova popped up behind me with her sweet voice, "Beautiful, isn't she?"

I could only nod my head in thought as I tried to calculate exactly who she resembled.

"Come on, I'll give you a tour of the place in the morning. Right now, you could use a warm bath, some clean clothes, and a bed." She took my hand again to lead me further down the hall, then down another set of stairs without spirals, before she stopped at a hall full of doors. "Here we are," she proclaimed as we reached the door furthest down the hall. A key was hanging by a purple ribbon from the knob. Nova gently lifted it and placed it into the lock, opening the door to a room so beautiful my mouth dropped open.

Every aspect of this space was a place of comfort. I was sucked into the room as if it was inviting me to come in to unwind and escape the stress of the outside world. The dark hues were a stark contrast to the gold and white I had become accustomed to in Solaris. Interior colors of purple, grey and black offered tranquility that already had my mind relaxing as I thought about dropping onto the bed that was stuffed with plush pillows and sumptuous linens. I was convinced they were waiting to pull me into a cloud-like embrace.

I slipped my shoes off before going in any further, not wanting to ruin the black fur-like rug that was laid out on the floor before me.

"That's not necessary. Even if you were to make a mess, we could easily clean it up with magic," Nova pointed out before grabbing my shoes and bringing them inside.

"I've never seen a room so beautiful," I exclaimed as I walked further in. I turned in a full circle to admire the room in its entirety.

"It's my favorite guest room here," she replied with a wide smile. "I'm happy you like it as much as I do."

I ran my fingers along the bedding before I came to an abrupt stop at the full-length mirror resting on the wall.

Fuck.

I looked like I'd just been through hell and back. "*Because you have been,*" I muttered to myself. Horror played across my face at the blood on my wrists from the chains placed upon me back in Solaris. My eyes wandered up to the scar on my cheek from Raine's hand.

I could've fought harder.

Tears sprang to the back of my eyes as the image of Millie and Ellie's dead bodies leaped into my mind.

"Why don't we get you washed up?" Nova offered as she guided me into the adjoining bathroom. She turned on the water to fill the large black tub as she threw in flower petals.

Flower petals? Where am I?

"That's truly not needed. You've already done so much for me. I can take care of myself," I said with pleading eyes. I was already ashamed that they had to save me, and now here she was running a bath for me like I was unable to do anything for myself.

"Of course you can take care of yourself, Amira. It is Amira, right?"

My mind raced, wondering how she learned of my name. Had Silas informed her? Was she aware before we even had a chance to meet?

"Yes," I answered with a quick, small smile before she continued speaking.

"I have no doubt that you can take care of yourself. But that's what we do here in Obsidian and especially in the House of Umbrion. We take care of our own. And right now, besides Raya, you don't have anyone else. So, I'm adopting you as my own. Now get undressed and let me help you," she said without a breath. "Unless you prefer to not be seen naked by someone you just met. Then I would completely understand." Her cheeks turned red at her statement, which made me produce a light chuckle. "No, no. I don't mind. There's nothing I have that you don't, so I could care less."

Nova eyed me up and down. "You are aware of the amount of curves you have in all the right places, right?" she asked while waving a hand over her petite build with a broad smile. I waved my hand in the air to dismiss her with a laugh, "You know what I meant."

I peeled my dress off without looking in the mirror, scared of any additional marks I might have seen. Holding it in my hands, I silently thanked the garment and Raya for saving my life during my last moments in Solaris. After carefully folding it and placing it on the countertop before me, I removed my undergarments and threw them to the floor in a pile. Standing before the tub, my hand reached up to rub the stone of my necklace between my thumb and forefinger.

Nova glanced at the necklace, smiled, and offered a hand to help me step inside. The warmth of the water forced me to release a thankful hum from my lips as I sank my entire body into the welcoming bath.

Dark red rose petals floated so heavily around me that I couldn't see my body through the water. With a deep breath, I slipped below the surface until the top of my head was submerged and pop back up within seconds.

I could stay in here forever.

"Do you mind?" Nova asked as she held two glass bottles in her hands and nodded at my hair.

My mind raced as I wondered if she knew how to care for the hundreds of curls atop my head. But I trusted Millie and Ellie, and neither of them had a curly hair on their head. My heart squeezed tight again at the thought of them.

"Are you sure? I can—" I offered before Nova cut me off.

"Do it yourself. Yea, yea I know. I don't mind. Lean back on the pad."

A soft rectangular pad was at the back of the tub for me to rest on as I leaned back for Nova to wash my hair. Gently, she separated my curls in sections to untangle it before she started washing. The feel of her slender fingers massaging my scalp almost sent me into a deep sleep before I forced myself to speak.

"So, are you and Thane together?"

Nova's hands froze on my scalp before a flurry of laughter erupted from her. She continued massaging my scalp while answering. "Thane is my brother. We're night and day but..." she huffed.

My mouth flopped open at her statement. They didn't even look alike, let alone their completely different personalities.

"Adopted sister, not actually blood related," she followed up. "His family took me in when I had no one else at a very young age."

I bit my lip at her explanation. Why did his family need to take her in?

"Don't let his hardshell and demeanor fool you. You tend to get like that after a few centuries of experiences like the ones he's endured. He's a lover not a fighter. Unless someone comes after those he loves," she added on.

Did she just say centuries?

"Did you say centuries?" I questioned her with a snap of my neck to see her from the edge of my vision. The corner of her lips tilted upwards. "How *many* centuries?"

She gently turned my head to face forward again. "Four or five. You lose track after the second one."

My eyes bulged while trying to evaluate the information she was providing me. If she lost track of Thane's age, that would mean that she was over two centuries old as well. I tucked away the additional questions about everyone's age for another time.

"And what about Silas and Xavier?" I continued with my interrogation.

Nova gently pushed me forward to rinse my hair.

"Xavier is... different. Dark. But he is the most trustworthy man I have ever met." After a slight pause, Nova continued feeding me information about her inner circle. "He's been through *a lot* before and during his time here. And he typically keeps to himself, but when he finally opens up, he's just as funny as Silas. Speaking of Silas, he's the idiot of the group if you can't tell." Her statement made me produce a real laugh that echoed throughout the room.

"I'm assuming his personality was portrayed back in Solaris?" she asked lightheartedly, and I could hear the smile in her tone.

"I mean, I was in distress and beyond despair. Two of my friends were just murdered," I said with a lump caught in my throat forcing me to pause. "And he was just so relaxed about everything." I thought about our interaction in Solaris a moment and realized that Silas' calm demeanor allowed for me to keep my usually full-blown panic at bay.

Nova finished rinsing the remaining wash from my curls before sliding back around to the side of the tub. "Sounds like Silas.

The look I gave Thane when he suggested sending him in to guard you was overly judgmental. But he's the only shape shifter we have in Obsidian, so he was perfect for the job," she informed me while capping the glass bottles. "He may be the relaxed one, but you can also count on him to always have your back and get the job done."

A smile graced her lips as she spoke about him. She handed me a circular cream-colored bar and cloth before standing.

"Are you and Thane the only ones that are related?" I asked while taking the items from her with a smile of thanks.

"Yes, but after all this time together, we're family at this point. Blood doesn't make you any more or less family. Not sure if it's like that in the mortal realms... but we would die for each other here," she said with the confidence of a thousand-manned army.

Our eyes locked in a serious gaze. Her deep, green eyes gleamed in the light of the sconces while her olive tone shimmered. The sharp features of her face would have been intimidating if she didn't have the sweetest voice I'd ever heard, and a heart of gold portrayed with every action so far. Her statement sent a dagger through my heart at the thought of my siblings and a faint smile brushed my lips as I released a breath.

"I would die two times over to save my family."

Chapter Three

When I hinted at the thought of the pillows begging to pull me into a cloud-like embrace, I was right.

After the relaxing bath and full scalp massage I received from Nova, I couldn't keep my eyes open if I tried. The moment my head landed on the overly comfortable pillows, and my body sank into the open invitation from the over-sized bed, I was whisked away to my dreams.

Unfortunately, those dreams turned to nightmares as all I could picture were Millie and Ellie being slain all over again. No matter how hard I fought to awaken before their blood spilled before me, I was forced to watch the bitter memory replay. Though I couldn't see Raine's face, I knew he was there. And every inch of me wished it was real, for just a moment, so I could make him pay for the pain he had caused.

Still caused.

The citizens of Solaris had no idea what was happening in their realm and may never know thanks to the power he held over them.

Once the nightmares subsided, I sank further into sleep and

only awakened due to the birds singing their morning melodies outside the gigantic windows of my room. Lying in bed, my thoughts roamed freely. And while I was thankful that it happened, I couldn't stop questioning why Thane and the others saved me from Solaris. My head began to pound from the stress of trying to figure out the recent events that had taken place.

Throwing back the covers, I glanced over the deep purple nightgown Nova loaned me and wrapped myself in the silk robe hanging in the bathroom. My stomach rumbled as I splashed water on my face to fully awaken. Running a cloth over my face, it dawned on me that I didn't have any clothes here. As if she could hear my thoughts, a knock at my door sounded.

I opened the heavy door to Nova's bright eyes as she held a stack of clothes in hand.

If this was what she looked like first thing in the morning, I wanted whatever magic she had.

"I wasn't quite sure of what size clothing you would wear, so I guessed. If it's wrong, nothing a bit of magic can't change," she said with a wink. "I also got the notion that you weren't the pink with frills type."

A smirk played on my lips at her comment, thinking about Tessa and how she would loathe someone else with the same style as me. "You assumed correctly," I confirmed, taking some of the clothes from her so she didn't have to peer around the large stack to walk inside. I placed the clothes on the bed as I walked over to the repository, opening its doors to store the clothes. But when I opened it, half of them were already placed within. I quickly turned to look back at the pile of clothes I placed on the bed still neatly stacked. Yet, the pile in Nova's hands were no longer there. She smiled at me with a mischievous, yet friendly twinkle in her eye.

"Sorry. I'm lazy and use magic for almost everything around here," she quipped with a flick of her middle and index fingers, sending my pile to hang neatly in the cabinet.

Jealously coursed through me at how everyone around me possessed such talents and I had nothing. *Was Nothing.* I unfurrowed my brow as Nova noticed me deep in thought. "Everything okay?" She asked with concerned eyes, stepping toward me.

"Absolutely," I answered with a lump in my throat. "Do you have any other...powers?"

Nova's expression never changed as she halted her steps. "Do...*powers* intimidate those in the mortal realm?"

She sounded as though she was embarrassed, or even afraid that I would fear her.

"Possibly. But if you're asking about me, I don't think it's possible for me to be intimidated by you. You're far too kind." A genuine smile graced my lips as she mirrored it.

"I'm glad you're not afraid of me," a feminine voice blared within my head. I threw my hands up to my ears due to the pitch and inexpectancy.

What the fuck was that?

"It was me," Nova said, shyly biting her lip.

"You can speak without—" I gaped at her. "Did you just—"

"Read your mind and answer your questions too? Yes. I figured it was better to show you rather than to tell you," she shrugged as she bounced back and forth on her feet. "To be clear, I don't read anyone's thoughts without their consent. Unless it's for the greater good. You can consider that the first *and last* time I do that. Can't promise I won't gossip with you silently though. Not everyone needs to know our secrets in the future." She winked again as her smile spread wider.

"Future?" I asked, concerned. I didn't want to be trapped like before.

"I just meant for as long as you're here. I'm not sure what you and Raya's plans are once she awakens."

"Raya," my mind drifted to my friend. "Do you mind if I visit her?"

"Of course, but I feel that you should know that the

medwitch still has her asleep to heal. Maybe we should get something in our stomachs first and then head over there?"

As she made her suggestion, my stomach roared in agreement which made both of us laugh. I quickly changed into the black slacks and dark blue top that Nova provided when she arrived. A large amount of happiness flowed through me when I saw that it wasn't a pile of dresses like back in Solaris.

Though the top was skintight with a bit of cleavage showing, I was comfortable and felt like myself. I looked into the floor-length mirror next to the door and threw my freshly washed curls into a loose bun, allowing a tendril or two to grace the sides of my face.

As we stepped out of my room, she pressed the key for the lock into the palm of my hand. "I forgot to give this to you last night," she said as we began walking the length of the hall.

"That's awfully kind, but I'm just a guest here," I said while tucking the key into the pocket of my slacks.

"Even a guest deserves privacy," she declared as we rounded a corner of the hall that opened into another. Artwork and chandeliers decorated the walls and ceilings as we walked along the long deep purple rug. She slowed her pace as we approached large black double doors to our left. Pressing her hands against them provided entrance into a room with a large table, wall of large windows and aromas of food that had my mouth watering.

We stepped further into the dining hall where Thane and Xavier were seated. Xavier nodded his head in greeting, returning to the papers before him before I could give a nod in return. My gaze flicked over to Thane who was reading a piece of paper and never raised his head to acknowledge either of us. I rolled my eyes and continued into the hall, not giving him the satisfaction of noticing his arrogance.

Taking in the ambiance of the room, I followed Nova to the dark marble table ingrained with subtle, twisting white lines. As I took my seat beside her, Silas entered with a big smile across his face, his eyes landing on me.

"Morning, Mirror!" He said while claiming a seat on the other side of Nova.

"It's, Ah-Meer-Ah. Amira. And good morning, Silas," I said with a deep smirk.

Nova smacked him on the back of the head at his greeting, her wings ruffling as she readjusted them behind her. Xavier chuckled, momentarily looking up from his reading to watch Silas rub the back of his head. I bit the inside of my cheek, realizing that this must have been a common occurrence between them.

"It was a joke!" he muttered.

Soon after, servants entered the room with eating utensils in hand. Nova and the others jumped out of their chairs to rush over to help. I stared at them, dumbfounded. Raine never once helped his servants in Solaris. I vividly remember him scolding me on one occasion whenever I attempted to assist.

The servants attempted to brush everyone away, but they were no match for the group that ambushed them. I watched with brows raised as Nova gently removed the silverware from the hands of a maid with greying temples who gave her a glare before laughing. Silas slipped behind another woman, grabbing a pile of plates from her hands before quickly darting away and dodging a towel she playfully swung in his direction. Xavier and Thane swooped in and helped with the remaining items as the younger servants swooned over them with wide, open mouths. I rolled my lips in to suppress a laugh when I noticed how oblivious they were to the admiration while the two of them chatted amongst themselves on the way back to the table.

My internal laughter subsided when I pulled myself from my stupor and noted how intently Xavier and Thane were speaking in a harsh whisper.

"Right, but the death toll is increasing daily. The amount of mortal disappearances is rising at an alarming rate. How many more until we step in?" I heard Xavier ask with an exasperated breath, and I swallowed the anxiety threatening to rise.

Thane cast him a warning glance when they finally took their seats at the table, leaning closer to him. "There is a treaty in place for a reason, Xavier. Who are we to step in and cause more of a disruption?"

Xavier rolled his eyes and focused back on his friend. "Don't act like the title of High King or a damn treaty changes your morals. I know you. And I know that you won't sit idly by while innocent people are being slayed during an uprising for Erebus knows what. You're practically itching to beam there right now as we speak."

Uprising.

They were speaking about Medlar. The last letter I received from my mother had mentioned an uprising. They had to be speaking about Medlar.

"I'm sorry, did you mention an uprising?" I asked louder than normal, causing the group to tense in unison.

Thane's eyes widened at my question, and I quickly averted my focus away from him and toward Xavier who cleared his throat. He eyed everyone in the room while poking at his food with his fork before setting it down and speaking.

"There's been word of an uprising in a mortal realm. We haven't located the exact location yet. But it seems they're fighting back against immortals that have infiltrated their land for reasons that we're not quite sure about." Thane shot a glare at Xavier once he finished speaking.

"My family..." I whispered to myself, slowly rising from my seat.

"What about your family?" Xavier asked through narrowed eyes.

"They're in Med—"

I was about to answer his question, when a black blur

appeared out of the corner of my eye before knocking me to the ground. A massive weight was atop me with my face being covered in saliva that was dripping from a wide mouth. Chairs scattered, and shouts rang through the room. Sharp, glistening teeth moved closer to my neck. His wet nose grazed my skin as he sniffed relentlessly. I yelped in panic. Moments later, the weight of the animal was removed and multiple hands helped me to my feet. The air knocked from within me returned as I eyed the figure that tackled me to the ground.

The melanistic animal stared at me with its tongue hanging from the side of its mouth, its large frame vibrating with restrained movement. Its eyes fixed on mine as if we had met before.

I stood, slack jawed and paralyzed.

Because we *had* met before, in the forest when I had lost my way leaving Lorena's cottage the first time I went there.

Why was he so happy to see me today when he wanted to have me for dinner in the forest?

"Apologies. Atlas has never behaved in that manner," Thane explained as he commanded the large, black wolf to sit with a sharp flick of his wrist. He sat for a moment before he sprinted back over to me, attempting to lick my face while Thane wrapped his arms around him, pulling him back.

"He was there," I blurted out.

"He was where?" Thane asked as annoyance rose in his facial expression while pointing a stern finger at the wolf.

"In the forest where I first met Raine. When he...saved me."

Thane rolled his eyes at my answer. "Didn't quite seem like he saved you to me," he quipped, making his way back to his seat. "Plus, Atlas doesn't leave Obsidian unless he's with me. Like I said, it's a first occurrence for him acting in that manner. On the contrary, he's quite unfriendly."

Nova lovingly patted the four-legged animal on the head. "She doesn't need you to remind her about Raine's bullshit, Thane,"

Nova reprimanded while reclaiming her seat. The wolf growled at Silas whenever he tried to pet him which made everyone at the table smirk.

"I also can speak for myself when I say I don't need you to be an asshole as well. I dealt with that enough in Solaris. Unless this is just a replica of where you graciously saved me from," I said as I remained standing. Everyone stiffened at my statement. Xavier let out a subtle *"oh fuck"* under his breath.

Thane forcefully bit his bottom lip, fighting every fiber within himself to not rip my head from my body. He slowly closed his eyes before speaking. "If you *ever* compare my home to Solaris again, I will make it my duty to drop you off right where we fucking found you. Is that understood, P—"

"Do not call me a fucking Pixie," I spat at him with a pointed finger. His eyes pinched at the sides as he narrowed them at me.

"*Princess.* I was going to say, *Princess.* What do you have against pixies?" He asked with his head cocked to the side. I swallowed as embarrassment tried to rear its ugly head.

"None of your business," I said, holding my head high despite his devouring stare. Those golden eyes never blinked as a subtle smirk played on his lips.

"Sure thing, Pix."

My blood broiled at his nickname. My fingers curling into fists as we held each other's gaze. Atlas prowled over to my side and buried his head into my hip with a subtle whine. I looked down at him in confusion just as the doors to the hall flew open and a beautiful slender woman with long dark hair rushed down the steps.

"Thank, Erebus! Are you okay?" She asked with arms outstretched wide.

The room spun as I focused on the figure before me, confused on if I was in Obsidian or Solaris. Was this all a dream? A Nightmare?

"Are you hurt?"

I licked my lips as she rushed over to me, internally yelling at myself to move, my voice to speak, to function properly instead of freezing up. We stood face-to-face, her arms already extended towards me, before my brain turned back on, and words slowly flowed from my mouth.

"Hello, Anya."

Chapter Four

My breathing threatened to cease as I tried to comprehend how Anya was here and not in Solaris. And better yet, *why was she here?*

A multitude of questions floated though my mind as she flung her arms around me in a motherly embrace and took a step back while still grasping both of my shoulders. She raised her hand, wanting to touch the small mark on my face from Raine's assault in the holding cell. Instead of following through, she drew her hand back to cover her mouth.

"I am so sorry, Amira," she sputtered while searching my face for what seemed like forgiveness.

"Why are you sorry? None of this is your fault."

I studied her inquisitively, wondering if she knew something that I didn't. Of course she did... she was a fucking witch. My stomach turned to knots as I wondered if she knew about Millie and Ellie. It twisted even tighter as I recalled her telling me how they were the last of her coven.

She was completely alone now.

"I should have just told you about Raine instead of letting you find out on your own. But I could see your love for him and was afraid you wouldn't believe me if I told you what a horrible being he is. You must believe me when I say that I never thought it would go that far, nor did I know about the hex on Solaris. I only believed that he had convinced them he was for the greater good. I never thought it would come to this. I never thought I would lose..." Her voice cracked at her last statement.

She knew.

I bit my lip as I tried to formulate words to let her know I tried to save them. That it was my fault they were no longer here because they willingly decided to help me. *Me.* A fucking nobody. They lost their lives for a nobody.

"I'm sorry... did you say *hex* on Solaris?" Thane asked with a confused expression. The others in the room that I could see from my peripherals looked just as bewildered about the issues taking place in Solaris.

Anya inhaled deeply and opened her mouth to answer Thane, but I threw my body into hers before she could utter a word. She faltered backwards with her small frame, yet still welcomed my embrace. Involuntarily, I wrapped my arms around Anya, squeezing so tightly I feared I might break her in half. I heard her grunt while mimicking the action and resting her head against mine.

Hot tears flowed down my cheeks as the reminder of losing Millie and Ellie pierced straight through me. The room fell silent as my soft sobs filled the void, and I didn't care.

I finally pulled myself back from Anya's embrace to see heartbreak in streams running down her face as well.

"They are gone because of me. Because I wasn't strong enough and now—"

"They are gone because they stood for what they believed in," Anya cut me off, raising her hand to wipe a tear from my cheek. "They knew what a wonderful being you were, and they would not be able to live with themselves if they just stood by while..."

Her words trailed off as her gaze washed over me.

Biting into her lip, fresh tears welled in her eyes, and I shook my head, silently pleading for her own heartbreak to stop. "I don't know how to repay them. How to repay you for the hurt that I have caused. They died for helping me and I couldn't do anything except beg for their lives to be spared."

Anya's hands grasped my biceps as I trembled from the force of recalling those final moments. The memory of their blood spilling across the stone ground was becoming too much to bear as we spoke.

"There was nothing you could do, Amira. They died with honor," she said while stepping back from our embrace. "I knew the moment they left this cruel world. Covens have a bond that can't be broken until death." Her voice broke when she reached the word death, pulling another muffled sob from my lips. "Our type of coven only fully leaves this world one way. We have a specific type of dark magic known as Chaos that won't allow us to simply *die*. I could have brought them back had Raine's men not..."

She couldn't finish her words, and I was hanging on to every single one of them.

"Had they not what?" I asked as I began chewing on my bottom lip in anticipation of an answer that I knew I didn't want to receive.

Anya gently squeezed my shoulder. "Had they not used Visbane to slay them," a familiar voice said solemnly from behind me. Stunned, I slowly turned my head with horrified eyes to see Silas standing there. "Same way I lost my sister and mother. All immortals have the same fate with it, even Fae. It is a banned substance in every realm except Solaris. It removes our immortality, leaving us mortal and halts all healing."

I forced my mouth shut, swallowing and casting glances between the two of them.

"Are you saying that you could have brought them back to life?" I asked as hate filled me. Hate for the bastard I was willing to give my heart to. The first person I had ever been open to the possibility of love with.

"Yes, I could have brought them back. When a dark witch of our caliber nears death, their spirit always finds a way back to their coven. Their Chaos is strong enough to call out to their coven for help even when they physically cannot," Anya replied quietly. I bit the inside of my cheek to control my emotions as she continued talking. "But, by the time I was able to break down the wards to leave the dark forest and enter the grounds of Solaris to retrieve their bodies, it was too late. Raine and his men knew what they were. *Who* they were by that time. Their glamour had already been lifted willingly." Anya stared off into the void before finally releasing me from her gentle grasp and staring up at the ceiling.

I hated everything about this conversation. But there was that word again... *Chaos.*

"Chaos?" I questioned as my head began to pound from so much information.

Anya's eyes dropped back down to mine. "Chaos is what others call the magic of a dark witch."

"Why not just call it magic?"

"Because, as witches of the Dark Forest, we can ignore the rules of traditional magic and control elements that are forbidden to be controlled, making us able to cause any amount of chaos we require or deem necessary. Unfortunately, if it can't be controlled, it can eventually consume its vessel." Anya's gaze hardened at the explanation, sending a chill down my arms.

Her eyes softened before continuing. "The pull that I usually had toward them let me know that somehow their Chaos was halted. And I knew... I knew in that moment they were no longer flourishing as they always had."

My heart had already cracked in different directions. But now I could feel it splintering off from its original cracks of pain. Chaos was their own form of dark magic that pulled them together. I couldn't imagine what Anya must have felt when they lost their lives, and the connection was severed.

"Did they see you?" I questioned her with wide eyes.

Her eyes snapped back up to meet mine. "I did not want to take a risk on endangering the dark forest," she answered, her head held high. "I will not rest until I get vengeance for my sisters. For you. For us."

My heart squeezed. She barely knew me, so why was she so loyal to me?

If there was one thing that I had learned during my time away from Medlar, it was that dark does not always lead to evil. I would pick the darkness a hundred times over if it always led me to Anya's Chaos and warmth.

"Don't take this the wrong way," I said with a crooked smile, the tears and sobs finally subsiding between the two of us. "But how...why are you here? In Obsidian."

To my surprise, Thane answered for Anya. "The Dark Forest is just a piece of Obsidian that happens to be conveniently placed and hidden in Solaris. Therefore, this is Anya's rightful realm and home," he said with a nod to her. "Her coven originated within Obsidian but relocated to Solaris to help find others of their kind and provide sanctuary from Raine."

My throat constricted at his words. A flash of warmth came across those golden eyes as he locked eyes with Anya.

Were they more than friends?

"Why didn't they use their Chaos before everything that happened?" Xavier asked with arms rested across his chest, breaking his usual silence. "They easily could have protected themselves and Amira."

Anya clenched her jaw and scanned the ceiling for a moment before landing back on Xavier who was now offering an apologetic expression.

"To answer your question Xavier, I can only assume that Cryo was used to suppress their Chaos in some sort of shackles used on them." She looked at me with anguish in her eyes, responding to my question before I could utter a single word. "It's a rare type of stone used to suppress our magic."

Silas threw his hands on top of his head in revelation as Xavier confirmed to Anya that Millie and Ellie were both shackled at the time of their death and prior.

Nova groaned as she leaned against the back of a chair. "Since when has such an element existed?"

Anya's shoulders sagged before answering. "Since the beginning of time my friend."

Silas closed his eyes as he looked away, muttering and muttered an apology of grievance before pulling a small glass bottle from the pocket of his clothing. Slowly, he stepped in front of Anya, grabbing her hand and placing it within her palm. Glancing at it, a tear from each eye fell down her cheeks.

As she raised the clear, glass bottle to look at it, I noticed the same purple dust that floated to Xavier in place of Millie and Ellie's bodies back in Solaris. Raising my palm to my lips, I did everything to refrain the sobs from coursing through me.

She studied the bottle for a few moments before clutching it tightly and pulling it toward her chest. "Your friendship to them meant the world," she informed me, sending an electrical charge to my heart before she faced the others.

"I- I didn't think you all would've had the time to..."

She clenched her eyes shut, shaking her head in gratitude. Opening them and scanning the faces in the room she followed up with a bow of her head and wiped the tears from her face. "And your devotion to the Dark Forest and my coven will forever be remembered."

Placing the bottle within the satchel on her hip, she smoothed her hair back from her face before addressing everyone again. "I will never be able to repay you all."

Leaning over the table, Xavier spoke for the group in confidence. "We always make time for the ones we care about. Especially the good ones," Xavier replied to Anya with a pitying smile.

After thanking them once more, she sauntered over to Thane and rested a hand on his shoulder. I had yet to see anyone touch him, but he didn't flinch as she placed a kiss atop his head. "I assume that Thanasis has welcomed you with open arms to Obsidian?" She inquired with a smirk and playful glare at the back of his head.

I snickered at her question. "Quite the opposite actually." His head whipped up with a glare twice as vicious as hers, but I didn't falter my stance. "Now that I think of it, you haven't actually informed me when I'll be returning to Medlar," I pointed out while tilting my chin.

Anya dropped her hand from his shoulder at my statement. The others became increasingly awkward, clearing throats and glancing around aimlessly.

"Ready for training?" Xavier asked Nova while standing from the table.

"Me? Don't you mean to ask Silas?" she joked while jerking her head in his direction.

Silas threw his hand to his chest and reared his head back. "Excuse me? The fuck is that supposed to mean? I'm the best fighter sitting at this table," he rebutted. Everyone stopped what they were doing and stared in his direction with a confused look.

He narrowed his eyes at his friends before rubbing the back of his neck and producing a sheepish smile.

"Maybe if you put more of an effort into your sparring rather than your jokes you would be able to take down his sister," Xavier said while walking behind Silas and slapping both of his hands down on the tops of his shoulders with a nod toward Thane.

I imagined Nova's petite build beating Silas in a fight and sputtered while trying not to laugh, earning me a glare from Silas before he smacked the table and rose from his chair. "Fuck you guys. She's not even that good," he replied under his breath and recoiled when he noticed Thane's fire-filled gaze on him. "Okay, maybe she's a little better than me. But I take it easy on her."

"Right," the entire room boasted in unison.

I waited until we were done laughing at Silas' loss in the argument before I followed up.

"What's the training for?" I asked, genuinely interested.

"Vaternian training," Nova answered nonchalantly and winced when I still looked confused. "Sorry, that's what Obsidian warriors are called. We train nearly every morning."

I snorted at her statement. "Aren't you guys like... one-hundred years old? How much practice could you possibly need?"

"Three-hundred and some change," Nova quipped with a wink. My mouth popped open at her age.

"Come train and find out," Silas added on with a wide grin.

"Stop it," Nova demanded with a glare. Silas shrugged his shoulders at me and waved a goodbye as they headed out the doors of the hall.

"I'll bet two rounds of drinks tonight that Nova puts you on your ass within the first five minutes," I heard Silas joke as he shoved Xavier from the side while they exited.

"You know, it's been some time since I trained with Vaternians. I think I'll join," Anya said as Thane looked at her with a quizzical look. She patted my cheek with a smile as she followed behind them, leaving just Thane, myself, and our inexplicable hate for each other in the gigantic hall alone.

Chapter Five

My heartbeat escalated as I surveyed the area, my eyes landing on the only other person in the room. *Thane.*

I swallowed hard and proceeded to bite my bottom lip as I shuffled through the questions in my head I planned to ask him in regard to my return home.

"Feel free to have a seat, Pixie," he said without a glance in my direction. Heat rose to my cheeks at his degrading nickname. I unclenched my teeth from my lip as I burned a hole into his soul with my glare. *If the fucker even had a soul.*

"You calling me that has no effect on me. Nor does your hostile attitude since I arrived in your realm," I stated. He noticeably stiffened at my words. "And I'd rather stand."

He finally raised his head to meet my continuous glare, narrowing his eyes before leaning back in his chair. His golden eyes caught my attention as the sun illuminated them through the large windows. I could only imagine the amount of women that fell under his spell while staring into their gleaming trance.

"Suit yourself," he said while shifting to a subtle gaze. The blank face he now wore annoyed me to my core.

Time to start asking the important questions.

"Back to my question of going home," I said before receiving a quick response.

"Say the word and I'll take you back before the next time your eyelids can blink," he informed me with a sarcastic smile.

I took a moment to study him. His perfectly handsome face. His broad and muscular stature. His perfect fucking jawline that I so badly wanted to make acquainted with my fist.

"Are you always this rude? Or is it because you so graciously saved me and want me to kiss your hands and feet in thanks?" I asked while crossing my arms over my chest.

A real, hearty laugh blared from him as he threw his head back. And as irritated as I was, the sight of his Adam's apple bobbing up and down turned my mouth dry. Bringing his head back up and straightening himself in his chair, he tilted his head to the side. "It's a little of both. Like I said, you are not being held captive here. You can leave whenever your little heart desires."

My heart fluttered at his words.

Now. I want to go home now.

"But I thought you should know," he said, his words floating to my ears, setting off an internal alarm as my stomach bottomed out. "Since you and your little friend got here, someone has been working diligently to get past our wards."

He ran his tongue between his full lips before continuing.

"Now, I'm going to go out on a limb and guess that you have some kind of idea about who that could be. Raine isn't dumb enough to attempt to come within these walls."

My eyes grew wide as I shuffled through the last few weeks I was in Solaris. Who the fuck would be willing to come here?

Eryx wouldn't dare leave Raine's side being the coward that he was. Especially not right now with trying to adjust with one less eye. The thought made me mentally chuckle at him clutching his face where his eye once was. I continued thinking until my brain finally worked.

Lorena.

I sucked in a breath at the realization.

"Mind telling me what's going through that pretty little head of yours?" Thane's voice brought me back. A sly smirk flitted across my face.

"So, you think I'm pretty?"

His face turned back to stone as his golden eyes pierced through me.

"Her name is Lorena. That's who's trying to break through your wards to get to me," I answered.

Thane's eyes grew wide at the sound of her name.

"Mind telling me exactly how you ended up in Solaris to begin with?" he questioned while crossing his arms over his broad chest. I could sense the judgement in his question, making me even more reluctant to open up to him.

"I'd rather not. I made some pretty dumb decisions and—"

"I'm shocked," he said with a loud huff. "Just answer the question, Pixie."

My eyes flared and narrowed at his arrogant tone. He may be a High King, but I'd be damned if he thought he could talk to me in such a tone and get away with it.

"Fuck you," I shot back with a sneer on my face. The words felt satisfying when leaving my lips, but that changed when I noticed Thane's response to them.

Thane's jaw clenched violently, a quick tick of the muscle the only indication of his mounting anger. His long, dark lashes fluttered shut, and he inhaled deeply, nostrils flaring as he released the breath violently. Whenever his eyes snapped back open, fixating on me, the words that had felt so satisfying when leaving my lips laid like ash in my mouth.

I could tell he was seething at the way I refused to answer his questions. But I was terrified to know what he was thinking while staring into his eyes filled with nothing but irritation and annoyance. I knew he was doing everything he could to refrain from leaping over the table and snapping my neck.

My breath caught in my throat when he slowly rose from his seat and rounded the long table. Placing both palms behind him on the table, he leaned back and rolled his lips inward while keeping his eyes pinned to mine.

I was still trying to force the breath caught in my throat to escape when his eyes trailed from my face down to my toes and back. The sound of his voice sent a rush of different emotions into the atmosphere, forcing me to ground myself and breathe.

"I'm not sure how things work in the mortal realm, but I'm going to tell you exactly how they work here in Obsidian," he started before clenching and unclenching his jaw and continuing. "Your attitude may have persuaded others to give you what you want, but not me. Whatever you spit out I can give back to you much, much heavier. I saved your ass once, and I won't do it again. Nor do I want a thank you. But what I do expect is when I ask you a simple *fucking* question, is to receive a simple *fucking* answer."

Despite the frustration he had previously shown, he seemed uncharacteristically calm and collected. Taking advantage of his tranquility, I let my fiery emotions get the best of me.

"Are you done throwing your testosterone around the room yet?" I questioned, popping out my hip with a satisfied grin resting on my face.

And that was the straw that broke the camel's back, changing the entire atmosphere.

Black smoke encapsulated me as a gust of wind blew the loose hairs from my face. I quickly lost sight of Thane and familiar panic filled me, tightening my throat. The room disappeared as the thick, viscous smoke blinded me completely. I blinked once, and he stood a single foot away from me with his golden eyes blaring in the darkness. That same sarcastic smirk thickly painted his tanned face.

What was he? Would he be considered Fae like the others?

"My shadows didn't quite like the tone you used, Pixie. Would you like to try again?"

Shadows.

This wasn't smoke. They were... his shadows? Multiple?

I reached my hand out to touch them, but a rough, calloused hand firmly, yet gently, wrapped around my wrist.

"They don't like to be touched by people they don't know," he quipped before dropping my hand back to my side. I nodded my head in understanding as fear flitted down my spine at the darkness surrounding me.

Would he hurt me like Raine had?

As if Thane could read my mind, his eyes softened along with his composure as his shadows slowly curled back into him. But before they fully returned, a slight caress dashed across the back of my neck, causing me to stiffen at the touch. I shifted my eyes to the corner as a lone trail of shadows retreated from where I felt the light touch and floated back to Thane.

Something like surprise flitted across his face before he glared at the lone shadows returning to him.

"Tomorrow," he said, turning his gaze back to me, a new wariness in the planes of his face.

"What about tomorrow?"

He sighed before shaking his head and walking back over to his seat. "Your friend should be awake by the end of the day. I will have you taken wherever you both wish to go. Unless you would like to leave today without her."

He studied me while trying to gauge my loyalty. His offer was a test to see if I would abandon someone—someone that I considered a friend.

"Her name is Raya. And I will wait for her before I leave," I answered hesitantly.

My usual panic was close by as I told myself it couldn't be this easy to return home. It was all too simple. Too quick.

"Raine specifically let me know I had to wait a certain number of days before beaming as a mortal. Is it okay to do it now?" I asked cautiously.

A confused expression washed over Thane's face. "Is that what he told you?"

I bit the inside of my cheek and slowly nodded my head in return.

It was my turn to look confused as his expression morphed into a knowing smirk. Resting an elbow on the table, he placed a finger against his temple. He studied me with pity in his eyes as if I was a lost animal in the forest before he chuckled, shaking his head in amusement. He dropped his hand back down to the table and clasped them together on top of it.

"Raine fed you lies, and you listened. I never took you to be so..." he trailed off before cocking his head. "Submissive."

The heat of embarrassment gnawing at my throat threatened to erupt. I peeled my lips back while my fists slowly clenched at my sides, reminding myself that he could break me in half at any time. *Reminding myself that I was in his home.* I clenched my teeth and swallowed to refrain from causing another encounter like the one moments before. Just as my temper was about to rear its ugly head, he spoke once more.

"Regardless, thanks to Anya's magic, we have portals in Obsidian. Anyone can travel anywhere, at any time, whenever they want."

My blood ran cold at his words.

"Even beaming a mortal at any time of day," he followed up.

My look of bewilderment must have struck something in Thane because he summoned a servant to my side to help me back to my room.

"Please see to it that Amira returns to her room with whatever essentials she needs to get her prepared for the rest of the night and tomorrow," Thane instructed with a genuine smile and thanks. The servant looked so happy to be in his presence that I wanted to vomit. If it hadn't been for the fact that she averted her attention to me with a wide smile, I would have pitied her for nearly begging him to fuck her on the table with her eyes.

I returned her smile before throwing a quick glare at Thane as I followed her to the doorway.

Turning back, I found Thane's eyes on me. I licked my lips, preparing to speak while trying to steady myself under his intense stare.

"Tomorrow."

His golden eyes held mine. The hand resting on the table before him curled into a tight fist as I noted the tick in his jaw.

Why was he hesitating to reply to my statement?

"Tomorrow," he repeated back to me with a nod of his head before the doors shut in front of my face with a flick of his wrist.

Chapter Six

The days' time passed slowly as I closed myself off in my room. The level of annoyance I felt from Thane's condescending words didn't put me in a socializing mood, and as much as I wanted to wander the halls, I was not motivated to do so.

The jumbled thoughts of missing my family, Lorena searching for me, and the hex on Solaris were having a never-ending battle for attention in my head. I had spent a majority of the day shifting aimlessly from the large, open window to the bed.

Just as I had rolled onto my belly and shoved my face into the plush pillow beneath my head, a knock rattled the door. A servant had already checked on me three times, bringing lunch and dinner to my room. I had avoided the dining hall because I didn't feel like seeing *him.*

I yelled a polite invitation for her to come in and then dropped my head back down into the pillow.

"That's the invite I get after returning from the dead?" the sweet voice I could never forget asked.

I raised my head up from my pillow so quickly I strained a muscle in my neck. Raya's bright teal eyes stared at me as a genuine smile stretched across her oval shaped face. She stretched her arms outward, and I launched myself from the bed and into her open arms before she could say another word.

Pulling myself away from our embrace, I searched her up and down for any injuries.

"I'm okay, Amira," she said with a flash of pain in her eyes. "Really, I'm okay."

I swallowed at the memory of seeing my friend beaten and bruised before me and my inability to do anything to save her. All I could do was beg, and even that didn't work. Reaching further back in my memories, I remembered her words to me as they threw her into my arms within our cell, *"He took what he couldn't have."* I stiffened at the reminder of what he did to her. What Eryx *took* from her.

"Raya, did you let them know that Eryx—"

"I'm not," she interjected. "They checked. I'm not pregnant. I'm... I'm in the clear."

Her words made everything within me drop to my stomach. Everything she endured in Solaris pained me to my core, so I could only imagine how she felt.

"Fae can tell within days if we're with child." Her eyes flitted to the far corner of the room at her statement, conveying her embarrassment. A deep burning sensation arose within me. She had nothing to be embarrassed about.

"If it's okay with you, I don't want to talk much about what happened. It will be a while before I can gather myself to speak of it again," she stated with a forced, tight smile. I nodded in agreement and gestured toward the balcony beyond the glass door. Raya's eyes widened as she finally took in the space around us. "They really know how to treat their guests here, huh?" she asked as she followed me outside.

"I thought the same when I was in Solaris...let's not put too much faith in them," I said as Raya winced at my words, filling me with regret for my callous response.

I ran my hands up and down my arms at the decline in temperature once we stepped foot outside. Raya noticed the small fire pit in the middle of the balcony and smiled as flames slowly rose from the pit.

"Did you see that? Those flames just—"

Pausing in utter silence, my eyes roamed over Raya. She didn't make any motions with her hands, so I knew she didn't summon her magic.

My questioning eyes met hers as she smiled widely.

"I guess the spirit wasn't only a part of the palace in Solaris," she said with a subtle shrug of a single shoulder. "Apparently it follows me and takes care of those close to me as well. Assuming it's still interacting with you here?" she inquired while claiming her seat next to the fire.

My jaw dropped in awe. She knew the entire time about the spirit interacting with me in Solaris and never said a word. I dropped down into my seat and faced Raya.

"So, you're telling me that I wasn't imagining things each time the lights in my room would dim or the fireplace in my room would light on its own back in Solaris?" I asked, bewildered.

"Nope, you weren't imagining things. I asked for it to watch over you as it would me. I'm sure it'll be the same here now that I'm awake." Her lips moved into a soft smile before she was lost in thought. "I'm not entirely sure what or who it is. But I like to believe that it's my mother or father watching over me. Still caring for me with their tenderness I still yearn for."

A sense of ease flowed through my veins at the thought of the same spirit caring for me within these walls as well.

That technically made it two friends that I had here... if a spirit could count as a friend.

She stared out into the palace grounds before continuing. "Don't ask me how it works. I have no idea. It's been with me ever since my parents went missing."

We both fell silent at her statement. Her entire family was...

gone. There was no way she could possibly claim Raine as her brother anymore after everything he put us through. Put *her* through. How would he have treated me as his wife if he could do that to his own flesh and blood? I sucked in a deep breath as I prepared to ask her where she wanted to go, what she wanted to do now that she was awake and mostly healed. Before I could get either question out, she turned to me with determination dancing in her bright, teal eyes.

"We must find, Ezra. We can't save Solaris without him. I don't want everything my parents worked for to..." she trailed off at the thought of her parents and eldest brother. I could hear the hurt in her voice as I reached my hand out to settle atop hers. "I don't want everything they worked so hard for to fall at the hands of Raine," she continued. "Ezra is the rightful heir and will restore everything that has been destroyed. He can mend what's been broken by Raine's hand."

While preparing to inform her of my plans for Thane to take us to Medlar tomorrow, a faint voice spoke from behind, causing us both to jump as Raya threw her hands out before her, the faint tang of magic suddenly in the air.

"Whoa, sorry! I thought you heard me come in," Nova said in protest, throwing her hands in the air as a truce. We both loosened our breath as we realized who was joining us. "That's my fault, I probably shouldn't do that after everything you two have been through."

She took a few steps closer and summoned a third chair with a quick gesture of her hand, taking a seat between Raya and me.

The three of us stared out into the dusky light in comfortable silence. Something about Nova's presence brought peace instantly. She cleared her throat, preparing to speak.

"I don't know how to say this, but I just want you two to know that I'm sorry for what you endured back in Solaris. We should have intervened with your brother's foolishness sooner rather than later," she said while glancing at Raya who nodded in agreement. "Anya just informed us of the hex placed on Solaris. I don't mean to intrude or sound brash, but is there reasoning you did nothing to stop him?"

Raya visibly tensed at Nova's question.

Though I knew Nova meant no harm and was only looking for answers, or reassurance in her trust with us, Raya clearly could not sense her intentions.

"Raine went as far as casting a hex on Raya as well, regardless of blood relation," I answered for her. Nova's jaw dropped at the information just provided to her. She offered her condolences for the pain Raya endured without asking for details. To my shock, Raya filled Nova in on the extent that the hex had on her.

"So, your powers. Can you use them now?" Nova asked. "His curse should have no latitude in this realm."

Raya dipped her head to look down at her hands as she flipped them over twice, holding them out in front of her. "I... I haven't actually tried."

Nova's brows shot up. "His stupidity has no reign here in Obsidian. There's no reason you shouldn't be able to activate your magic freely now. Although, if you ever go back, I'm unsure how that would work." She offered a low smile to Raya, "What is your power? If you don't mind me asking."

I searched Raya's face at the question she was just asked. After all this time, I never inquired about her powers or what her magic could produce.

Without glancing at either of us, Raya answered with a faint smile on her lips, "Light."

Her throwing a forceful bit of magic consumed with light toward Raine during Solstice flitted through my memory.

Raya slowly stood from her chair with her palms still stretched outward in front of her. With a deep gasp we threw our arms over our eyes at the flash that surrounded us.

That would explain why she threw her hands in front of her when Nova startled us.

"Heavens above... did you just try to fucking blind us?" I asked while leaning back in my chair and rubbing my eyes.

Raya stammered as she reeled the light back into her palms.

"I'm so sorry, it's never been that bright before. Did I hurt either of you?" she asked while dropping to her knees between the two of us and placing a hand on both of our knees.

Nova and I locked eyes and began laughing hysterically at what just happened. Raya observed us in bewilderment before joining our laughing fit as well. "It's not funny you guys... what if I would've blinded you?" she yelled frantically while wiping the tears of laughter from her eyes.

"Then I wouldn't have to witness the outcomes of my stupid decisions anymore," I murmured which threw us into another laughing fit.

"And I wouldn't have to look at the scowl on Thane's face every damn day," Nova exclaimed which was my ultimate undoing until Raya's expression turned to confusion. I quickly realized that she had yet to meet Thane. With a dramatic sigh, I once again leaned back in my chair as Nova and I filled her in on the High King of Obsidian.

When we were done answering her questions about Thane, and finally gathered ourselves after our laughter, the three of us wore wide grins across our faces.

"What do you girls say to a relaxing night in my favorite place?"

Raya and I exchanged nervous glances.

What if we put our trust in Nova and it ends up being a mistake?

Nova's smile faltered as if she knew exactly what we were thinking. "I'm sorry, it was a stupid thought. I haven't given you two enough reason to trust me yet. I just thought you could use some relaxation and freedom after well... you know," she stated sheepishly as she stood from her chair, teetering from foot to foot.

My heart squeezed at her statement. She was making an effort to make us feel comfortable and here we were judging her. She did assist in saving both of our asses after all.

"Let's go," I said enthusiastically as I stood from my chair. Nova's eyes lit up with a matching smile. "Really?" she asked. "It's not that far from here, but I'll have Xavier walk us to be safe since I've heard someone is trying to break through our wards since we brought you guys here." She grimaced at her statement before smiling again. "No one has ever broken through, but better to be safe than sorry."

Moments later, we were following Xavier through a thickly wooded area until we reached a large body of water that was illuminated under the moonlight. My brow furrowed, confused as to why we were at a large body of water after sundown.

"You ladies have fun," Xavier said before dipping his head as a goodbye. "I'll be nearby if you need me."

Nova protested him having to remain in the area, stating that he should go enjoy his night. He waved her off with a smirk and vanished from our sight.

"Um...mind telling us what we're doing here?" Raya inquired with a raise of a single brow.

Without an explanation, Nova unclasped her vest and raised her undershirt over her head. I swallowed waiting for her to speak and snuck a glance at Raya who was locked in on Nova's every movement as she rubbed her palms on her pants.

"I'm assuming you guys aren't modest?" Nova inquired as she started unbuttoning her pants.

"Well...no. I'm not b-but," Raya stammered in an attempt to answer the question.

Nova giggled before fully removing her pants and pointing at the open body of water. "It's a hot spring."

Raya and I glanced at each other and back to Nova in confusion.

"Do they not have hot springs where you guys are from?" she asked cautiously. We shook our heads in unison. Nova nodded with an expression of surprise. "Well to put it simply, the water is comfortably warm and extremely relaxing." Her eyes beamed with excitement as she removed the remainder of her clothing.

Naked.

She was completely naked.

I'd never been with another woman before, but heavens above if Nova didn't make me consider my sexuality. I felt intrusive as I stared at her body before she pranced over to the hot spring and fully dipped beneath the water's surface. Glancing at Raya who might as well have had a string of drool falling from her mouth, I elbowed her in the ribs to bring her back to earth. "Thanks," she muttered before pulling at her clothing to remove it. I raised my own brows at her actions before shrugging my shoulders and doing the same.

Nova told no lies about the comfort of the dark waters. My muscles immediately relaxed as I submerged myself in the warm water, followed by Raya doing the same.

"I come out here when I need to clear my mind. Or just relax after a stressful day in training," Nova stated as she shook the water from her short, dark hair. Her bright white teeth flashed in the moonlight.

"I can see why," I responded while floating on my back. I didn't have a care in the world about my freshly washed curls getting wet.

The night sky was filled with stars, and I instinctively searched for the constellations that I knew—something familiar in this realm of uncertainty, magic, and darkness. My father had spoken of a specific constellation many times, yet he nor I had ever seen it ourselves. With celestial maps laid out before us, we studied constellations together since no one else in our miniature family had been interested. The fond memory had me naming the ones I found above in my head.

The little dipper.

Orion's Belt.

Leo.

My breath hitched as I noted the last constellation, the only one my father and I were never able to locate.

Andromeda.

I swallowed hard as I remembered its alternative name. *"The Chained Lady."*

For the first time since I set foot in Obsidian, my anxiety crept its way in through the surrounding calm. A feeling of chains wrapped around my limbs, sending me to an inescapable dark void. The darkness from my time in Solaris wrapped itself around my mind, holding me prisoner, frozen, in my own memories.

The recollection of having to see my friends humiliated and abused while I remained chained to a throne forced my heart to beat so rapidly, I feared it was about to break bones to escape. The subtle whooshing from my heart pumping mixed with the sounds of the water caused an imbalance I could no longer control. My focus settled on the constellation again, a reminder of Raine's promise to force me to carry his heir. Bound to him by our child. Truly trapped. A *Chained Lady.*

I suddenly forgot how to breathe.

My body bolted upwards as my panting and gasping for air forced its presence.

"Hey, you okay?" Raya asked with narrowed eyes as she floated over to me, Nova not far behind her. "Did you see something? Someone?" she asked as Nova began surveying the area around us.

Catching my breath, I reminded myself that I was in my own head. *"Raine isn't here. You're in Obsidian,"* I said over and over to myself until I believed it. Wiping the water from my face, I focused on Nova and Raya who had repeated their question again since I had yet to answer.

"No, no. I'm fine. Everything is fine. Sorry, I'm just getting in my own head," I replied with a forced laugh.

Raya tilted her head at my answer. The quick squint of her

eyes let me know that she sensed I was lying, and I tensed, awaiting her next words.

Saving me from her interrogation, a noise rustled in the trees beyond, causing us all to focus in the same direction as Raya raised her palms.

"Mind if we join you ladies?" Silas chimed, stepping through the crowded brush towards the edge of the spring. An enthusiastic smile consumed his handsome face.

Xavier came running after him. "I'm so sorry. I tried to stop him to give you privacy, but this idiot doesn't understand what that word means," he explained with a considerable amount of irritation.

Before we could protest, Silas was already halfway naked without a care in the world.

Part of me, the teensy conservative part of me that has been dormant since... well, forever, knew I should look away. But I watched as he quickly stripped before us.

Heavens above...

Every inch of him was covered in muscle. My gaze badly wanted to dip below his waist, but before I could turn into a full-blown creep, Nova snapped me out of my thoughts.

"Erebus save us, put your fucking clothes back on, Silas. They don't want to see that," Nova said with a grimace.

"Speak for yourself," Raya and I muttered in unison under our breaths.

Silas came running to the open water in all his glory before jumping in with a huge splash. We all laughed before noticing an additional shadow behind Xavier.

Thane.

There was no way in hell his tightly wound demeanor would allow him to relax in here with us.

There was no way I wanted him in here with us.

In here with us while I was naked.

As if he could read my mind, he began unbuttoning his dark

shirt. The planes of his muscles flexed with each small flick of his wrist. The arms of his shirt were tight, making every movement visible and alluring. His eyes never left mine as his hands slid slowly down the front of his body, each button loosening under his deft fingers. Biting the inside of my cheek, I knew he was taunting me to see if I would turn away.

The lump stuck in my throat caused me to cough as Raya patted my back. Thank heavens the others weren't paying attention to me. Silas and Nova were now splashing each other, and Xavier had somehow slipped under our radar and joined in on the fun. A pang of disappointment hit me at the realization that I had missed him stripping down to join us. All of these men were overly attractive.

Nova grabbed Raya and threw her into the middle of the fight, leaving me to continue my stare down with Thane. Somehow, I knew he wanted me to watch him undress.

Every fiber within me wanted to watch him undress.

If I could see his muscles through his clothing, he had to be godlike when naked.

Snapping myself back to reality, I stopped biting my lower lip and shook my head. I could've sworn I saw a smile flash on his tanned face.

Before he could loosen the last button, I turned my back.

He wouldn't get a reaction out of me. But I had to fight every muscle within me not to turn around to see what he possessed under those clothes.

An audible splash emerged from behind me as I braced myself. Waves surrounded me from his body entering the dark, warm water.

"Should've watched the show, Pixie," he said as he floated past me.

I inwardly snarled at his words, but acted as if I didn't hear him. I knew if I responded I'd be giving him exactly what he wanted—my anger.

I watched as he floated over to his friends, the defined muscles of his broad back glistening under the moonlight. I swallowed as he stood, running his hands through his dark, shoulder length locs. My gaze refused to look away from the black swirls and designs inked across his back.

"If you stare any harder, he may fuck you tonight," Raya whispered in my ear, causing me to lose my footing and almost slip under the water's surface.

"Oh, piss off," I spat back with a splash to her face. She laughed as she wiped the water from her eyes.

"He is a sight to see though... they all are," she said as her eyes flitted over to Nova.

I quickly noted the intensity of Nova's stare toward Thane. My focus bounced back and forth between them while trying to figure out what was triggering her. The anger in her eyes intensified as she whispers to him with a stern look on her face.

"Now is not the time, Thane," Nova reprimanded, glancing quickly towards us before glaring at Thane. "We came out here to relax."

His whispers became louder as he continued speaking. I began chewing on the inside of my cheek when I barely heard him mention my name.

Sensing my eyes on him, he whipped his head in my direction with a deep sneer on his face. My gaze never faltered as I raised a brow before narrowing my eyes at his annoyingly handsome face.

"If she's so worried about it, let's get the details together now," he remarked louder than before while keeping his focus on me in a challenge.

"Details of what?" I questioned with narrowed eyes.

Thane tilted his head to survey me, though there was nothing to survey as I purposefully kept everything below my neck underwater. I was not shy, but I'd be damned if I graced him with a view of my assets given his shitty attitude.

"To inquire if you informed Raya about your plans for tomorrow," he said cooly.

"What's he talking about?" Raya inquired. I fought to find the words to explain how I was going to talk to her about our plans to leave Obsidian earlier, but it had slipped my mind.

Even the water remained silent at Raya's question, prompting her to repeat herself. Her innocence ate me alive as I floated in self-disappointment. "Raya, I was going to tell you earlier, but we—"

"Your friend didn't inform you about her plan to take you both back to Medlar tomorrow?" Thane questioned her in a derisive tone, cutting me off from my explanation.

Raya's eyes widen as she looked back and forth between me and Thane.

Finally, her gaze rested on me before her teal eyes narrowed. I opened and closed my mouth, trying to force myself to respond and dig myself out of this hole.

"You... you were just going to abandon my people in Solaris?" she questioned.

Blood drained from my face, and Thane knew, in that moment, that he had won whatever game he was playing.

"Raya, I was going to speak with you earlier but—"

She held up a hand to stop me from speaking. I could see her questioning the loyalty in our friendship, her expression filled with shock at my betrayal. She stepped away from me, and I felt a sharp tug in my chest.

"You listened to me earlier about everything my parents worked for...while planning to tear me away from my home?"

Hurt drips from her words. She turned away from me, the water rippling as she moved towards the bank.

I shot a sharp look at Thane, who surprisingly cringed at my glare before regaining his stoned face composure.

"She was so adamant about the situation that I had assumed she would have told you by now." I gawked at his statement, the lump in my throat working to be released in the form of a frustrated scream.

I swallowed my rage, blinking multiple times to regain my composure. Just as I reached for Raya's arm to explain this misunderstanding, she floated out of my reach.

"I'd like to go back now," she informed Nova while moving past her. Nova nodded in agreement as she flashed a look of pity in my direction with a shrug of her shoulders. She was just as bewildered by the entire situation as I was.

They both scurried out of the water, and Silas cleared his throat at the sight of the two women rising from the water completely naked.

I clenched my eyes shut before opening them with a look of fire focused on Thane.

"You piece of shit," I spat as my breathing increased.

Xavier and Silas visibly tensed at my statement, glancing between Thane and I with wide eyes.

"Thane, I think maybe you were in the wrong with how you —," Silas spoke.

"Leave us," Thane snapped at his friends.

Xavier hesitated to follow the command, but without dispute, they both swam to land and followed Raya and Nova into the night.

My skin prickled with anticipation as fire roared within me. Thane stared at me with his lips curled upward.

Regardless of if he saved me or not, I would drown this motherfucker before I accepted having to deal with his bullshit another day.

Slowly, he began floating toward me.

"You don't scare me," I announced. *And I meant it*. The only thing that scared me in this world was the thought of never seeing my family again. The mere thought of them squeezed my heart tightly as I placed my attention on the night sky that now held hints of deep purple among the stars.

A sinister laugh left his lips as his shadows began to rise above the warm water and encapsulate the space around us.

There was no way I could hold my own against him in a fight with that type of strength.

He was only a few feet away when he stopped and glanced up at the moon.

"It's just you and me now, Pixie."

Chapter Seven

The venomous look in his eyes as he slowly brought his gaze back down from the night sky to focus on my rage had me clenching my jaw at the anticipation of his next move. His bright golden eyes never veered from my face as they darkened. Whatever venom he wanted to spit out, I could match it. But what I couldn't match – if he had any malicious intent — was his strength and speed if he were in fact Fae.

On top of that, the thought of both of us being completely naked was not helping me focus.

A sinister grin swept across his ungodly, handsome face. He dipped his head beneath the surface, and came back up once more, running his hand through those wet, thick locs that I had noted earlier. Each bead of water that dripped down his defined chest muscles had me fighting to keep my focus on the issue at hand, especially after noticing how the swirls of ink on his back crept around to cover the ridges of muscles across his chest.

"What is your problem, Thane?" I asked in annoyance.

He licked the dripping water from his lips, and I did my best to stay focused on how angry I was instead of his perfectly sculpted lips. "You don't even know me, yet you already hate me."

His eyes narrowed slightly, scrutinizing me without any spoken words. The expression on his face was unreadable as he tilted his head, studying me in the moonlight.

"You get three questions, Pixie," he stated before licking his lips once again. My gaze lingered on his full bottom lip, and I couldn't stop myself from thinking about what it would be like to sink my teeth into it. The trance ended when his statement about three questions registered.

"Excuse me?" I responded, confused at his statement. "You just caused a massive argument between Raya and me, and now you want to play a fucking game?!"

I was so angry that I wasn't sure if the heat on my skin was coming from the hot springs or myself.

Thane let out a frustrated breath before repeating himself.

"You get three questions. I get three questions. You said I don't know you. So, this will be my chance and your chance. If that's too hard for you to understand, let me know and I can do my best to simplify it for you" he smirked. "I'll try to use really, really small words."

"You're insufferable, you know that?"

"And you're nothing more than a damsel in distress. What's your point?"

Fire bubbled over in my veins. The insistent yearning to gouge his eyes out was about to become a reality if I didn't calm myself down. "What you think of me isn't my concern," I retorted.

"Great, let's begin," he said with a monotonous voice.

As nervous as I was to be alone with him in the night, I wasn't going to let it show.

"You first, prince charming," I offered mockingly while batting my lashes excessively.

Irritation flashed in his darkened eyes, but he nodded with a clench of his jaw.

"We will start by trying again with my original question from this morning. How did you end up in Solaris?"

I clenched my teeth together, grinding them thoroughly at his question. Before I could protest, he chimed in, "If you decline any questions, the game is over, and you don't get to ask your three." His lips curled in the corner as his eyes narrowed. I grunted in frustration, licking my lips as I glanced upward, preparing to provide my story.

I gave him every detail of the events that took place right before and during my time in Solaris—from Lorena, to falling for Raine, to our captivity to being rescued by yours truly, only leaving out certain details that didn't need to be disclosed.

"Next question," I demanded when I didn't receive a reply after answering his question in full detail. He just stared at me with his usual cool expression. *He was painfully irritating.*

"Did he hurt you?"

I narrowed my eyes at his question, confused.

"That mark on your face. Did he do that?" he asked. His voice so dark that a chill ran up my spine despite being submerged in warm water. I raised my hand to my cheek where Raine had back-handed me.

"The marks on your wrists. I'm assuming they're from chains that were used to keep you where he wanted you," Thane stated while dragging his teeth over his bottom lip. Anger flared in his eyes as he waited for me to answer. I stared helplessly into the water. Seconds passed in silence and I flinched when a growl escaped him.

"Did he touch you unwarranted?"

I sucked in a breath at his prying question. "Boundaries, Thane. You're on thin ice," I warned. I didn't need to put my hand to my face to know embarrassment was showing on my cheeks.

"Or you could just trust me and answer the question. Not everything has an underlying purpose to attack you."

"Yet, that's all you've done since you brought me here," I snapped back. "*And trust you?* I don't even know you."

He tsked as his gaze drifted to the side and back to me. "So, is that a pass on the question? Great, see you back at the palace," he said as he turned to get out of the water.

"Stop," I snapped, flustered and angry. I had fully intended to ask questions of my own, had supplied my entire story to get something useful from the taciturn man in front of me. I would not stop now.

Thane turned around, a look of gentle expectation on his face.

"He... Raine, tried to in the end. Tried... to take advantage of me. Threatened that..."

My hands intertwined in panic beneath the water as I tried to figure out the words to describe his threat to me in the holding cell. Raine and I had intimate moments but had never had intercourse despite all my attempts to persuade him.

"Threatened what, Pixie?"

"Stop fucking calling me that," I hissed through gritted teeth.

"I thought it didn't bother you?"

"It doesn't," I grunted. Collecting myself, I continued my answer, "He threatened to take what *belonged* to him." Embarrassed by my answer, I focused back on the stars, the calming darkness that surrounded us. I prepared myself to bask in the silence that Thane would bring by not replying, but his deep voice caused me to jerk my attention back in his direction.

"I already knew," he said in an angered tone. I studied his face in confusion, waiting for him to clarify.

"You knew he tried to take advantage of me?" I asked angrily. I narrowed my eyes at him, waiting for an answer that I knew would make me even angrier than I already was.

Rolling his lips inward, his eyes darkened further until they were almost black. I noted another tick of his jaw in the moonlight.

"I already knew he wasn't a real man," he clarified while rolling his neck.

I stared at him with parted lips as he turned away from me in the water.

"My turn," I whispered into the comfortable night air. I sucked in a sharp breath as I noticed multiple small, healed scars on his back within the black ink. There were so many, but it wasn't my place to ask him how he got them.

He looked over his shoulder and nodded once, permission to begin my line of questioning.

As much as he annoyed me, as much as I couldn't stand him in my presence, to look at him was a privilege. The man was a sight to see with his tanned skin dripping in the water and glistening under the bright moonlight. If I thought Raine looked godly, Thane was a different type of cosmic-being above him.

How could a man be sculpted so perfectly?

He turned back around to face me when I didn't follow up with a question. The angle of the moonlight shining on his ribs showed swirls of ink that led all the way back up over his shoulder, up the side of his neck and ended behind his left ear. How did I not notice that before?

Noting where my gaze was fixed, he cleared his throat, breaking me out of my trance. "See something you like?" he asked with a smug look smothered in confidence.

Ignoring his question, I rolled my eyes. "Why are you not bothered by me being human?"

"Is it something I should be concerned about?" he responded with knitted brows and a tilt of is head.

"No," I answered, feeling like an idiot.

"Okay then," he answered. Noting my frustration with his simple answer, he continued. "I don't care what any living being is as long as they don't cause harm to what I love most."

"Which is?" I asked, intrigued.

He glared at me as if I should already know the answer.

"My friends and what little family that I have left."

He lifted one hand from under the water's surface and held it up to the moonlight, studying it. "And that's two questions, Pixie."

I cursed under my breath.

"What are you?" I finished up my round of questioning, failing to ask a single important one thanks to my rambling.

For the first time since I landed in Obsidian, Thane looked utterly confused.

"Are you... Fae?" I asked to clarify.

"Obviously," he answered, annoyed.

"I'm sorry that I don't know every fucking thing in every fucking realm," I snapped back. His eyes quickly widened at my reply.

"Your wings. Do they retract on command? I haven't seen any of you with them except for Nova since we landed," I inquired and began chewing on my lip. Thane's focus dropped to my lips and I saw his chest rise and fall before he nodded his head. He must have read the annoyance of his short answers on my face because he huffed and resumed speaking.

"Divine Fae," he followed up with an exaggerated eyeroll.

"I'm sorry?" I asked, confused.

"I'm what is considered *Divine Fae*. Some Fae are... stronger. More powerful. They're known as Divine Fae," he answered with a grunt. "And yes, all of us can produce or retract our wings as we wish. Except for Nova."

"Why don't hers retract?"

"That is her story to tell. Not mine," he answered harshly.

I processed his information for a moment. "So, you're a high king then? Like Raine?" I inquired.

He sneered before snapping at me. "Game's over."

"What's your deal? I was just trying to piece everything— "

"Do not fucking compare me to that revolting piece of shit," he hissed with a snarl on his face.

"I wasn't comparing you, asshole. It's the only example I have. Does everything always have to be a fucking argument with you?"

We glared at each other, both of our submerged chests visually heaving in the overly warm water that was now bubbling around us.

"Forget it. I don't need this," I spat and turned to get out of the water but suddenly froze in place, remembering we were both naked. I wasn't ashamed of nudity, but I wasn't willing to give the grumpy male behind me a free show.

"Go ahead. Run away, Pixie. I'm so shocked," he said with a sarcastic drip in his tone.

"Piss off, Thane," I yelled while spinning back around to face him. "Share your little dick energy with someone else. Your less-than-intimidating shadows don't scare me. Your temper doesn't scare me. And I'm sure as fuck not intimidated by your childish insults. I can spot a man that hasn't been fucked from a mile away. Take your frustration out on someone that cares. Because it's not me, your fucking highness," I said with a fake curtsy beneath the water's surface, dipping my head low to imitate the title I gave to him.

When I stood back up and raised my head, we were inches apart. Shocked, I stumbled backwards, almost going under water before Thane snatched my wrist, yanking me back up and toward him.

I glanced down to see my bare breasts pressed against his chest.

His rock-solid chest.

I swallowed as we both stared at each other with heat from a thousand flames flowing between the contact of our bare skin. The thought of him naked below the water sent an additional flash of heat through my veins. Surely, he wouldn't be like Raine, attempting to take advantage of me. He could easily overpower me with immortal strength, and I wouldn't be able to defend myself like back in Medlar with other mortals.

I swallowed at the thought. I was out there alone with a man I didn't know.

How long had we been staring at each other? Seconds? Minutes?

He dipped his head low, bringing those lips I had stared at multiple times to my ear. His breath, hot against the cool night air, caused me to shiver. At some point, his free hand had slipped around my waist and was resting on the middle of my back while the other still clutched my wrist.

"I didn't get to ask my third question," he hummed in my ear. "But it seems there's a more pressing matter on your mind." He squeezed me tighter to his body yet carefully kept our lower halves from touching. My eyes flicked above his shoulder, and my stomach took a leap as I noticed his shadows taunting from behind him. Another shudder rolled through me. "Who I fuck, and when I fuck isn't your concern. Nor will it ever be. But if you weren't so fucking irritating, I would devour every single curve of your body while you beg for me to stop. While you beg for me to let you come. While you *plead* with me to fuck you until the sun rises." Releasing my wrist to tuck a stray curl behind my ear, he brought his face back in front of mine. "I'll save my last question for a later time."

His erratic breaths starkly contrasted with my shallow ones as our eyes remained locked on one another, the touch of his hand on my back now firm. Slowly, his eyes shifted to a darker hue and a gasp released from my lips.

The hand on my back softened to a gentle touch before he removed it, backing away. My mouth hung open; my breaths heavy from his words. I forced the lustful haze away and closed my mouth, trying to steady my breathing as he watched me with a knowing look.

"You thinking I'd want any of that from you screams that you're delusional," I said once I'd calmed down. Turning away from him, I began to make my way toward land. I didn't care if I didn't know my way back. I would rather spend the night among the trees than remain in the pool with him.

A deep growl boomed from Thane, and my legs began moving faster.

"Stop fucking running, Pixie."

That lone sentence made me stop cold in my tracks. I was a lot of things, but being someone that ran from their problems was not one of them. Turning around, I saw him glistening under the moonlight and bit the inside of my cheek. "Stop being a delusional, self-absorbed prick."

Thane's eyes narrowed before producing a rough, mocking laugh while he stared at the moon. "I can do that. And I can even keep my promise to take you back home when you stop being a pretentious brat that can't handle when you're not in control."

I observed him studying the stars for a moment, attempting to no longer acknowledge my presence. My frustration had reached its ceiling, and I had to catch myself from biting through my cheek when he didn't even have the courtesy to look at me while insulting me. As I turned to leave again, his voice projected from behind me.

"Andromeda."

The fire in my veins was smothered by cold, hard ice. My eyes narrowed, waiting for him to continue.

"The constellation. I'm sure you're aware of that story. Kind of like your own," he said. I blinked, frozen in place. "A beautiful, young woman who was placed in a dangerous situation and had to be saved by her knight in shining armor because she was *fucking helpless*."

I bared my teeth. Thane knew nothing about me, yet he remained adamant that I was helpless in every aspect of life.

"Prove me wrong, Amira."

I flared my eyes as I prepared to give him a piece of my mind, to inform him that he didn't know me and would never be given the privilege to do so. That my inability to put up a fight against a witch or immortal didn't make me helpless. That I was not afraid to fight. But before I could counter his remark, he raised a hand in the air and motioned it in a counterclockwise circle.

Within a blink, I was beamed back into my room at the palace. Water fell in heavy droplets onto the floor beneath me from my wet, naked body.

I seethed at the thought of him getting the last word.

I. Fucking. Hated. Him.

Chapter Eight

As much as I wanted to hunt Thane down in his own home to give him a piece of my mind, Raya was my priority. Without trying, I always somehow found a way to betray her trust. I wanted to mention my plans to return to Medlar tomorrow immediately after her recovery, but it had slipped my mind with everything else that we needed to discuss.

I threw on clothes from the pile Nova supplied me with when we first arrived and headed out the door of my room, quickly realizing a major issue in my search.

I had no idea where Raya's room was.

I began the search on my floor, opening door after door only to find empty room after empty room.

On the eighth door, I found Xavier sitting at a desk in his room, sharpening his weapons.

Shirtless.

I covered my eyes like a child and apologized for intruding. I turned to leave, but pivoted back around with my hand still clamped over my eyes to ask if he knew where I could find Raya's room.

His warm laugh made me smile.

"You can take your hand down, Amira. It's just a bare chest and you already saw it in the hot springs," he said in his deep, calming voice. I peeked through slightly cracked fingers before I removed my hand slowly as the warmth of my embarrassment flooded me.

"When we returned, she headed to the observatory with Nova," he informed me before raising a thick brow. "Everything okay with you and Thane?"

I lifted a corner of my lips and shrugged my shoulders.

"Any idea how to remove the stick that's shoved up his ass?"

Xavier laughed loudly and slammed his hand down on the desk, causing multiple things to fall to the ground. I walked over to help him place things back onto the desk, but he demanded that I leave them.

"I've got it, princess," he said as he threw the objects back onto the wooden surface.

He ran a hand through his long brown hair, blowing out a breath of air. "Thane has been through a lot. Seen a lot. It takes time for him to put his trust in people. But once he does, it's hard to get rid of him. He will have your back until the end of time."

I nodded my head in understanding even though I wanted to call bullshit. I couldn't ever see Thane trusting me or having my back for *anything* in the future.

"But he also doesn't know how to act around beautiful women as well. Little dick energy is what I like to call it," he said with a wink and a broad smile.

Xavier spoke the least when I arrived in Obsidian, so for him to make an exact joke of mine caught me off guard. A wide grin spread across my face before I laughed out loud. He offered to walk me to the observatory to meet with Nova and Raya, and I gratefully accepted , letting him know I'd rather not get lost in there at night. He chuckled, arranging his weapons neatly on the desk, holstering a few on him, before leading the way out of his room. *Did he always carry them with him?*

As we walked in silence through halls and winding staircases –
How massive is this place? – I noticed the comfortable silence
between Xavier and I. Why was I so much more comfortable here
than I was in Solaris?

I peeked up at him from the corner of my eye. Xavier was the
tallest and largest in the group with the most intimidating look.
Everything about him screamed *warrior,* and he had the muscles
to prove it. A faint cut settled on his right cheek, barely visible
beneath his beard.

As if he could sense me staring at him, he cleared his throat.
"Don't let Thane's antics get to you. You casually handing him
back the same bullshit he gives you is something he's not used to.
And honestly, it'd make us happy to see him explode from frustration," he said with a small grin.

"I just hate that he thinks I'm some helpless human that can't
defend themselves. What exactly was I supposed to do against
immortal strength? And I don't have an ounce of magic to fight
back with," I explained, my previous irritation returning in full
force.

Xavier stopped walking and turned to face me. His large hazel
eyes settled on me as he sighed. "I've known you less than a week
and I know for a fact that you're not helpless. Meaning that
Thane knows the same. He's just trying to get under your skin."

The gratification of his statement was short lived.

As if we weren't just in deep conversation, Xavier swiftly
raised his hand and swung it toward my face. Mindlessly, I dodged
his blow and kicked my leg out to bring him down onto his back
before standing over him with my own fist raised above his face.

The rush of adrenaline had my heart pushing against my ribs
while I tried to figure out what just happened.

*Xavier had just tried to hit me. And why wasn't he defending
himself?*

With a heaving chest I glanced at my clenched fist and back
down to Xavier.

Frozen, I noticed the smirk on his face.

"Someone that is defenseless wouldn't have acted as swiftly in that scenario," he said with a hint of satisfaction. *He planned that... with zero intentions of hitting me.* My mouth dropped open at the realization as I offered my hand to help him up.

As if he needed it.

He stood from the floor, brushing off his all-black ensemble, and raised a hand outward to gesture that we continue walking.

"Why?" I asked, confused.

"Why what?" he countered with a raised brow.

"Why are you telling me things about Thane? Why are you showing me that I'm not as helpless as he implies?" He shook his head at my question while we continued to walk. "Because I know what it's like to feel worthless. To feel like you're the weakest link in a place that you don't know," his voice faded into a whisper. "You should consider training with us while you're here."

"No thanks," I responded quickly. *Training with immortals? Did he want me to die?* If I wanted that outcome I would've just stayed in Solaris. "I plan on leaving tomorrow anyway, but thanks for the offer," I said apologetically.

Xavier nodded his head in understanding before turning left and opening a gigantic, dark wooden door to a room with a glass ceiling.

The grey flooring shone in the moonlight from above with hints of sparkle. I tilted my head upward to gaze at the clear ceiling above. My lips parted in awe as I took in the view provided by the wide range of glass. Stars littered the beautiful, dark night sky, boasting a moon that fully illuminated the otherwise darkened room. My eyes shifted in every direction, absorbing each small detail until my attention landed on a telescope in the center of the room that held Raya's attention. Nova lay next to it with her arms spread wide, taking in the sky above.

Raya popped her head back from the eyepiece of the telescope to speak to Nova but noticed Xavier and me instead. Her face turned into a visible frown as her eyes slightly narrowed, causing me to deflate. We stared at each other for a moment before Xavier cleared his throat and announced to Nova that she was needed in the courtyard.

Lie.

"For what exactly?" she questioned, turning her head in his direction. Noting the scowl on his face, portraying that he was obviously trying to give Raya and me alone time to sort out our pressing issue, she blurted out an additional reply. "Right. I forgot about that thing we said we would take care of."

Nova gracefully hopped up from where she was laying and glided over to Xavier. She leaned into me while whispering, "I tried to talk to her before you found us. I think I worked some of my charm on her a little bit." Leaning back, she hooked her arm around Xavier's. He threw a wink at me before they disappeared through the door and into the hall.

I took a moment to glance up at the sky once more before focusing back on Raya who was now staring at me with her arms crossed in front of her chest. Studying her for a moment, I sucked in a deep breath and began to plead my case.

"Raya, look... I'm going to put it all out in the open before you get even more mad at my stupidity. I wanted to tell you. And I was going to tell you. But I was just so happy to see you were awake and at the same time I was hurt because we revisited everything that happened to you that I didn't want to bring up such a serious subject right away. And then Nova came and invited us to the hot spring and then I got stuck with Thane which.... Yea," I word vomited to her in one breath. Chewing on my lip, I surveyed her face and remembered I forgot to say the most important bit of information that was necessary to hopefully fix my mistake. "I'm sorry," I said while scrunching my nose.

My heart stopped beating for a moment when she didn't reply, nor move, until a fleeting smile crossed her beautiful face. "I know you are. I just wanted to hear you say it," she retorted while pursing her lips followed by a much wider smile.

"I hate you," I muttered, which caused her to laugh and walk over to me.

After we hugged and exchanged apologies, she asked a question I was wholly unprepared for: "Are you... are you really leaving tomorrow?" The vulnerability in that small waver filled me with dread.

I swallowed, trying to figure out how to answer her question.

"I'm... I'm not sure. I don't want the people of Medlar to suffer because of me. And I don't know what Raine will do if he gets ahold of my family. But I should have spoken with you about Solaris before making such a brash decision. My realm is not more or less important than yours. Innocent people are at risk in both," I rushed out and waited for her response. I intertwined my fingers and fidgeted with my clothing when the silence became overbearing.

She ran her tongue across her bottom lip before biting it, nodding her head. "You're right. Both realms possess innocent people that are at risk of suffering," she affirmed, and I held my breath. "But if it were my family, I would choose them. So, Medlar is where we will go first. But we must have a plan."

I was at a loss for words. Was she offering to return to Medlar with me? She held a finger in the air before continuing, "And we will make our way back to Solaris with a plan after we sort everything out with your family."

My eyes widened at her answer. "You're willing to return to Medlar with me?"

She seemed taken aback at my question with a furrow brow and a tilt of her head. "Would you not return to Solaris with me if the roles were reversed?"

I rolled my lips inward, fighting against the toothy smile threatening to surface across my face. If it were possible for a heart to burst from feeling so many emotions, mine would have exploded in that very moment. "You know that I would," I said without question.

"Then it is settled," she confirmed, swiftly moved on from the conversation to show me how to use the telescope. It must've been a full hour before I finally pulled my eye away from the lens.

We laid in the space on the floor that Nova had occupied before she left and gazed at the stars providing us light in the sea of darkness. The calmness flowing through me had my eyelids feeling heavy. I turned my head to look at Raya who had a faint smile playing on her lips, her unwavering attention on the sky above.

"What are you thinking about?" I inquired.

Raya turned her head to look at me, still wearing the same smile.

"Thinking about the memories I shared with Ezra."

My stomach did a flip while I thought about how much loss she had experienced. At the same time, a twinge of pain surrounded my heart as I thought about my own siblings. *Did they think I was dead by now?* I had already considered asking Nova to help me send them a letter but thought it would be too risky.

"Did you two get along?"

She nodded her head with a chuckle. "He was the best," she said as her smile faltered.

Was.

It hurt to breathe as I absorbed the pain from her. I missed my own brother and knew exactly where he was. I couldn't imagine what it must feel like for your mother, father and brother to go missing.

"Do you mind if I ask exactly what happened to him?"

Raya released a deep sigh and lifted one side of her mouth. "We had breakfast as usual in the dining hall and he asked if I wanted to go for a ride into town. I agreed and told him to meet me at the palace gates in twenty minutes so that I could change into the proper attire for a horse ride. When I came outside, his horse was gone and mine was in a panicked frenzy. I screamed for Raine, and the two of us frantically rode our horses through every single path of the forest yelling his name but..." she trailed off. "Our men searched day and night for him as they did our parents, but to no avail. He and his horse were gone without a trace."

I reached out to grab her hand lying at her side. "We will find him." She turned her head to meet my gaze before she replied.

"I know."

I rubbed my lips together as I battled with my anxiety to ask the question that had been burning a hole through the back of my mind since we'd been laying there. I blew out a silent breath before finally speaking again.

"Can I ask you a question?"

"Always," Raya replied confidently. My heart surged with gratitude for her friendship.

"What was supposed to happen on that third night of Solstice back in Solaris?"

Raya flipped her hand so that we were now palm to palm and gripped tightly. Minutes passed without her uttering a single word. "Raya, tell me. Please," I begged as my heart raced and goosebumps rose on my skin at the thought of what she could possibly say. When I finally glanced over at her, a single tear rolled down her cheek. I sat up quickly and swiped it away. "Hey, I'm sorry, I didn't mean to upset you. I just wanted to know what—" she shook her head to cut me off.

"No, I'm sorry. I'm sorry I wasn't strong enough to break my brother's—" Raya paused at the title she gave Raine. "I'm sorry I wasn't strong enough to break *Raine's* hold on me," she said with empathetic eyes. "I fought so hard to try to tell you to run. To not listen to his lies and deceit, but I couldn't break the hex that was placed on me for a long enough period of time."

"Raya, I don't blame you at all. For any of it."

"I know, I know. I just hate myself for it."

Another moment of silence swept through the room before she groaned and gave me the answer I asked for, but desperately didn't want to hear.

"On the third night of Solstice, mates do their very best to conceive before the night is over. It's believed that the strongest of heirs are conceived on the third night of Solstice. And since you two were mates—so you say—he would have..."

I searched her eyes with confusion as the realization slowly began to settle in.

"He would have what, Raya?" I whispered, fire consuming every vein woven within me.

She swallowed once more before providing the rest of the details.

"He would have taken you to bed to become pregnant with his child whether you agreed to or not. Regardless of what you wished for in your relationship at that time, he would have followed through to conceive an heir to the throne," she whispered and swept away another tear. "How he figured that would have happened I'm not sure, as I told you before that a mortal would not be able to carry the offspring of an immortal. It's simply unheard of outside of tales."

I opened and closed my mouth like a fish out of water. Words escaped me as I tried to register the information she had just provided me. The room remained silent, broken only by the pounding of my own heart.

He intended to take me, and in the haze of my own hexed mind, I might have even given myself to that monster. In either case, my will would not have been my own.

Damsel. I heard Thane's words from the hot springs echo, beating in time to my steady heartbeat. A fire began coursing through my veins, pulsing to the same tempo as my heartbeat that thrummed loudly in my head. The heat seemed to rush through my body, building in its intensity, its rhythm. A song of wrath and rage began to crescendo as I thought of my own helplessness.

Damsel.

A boisterous laugh broke free from Raya's mouth, startling me. The inferno building in my chest retreated at the sight of her head thrown back, peals of laughter reverberating throughout the room.

"What could you possibly be laughing about right now?" I snapped as I stood to my feet.

Did she just make that up? How could something so monstrous be funny to her?

Raya mimicked my action, rising to her feet before placing a hand on my shoulder.

"I'm laughing because I can't wait for us to get our revenge. Because I know it's going to be perfectly dark and twisted."

The spark of life that ignited at her words had never shone so bright.

Her people deserved to be saved from Raine's hand. She deserved to have her brother beg for mercy at her hand. And I deserved to hold him by the balls while he did the begging.

And I'd be damned if I didn't see it come to fruition.

Chapter Nine

Morning came accompanied by loud noises and harsh yelling outside. I threw on the robe I had been gifted by Nova the first night I arrived and rushed out onto the balcony to survey the area before me.

In the distance, I glimpsed Xavier and Thane standing off to the side of a large platform while Nova clapped, staring at the center of what appeared to be a sparring ring. Focusing my sight on the same location, I saw Silas sprawled on his stomach with a woman firmly holding his head locked in place with her forearm. I grimaced as I watched his body resemble a scorpion, making me recoil into myself.

"Damnit Silas, you're embarrassing me. Get the fuck up!" Xavier spat while crouching down with his hands behind his head. "Use your hips and buck her off of you! She's a quarter of your size for crying out loud."

The raven-haired woman turned her head to Xavier and threw her head back in laughter. I had no idea who she was, but I liked her already.

My eyes flicked to Thane who flashed the widest smile I had seen on him since we met. "For the love of Erebus, Silas. Tap out before she rips your head from your shoulders. You're not going to win," he said in between laughs as he stepped forward.

I stopped breathing as Silas slowly began to go limp. Reluctantly, his hand stretched out before him and quickly tapped the ground three times. The woman released him and lightly placed one foot on his back with her arms straight in the air before Thane wrapped his arms around her waist and hoisted her into the air.

My stomach plummeted as Thane swung her around, chuckling at her squeal of victory. The broad smiles stretched across both of their faces was the happiest I had seen him during my time here. The laughter never seemed to end, and I couldn't roll my eyes any further back in my head, even though I tried.

I don't care who he's with. I barely know him.

But the irritation that bubbled over inside of me wouldn't back down. Maybe informing her that I had my bare breasts pressed to his chest last night while believing he was not in a relationship would wipe the smirk off his face.

Typical man.

Taking a deep breath and resting my palms on the ledge of the wall, I smiled to myself. The thought of getting revenge for his actions in the hot springs brought a sense of enjoyment to the forefront.

I was pulled from my own thoughts when the raven-haired woman released a boisterous burst of laughter. Leaning over the ledge a bit more, I saw Thane had her hoisted onto his shoulders as she flexed and kissed her biceps and then pointed to Xavier with a wink.

"Damnit, Silas," Xavier yelled as he smacked both hands on the ground from where he was still crouching down.

"Oh, blow it out your ass, Xavier. You jump in and fight her then you pussy," Silas spat as he rubbed his shoulder.

I threw on my clothes and swung my door open to see Elora, the sweet servant who had been caring for me since my arrival, with her fist raised in the air to knock. I had learned yesterday that her name was Elora and had made every effort to memorize it since I was so awful with names. She smiled warmly before dropping her hand.

"Good morning, Elora. Would you be able to point me in the direction where the others are training this morning?" I asked since I don't quite know my way around the giant palace yet. She nodded fervently. Not only did she tell me where to go, but she guided me there.

Stepping out onto the platform, I caught a glimpse of Thane's sword leaning against the stone wall, its shiny black stone glimmering in the sunlight. Seconds later, I noticed everyone had gone from cheering and playfully cursing each other to staring at me in silence.

My gaze swept the area until I landed on Thane who had one arm slung around the raven-haired girl's shoulder. His deep golden eyes burned through me as he had gone from smiling to glaring in my direction.

She was just as beautiful as I was afraid she would be up close. Her light brown eyes twinkled with mirth, and her bronzed complexion was littered with dark freckles that sprayed across her nose and cheeks. She swept her long tresses behind her back and offered me a friendly smile.

Searching for words, I stammered as all eyes remained focused on me. "I-I didn't know this training was for immortals only. Sorry."

I turned to leave.

"Did we wake the princess? Sorry, we'll try to remain quiet and lazy like you mortals," Thane ridiculed. His words caused my heart to pump with rage despite the early hour. "We woke up hours ago. What were you doing? Dreaming about being saved again?"

The anger in me turned from ice to flames as I spun around ready to lay into him with lethal words, but the girl in his grasp beat me to it. "Uh... I'm sorry. Since when do you speak to women that way?" she asked him with a scowl sketched across her face.

Thane winced at her question as she stepped out of his grasp.

The girl basically bounced over to me in excitement. "Hi! I'm Athena, Thanasis' sister," she exclaimed while sticking out her hand to greet me. Shaking it, I introduced myself and returned her smile. I didn't have a reason why, but my shoulders relaxed at the word *sister*.

"Did we wake you? I'm so sorry. Thanasis said he had a visitor here but failed to mention you were mortal. I've heard your kind needs more sleep than we do."

"It's okay, I needed to be up anyway," I responded.

Thane snorted, resulting in Nova snapping at him to cut his bullshit.

Have I mentioned how much I love the women of Obsidian so far?

"Unless you're going to jump in the circle, Pixie, you can head to the dining hall for breakfast," Thane said coolly. Embarrassment flooded me internally, but the rising bout of hate I had for him ignited in my veins.

"What's wrong? Can't match anyone here?"

His words made me feel insignificant, and even though I was in this realm, it didn't need to be proclaimed. I was about to take a step toward him when a voice projected from behind me.

"She may not be able to, but I can," Raya announced.

She stepped out into the morning sun, her deep tan skin and snow-white hair glowing. Her hair was pleated in an intricate braid that hung over her shoulder. "You love talking shit to someone that doesn't possess your strength don't you, tough guy?"

Thane's expression hardened at her taunt, making me smile so wide my face hurt.

"Let's see what you've got with all that talk, and step into that circle with me," she said with a tilt of her head. I don't think Raya is aware of Thane's status as Divine Fae, or perhaps she just didn't care? She stepped closer to him with raised brows.

Oh shit... she was serious.

"Or do you reserve all that bark and no bite for mortals?" Raya taunted again, and I could see Thane's fists clenched at his sides. She tilted her head in the direction of the circle and waited for Thane to move. Crossing her arms over her chest, she shrugged her shoulders. "Or we can spar right here. I have no problem putting you on your ass in front of your friends if that means you stop speaking to mine like a complete asshole."

That did it.

Thane flashed his teeth with a mocking smile and strode toward Raya who stood with her feet firmly planted, refusing to back down.

Before I could decide on whether or not I should intervene, Thane's sister stepped between the two and held up both hands as a peace offering. "Hi, I'm Athena, also known as this asshole's sister," she proclaimed while gesturing a thumb over her shoulder in Thane's direction. "Why don't we all calm down and start over? Let's not waste this beautiful morning."

Raya looked from Athena to Thane and back, visibly processing that she was meeting his sister. Raya offered a greeting and glanced at Silas who was still grimacing in pain.

"He already got the shit beat out of him. Let's not ruin anyone else's day," Athena followed up with a grin and nod in Silas' direction.

All eyes landed on Silas who was now leaning against the stone wall, rubbing his other shoulder. "If you guys mention this one more time today, I swear I'll jump over this wall."

"You can fly, dumbass," Xavier retorted, causing all of us to laugh, including Silas.

Amid our laughter, multiple servants came out to inform us breakfast was prepared and awaiting us. No one moved until the servants assured everyone in the room that they had already eaten themselves.

They were so kind to their servants here, unlike in Solaris. The memory of their mistreatment caused me to clench my teeth together.

Raya and I followed the others back into the palace to the dining hall where we found our seats at the table and began chatting like Thane and I hadn't wanted to slit each other's throats just moments ago. Thank the heavens Nova and Raya flanked me on either side so I didn't have to put up with his bullshit alone.

"So, Amira, right?" Athena asked to ensure she had my name right. I nodded my head with a sincere smile. "How is it that you haven't knocked my brother's head off yet?" she questioned while popping a fork-full of eggs into her mouth. Thane grunted at his sister's question and glared at her before sipping from his cup of steaming hot coffee, averting his eyes from me.

My attention was snatched away when the doors to the dining hall were thrust open and Anya walked in with a small, four-legged friend behind her. Once again, I became light-headed as I watched the small, black ball of fur prance in.

Am I seeing this correctly?

The black cat from Lorena's cottage sat at Anya's side, staring at the table. Before I could ask any questions, Thackery scurried across the floor and landed in Raya's lap, causing her to slide her seat back from the table with a shriek.

"Hey buddy," I said as the cat placed its front paws on her chest and stared into her eyes before resting his round, furry head under her chin, purring non-stop.

"Uh, okay," Anya drawled out as she eyed the cat, and Raya, suspiciously.

"This is the cat that dropped the crystal into the cell that night," I exclaimed to Raya as I patted its soft head. Everyone at the table froze at my mention of the crystal, but I tried to ignore them.

"How is he with you? Doesn't he belong to Lorena?" I asked as I remembered seeing him in the dark forest with Anya back in Solaris.

Anya sighed before taking the seat next to Thane that everyone had obviously avoided to steer clear of his bad mood.

"Technically... he does. But I found him wandering outside the wall of the dark forest one day and brought him in. He seems to like staying with me more, so I let him come and go as he pleases," she said while a servant poured her coffee. She thanked him before continuing. "Thackery here can astral project whenever he wants. I wish he could talk though. It would be extremely useful in our current situation."

The cat meowed and tried its best to rebel as Raya sat him on the ground before scooting back up to the table. "Yea... cats aren't my thing. He's cute and all, but I sneeze like crazy when I'm around them." As if on cue, she sneezed right into her plate of food. Xavier chuckled quietly, receiving a playful glare from Raya.

Thackery accepted his defeat and stalked to the stairs just as Atlas burst through the door, paws sliding across the marble floor. The wolf quickly bounded toward him, pulling a screech from Thackery.

A chase between the two animals broke out in the dining hall.

While the men were entertained, I panicked. Afraid that Atlas might unintentionally hurt him, I jumped from my seat to grab Thackery. The four-legged ball of fur slipped between my legs, and I threw myself to the side just in time before Atlas barreled past me to get to his prize.

Thankfully, after multiple laps around the room, it was made known that Atlas just wanted to play. Unfortunately for him, Thackery was now perched on top of a shelf that held two vases. It was his way of saying that he wanted no part of the interaction. Once the giant wolf realized he wasn't going to get the playmate he hoped for, he padded over to me instead of his owner. Thane's jaw ticked, showing his irritation toward his companion.

"Morning cutie, how are you?" I asked while scratching behind his ears. The comforting scratches granted me a reward of a lick straight across my face before he moved onto his owner and laid at his side. When I faced Anya again, she stared at me, bewildered by my interaction with Atlas.

"He doesn't typically interact with anyone like that except for Thane," she pointed out. Silence fell at the table once again before Raya spoke.

"I can't believe you weren't hallucinating when you said a black cat brought that crystal to you."

"Ah, yes. That coveted obsidian crystal," Anya said.

Obsidian crystal. We're in Obsidian.

How the fuck did I not put two and two together before now?

Thane groaned before standing. "I'm going to get some fresh air."

"Have a seat," Anya barked, glaring at him from the corner of her eye. Thane bared his teeth but reclaimed his seat.

"What is the big deal about the crystal? I mean... I put the puzzle pieces together that it's what most likely lead you to where I was. But..." I trailed off, waiting for someone to inform me.

Nova cleared her throat before speaking. "When broken, a *rare* obsidian crystal summons its true High King." She glanced back down to her half-eaten plate and poked her fork around in her food before continuing. "Thanasis may decline to claim his true title, but Obsidian crystal never lies. Just like the sword he's attached to," she informed while passing a side glance to him. "If summoned, he—and anyone he wills—can access any realm."

Why would he *not* claim his title as High King?

"It's why Silas demanded that you smash the crystal," Nova interjected, disrupting my thoughts. "The wards to get into Solaris were too strong. Even for Thane to penetrate without the calling of the crystal."

Why were they so concerned for my well-being that they would risk sending one of their own?

My head spun frantically, swirling with too many questions and theories. I pushed aside my confusion and focused on my most pressing concern. "How did you all know I was in Solaris in the first place?" I asked.

Everyone at the table stiffened as Silas choked on his food.

"And why..." my words drifted as my gaze settled on Silas. "Why, and how was Silas already stationed in Solaris as someone else? That's your magic, isn't it? To look like someone else at any given time."

In answer, Silas shifted into an exact replica of Raya before our eyes.

"Correct. I'm a shapeshifter."

An audible gasp left my lips as he responded in her exact voice.

I shook my head as I tried and failed to piece everything together. Raya exploded, begging Silas to change back to himself. Panic flooded within me, causing flames to ignite with it. And those flames of anger only increased when no one spoke.

Not a single word could be heard at the table regarding my question.

Slamming both hands on the table, I allowed my anger to come to the forefront, "Someone here is going to answer my fucking question. I am so sick of everyone acting like I'm a fragile child."

My hands shook as anger seeped from me. Anger from everyone constantly holding secrets. From everyone constantly thinking they knew what was best for me. Anger from just wanting to go home.

I shoved my chair back from the table as I stood and marched to Thane. Thrusting my finger in his face, I made my demands. "Today. You said tomorrow yesterday, and here we are. I am done playing your stupid little games. Take me back to Medlar you arrogant—"

I was cut off by Raya's hand on my shoulder, "Amira, calm down. Let's go upstairs and talk—"

"No!" My shout was so loud it seemed to ring throughout the hall.

Thane shot up from his seat at the same time as Xavier and Silas, their movements indicating a wariness of his unpredictability. Deep down, my heart warmed at the thought of those two men willing to come to my aid regardless of being Thane's closest friends.

"You want to go home? Then I'll fucking take you myself," he spat, grabbing my wrist and tugging in the direction of the double doors at the entrance of the dining hall.

Doing my best to plant my feet to the floor, my eyes darted around the room until they landed on Raya, her teal eyes round and filled with a panic of her own at the sight of Thane dragging me toward the hallway. Before I could yell in protest, a blast of light flashed, and a wave of power flowed through the air. I threw my free arm over my eyes instinctively.

With clenched eyes, I could feel Thane's grasp drop from my wrist. Slowly removing my arm and opening my eyes, I blinked rapidly until I found Raya once more. The cold, hard look on her face was out of the ordinary for her.

"Touch her like that again and I'll fucking kill you. High King or not," Raya said with her hands still raised, a dim light flickering in her palms.

A low crackle sound from beside me caught my attention.

I turned to find Anya standing behind Thane with a hand to each side of his head. Thane stood completely stiff, his eyes now a dull color instead of their usual brightness. I took a small step backwards at the sight. Anya caught my gaze and subtly shrugged her shoulders with a disappointed look on her face before addressing Thane. "I'm going to release you, but if you so much as raise your voice, I will pin you to this exact spot for the remainder of the day."

I stood slack jawed at the power both women exuded while Athena moved closer, gently wrapping an arm around my shoulders and pulling me back.

Anya removed her hands from both sides of Thane's head as life came back into his golden eyes. His focus landed on Raya who still had her palms raised. "You're lucky Anya has the power that she does. Otherwise, your lightshow would have ended differently," he seethed.

"Are you sure about that? Atlas would beg to differ," she replied. All eyes landed on the black wolf standing defiantly with his teeth bared, ready to pounce on Thane. Shocked, Thane stared at the black wolf in astonishment.

"I'm okay, Atlas. I promise," I whispered. The wolf glanced at me before easing back down into his original spot, sprawled out on the floor.

Thane's jaw tensed so hard at the actions of his four-legged friend that a vein appeared in his right temple. He whipped his attention back to me. "You," he seethed. "We're leaving. *NOW*. And whoever the fuck else wants to go to that fucking mortal realm you call home."

My heart sank at his words. Did I speak too soon? I had promised Raya that I would fight for Solaris by her side. I peeked over at my friend who had supported and defended me since we had met.

"Raya I—"

"Let's go to Medlar first, Amira. Your family needs you," she said.

My shoulders slouched forward at her words. I didn't want to put my realm above hers, but I couldn't put my family second either.

"Yes, in the name of Erebus, please go home," Thane mumbled toward me.

I turned to unleash the rest of my anger before a cloud of purple dust formed in the corner of the room, commanding everyone's attention. As it faded, a tall, older man with dark hair appeared. "Fucking fantastic," Thane muttered under his breath.

As the man walked toward us in his black and white ensemble, a dominant thick, white streak presented itself within his full head of hair. His bright green eyes crinkled in the corners as he surveyed me, a flash of a smile showing before it disappeared.

"Your whining does get quite tiresome, Thanasis. Just tell the poor girl the truth," he said while placing a kiss atop Athena, Anya, and Nova's heads.

"I'm the one that sent them to Solaris to rescue you."

Chapter Ten

My eyes narrowed in hesitation as I surveyed the older gentleman standing before us. I opened and closed my mouth with ten questions on the tip of my tongue before one finally escaped.

"You sent them? I don't even know you," I said in a gentle whisper.

The older man tipped the corners of his lips upwards before continuing his path toward us. The power in his presence made me take a step back as he neared. Everything about him oozed authority and strength as if power rested at his very fingertips. He could command a room based off his presence alone. But once he stopped directly in front of me, his entire demeaner calmed me in a way that was unexplainable.

His soft, green eyes lingered on my face as his shoulders relaxed. And involuntarily, I mimicked his actions.

"You're correct. You don't know me, but I do know your mother," he said calmly. "I'm an old friend of hers and when she received your letter, she got the sense that something was... off. Therefore, she reached out to me to check on your well-being. We sent Silas to check on you because of his shapeshifting abilities and since he has clearance through Thane to travel to any realm."

I stood before him, dumbfounded, my jaw nearly touching the floor. My fingers intertwined with each other, twisting in apprehension.

"You... you know my mother?"

Another smile graced his handsome face before he connected his hands behind his back, nodding. "Yes. Your mother and I go quite a way back. I'm assuming she never spoke of me?" he asked with a lighthearted chuckle.

I squinted my eyes, questioning the truth in his words. If I learned anything during my time in Solaris, it was to keep my walls in place with anyone new until they proved their trustworthiness.

"My mother never mentioned anyone from another realm. Let alone a—" I cut my sentence short, as I wasn't sure if he was Fae like the others.

A short chuckle escaped him.

"Fae?" he finished my sentence for me, and I nodded my head. "Ah, yes. Well... we had an agreement that we would never speak of each other to anyone else in our realms. There are enough unfavorable rumors about immortals floating around in the mortal realms."

He reached a hand outward to cup the side of my face.

Standing frozen in time, I didn't retreat. The expression on his face was unreadable as his hand rested on my skin. The peacefulness that radiated from his touch on my cheek was gone in a flash once he removed his hand and I yearned to have it back, if only for a few more seconds.

He stared at me for a moment before nodding and looking away.

"Unfortunately, I'm here with additional horrifying news," he announced. "Your mother has sent an additional letter about an uprising. It seems that their new king is not quite as ethical as they had hoped for."

My breathing halted at his words as my eyes roamed around the room, noticing everyone else groaning and leaning closer to the dark-haired male, waiting for him to speak. Forcing myself to remember how to breathe, I attempted to string words together to form a coherent sentence.

"My mother... did she—?" My words fell short with hesitancy taking over. I forced myself to take a breath before continuing. "Did she ask about me?"

The dark-haired male's gaze glided over me and across the rest of the room before resting back on me. My thoughts swirled heavily while trying to piece everything together.

How did he know my mother? How did he know who I was?

Licking his lips, he rolled them in before pursing them with a shake of his head and continued to provide us information.

"Additionally, it seems that Solaris has not taken kindly to us extracting you from their grasp. With permission from the king of Medlar, they're currently searching every home for..." his eyes flared and softened on me. "You, Amira."

My heart might as well have fallen out of my ass and splattered onto the floor the way it irregularly beat within my chest. If Raine so much as touched a hair on my family's head, I'd...

I didn't know what I'd do because I was mortal.

Medlar was burning while I resided in another realm. I should have been there. I should turn myself in instead of having them suffer because of me. My eyes flicked upward toward Thane who was glaring at me as if he could read my mind. I cast my focus back down to avoid his burning stare.

After letting my thoughts run wild while staring at the floor for what seemed like an eternity as the others threw questions around, I met the older man's gaze once again.

"I'm sorry, I don't think I ever caught your name?" I asked.

"Ah, apologies. My name is Aravis," he said with a genuine

smile as my heart skipped several beats once more. My memory raced back to the final letter my mother had sent to me.

"If anyone can get you to Aravis, you are safe with him."

I pondered heavily, trying to remember anything else she said in the letter about him and failed.

"You're Aravis..." I whispered into the quiet room.

As he formed his mouth to reply, Anya interrupted with a panicked voice from behind us. "We may be too late." A pained expression washed over her face as she stared into a green ball of light floating between her palms.

"All of you may want to come look at this..." she said hesitantly.

As we all gathered behind her, a cry left my lips as Raya held me upright.

Within the ball of magic, Eryx could be seen holding my sister by her hair as he dragged her onto the wooden floor of our home in Medlar. Three additional soldiers stood in the same room while another pummeled my father in the corner. My mother was held nearby with tears streaming down her cheeks, begging for them to stop.

Screams flowed from my mouth like a river as everything unfolded before me. My heart was breaking into a million pieces as I watched them attempt to tear my family apart to get to *me*.

My eyes scanned the room for Aravis. "Do something," I pleaded.

A rustling of movements came from behind me as three large bodies stood tall.

"We leave now," Thane ordered. Xavier and Silas nodded their head in agreement as they finished concealing their swords and daggers. My heart squeezed at his words. For as mean as he had been, he was willing to save my family without question?

"I'm coming with you," I said.

"Like fucking hell you are," he spat back while latching his long, dark sword onto the middle of his back. "They are there looking for *you*. And you think we're just going to hand you over that easily? You may be an annoying, fucking brat but I'm not that coldhearted."

There's the Thane I knew.

"And mortal or immortal, no woman should have a male's hands laid on her," Xavier snarled while looking at my sister struggling with the guard from Solaris. I began to tremble as I focused back on my sister struggling to regain her footing. I felt a soft brush on my arm and turned to see Raya had linked her arm with mine in support.

I wanted to rip that guard's head from his shoulders.

"I will accompany them," Aravis announced. "Nova and..." he surveyed Raya, unsure of her name until she informed him.

"Raya, nice to meet you. Nova and Raya, you two stay here to ensure her safety."

As badly as I wanted to argue that I should be going with them, what could I do as a mortal in a room full of immortals? Irritation, annoyance, and anger rose within me so ferociously that the room started to spin.

Raya swiftly released my arm with widened eyes.

"Are you okay?" she asked while surveying me from head to toe.

I regained my focus, resting my hand on a nearby chair and nodded. Unfortunately, her question had landed all eyes on me. The additional observation of everyone else had my heart pumping with anxiety.

"You're warm to the touch. Are you sure you're, okay? There's a lot going on and I'm sure you're overwhelmed," she continued while still studying me as if I was an endangered animal that was on its last leg.

I reassured her that I was okay, forcing a comforting smile until she accepted my answer. My eyes connected with Thane who squinted and quickly scanned over me before turning back to Anya. Thankfully, he and the others jumped into voicing their plans and halted our conversation.

"Anya, we may need some of your dark magic depending on how many they have surrounding their home," Thane spoke. A sinister smile graced her slender face, "I thought you'd never ask. Shall I transport us?"

"I'm coming with," Athena interjected, and Thane cast a cold glare.

"You know as well as I do that them seeing you will make things worse. Stay here and stand guard in case anything happens," he commanded his sister who glared back and rolled her eyes.

I swallowed, holding my breath as Thane made his way over to me. Reaching for me, his hand lifted and dropped back down to his side. "I know that we haven't seen eye-to-eye. But I promise... " his words trailed off as I watched his golden eyes roam over my face. "I promise to bring your family back here. Every single one of them."

My chest rose and fell as I inhaled and released a deep breath. "Please, Thane. Please."

I never imagined myself begging Thane to his face, but there was nothing I wouldn't do for my family. "I can't lose them," I said with a crack in my voice. I could see the tick in his jaw as he clenched his teeth and nodded his head before striding over to Anya who mouthed an apology toward Athena before her focus landed on me. She placed her hand over her heart with a subtle nod of her head before conjuring a green ball of dust that expanded to surround those that agreed to leave.

My gaze connected with Thane's golden eyes as it encapsulated them. "You can trust us," he said with a nod of his head.

And before I could respond, they were gone.

Chapter Eleven

THANE

As we landed in Medlar, a completely foreign realm to me, I couldn't stop thinking about her big, bright brown eyes staring at me before we left. For as badly as she got under my skin, *I couldn't get her out of my fucking head*. I could still smell her sweet aroma of lavender and honey even though we were realms apart.

I surveyed the area around us, shaking my head to get the thought of her out of my mind and snap back to reality. The scent of lavender and honey was whisked away by a heavy smell of sulfur and decay. Xavier scrunched his nose and squinted his eyes, "Do you smell that?"

I nodded my head with a disgusted face. "Definitely a hint of some sort of dark magic running through here. And not the good kind."

Anya raised her brows and pursed her lips. "It's definitely the smell of uncontrolled chaos." It was now my turn to raise my brows to my hairline. *Uncontrolled chaos?* That couldn't be good for any realm. "You don't think it could be the Reaper, do you?" I followed up, throwing a prayer to Erebus that I was wrong.

She sucked in a deep breath, taking in the foul smell with clenched eyes. Popping them open, she scrunched her nose as well. "It's too prominent for the Reaper. Someone with as much power and experience as him would know how to mask it."

The thought of the Reaper made me grit my teeth, accompanied by a mild bout of unease.

"The home directly in front of us," Anya pointed out, urging us to keep moving while passively changing the subject.

Aravis growled as he clenched his fists together with a stone-cold look in his eyes.

I drew my blade from my back as the others brandished their weapons, save for Anya and Aravis. Erebus help those that went up against their magic.

"Xavier and I will go through the roof. Anya and Aravis, use whatever weird dark magic you desire," I said with a tight smile, knowing they'd both glare at my joke. Aravis hadn't used his dark magic for so long that I forgot he possessed it at times.

Out of the corner of my eye, I saw Silas rubbing his palms together while his shoulders bounced up and down. "Fuck yes, does this mean you're going to let me do *who's there*?" he asked in a gleeful tone.

I rolled my eyes before answering him. "Yes, Silas. Please don't fuck it up."

He bounced up and down on his toes like a child getting a forbidden sweet treat for breakfast.

"Priority is the mother and sister," I announced. "Women first. Those are the rules that we uphold."

Everyone nodded in agreement.

"We meet back here to have Anya beam us back. I don't want to open a portal within this realm. Erebus knows what that could bring here or back to us," I said with a wince.

With a deep breath, I spread my wings and shot into the sky

after watching Silas shape-shift into a hunched over, mortal woman with tattered clothes, bringing a silent chuckle from my lips as I shook my head.

Xavier was right behind me in the air as two clouds of dust surrounded Aravis and Anya. With the amount of magic we were using, I was thankful there was no one around to question who we were or what was going on.

Quietly, we landed on the roof, lying flat on our stomachs as we watched Silas saunter up the five steps to the small porch of the cabin. The silence of the town cast a blanket of darkness over us. There wasn't a single mortal in sight, leaving the pathways empty.

I was pulled from my wandering mind when screams came from under us as guards shouted from inside.

"Where is your sister?" I heard a man yell before a distinctive slap was heard, causing me to bare my teeth and wish Silas would hurry the fuck up.

Once he reached the door, he knocked three times before a disgruntled, "Who's there?" bellowed from inside. Silas didn't reply and proceeded to knock three more times. Grumbles and movement from inside got louder and the door swung open as a male grabbed Silas by the front of his clothing.

"Do you not know how to fuckin' speak, woman?" the guard shouted in Silas' face. If anything, this showed me they really didn't give a damn about putting their hands on women, which only infuriated me further.

"I-I was just wondering if anyone has seen Amira lately?" he asked.

My hand flew to my face at his question. This idiot knew he was just adding fuel to the fire. I heard Xavier trying to hold his laughter in beside me.

The burly male Fae moved his hold to Silas' throat. "What the fuck do you know about Amira you old hag?"

Silas purposefully didn't fight back, causing him to sputter under the guard's hold. And just like we wanted, each guard rallied behind the one holding Silas. He portrayed like he was still struggling for air until the guard released him and he bent over panting.

"Well?" the guard spat. "Speak!"

Silas straightened his stance before brandishing a devilish smile.

"Show time," he said with both arms spread out wide. *He loved that fucking saying.*

Before the guards could act, Anya appeared in a cloud of smoke in front of Silas, lashing out her magic to throw the guards back into the cabin. Aravis appeared shortly after, releasing a dark magic of his own to keep them from talking. They clawed at their own throats, eyes moving wildly in panic.

Dropping in from the roof, Xavier and I landed right in front of the soldier that had his hand twisted in Amira's sister's hair. Without hesitation, Xavier removed a dagger from his belt, swiftly bringing it upward and under the chin of the soldier. Removing the dagger, Xavier plunged it into the man's heart, removing it once more before he dropped to the floor.

Instead of screaming at the sight of the blood that had spurted across her face from the assault, her sister lifted her leg and drove her foot right between the guard's eyes. She sprang to her feet, sending her fist into the side of the dead man's face.

"Asshole," she spat as she prepared to lunge at him again before I caught her, wrapping an arm firmly around her waist.

"Easy there..." I blanked, remembering I never asked Amira for her sister's name.

"Tessa. Who the fuck are you?" she asked cautiously as she balled her fist again preparing to strike me. "W-What are you?"

I released her, studying the petite woman as she turned around to face me. Standing to her full height, she only reached the middle of my chest. She was only an inch or two taller than Amira, but her presence resembled her sister, nonetheless. Her thick hair was pulled back, lacking the curls that I was used to seeing on Amira, and not a freckle in sight. Tessa's face twisted in annoyance, and I almost cracked a smile at the significant resemblance of Amira sprinkled throughout her pretty face.

"Your sister sent me," I informed her and the look of shock on her face was instantaneous. Realizing that her shock could also have been because my wings were still slightly jutting from my back, I took a step back, my wings fluttering before I fully retracted them.

Before we could go any further with introductions, I heard a sputter from the corner of the room. A swivel of my head showed that Silas had broken the neck of the guard that was attacking Amira's father, but the older man laid immobile on the floor, blood filling his mouth.

"No, no, no, no, no," Tessa wailed as she ran and dropped to the side of her father. "Please, no." Tears were immediately falling from her face as she clutched his clothing.

I surveyed the room where the remaining soldiers were still clawing at their throats.

The mother. Where was the mother?

"Your mother. Where is she?" Aravis bellowed from the other side of the room.

"The white-haired one took her," Tessa hissed with bared teeth.

The color drained from Aravis' face; his fists tightly clenched at his sides. Subtly, the ground beneath us shook. Our eyes grew wide as Anya rested a hand on Aravis' shoulder in an effort to calm him. After a moment the shaking subsided and we were able to find our footing.

"Did he say anything before he took her?" I questioned.

"*They'll come for her,*" she said. "I lunged for both of them, but that asshole still had me by my hair."

I rubbed my hand over my face and kicked the chair closest to me, sending it flying against the wall where it broke into pieces. I immediately made a mental note to have it replaced.

I had made Amira a fucking promise and I broke it. I promised her we would bring them back safely. How the fuck could I do that when her mother wasn't here and with the possibility of her father not making it out alive?

I was too fucking late.

Regaining my composure the best I could, I glanced around the home. My eyes bounced from each piece of well-used furniture to the chipped cups and plates, and back to the fabric that was hanging in the small window with more stitches than fabric. I turned my head to see the additional rooms available in the house.

Two additional rooms.

There were only two additional rooms in the home for a family of five.

I tilted my head back and cast my eyes toward the gaping hole in the ceiling. *Had I really misjudged Amira and the life she lived in Medlar?*

The sound of footsteps from outside caused us all to prepare to fight with weapons in hand. But a male with disheveled hair and tall stature stumbled into the doorway. At the sight of us, he raised both hands in front of him, indicating peace.

"Who the fuck are you?" he asked in bewilderment as he quickly scanned over each of us. The fact that he was sizing each of us up to see if he could take us on in a fight was laughable. His gaze bounced to each one of us until he noticed Tessa surrounded by unknown men. His impulsive response led him to lunge at the male closest to him.

Me.

Unbothered by a mortal male, I casually stepped to the side. The male's eyes flared and narrowed, preparing to lunge at me again before Tessa stepped between us, placing her hands on the male's chest. "Relax, they all saved me," she explained while attempting to push him backwards. "They are on our side. Back the fuck down."

The male's gaze connected with mine and I raised a brow, keeping my hands at my sides. "And you are?" I asked in a condescending tone.

He snarled at my arrogance while removing Tessa's hands from his body, straightening his stance and puffing out his chest. "I'm her brother. Alix," he answered. "And I'll ask again, who the fuck are you?"

This time I released a snarl of my own before I realized I was in his home, and he had a right to be defensive. The brother was much taller than Amira and Tessa, but still much shorter than me. His hair was as dark as night, a stark contrast from his sisters' light, warm brown. I was about to introduce myself when a loud gasp and gurgle broke me from my train of thought.

Our focus pivoted to their father, gasping for air on the floor.

"Do something," Tessa screamed at us collectively as she sat her father up to let the blood drain from his mouth. My eyes flicked back up to Alix who had turned ashen at the sight of his father.

Xavier bent down next to Tessa and checked his pulse. "He's still alive. But his pulse is extremely weak."

A spike of dread dug into my chest at his words. Within seconds her father drew a deep, strangled breath and fell limp in his daughter's arms. My heart stopped beating as silence sliced through the room. Tessa began to shake violently as Silas walked over, grabbing her by the shoulders to pull her upwards while Xavier gently removed her father from her arms.

"Let me go, I won't leave him like this. Let me go," she yelled as she shook and thrashed in Silas' grasp.

Xavier carefully lowered the limp body to the ground with saddened eyes.

Both hands were clasped behind my head at the events unfolding before me. This wasn't my family; this wasn't even my realm. *But I made a fucking promise*, and I couldn't go back to Obsidian with only a fraction of her family when I promised Amira everyone would be safe.

I turned to beg Aravis and Anya for help, but Aravis was already striding toward the limp body on the floor.

"This can only be used once. And has never been used on a mortal, but I will do my best," he exclaimed before running a hand through his full head of hair.

If it could only be done once, why was he using it on a man he didn't even know?

Silence fell as Aravis extended his palm to the side of the man's head. I had seen Aravis use extreme parts of dark magic during my lifetime, but I had never in my many years of life seen him save a mortal life.

As he settled the palm of his other hand on the forehead of Amira's father, a silver ring of light encapsulated the two of them. I started as Anya began chanting words in a foreign language with her hands held up at her sides.

Could a mortal even be brought back to life under immortal magic?

The only other sound in the room was Tessa's sobs as she curled into Silas' embrace. My chest tightened as he stroked her hair soothingly while her brother, who was still an ashen mess, wandered near where their father lay.

The silver light shone so brightly we had to shield our eyes before we heard loud bouts of coughing and wheezing from the floor. The light dissipated as Aravis lifted the man to sit upright on the floor and handed him a handkerchief from his pocket to catch the blood spilling from his mouth.

Amira's father gathered himself from nearly experiencing a mortal death and eventually looked over at the man who saved his life. His eyes grew so wide I feared they would pop out and roll onto the floor. Aravis mentioned that Amira's mother knew him, but had her father known him as well? His mouth formed to speak but Aravis beat him to it. "Kethien," he greeted with a nod toward her father. "Glad to see you're alright."

Aravis stood from his position and started towards the front of the cabin. "I'll be out here standing watch. I wouldn't stay much longer than we already have. Surely Raine knew we would come and will send additional soldiers. Anya, you know what to do with the rest of them," he said as he headed out the front door.

I rested both hands on the back of another chair, careful not to break it. How was I going to explain to them that I had to take them back to Obsidian to be safe? Did they even know other realms existed? Did they even know what a Fae was?

"So... as I explained to Tessa," I started out, focusing on Kethien who still stared at the door where Aravis had just stood. "Amira sent us here to save you. Unfortunately, we were a little too late for your wife. But to keep our promise to her, we would need to take you back to our realm, Obsidian, to ensure your safety."

Tessa scoffed at my words as she finally broke free from Silas' gentle grasp.

"Like hell I am. Those men won't scare me out of my own home. We'll be prepared next time," she said forcefully, crossing her arms over her chest.

I released an irritated laugh at her thinking she had a chance against Raine and his men. "While I understand not wanting to leave your realm, you are no match for an immortal. Your sister being the damsel in distress that she is thought though the same when—"

I was caught off guard when she stomped over to me, firmly pressing her finger into my chest. "You have no idea what Amira has done for this family. The sacrifices she has made. You don't speak down—"

Her words trailed off as she reared her head back, taking tiny step backwards to look up at me.

"I'm sorry... did you say *immortal?* As in people that never die?" she asked with a slacked jaw. "What the fuck is going on right now?"

I nodded my head in confirmation.

"So, like I was saying before I was cut off," I hissed. Her resemblance to Amira was remarkably irritating. "I understand you don't want to leave, but for all parties involved, it would be in your best interest."

Tessa tilted her head, preparing a snide remark, before her father chimed in.

"Tessa and Alix will go with you. I will stay here. I will not abandon my family's home that I built."

Tessa balked at her father before her protesting began in earnest.

"Absolutely not. I will not leave my father to die *again* at the hands of some freaks with wings," she spat. The rest of us winced at her words before glaring. I knew she was referencing Raine's soldiers, but the insult stung regardless.

"Well, freaks with wings also saved your ass just now," Silas refuted before expanding his wings, knocking over a side table and a vase. Tessa snapped her mouth shut at the action.

"I do not want Amira alone in a random realm. Aravis... he was a good friend of your mother's," their father spoke quietly. I watched idly, observing how Tessa was taken aback at his words about Aravis, while the brother remained silent. "If he is working with these men, I trust them."

Tessa still protested, shaking her head with parted lips.

"I will put a charm around your home so that no one can enter without permission," Anya spoke from behind us while mending the gaping hole in the roof. "Your father will be safe here. We can have someone bring him supplies so that he does not need to leave."

The siblings' shoulders relaxed at the protections put in place around their home. For a witch with such dark powers, Anya had always possessed a heart of gold.

Tessa ran to hug her father goodbye. The three of them exchanged whispered words as I surveyed the far wall by the door. Little white lines were marked next to the doorframe. Squinting, I made out the names of each of them.

Alix, Amira, and Tessa.

Next to the names were their ages. My heart clenched when I landed on the height of three-year-old Amira. The emotions consuming me were foreign as I looked away from the measurements to see Silas extending his hand to Tessa. She glanced at his palm and back to his face before placing her hand in his.

After remaining silent during our time here, Alix began to protest leaving their father, earning him a dark glare from Tessa. "And exactly where were you *brother*?" she asked, her tone ice cold. He blanched away from her.

"Before you go," Kethien interrupted them. "A word with Aravis, please."

My brow furrowed at his request, but I dipped outside, relaying the message. Aravis looked unsettled at the request but obliged. When he entered the house, the rest of us took our exit and waited on the porch.

Minutes later, Aravis exited the home and slammed the door shut behind him before walking past us and waiting at the bottom of the stairs.

"Okay then..." Silas said with a raised brow.

"Maybe I should stay for a bit," Tessa stated.

"Not happening gorgeous," Silas declared before sweeping her into his arms, extending his wings, and catapulting into the air. "What the —" Tessa yelped as they ascended.

Xavier and I slapped our palms to our faces at the sight. Silas didn't even give her a warning or a chance to understand what he was doing. Alix snapped his head to stare at the two of us, hoping for answers that we didn't supply.

Anya walked next to Aravis and extended her palms outward toward the cabin. I was anxious and excited to watch her in action. But with a few chants and hand motions, nothing out of the ordinary happened.

"That's it?" I asked in bewilderment.

Anya smirked. "Open the door, tough guy."

I rolled my eyes and extended my hand to the doorhandle. A shock extended up my arm so fiercely that I dropped to my knees, panting. Xavier laughed so hard he bent over, gasping for air.

"Fuck off," I spat at everyone while rising to my feet on wobbly legs, extending my wings to head to our meeting spot. I could hear Anya explaining to Alix how she was going to get him to the location as I ascended into the sky.

When we all reunited in the woods behind Amira's cabin, Tessa had her finger pointed in Silas' face, reprimanding him about launching them into the air without warning. Silas smiled in her face as though he was enjoying her scolding.

"Everything go okay back there?" I asked Aravis, who still had a scowl on his face. The only reply I got was a grunt. "Did you know him as well?"

Aravis looked at me with narrowed eyes and I threw my hands up in a truce.

"I do not want to be the one to tell Amira that Raine took her mother," Xavier murmured in worry.

"Do you think he will hurt them?" Tessa asked with worried eyes.

"I've never been one to lie, so I will be honest and say I'm unsure. What we need to do right now is get back to Obsidian and secure a plan in place to get her back." I knew that wasn't the statement Tessa wanted to hear, but I had already broken one promise today, and I wasn't about to make another that I wasn't certain I could keep.

Anya asked if everyone was ready, and Tessa groaned as she prepared to be launched back into the air.

"Oh no sweetie, no more flight for you today," Anya said with a smile as she walked up to Tessa and placed her hand on the back of her arm. "I'll beam us there."

"You'll what?" Tessa asked.

Anya smiled before a cloud of green dust formed around all of us as we stood in a tight circle. Before Anya completed her spell, we looked toward the sky as we heard multiple flapping wings overheard. Over thirty white-winged Fae were doing a downward dive in our direction.

Saurians.

Just as Aravis had warned, Raine sent more of his army for us because he knew we would come.

"Not today fuckers," Silas yelled at them while throwing two middle fingers in the air.

A random arrow flew in our direction, and I flinched when Aravis caught it in one hand, thrusting it back into the sky. I watched in awe at his precision as it pierced through a white wing, the soldier free-falling through the air as fire spread throughout his feathers.

I gaped at Aravis who gave me a shrug of his shoulder before the green dust surrounded us, thrusting us back into Obsidian.

Chapter Twelve

I paced from wall to wall within my room as Raya and Nova sat on the balcony, watching me like hawks. Athena remained on the sparring platform to keep watch with additional Vaternians at her side.

How could I have let them go to save *my* family without me?

Was it in the best interest of everyone to leave me here since I was of no real help against immortals? Yes, but it still made me feel worthless and helpless—the two things that made my skin crawl.

I marched outside. "There has to be some sort of way for you to contact them." Nova shifted in her seat as she placed her drink upon the small table. Rubbing her slender fingers over her brows, she leaned back and let out a sigh.

"Thane's powers are strong but not strong enough to contact us from so far away."

An apologetic look washed over her gentle face before she spoke again. "I assure you that he will be back soon. Thane likes to get in and out as soon as possible with these types of situations."

Normally I would have made a wildly inappropriate joke at her statement, but the hollow feeling in my stomach wouldn't allow it. Just as I was about to insist that there was something she could do, Atlas burst through my bedroom door head-first and began howling. "I'm assuming that means they're back. Atlas isn't too happy that Thane left him again," Nova said as she quickly stood from her seat.

I walked over to the ball of fur that came to summon me. He nudged my hip and turned to the door. Without waiting for the others, I followed his fast pace throughout the castle in a full sprint until my feet hit the concrete of the sparring deck.

I locked eyes with my brother and sister before the three of us moved at lightning speed to embrace each other. I brushed Tessa's dark hair away from her face to examine the marks left on her and glanced over Alix as I held my hand to his cheek. "You should see the other guy," Tessa joked with a soft smile. "Knife to the heart and everything." She threw a glance over her shoulder at Xavier, who flashed a matching smile but immediately went back to his usual nonchalant demeanor.

My eyes roamed the remaining space, looking for the rest of my family.

"Before you ask—" Tessa began, but her words faded as I continued to search for specific people in the group. After looking over everyone multiple times, my heart tightened when I accepted that my mother nor my father were in sight.

"No. No no no no no.... you fucking promised me," I spat at Thane who was clenching his jaw.

I marched up to him and stuck my index finger into his chest. My fragile finger felt like it broke in half when I thrust it into his hard muscles, but I ignored it.

"You said you would bring them back. *All of them.* I *trusted* you."

Thane winced at my words before looking off to the side and back down at me. "Why don't we go inside so I can explain everything to you?" he whispered in a gravelly voice so only I could hear.

"Whatever you have to say to me can be said in front of every-one. Where the hell is the rest of my family?" I screamed into the open air.

"The situation had already escalated before we got there and ——-" He stopped mid explanation, forcefully clenching his teeth before taking a deep breath and stepping back from me. "You are unbearably frustrating."

I took a step toward him when a light touch fell on my shoulder causing me to turn around. Raya's soft look through her teal eyes had me squeezing mine shut for a moment. "Amira, he was only helping. Whatever happened can't possibly be his fault. Let's hear him out," she commented with a gentle squeeze.

I glanced over at Tessa, whose usual demeanor was as unwound as mine, bouncing from foot-to-foot while biting her bottom lip like I typically did. Stepping out of Raya's grasp, I narrowed my eyes at my sister. She finally observed my stare and I could see her visually swallow before speaking.

"I'm sorry."

Those two words sent every emotion weaving through every vein in my body. Shaking my head, my chest became tight with each passing second.

"You didn't," I whispered.

Tessa stopped bouncing and stood frozen. Licking her lips she glanced from Alix, who had yet to speak, back to me. "Amira, father insisted that we leave to be with you. He's protected and—"

The rest of her excuse was a stuttering blur of background noise. Rage consumed me at the thought of them leaving our father behind. Tessa was the eldest of the three of us. She should be better at making decisions to help our family.

"You fucking idiot," I spat before lunging to tackle her. Before I got a chance, Thane grabbed my arm. "Leave us," he commanded. "Now."

How could they leave our father in Medlar?

"Your childish act stops now," he reprimanded while tightening his grip. I attempted to snatch my arm from his hold, but he only pulled me closer to him.

"*ENOUGH,*" he roared.

Everyone surrounding us scattered like flies. The authority in his voice had my rage evaporating as I swallowed, my eyes widening in fear.

Tessa and Alix refused to leave me, their fear for my safety outweighing their fear of Thane's anger. Raya and Nova introduced themselves and assured them that I would be okay while alone with Thane. Both of my siblings held their stare on me until they vanished inside.

Once everyone was gone, I noticed Thane still held a firm grasp on my arm. I pulled my arm back toward my body once more, but he still didn't let go. Instead, he dragged me over to two stone boulders and forced me to sit down as he placed a foot atop the other. Taking a deep breath and peeling back his upper lip, he leaned on his elevated knee toward me. "If you're going to act like a fucking child, I'll treat you like one," he said. I attempted to stand up, refusing to let him speak to me in such a demeaning tone. His large hands shot out, landing on both of my shoulders and pressing me back down to the stone effortlessly.

"I know I made a promise. I know I didn't uphold that promise. The only thing that I can do now is work to make it right," he said before turning away from me. "I understand how upset you are right now. Trust me, I get it."

I reared my head back at his statement. *How* could *anyone understand this type of pain?*

He ran his hands through his thick dark hair that shone in the sunlight before facing me again. I watched as it gently fell back into place upon his shoulders. "I know we don't get along. But family is not something I take lightly. So, we can either work together to save your family, or they can die because you refused to put your hatred for me aside."

I opened and closed my mouth, trying to decide on what words to piece together. The fact that he was acting like the hate I had for him wasn't also flowing through his veins toward me only fueled my irritation.

"Where are they, Thane?" I finally asked.

I could see his Adam's apple bob as he swallowed before he answered.

"Raine took your mother before we landed in Medlar," he answered quietly, and my chest felt like it caved in on itself. "And your father refused to leave with us. So, Anya placed an enchantment on your home to keep him safe."

The blood running through my veins ran cold. The tips of my fingers felt as though they had frostbite and were ready to fall to the ground. I trembled as I processed his words over and over in my head.

He would kill her to get to me.

I didn't know when it happened, but Thane now knelt in front of me holding my face. "Amira, what do you have that Raine wants? I can't help you unless I know."

Tears rimmed my eyes as I surveyed his honey-colored ones.

"I don't know," I answered honestly.

"For the love of everything Amira, be fucking honest with me for once."

"I'm being fucking honest with you, Thane," I snapped back as I snatched my face from his hands. "And don't fucking touch me. I'm grateful that you are willing to help me and my family. But don't act like you haven't been anything except hostile toward me since I got here."

He began to reply as we heard a rustling at the entrance of the deck.

Aravis.

Had he remained there the whole time when everyone else left?

"Meeting. Observatory. Now."

Aravis' words were clipped as he turned and disappeared through the entryway.

Thane and I exchanged glares, our chests heaving in anger. "We're not done with this conversation," he concluded and lead the way to the observatory.

When we arrived at the large oak door, Anya halted us. "Aravis has stated it is a closed meeting," she uttered and flashed a helpless smile my way.

"Meaning what, exactly?" I asked as I crossed my arms over my chest and glowered at Thane.

"Only those of Obsidian are requested at the meeting."

I looked around Anya to see Xavier, Silas, Nova, Athena and Aravis standing on the center platform in a circle. None of them would even glance in my direction.

"It wasn't my call to make," Anya said with an apologetic tone.

I nodded my head in understanding as a pang of jealously pierced through the center of my chest. Thane took a side glance at me and stepped forward. I caught him by the arm and narrowed my eyes. "Our conversation about your broken promise isn't done."

He narrowed his eyes to match mine and snatched his arm from my grasp as he walked past Anya to enter the meeting.

The dark witch that I now considered a friend, mouthed an apology before closing the door where I heard a lock move into place. I waited a few minutes before I pressed my ear to the thick wood, hoping to hear pieces of a conversation.

"Wishful thinking," a soft voice sang from behind me, causing me to bang my head on the door.

"Fuck me," I spat as I rubbed my head. "You're still doing this shit?"

Raya was holding her hand over her mouth to keep her laugh from echoing in the halls. "They've most likely placed a charm on the room so that nothing can be heard from the outside."

I rolled my eyes at their stupid magic. "Where's Tessa and Alix?"

"They're getting cleaned up by two of the kind servants. I told them we would come back in a bit."

Raya placed her back against the wall and slid herself down to the marble flooring. "Might as well wait until they're done. I'd say we could snoop around, but this place is way too big, and I'm scared we may never be found if we get lost."

She wasn't lying. This place was massive.

"He didn't lay into you too hard up there, did he?" she asked.

After a confused look, I realized she was talking about when Thane demanded the two of us be left alone on the sparring deck. I looked at the ceiling and sighed. "I realize that it's not his fault Raine took my mother and that they left my father behind. I just had so much hope that he would bring them back to me," I said before sliding down to meet her on the cool marble flooring. Resting my head on the wall behind me, tears sprang to my eyes. "Raine took my mother, Raya. He knows no bounds."

Raya leaned her head on my shoulder and clasped her hand in mine. "We will get her back, Amira,"

A long silence passed between us while we remained lost in our own thoughts. Thoughts that were filled with darkness. So dark that I was biting on my lip so hard I raised my fingertips to find that I had drawn blood. I cleared my throat as Raya lifted her head and peered over at me.

"For the first time in a long time...I'm scared," I confessed as my breathing increased and I fought inwardly to keep the panic away.

Raya reached out and tucked a lose curl behind my ear. The corners of her mouth slowly tipped upward.

"Use it to fuel your fire," she replied as the door swung open to the observatory.

Chapter Thirteen

Nova was the first one to enter the hallway from the Observatory. Raya and I scrambled to our feet and ruthlessly bombarded her with questions as she stood there, caught off guard, with her mouth open and eyes wide. Saving her from answering, Aravis stepped in front of her. "It was an emergency meeting in regard to Merakai."

I blinked a thousand times, trying to process his reasoning for the emergency meeting. "I'm sorry, are you telling me that you decided to have an *emergency* meeting about a celebration when my mother could possibly be being tortured as we speak?" Tessa asked from behind me, with Alix not far behind. The servant that guided them to us scurried off down the hall, away from the conflict.

Aravis barely glanced at Tessa as he summoned Thane before departing.

"We will discuss the plans for rescuing your mother at dinner. If we rush into Solaris, they will be expecting us this time," Thane attempted to reason.

"This time?" Tessa questioned with bulging eyes.

Thane and I both looked at her and back to each other. Just looking at his overly handsome face made me angry all over again.

"Your sister can catch you up on everything before dinner," Thane said before walking down the hall. A few steps away he turned around, his eyes landing on Tessa and Alix. "Welcome to Obsidian."

Once Thane departed, Nova flagged down a servant to lead Raya, my siblings, and me out to the gardens since she had prior obligations, but she promised to catch up with us at dinner. Though I was still irritated from wanting to rip Thane's head from his shoulders, a small part of me was interested to see how the palace grounds compared to Solaris.

After traversing a long staircase and three hallways, we stepped outside onto stone steps that overlooked a garden with a plethora of eye-catching blooms. Whereas Solaris was filled with vibrant colored flowers, each one in this garden was of darker shades. The only color to break up the darkness were the white tulips scattered throughout. The sweet fragrance of the hundreds of flowers hit the tip of my nose and roped me in.

"If you need anything at all, we're scattered throughout the garden and grounds. We would be happy to assist," the servant offered and slightly bowed before leaving with a smile on his face as we thanked him.

Slowly, we descended the stone steps in silence as we took in the tranquility surrounding us. Following the cobblestone pathway, we found a miniature waterfall where birds were bathing and chirping in harmony. Surrounding it were deep red roses in full bloom. I bent down to admire them when Tessa tapped my shoulder and pointed to the far corner of the landscape where a garden pond was tucked away behind dozens of black dahlias.

The four of us followed the pathway until we reached the small pond that was the home to multicolored fish and settled onto the stone bench next to it. Glancing up, I noticed the giant weeping willow tree perfectly settled in the middle of the garden.

I had to admit to myself, this had Solaris' garden beat.

"Well, now is as good as ever to explain to me how the hell you ended up here," Tessa announced from the right side of me with Alix seated on the stone path in front of us, nodding his head in agreement. "Also, it would be nice to know who the gorgeous lady to your left is."

Raya cleared her throat at the compliment and reached around me to offer her hand to Tessa as she introduced herself, then did the same with Alix. Once they were done exchanging pleasantries, I laid everything out on the table for my brother and sister.

From Lorena attacking me at the cottage, to Raine pretending to be my knight in shining armor, to him forcing me into marriage, and how Thane and the others rescued us.

I even filled them in on the hex placed on Solaris.

Tessa and Alix stared at me dumbfounded when I stopped talking. Instead of questioning me further, Tessa leaned forward to look at Raya. "So... you're this Raine guy's sister, and you chose to side with Amira?"

Raya released a soft chuckle before telling her everything that Raine had done to her as well. She even sprinkled in small bits and pieces about Eryx.

Alix spewed a few words under his breath while Tessa leaned back, bobbing her head up and down. "Yea, I'd leave my brother too if I were you."

After a moment of silence, I finally asked my siblings what was burning me alive. "Why did you leave our father by himself?"

Tessa snapped her head in my direction with a glare, cutting Alix's explanation off.

"He is our father, but you are my sister. I told you once before when you left with Lorena that I would always come for you. Did you think that was a lie?"

I sat in silence as she scolded me.

"Father is fine. The kind uh...I don't know what she is, put a spell on our home that made it impossible for anyone to enter," Alix insisted.

He had to be referring to Anya.

"Her name is Anya. And she is quite sweet; you're right about that."

"Well, could someone explain to me what the fuck everyone is? One moment I'm in my home fighting for my life, and the next moment there's men with wings coming to save me and a woman that can wield magic," Tessa pleaded while rubbing her temples with her eyes closed.

Raya and I explained everything to them regarding Obsidian and Solaris, as well as what type of immortal being everyone was that they had met so far. To my disbelief, neither were shocked by any of the information.

We talked for so long that the sun began to set and multiple servants had stopped by to ask if we needed anything. The large doors opened to the back entrance of the castle, showing Nova in her all-black attire as she waved fervently at us.

"Time for dinner," she yelled with both hands cupping the sides of her mouth. The four of us waved back and stood to walk over to her. Reaching her, she let us know that she would take us out into town at some point, so we didn't have to be stuck in the same place for so long.

Halfway to the dining hall, I gave myself an invisible pat on the back. Somehow, I was slowly learning my way around this place. When we entered, everyone else was already seated at the long, marble table. I sat in my usual spot as Nova sat next to Tessa who was being heavily eyed by Silas until we made eye contact. He cleared his throat and looked away from my sister. Alix claimed a seat at the end of the table by Anya.

Once dinner was served, Thane jumped right into conversation about my mother. "Thanks to Anya here, we have some insight on your mother."

My heart skipped several beats before I began to breathe correctly again.

"She went back to the dark forest and got as close to the castle grounds as possible without being caught."

My gaze snapped over to her.

She would do that for my family?

"Anya was able to see your mother in the garden of Raine's palace, untouched. He is most likely hoping for us to come at any moment to retrieve her."

"So, then what exactly are we waiting for?" I questioned anxiously.

"My brother may be an asshole, but he's smart. Raine will know you're coming," Raya said from across the table.

"So, we make a fucking plan," Tessa countered.

"Plans take time," Aravis said from the opposite end of the table. "We will get your mother back, but you have to trust us to make the right moves."

"I trusted him once, I won't do it again," I said as I jerked my head in Thane's direction.

A sudden snap echoed through the air as little shards of glass sprayed across the table. The glass that Thane was holding now lay in a hundred tiny pieces strewn across the table and trickled down to the floor.

I straightened my shoulders, studying the man that now had blood dripping from his clenched fist where the glass once was. The harsh rise and fall of his chest let me know he was doing everything he could not to snatch me from where I sat. And even though I'd lived my entire life with a slick mouth and fists to back me up, I was unsure about this moment.

"Listen here you little—" Thane seethed, baring his teeth before Aravis held up a hand, attempting to stop him. "I don't owe this damsel shit. I saved her once; I don't owe anyone else a damn thing."

Aravis glared at Thane with fire in his eyes.

My gaze flitted down to Thane's hand that he was now opening and closing. I blinked, focusing on the cuts that were healing themselves in seconds as the blood dried and crusted around them.

I jumped in my seat at the sound of the dining hall doors being thrown open, a servant descending the stairs with a letter in hand.

"Sir, an urgent letter came addressed to the High King of Obsidian moments ago."

Thane grumbled, placing his elbow on the table and smacking his palm to his forehead. "I am not the High King. Please give it to Aravis," he replied and pointed in Aravis' direction who fumed at Thane's dismissal of his duties.

"At some point you will have to realize I do not accept the title you keep trying to hand down to me," Aravis said to Thane as he took the letter from the servant and ripped it open. His body stiffened as he read the piece of parchment.

Each one of us shifted in our seats waiting for him to speak.

"What? What is it?" Silas asked anxiously.

Aravis glanced around the table and lingered on my siblings and me. Clearing his throat and wiping his brow, he settled his forearms on the table with the paper in front of him. "It's a letter from Raine demanding a meeting in three days at Bavaria."

My breathing turned rapid as Thane slammed his fists onto the table. "That fucker knows why he chose there," he said. My brow furrowed in confusion. Thankfully, Xavier took pity on us mortals and proceeded to explain the location.

"Bavaria was deemed neutral territory centuries ago through a treaty that was signed by each realm. Magic is forbidden there, and those that use it are sentenced to death by the High Kings of each realm," Xavier said before resting his hands behind his head and leaning backwards.

"He says that he would like to discuss a truce and laws that were broken for...."

We all leaned forward on shallow breaths, waiting for him to finish reading Raine's request.

"For what?" I begged.

"For his *mate* being stolen from him by another male," Aravis answered as he swallowed before continuing. "The mother of Amira will be returned once..." he stalled once again, not wanting to say the words written before him.

"Heavens above! Stop pausing," Tessa spat.

"Once Amira and Raya are returned to Solaris," Aravis finished with squinted eyes.

Audible gasps and curses were heard around the table. Atlas growled at the commotion and padded over to plop down behind me, which made Thane roll his eyes.

After a long silence carried throughout the room, I voiced my decision.

"So, we meet with him," I said with my head held high.

Everyone at the table quickly said "no" except for Thane who only stared at me with no expression.

"I am so sick of everyone telling me what I can and cannot do my entire life. Making every single choice for me. I will be twenty-five soon and I still can't make my own fucking decisions," I said, my words laced with venom. "If I want to sacrifice myself for my mother then I will fucking do it. And I will do it alone if I must."

Rage had once again consumed me as I began to shake, the same fire I always felt in my veins more dominant this time.

"Training," Thane said from across the table into the once again silent room.

"What?" I questioned to his one-word reply.

"We begin training tomorrow morning. If you want to go to Bavaria, then you need to learn to fight. Magic is not permitted on those grounds, but combat is."

"I know how to fight," I retorted.

"You are beyond irritating," he gritted out. "You will train like a Vaternian. And learn to fight like a Vaternian."

I tilted my head in confusion. "If I'm so irritating, why are you willing to train me like one of your own?"

The stiffness in Thane's shoulders dissipated as he pulled his bottom lip between his teeth and released it. Running his tongue across his teeth he let out a huff before looking at Nova to chime in.

I had finally stumped him.

"As I said before, it is what we are in Obsidian," Nova said with pride. "Our people are known to be warriors and fight for what is right." She leaned over and gently pressed her index finger into my chest, atop my heart. "I know you have the same spirit as us deep down in there."

She sat back with a wink and my soul warmed at her confidence. I rolled my lips inward and bit down, fighting the smile that desperately wanted to bloom.

"We may not be able to use magic in Bavaria, but if that fucker lays a hand on any of us, we all need to know how to fight," Xavier chimed in from across the table.

"Meet us out at the sparring deck at sunrise. That goes for you *and* your siblings," he said, pointing his index finger at each of us. Tessa who usually didn't do well with being told what to do, just narrowed her eyes at Thane. "Xavier, you know what to do if they're not on time," he added, which caused Silas and Nova to wince.

"If you hurt any of them during training, you'll regret you were ever born," Anya said with a raised brow.

"I second that," Aravis stated with a nod of his head.

"Define *hurt*," Thane said. A devilish smile spread across his handsome tanned face.

Chapter Fourteen

The screams of my mother filled the room as we glanced over at my dead brother's body. I opened and closed my mouth to speak, but only silent cries came out. "Save him," my mother wails from behind me. I walked over to cradle his head in my lap. His lifeless, green eyes stared up at the ceiling. "This is your fault," she screamed again as I turned to face her. "You can't even defend your family after everything that was given to you. What good are you?"

I peeled my lips back before screaming my own words at her. I'm silenced by a cold, cynical laugh. My eyes trailed up the stairs to the dais where Raine sat next to Eryx. They laughed in unison at the sight of me holding Alix close to my chest.

Gently, I laid his head back down and stood to storm the platform. Raine raised his index finger, waving it at me as if I was a naughty child and pointed it in the direction of my mother. I shook my head viciously, begging him to spare her life. "Here we go again with the begging, Amira," he said with a cruel smile. "Your actions have consequences. And the worst action you took is when you failed to be my bride," he hissed before waving his hand to the side and a loud crack echoed throughout the room followed by a thud.

Tears fell from my eyes as I slowly turned around to see my mother's neck snapped as her body lay on the ground behind me...

I woke up gasping for air.

My hands fisted the bedsheets as my chest heaved. Air felt foreign to my lungs as I fought to force myself to focus on my surroundings. I felt a trickle of liquid slowly making its way down the side of my face and lifted my fingertips to it. My eyes widened in realization when I noticed my hair plastered to my head from the ice-cold liquid that was thrown on me.

Ice cold water dropped over every inch of my body, causing me to shiver underneath soaking wet sheets.

"Sorry about that," a man murmured from above me as he held a giant bucket at his side. Wiping my eyes, I saw that it was Xavier standing there with an amused grin on his face. The servant at his side glanced at Tessa as he held a similar bucket.

"I wouldn't even think about it if I were you," she said with her eyes still closed.

Throwing the sheets off my body I jumped up and almost slipped on the marble flooring as Xavier caught my arm.

"What the fuck is wrong with you? A simple *'Hey Amira, wake up'* would have sufficed," I snapped at him. He shrugged with a sheepish smile on his face. "Thane's orders. I suggest you get dressed and out to the sparring platform before he makes me do step two."

"*Step two?* Am I in a fucking army or something?" I asked with a scowl on my face.

Xavier let go of my arm and walked to the door. "That would be easier in my opinion."

He stared behind me, and I looked to see Tessa standing in her nightgown.

While Alix had opted for his own room to give us privacy, the servants used their minute magic to produce an additional bed for Tessa in my room so she wouldn't have to sleep alone last night.

Seeing her in the dark blue satin nightgown clinging to her body made me realize exactly what Xavier was looking at.

Whipping my head back around, I glared at him while flashing my teeth.

He huffed a laugh with a nod of his head, "Ten minutes. See you out there."

~

I'd never let them know it, but I was scared to find out what step two was if we weren't on time for training. Tessa and I swiftly threw on pants and tank tops, with boots that were provided to us the night before and hurried out to the platform. The entire way there I had to listen to Tessa complain about the lack of colors for the clothing. I inwardly smiled at her having to wear dark colors for the remainder of our time here.

Raya was already having a friendly sparring session with Nova when we stepped out onto the tan, stone ground. The sun beamed down on them as their sweat glistened in the light.

Just as I was admiring their skills, a slow clap began in the far-right corner.

Thane.

"How nice of you to be on time this morning. Oh wait, you're forty minutes late," he said with a scowl on his face.

"Are you telling me that you couldn't wait to see my face this morning, Thane? Was it because of your wet dream about me last night?" I asked with the fakest smile I could muster this early in the morning.

His jaw clenched at my sarcasm, followed by him barking orders.

"Tessa you'll be with Xavier."

Xavier's stern face never faltered, but I noted a small twitch in the corner of his lips. I looked at Tessa who looked slightly terrified of the giant, muscular Fae that was placing his daggers on the ledge and tightening his boots.

"Raya is already with Nova and Alix, so that leaves me and you," Thane said in my direction with a devious smile plastered on his face. My eyes scan Alix who has now joined from the side where he was re-lacing his boots. *I let Alix get here before me?*

My gaze wanders over to Silas who was resting on one of the stone boulders. "Thanks, but I'm going to train with Silas," I said, hope lacing my words. Silas raised his brows before shrugging both of his shoulders apologetically.

"Sorry gorgeous, but I have a meeting with Anya and Aravis to head to," he said as he sauntered over and slapped his large hand on the middle of my back. "Aim for his knees, he's old as fuck."

I swallowed as I turned back to face Thane.

"Head to the yellow circle," he said with a neutral expression.

I noticed Tessa already standing next to Xavier who was showing her correct fighting stances as he gently moved her limbs to correct her. We both knew how to defend ourselves, but not against immortals. And I could see in her face that she was eager to learn.

Thane walked past me and set his long, black blade in the corner of the platform before stepping into the circle. I glanced at the blade that I remembered seeing when they rescued us from Solaris. Studying its beauty in the sunlight as its black crystal blade glistened, I wanted nothing more than to feel the weight of it in my hands.

"Focus, Amira," Thane snapped to bring me out of my trance.

I clenched my jaw as tight as I could. "Then start teaching, *oh great master.*"

His tongue came out to lick his bottom lip before a growl came from his throat.

"Can't I train with Athena instead?" I asked with my hands

on my hips. Thane's eyes flared and relaxed as my head swiveled to look around the platform. "Wait. Where is Athena?"

I hadn't seen her at dinner last night and figured she had called it an early night. Thane blew out an annoyed breath. "Gone."

I jerked my head backwards. Cocking my head to the side, I waited for an explanation.

Running a large hand down his face, he stood upright. "Athena lives in the mountains of Obsidian. Now attack me like you can actually hurt me."

"Where?" I inquired, ignoring his command. I could hear a low growl slip from his lips as he tried to mask his annoyance.

"I don't know. Athena is a free spirit that travels a lot and comes down to visit when she feels like she has nothing better to do," he said through gritted teeth. "Any other unimportant questions, Pixie?"

I clenched my teeth at the nickname that transferred from Solaris. "Does she have a specific power that could help us?"

And that was the question that broke Thane's patience.

"Attack me or, so help me Erebus, I'll throw you over this wall and forbid anyone to go after you," he hissed. I was ready to decline and continue asking him about Athena until he made an offer I couldn't refuse. "If you can land a single blow to any part of my body, I'll stop all training."

A wicked smile surfaced on my face.

This idiot had no idea that I'd had combat training in the past. He may be Fae, but I could at least land an accurate blow to that immaculate face of his. As if he could read my mind, a low, sinical laugh came from him. "Aim for the face if you want. I know how much you love admiring it."

Every part of my body, from my ears to the tips of my toes, began to tingle from his irksome words.

Glancing at the circle where he stood, my heart skipped a beat or two at how it resembled the circle Tessa and I used to make before going at each other while Alix looked on in awe.

Raising his arm palm side up, he flexed his fingers toward himself twice, telling me to begin.

Walking up to him, I got in a fighting stance, my body trembling from the excitement of getting a free shot at the arrogant prick. Faking like I was going to throw a left hook, I swung with my right fist and met air.

What the fuck?

A tap on my right shoulder had me swiftly turning around to where Thane was standing.

Behind me.

He pressed his palm to my forehead and pushed me backwards onto my ass as he laughed.

"Fuck you," I seethed through gritted teeth as I jumped back up to my feet.

"You're right, my apologies. I forgot that mortals don't possess a thread of magic in those fragile bones of yours."

I lunged at him, swinging my fists in his direction as he easily veered out of their paths without moving from his standing position.

Palming my right fist in his hand, I threw my left. He caught that one as well.

"Look at that. I didn't use an ounce of magic, and you still haven't landed one hit," he said as his golden eyes shone bright with amusement. He leaned down toward my ear and whispered, "And you think you can save your mother? She might as well already be dead."

Fury rushed from the tips of my toes to the tips of my ears as I screamed with a rage that fueled me. I ripped my fists from his grip and dropped down to sweep his legs from under him. How fast Fae move did not give me any type of advantage as he jumped to avoid my leg and landed behind me, pinning my arms to my side while forcing me to drop down further.

I felt the brush of his lips against my ear as he held me down onto the stone ground. "Who would have thought that someone with such a large attitude would have so little to back it up," he said with a sullen laugh. I shook as anger consumed me and threw my head back, hoping to connect with his face. I fell forward onto my hands, pain splintering up my arms and legs. I opened my eyes to see him crouched down in front of me. *They move so fast.* Our eyes connected as he continued to laugh.

"Pathetic," he hissed while jumping up to flip me onto my back as he straddled my body.

I bucked my hips to flip him off me, but he was far too big for me to be successful. I clawed at his chest and gripped at his black shirt as his eyes bore into mine. I reached my fingers into the collar of his shirt and tugged; my efforts were rewarded with the sound of a small tear. Happy with the sound, I yanked again, and the shirt tore down the front of him. Carelessly, he grabbed the tattered shirt and ripped it from his torso. Different types of swirls and patterns that I missed that night in the hot springs covered his chest and branched out to the top of his biceps and down his ribs.

The sweat that had now formed on his tanned skin made every single groove of muscle glisten as he hovered over me. My eyes finally left his body to trail up to his eyes that had darkened, snapping me out of my daze.

I curled my fingers in and threw a fist at his torso, but before it connected, he grabbed it, pinning my arm above my head. Taking my chances again, I threw my other fist, and it ended up right next to the first one.

Both my arms were pinned above my head as I flailed my legs to get him off me. He leaned his face down to mine, his heavy body crushing me beneath him.

"I knew you wanted to fuck me, but I never thought you'd be the type to do it in front of other people," he said before leaning down even further and pressing his tongue to the side of my face, licking me from the bottom of my jaw to my temple and bringing his darkened eyes back in front of mine.

My heart was hammering in my chest.

Could the others see what he did? Why would he do that?

My anger triumphed as I trembled beneath him and my body felt like it was on fire. A look of shock washed over him as I screamed, and he let go of my arms, grabbing his right hand. I bucked my hips as he rolled backwards onto the stone beneath us and his shadows seeped from around him. I crawled on top of him and prepared to drill my fists into his face before his shadows wrapped around my arms, pulling me down to him, resting my chest on top of his.

"You lost, Pixie," he said while flaring his nostrils.

A set of arms wrapped around my waist and lifted me up into the air as the shadows released me. I yelled for whoever had grabbed me to put me down, and as they did, I saw that it was Raya. Before I could yell at her about stepping in, I heard Tessa's voice from behind me.

I turned around to see her on top of Thane, throwing her fists into him wherever they would land as Xavier stood a few feet away, laughing with his hands on his hips.

"You bastard! Don't you ever put your hands on my sister again. I don't know who the fuck you think you are but—" she ranted, landing punch after punch until Alix pulled her off of Thane who never tried to fight back.

He got to his feet, touching his fingertips to his lip where a small amount of blood formed, and he smiled at my sister who was doing her best to be released from Alix's hold.

"I'll fucking kill you," Tessa spat at Thane.

He tilted his head to the side, "Looking forward to it."

Thane reeled his shadows in as he faced me again. "Nova, see to it that she works on the board until lunch."

I whipped my head in Nova's direction.

"Thane come on. I don't think—" Nova started before she was cut off.

"That's an order," Thane barked, causing all of us to flinch before she nodded in agreement. "I'll step in to train with Raya."

He gave one last glare in my direction before striding over to Raya who looked bewildered as her teal eyes bore into Thane. She straightened her shoulders, crossing her arms and resting them across her chest as he stopped in front of her. She raised an eyebrow, waiting for him to speak. Her expression showed she was less than amused by his broody behavior, and the way she didn't back down or cower away from him gave me a sliver of joy.

Xavier took over and instructed everyone to get back to training as he lead Tessa back to their area. Her demeanor showed that she was still fuming, and I heard Xavier tell her to take her anger out on him.

Nova lead me over to a flat, dark wooden board that was nailed into two thick wooden legs. Next to it was a pile of additional boards. My eyes trailed to hers in confusion about what I was supposed to do.

"Break it," she said while wincing and biting her bottom lip. My eyes flared with panic at her instructions, and I looked back at the thick board.

"With what?" I asked loudly. She swallowed and slowly held up her fists. A maniacal laugh erupted from me, causing Tessa and Xavier to look over at us. And at some point, Silas' meeting must have ended because he and Anya had migrated out to the platform where they stood staring.

When I was done laughing, I waited for Nova to tell me this was all a big joke. She shrugged her shoulders as I surveyed her. "I can't do that, and I'm not going to break my hand trying just because that asshole told me to."

Nova opened her mouth to speak but was cut off when Thane came storming over. She placed her hands on his chest, attempting to hold him back. "Too pretty to put some sweat and blood on the board, Pixie?"

"Fuck you," I said and spat at his feet.

He looked at the spit next to his boots and slowly back to my face. "Weak."

"Excuse me?" I asked, appalled.

"Fucking weak," he hissed before moving Nova out of the way and advancing toward me, causing me to jump out of the way before rearing his fist back and connecting it with the wooden board, sending his fist straight through. He ripped the remainder of the board from the legs and nailed a new one up.

Turning around, he made an announcement to the entire platform.

"Training is over for everyone except this one right here," he said, pointing at me. Everyone's attention was now shifted to me, causing heat from embarrassment to take over. His gaze returned to mine as he planted himself directly in front of me. I stopped moving with only a breath of air between us. "She doesn't fucking leave until sundown. Until every single one of her knuckles are raw. And so help me, Erebus, if you don't try to break that board, I swear on my life—I will break *you* instead."

Blood rushed to my ears. The only sound I could hear was my heartbeat as my nose twitched and my fists tightened. Silas opened his mouth to speak with a pained expression as Xavier shook his head to tell him to shut up.

"Anyone that objects to my training methods can step into the circle to go against me," he announced. Raya took a step forward as I shook my head no, causing her to drop her head in frustration. "Didn't think so. Clear the platform."

"I'm staying," a strong-willed voice announced from the side of the platform where Tessa stood. "She is my sister, and I will stay."

"Mine as well. I will stay, or you can meet me in the center of the circle," Raya said defiantly.

"Same here," Alix said from behind everyone.

Thane's upper lip curled back as his tongue ran across his bottom lip. With a deep breath to level himself, he picked up his blade and sheathed it to the middle of his back. "Everyone else, out."

As the others filtered out through the wooden door, Xavier opened his large black wings that I forgot he possessed and shot into the air. Nova and Tessa sat on the stone ground next to me with anger sketched on their faces. Alix was unlacing his boots while glaring in Thane's direction. "I really don't like him," he spat as we all watched Thane stop at the door and look back in my direction.

My blood boiled at the subtle smirk that crept onto his face.

"Pussy!" I yelled at him from across the platform.

His smirk dropped as I watched his hand grip the door in anger, a sneer on his face, before he slammed it shut behind him.

Chapter Fifteen

I stared at the wooden board for eternity. I hadn't noticed Raya's presence next to me. "I know that you and your sister said you know how to defend yourselves, but these realms are an entirely different breed."

I rolled my lips inward and closed my eyes, knowing that her words held truth. But my stubbornness wouldn't allow me to admit I needed help when it came to *this* type of fighting. *And what exactly would breaking a board do for me anyway?* Slowly, she moved herself into a stance and instructed me to copy her. With my left foot in front and my right foot behind me on the ball of my foot, I raised my fists to mimic her stance. "Your strength comes from your entire body, not here or here," she said while pointing at her forearms and biceps. "Bring that strength from within, from the ground up."

I nodded in understanding as Tessa stood to mimic the exact stance while Alix looked on with wide eyes.

"Now each punch you take, push a breath out," she commanded as she threw a punch to the air in front of her. I followed suit and did the same as her, Tessa completing the same motions. "Put all of that into that board."

Tessa and Raya reclaimed their seats as I stared down the piece of lumber in front of me. I took one last glance at Raya —who was doing her best to get Thackery to leave her alone—for reassurance before I threw my right fist into the center of the board.

Pain shot up my wrist and into my forearm as I jumped back, hopping up and down while holding my wrist. "This shit is almost five inches thick. Is this some kind of sick Fae joke?" I asked in frustration.

"She's not doing this shit," Tessa said as she stood. "What's he going to do if she doesn't? We're not afraid of him."

I glanced at my sister. I didn't have the heart to tell her that I might be slightly afraid of him at this point.

"She's got this. I know she's got this," Raya said while she studied my face. "I saw what she handled back in Solaris. A piece of wood is nothing compared to that." My breathing evened out as her words sank in. "Stop letting him get in your head, and do the work," she added on with a raise of her brows.

I gritted my teeth and stood back again to study the piece of wood.

Despite the pain radiating throughout my right arm, I threw another punch into the wood, and I cried out in pain. I snuck a glance at Raya who still looked stern while Tessa looked concerned, her arms crossed over her chest in frustration.

Hours.

That's how long I put blood and sweat into that piece of fucking wood that never even cracked.

Servants brought us lunch and water during our time out there, but as I brought the container of water to my lips, all I could see were my knuckles.

Bruised. Battered. Bloodied.

On my last attempt, a final searing pain shot up my arm and into my collarbone, causing me to drop to my knees. Tessa and Raya dropped next to me while Alix held me upright on the ground. Attempting to raise my arm, I screamed in pain, lowering my head down to the stone.

"Stay still," Raya demanded. She raised both hands up to hover near my arm. Closing her eyes, the familiar feeling returned as it felt like magnets were pulling my bones in different directions, but no additional pain. After a few minutes, I was able to raise my arm again even though it still tingled and felt slightly numb. "Give it a few hours and it should feel as good as new."

Tessa's mouth hung open while I hugged Raya, thanking her. "You... you can heal people?" she asked Raya who nodded with a shrug of one shoulder. "Why does she get to be gorgeous *and* possess badass powers?"

"And that's only one of them," I said, causing Raya to blush and roll her eyes.

We whipped our heads in the direction of the sound of the wooden door opening from the entry to the palace.

"Dinner time," Nova bellowed from the doorway.

I glanced up at the sky, and in the chaos of everything, the sun had gone down.

Chapter Sixteen

The days had come and gone so quickly that in the blink of an eye, it was time for the meeting in Bavaria.

The training that Thane mandated for me was going well, except for that fucking wooden board and the fact that he wouldn't let me train with anyone but himself. My body was covered in bruises, evidence of him not going easy on me. He swore it was to have me prepared in case anything went south at the meeting, but I knew it was truly because he hated me.

Whatever I did to him in a past life had clearly carried over into this one.

We all stood on the training platform as we waited for Aravis to join us.

Anya had informed me that all of us would be going to Bavaria except for Tessa and Alix, who were not happy about the decision. No one wanted to stay behind in case Raine tried anything, even though magic wasn't allowed in that territory. I wasn't elated about leaving my siblings behind, but I understood it would already be enough to ensure one mortal wasn't harmed, let alone three.

As Aravis made his way over to us, we all fell silent when he cleared his throat to speak.

"When we arrive in Bavaria, we must think with our heads and as a team before making any brash decisions," he announced before turning his attention to Thane. "Regardless of you claiming the throne or not, you will be the leader of today's meeting."

Thane opened his mouth to refuse but was met by a fierce glare from Aravis that made all of us cringe. With a nod of understanding from Thane, Aravis continued speaking. "We don't make any deals without discussing with each other first. Amira, I know how much your mother means to you, but do not fall for Raine's empty promises."

I nodded in understanding as Anya stepped forward. "Everyone ready?"

Footsteps were heard from behind us. "We're coming. We're coming, and you can't stop us."

My shoulders slumped forward at Tessa's voice. I didn't need to turn around to know that Alix was in tow as well. "It's not safe for the three of us to be there together," I reasoned. Alix shook his head in response.

"We were separated once. I won't allow for it to happen again. I'll die before having to wait for you to come back again."

My chest tightened. I cast a glance upward to Thane, and for once, those golden eyes held understanding. He nodded to my siblings and threw his head back to look up at the bright blue sky above. "Stay close and do not wander off."

As my siblings agreed with Thane's demand, Anya conjured her usual green dust to beam us to the neutral territory that was agreed upon for the meeting.

Within seconds, we were on unknown ground.

A few of us stumbled as we landed, and Thane used his hands to balance me. My boots dug into the sand as my eyes wandered over the vast, open landscape. I squinted as I surveyed the rocky formations in the distance that looked like mountains.

"This is not what I had in mind," Tessa commented while attempting to brush the sand from her wavy hair. I held in my laugh as I watched her scramble to her feet as she was the only one that had fallen.

Though clouds packed together overhead, providing ample shade, the sweltering heat was already taking a toll on me. "Where is this asshole?" Nova questioned while tugging at her top.

"Let's not summon him," Xavier countered while swiping sweat from his brow.

While we waited for Raine to arrive, my breaths became shallower at the thought of seeing him again. Raya's hand rested on my shoulder as she smiled at me. "Don't worry about him. He may be powerful, but he can't get through all of us."

Thane glanced over at us before focusing on Anya. "If anything happens, you take Amira and leave."

My mouth fell open at his command.

Before I could refuse his order, a golden cloud of dust appeared several yards in front of us. My breathing ceased all together as Raya wrapped her arm around my shoulders in comfort.

A tall male with dark hair streaked with grey stepped out of the portal, and my body jerked in shock as Raya dropped her arm from my shoulders.

Eryx.

"Well, well, well... not only did you actually show up, you brought the property with you as well," he said with a sardonic smile.

Did he just refer to me as property?

Laughter erupted from my left. I glanced over to see Xavier and Silas chuckling. "Nice entrance... say, I like what that eye patch is doing for ya," Silas said between laughs. The corner of

Thane's mouth tipped upwards at Silas' joke. Eryx sneered at the three men.

"Shut your mouth. Since when are sentries allowed to speak before their King?"

Silas and Xavier laughed even louder.

Doing his best to ignore their laughter, Eryx surveyed the rest of us. "Had I known you were bringing the calvary, I would've brought our men as well."

"I guess one could say that you never saw it coming," Silas commented calmly before he and Xavier doubled over with laughter.

Eryx lunged forward as Thane drew his sleek, obsidian blade from his back.

"Uh, uh. I wouldn't if I were you. Magic may not be allowed on these grounds, but we outnumber you here. Where is your high and mighty *king* anyway?" Thane said with a fake smile.

"Is that blade not considered magic, Thanasis?"

Thane growled in frustration and sheathed his blade. I watched closely as the blade shimmered before going dull in the middle of Thane's back.

Eryx cocked a brow and cleared his throat in an attempt to collect himself. "My high king had important duties to handle within town. Had he known his *mate* would actually show, I'm sure he would have changed his plans."

He tilted his head as he surveyed Raya from head to toe. Xavier noticed the gesture and stepped toward her, their shoulders nearly touching.

"You came to discuss something, so get on with it," Aravis said from in front of us.

Eryx's eyes shifted from Aravis to me and back again.

"Yes. The High King of Solaris would like to offer a truce to the High King of Obsidian rather than retaliate for your little... *stunt*," he proclaimed while straightening his tunic.

"I'm sorry, are you referring to when he tried to force

someone to marry him against their will?" Thane inquired with a look of confusion. Eryx huffed and ran his tongue across the front of his teeth. "Apologies, perhaps you were referring to when he slayed two innocent witches."

Eryx's glare could cut glass as Thane spoke.

"Am I still wrong? Was it when he put a hex over your entire fucking realm? Enlighten me to which stunt you're referring to because there's so many, I'm getting confused here." Thane cocked a brow while waiting for a reply.

"Watch it," Eryx said through gritted teeth.

"Or what?" Thane snapped back "You're outnumbered in case you forgot how to count."

As Eryx tried to suppress his anger, another burst of gold dust came from behind him. My blood ran cold as I saw the form of an exceptionally tall figure erupt from the shadows of the portal.

All blood drained from my face as Raya grabbed my hand and squeezed tightly.

"Ah, exactly who I was looking for," Thane remarked as the figure came into view while brushing the long, white hair from his face, searching the area until his ice blue eyes found mine.

Raine.

Chapter Seventeen

Brushing the sand carried by the wind from his clothes, Raine looked directly at me, then to Raya. "Well, hello sister. Miss me?"

Her grip on my hand tightened as I whispered to not let him get to her.

"Do I miss being controlled like a pitiful rat because you're afraid of me overpowering you? No. No, I don't," Raya replied with a scornful smile.

Raine's quick glare sent chills down my spine as Thane moved in front of me.

"How kind of you to join us, Raine. I was just asking your jester here what *stunt* you were referring to when we visited your realm," Thane stated while crossing his arms over his chest and widening his stance. From behind, I could see his muscles move under his leather and swallowed whatever thoughts came to mind. Forcing myself to focus back on Raine, I took note of how his eyes never left the hilt of Thane's shiny black blade strapped to his back. One could only assume that Thane showing he didn't need his weapon in Raine's presence was a blow to his ego.

"Under immortal and Fae law, you cannot take someone's

mate without both parties in agreement," Raine stated as he stepped forward, causing Silas and Xavier to mimic his movement.

Thane turned to face me with a twisted expression. "Did you sleep with him?"

Heat from embarrassment spread through my body and built in my cheeks. "W-What?" I asked, baffled at his direct question.

"Did you sleep with him, Amira?" He grilled again, his impatience growing.

"That's a personal question. I—"

An exasperated breath came from him while he tried to keep his cool. "For fuck's sake. For once in your life, answer the question. Did you sleep with him?"

"No!" I shout.

A genuine laugh erupted from Thane as Raine looked like he wanted to set all of us ablaze.

"So, what I'm hearing is that you have no idea at all if the mating bond is mutual," he asserted while turning back to face Raine and Eryx.

"W-What is he talking about?" I asked Raya who was staring at me with wide eyes.

"I...I thought you slept with him?" she asked. I shook my head before Thane began speaking again.

"What the *High King of Solaris* forgot to mention to you is that, when mates sleep together, the bond snaps into place."

"*Shut your fucking mouth*," Raine hissed as Eryx observed him in bewilderment.

"Basically, he claimed you under false pretense. If fate finds true, you will know the moment you fuck. Or did Raine here leave that bit of info out as well?" Thane asked with fake sincerity.

"Fuck you," Raine seethed while drawing the dagger at his hip that Thane eyed carelessly.

"Looks like you should've been fucking *her*. Or were you scared you wouldn't be up to par?"

Raine sprang toward Thane but Eryx wrapped his arms around him. "We're outnumbered," he said quietly. "And if we slip any bit of magic on these grounds, we will face serious consequences." Raine regained his composure and placed his dagger back on his hip, flexing his hands impatiently. "Well...since we want to tell secrets."

Thane's entire body went from a relaxed to rigid state. "Don't cross a line you can't come back from Raine."

"Oh, we're leaping across lines now at this point, *Thanasis*," Raine said with a click of his tongue. Thane released a warning growl as I tried to figure out what he was so upset about.

"Did he let you know about your father?"

"What's he talking about?" I addressed my group. I glanced over at my siblings who looked just as confused as I was. Raine followed my gaze and tittered while surveying Tessa from head to two.

"You're just as beautiful as when I saw you in Medlar. A shame I chose to take your mother instead of you. You would have been a great asset to my sentries' *needs* instead of my sister," Raine announced, causing Eryx to laugh while winking at my sister.

"That's enough," Anya said sternly.

Raine sneered and squared his shoulders. "I enjoyed killing the remainder of your coven in case you were wondering."

I gasped and glanced at Anya who trembled as she fought to contain her magic. I would have done anything to be able to dig my fingers into his eyes at that very moment.

"Don't you wonder why Lorena wanted you so badly for herself?" he cooed while watching me.

"B-because she wanted my youth..." I answered hesitantly.

"Oh, but it's so much more than that, my mate."

"You're not my fucking mate. Thane, answer me. What does he know about my father?" I begged the man standing in front of me.

"He's bullshitting, Amira," Thane hissed between clenched teeth.

"Am I? Don't you want to know what I know? Don't you want your family to live happily?" Raine fired off questions as he stepped toward me.

Thane drew his sword. "If you take one more step toward her, I'll gut you where you stand."

Raine looked over Thane, and his eyes trailed to the tip of his blade. "If you draw it, you better use it."

"I intend to," Thane said as he stalked toward Raine.

Panic flared as I thought about Thane being sentenced to death. I shuffled forward in a stupor and Raya gripped my wrist. I blinked to see Aravis stepping in front of Thane. "Enough of this. What is it that you want?"

Raine settled his stare on me as he flashed a smile so wide that every single tooth showed. "Return my mate and sister to Solaris and we can forget any of this ever happened."

A menacing smile spread across Eryx's face before his focus settled on Raya. An audible growl escaped from Xavier as he pushed Raya and I behind him.

Raine's smile faded as he noticed that no one was moving to hand us over.

"Very well then," he said before snapping his fingers. A guard stepped through the portal with my mother in tow. I gasped as I leapt toward her, but I was halted when Thane wrapped his arm around my waist.

"Ah, that's all it took for you to act accordingly," Raine commented with a smug expression.

The guard threw my mother down to her knees as she fought to remain standing.

Raine stalked behind her as he drew his dagger, yanking her head back by her dark hair while I screamed so loudly my own ears rang. "Please no, please. I'll go. Just spare her," I begged as a tear slipped free at the sight of my mother near death.

"Shut the fuck up," Thane hissed in my ear. I threw my elbow into his abdomen which did absolutely nothing.

My eyes fell to the pendant hanging around her neck as I subtly clutched at the exact replica around my own.

"Take me," Aravis said as he stepped forward. "Let the woman go and take me."

What happened to not making any agreements or bargains?

The anguish and terror worn on Aravis' face as he eyed the dagger near my mother's throat sent waves of emotion through me. "Let her go and take me. Don't do anything you cannot repair, Raine. I'm more valuable than a mere mortal. *Take me.*"

Raine's eyes flared with excitement at Aravis' offer paired with his begging. "I don't think so. But, if you'd like for me to spare her life at this moment, you can hand over a spare."

Multiple pairs of eyes slowly turned their gaze toward my siblings and back to Raine before my mother and I protested the request. "Very well then, I'll slit her throat right here," Raine informed while pressing the dagger into my mother's slender neck as she squeezed her eyes shut. A single trail of blood ran down to her collar bone.

"I'll go," Alix shouted from behind.

"Don't do this Alix," I begged while turning to grip his shoulders. "He'll kill you to get to me."

My baby brother removed my hands and began walking toward Eryx. Tessa and I grabbed onto him as the others told him to stop. He halted his stride before turning to face us. "Please... let me make things right for once. You pulled me out from the dark before. It's my turn to protect what's ours," he said before grabbing our hands, squeezing them once and letting go. "I cannot watch on while sending my sister to be in harm's way."

Tessa gawked at Alix before dropping to her knees, begging him to stay. Aravis and Thane exchanged glances and nodded their heads in agreement. Knowing that blood would be shed if one didn't go in addition to my mother.

"Place the shackles on him," Raine instructed Eryx who placed glowing metal shackles tightly around Alix's wrists and ankles. "Can never be too sure."

The additional guard waited for Raine's command before forcefully pulling my mother to her feet while she continued to beg for Alix's freedom.

"As a gift, I'll show you how courteous and understanding I can be." Raine remarked. I sneered at him while fighting the mounds of emotions running through me. "You have until three days after Merakai to return my bride and sister to me, or I start killing—beginning with the mother," Raine declared. The sob that I had been fighting to hold in racked through me. "I will personally have her head sent to you before the blood finishes draining from her body."

I clenched my teeth at his words as I observed Aravis staring at my mother with sad eyes before glancing at Alix and back to me. The look in his eyes said everything I needed to know—*this is a mistake, but they* had *no other choice.*

Eryx kicked Alix in the back before instructing him to move along. The action sent my heart into overdrive and my vision began to blur.

Alix spat in Eryx's face before following the guard through the tunnel after nodding at us. He took one last look at Tessa and I before mouthing that he loved us and followed behind our mother who did the same.

"One last thing," Raine said while holding a single finger in the air and turning back around to face us. "When I brought your beautiful mother to my home in Solaris, Eryx encountered a rather peculiar, yet familiar issue."

His head tilted from left to right as he eyed me once again. "He can't read your mother's mind either. Now that can't be a coincidence can it, Amira?"

His question caused my eyes to bulge.

"Figured you wouldn't have an answer for me. But no worries,

I'll get it out of her. *Or your brother.* One way or another," he said with an intimidating laugh while walking through the portal.

As they all disappeared through the portal, Aravis paced in panic. "We shouldn't have allowed for that to happen." Anya gripped his shoulders, steadying him and stopping his wandering. "We will figure out a way to get them back to us."

Thane kicked sand into the air while releasing every curse word he could think of into the air. "Let's get back to Obsidian and figure out our next steps."

Before Anya beamed us back to Obsidian, Thane's stare was so dark and heavy that I feared he would take my soul where I stood. My head throbbed as my mind pressured me to ask questions.

What did they know about our father that my siblings and I didn't?

With deep thoughts floating in my mind, a cloud of green floated into the thick air, sending us back to Obsidian.

Chapter Eighteen

Anya beamed us back into the dining hall where Thackery and Atlas scurried up to the group of us.

Fear and panic consumed Tessa and I as we claimed seats at the table, trying to process what just happened in Bavaria.

"I should have killed him when we had the chance in Obsidian," Thane announced from the corner of the room. The way he paced in a circle in front of the large windows made him look like a mad man.

I grimaced when I noticed Aravis doing the same thing. He was pacing back and forth in the middle of the room while digging his hands into his hair, spiking my anxiety even further. "I have to step away," he said frantically. Thane tried to stop him, walking over and reaching a hand out for his shoulder but he was met with a dark cloud of smoke. Aravis had vanished from sight within seconds.

How can he leave at a time like this?

Everyone's sporadic movements and decisions were sending my unease into overdrive. My emotions were riding high, and could no longer be tamed, as I slapped my hands to the top of the table, causing Tessa to jump from her silent stupor. "How about you tell me what the fuck Raine was talking about back there? What secret do you know about our father?" I demanded out of pure anger.

Thane whipped his head around to study me as shadows poured out of him. Forgetting how fast Fae could move, I stumbled backwards when, in a second, he stood inches away from me. Grabbing my arm to steady me, he glared at everyone else in the room that quickly shifted to come to my defense. His eyes found mine again, and I swallow at how dark they'd turned. "You want fucking answers, Amira?"

I was so stunned that I didn't respond.

Aggravated with my silence, he grabbed my other arm and shook me. "I asked you a fucking question."

Anya was behind him in a flash as she held her palms up to his temples. "When I let you go, you're going to calm yourself. Or, you're going to have to deal with all of us."

Before she released him, I wiggled my way out of his grasp and stepped a few feet away. My body wanted to tremble in response, but I would rather be burned alive than give him the satisfaction of showing how much he scared me. Removing her hands, Thane stumbled forward. "For fucks sake Anya, I asked you to stop doing that."

"And I wouldn't need to if you knew how to control yourself," she replied, sarcasm saturating her tone.

His agitation had only grown now as his eyes were even darker than moments before, mimicking a night sky free of stars. Slowly, he took his usual seat at the long table. Reaching for an apple from the fruit bowl, he twisted and turned it in his hand while surveying it.

"So, the pretty princess wants answers."

His statement sent a wave of heated irritation through me. His constant ridicule, trying to paint me as nothing more than a pretty face, was the insult that got under my skin just as much as "damsel in distress".

"How many times have you broken the board?" he questioned as the room fell to an uncanny silence.

Raya and Tessa pretended not to hear him as they stared at each other. I glanced up to see Nova, Silas, and Xavier with pained expressions on their faces. When he didn't receive an answer, his fists slammed down on the granite table, causing me to jump. My eyes averted to the small, hairline crack in the table where his right fist connected.

An eerie calmness exuded from him as he settled his gaze on me. Running his tongue across his bottom lip, he tilted his head and furrowed his brows. "Did you break the board *at all*, Amira?"

On the outside, I portrayed the same calmness as him. On the inside, my blood was set ablaze from panic and shame—shame from not being able to break the board because of how weak I was. I gave one shake of my head to answer his question and took in a breath to calm myself. Before I could release it, the sound of his chair skidding across the floor pierced my ears and a grasp on my elbow was pulling me toward the door.

"Get your hands off of her," Tessa snapped, standing from her seat.

"Thane, what the hell are you doing?" Nova questioned as she rushed to my side while Anya moved to place her hands at his temples again but were met by his shadows. When I peeked up at him to ask the same thing, the sight of his jet-black eyes up close caused me to lose my words, my mouth falling agape.

With his lips peeled back, he yanked me to stand in front of him. "If you all want to stand around while she barely puts any effort into finding answers, then you do that. But it's not my family that needs saving." His vicious glare shifted back to me before he yanked my arm once more, causing me to fall into his chest while he crouched down and threw me over his shoulder.

Preparing to beat my fists into his back, a cloud of dark smoke surrounds us. When it dissipated, we were standing on the sparring platform. His dark, dead eyes still ablaze on me.

Did he just beam us using his shadows?

"Break. The fucking. Board," he seethed while pointing at it.

"What do you think I've been trying to do every damn night out here? Braid my fucking hair?" I snapped back at him. Grabbing my shoulders, he pushed me directly in front of the board. I dug my feet in the ground to prevent him from moving me, which did nothing against his strength. Bringing his face down to my level, his frown deepened. "If you know you're not strong enough then just say that. But if you want answers to secrets, then do what the fuck you're told."

My eyes flared as rage consumed me. I flexed my hands, letting the numbness that I felt run throughout my fingers and forearms. The movement sent chills throughout my body.

I'd worship Erebus before I ever took orders from a man.

"You say you want your family back. You offered yourself up to go back to Solaris, but you can't even break a fucking board," he hissed, followed by him throwing his head back with a mocking laugh. "Pathetic little human."

My emotions bubbled over from rage, and I raised my fist to hit him. Mid-swing, he caught my fist in his hand.

"Cute," he exclaimed, and launched me toward the wooden board.

A single droplet of rain landed on my cheek as I stumbled. I reached up to swipe it away and let out a guttural scream. Standing in silence, I let a dozen more droplets of rain fall on my face before I faced him.

"Why do you hate me so much?"

His silence only fueled my rage. Every emotion and tingling feeling I had was about to explode if he didn't speak.

"Since the moment you brought me here, you have only been

hard on *me*. Not Raya, just *me*. If you don't like humans, just say that."

He opened his mouth to speak, but then snapped it shut. For a faint moment, a look of empathy washed over him before the cold, vicious Thane reemerged. "Because you're weak, and I knew it the moment I laid eyes on you on that dais next to Raine."

My stomach sank. I started visualizing how helpless I looked the night he saw me for the first time. Bloodied and bruised. Chained by a man that I had given my heart to. But nothing cut as deep as Thane's follow-up:

"Right where you belonged."

The clouds opened way for the rainfall as we glowered at each other, the rain vicious and bitter cold. His words cut deep, and it killed me to know that he could see it on my face. I turned back towards the board to focus on something else. Anything else besides *him*.

His dark hair plastered to his head from the rain. His shirt stuck to him and outlined every single deep groove of muscle that he possessed. Even when his words hurt, he was still a wonder to look at, and that alone sent ice through my veins at the disgust I had for myself.

Placing both palms flat against the thick wood, I leaned forward, resting my forehead between my hands.

"A fucking damsel in distress that wants to hide behind a tough persona," he finished with a grunt, followed by another low menacing laugh. My shoulders began to shake in torment, the numbness flowing to my ears. I couldn't shake the icy feeling that constantly consumed me when I let my anxiety win.

I could hear him moving, stepping closer to me as the rain pelted the top of my head and back. He dipped his head, his warm breath on my ear sending a shudder down my spine. "And now your family is going to die for your mistakes, Pixie."

My breathing ceased

Those words...they were the ones to cut deep, severing me in half.

I released another hoarse, distorted scream as tremors racked my body. I pressed my hands as hard as I could into that impenetrable wood. Out of the corner of my eye, I could see Thane cautiously backing away.

With every fiber of my being, I pushed my anxiety and anger, the numb helplessness that had kept me frozen in the face of my fear, to the tips of my fingers.

Slowly, ice began to creep along the thick wooden board as I continued to push. My ears perked up with every snap, crackle, and pop that sounded from in front of me. I screamed louder and heard one last pop before the board shattered to pieces, falling at my feet.

I didn't move. *My mind hadn't resynced with my body to allow me to.*

I remained standing with my hands held up where the board once was, breathing heavily at the sight before me. I heard multiple gasps behind me as I turned my head to face Thane. A satisfied smirk twisted his lips. I pivoted my body until my palms were held up in his direction and released dozens of shards of ice toward him.

A layer of shadows quickly shielded him, the shards dropping to the ground.

Cognizance fell on top of me with a weight I could no longer bear. I dropped to my knees on the hard ground. The sobs racking through my body wouldn't allow for me to open my eyes as two large arms wrapped around me. I'd never felt the warmth of this specific embrace before as I tried to figure out who it was while my eyes remained clamped tight.

"I didn't mean any of it. Not a single word."

The heavy rain distorted the voice, and my cries were so harsh that I struggled to catch my breath when trying to decipher it.

"I promise you, every word I just said to you was a lie."

My eyes snapped open as the hard body pressed against mine brought me as close as possible. He embraced me like he'd never see me again, like I was precious and coveted. Turning my head to focus on the man that held me so tenderly, the sobs returned, and I dropped my head to his chest.

Thane's chest.

Chapter Nineteen

My surroundings were a colorless blur through my tears as I was carried through the palace. Thane cradled me against his chest while quickly moving us into a part of the palace I wasn't familiar with. When we reached the center of the room, I forced my eyes open to see a room that resembled a library before squeezing them shut once again. Carefully, he laid me onto a daybed where I curled into a ball on my side, my sobs barely subsiding.

Rustling could be heard around me as my eyes remained shut. *Had I fallen asleep?*

For a split second I opened my eyes to see Tessa perched on the edge of the daybed, Raya and Nova standing behind her, and the remainder of the room standing by the far wall. I shut them again, wondering when they had arrived. *Had I been asleep that long?* Opening my eyes once more, my gaze roamed the room freely, searching for a specific person that wasn't coming into view.

Why was I desperately searching the room for Thane?

"Are you okay, sister?" Tessa stammered in a whisper while she rubbed my back in soothing circles.

I snapped my eyes shut at her question. Am I okay? *AM I OKAY?*

My mind was working at lightning speed to figure out what just happened. For a split second, Thane showed an affectionate side. *And* cold, hard *ice just shot out of my hands.* No, I'm not okay.

"She needs time," Thane said from a corner of the room, causing me to open my eyes again while raising my head to search for him.

"Don't tell me what *my* sister needs pretty boy," Tessa snapped while inching closer to me.

"The last thing we need right now is an unnecessary argument. We need to figure out what just happened to her," Raya spoke. An apologetic smile gracing her face as she glanced down at me. "Let's see if we can sit her up." Before I could protest, three sets of female hands assisted me as Anya and Thackery burst through the entrance.

"What happened?" Anya questioned with narrowed eyes cast in Thane's direction. Thackery skuttled up to us and rubbed his entire body against Raya's leg. She shook him off and shooed him away, forcing him to leap onto the daybed next to me. Atlas stood, growling at the cat before plopping back down and focusing his large eyes on me.

"Shards of ice shot out from... um... from Amira's palms. I think someone must have cast a spell on her when we went to that meeting because— " Raya tried to reason but was cut short by Anya raising her palm to speak instead.

"This has gone on for far too long," she said while lowering her hand. I curled into myself as I questioned what that meant. She stared at Thane until he rolled his eyes and released a breath, pushing himself away from the wall he was leaning on.

"Everyone out. Amira and I need to talk."

My fingertips turned numb again at his command. Afraid

that I'd shoot shards of ice at any moment, I slipped my hands beneath my thighs.

Glancing around the room, I noticed a grimace on everyone's face except Raya and Tessa. And as I tried to process what just happened, no one else seemed extremely concerned except for them. "No. No one leaves this room. I am so fucking sick of these secrets," I said before standing on wobbly legs. Tessa reached her hand out to steady me, but I swat it away. "If there's something you need to tell me then say it now. In front of everyone."

Thane's expression never faltered, but I could tell by his body language that he was nervous to speak. But he didn't back down from my demand. He didn't even look around the room. His golden eyes were only focused on me as I fought to control my breathing.

"You are not fully mortal, Amira."

Numb.

That's what I felt after his words played over and over in my head like a well-known song.

"You're lying," I declared after what felt like a lifetime of silence. When Thane didn't reply, I surveyed the entire room as the others hung their heads. "Tell me that he's playing a mind game on me right now. I was clearly placed under some sort of—"

"Amira, stop. You asked for the truth and I'm going to give it to you," Thane interrupted as he ran his large hand down his face.

"Your mother... she...."

"Spit it out," I said angrily.

Thane only stared at me with eyes that began to soften. The roll of his throat as he swallowed turned my breathing shallow.

"Had an affair with an immortal," Tessa completed his statement softly from behind me. I whipped around to face her. Nothing but regret and sorrow portrayed in her eyes as she cleared her throat and began twisting a strand of hair around her finger.

"When I was younger, I heard our parents discussing what they would do if you were to develop any type of...magic. When I asked mother about it, she told me I imagined the whole thing and heard what I wanted to hear," Tessa explained with tears lining her eyes. My mind refused to process my sister's information. She reached out to touch me, but I flinched away from her.

"Your mother demanded that your biological father never return to Medlar," Thane added on.

I shook my head at the nonsense I was hearing. "Liar."

"Who do you think it was that sent us to Solaris, Amira? Fucking think."

"You do *not* get to speak to me like that," I screamed while pointing my finger in his direction. "You do *not* get to make up some story about my family. My father is—"

"Your father is Aravis."

I stumbled backwards at his words. The ringing in my ears began to blare as I tried to focus on the man standing in front of me. The man that was ruining every aspect of my life as he fed me more lies.

"I promised him that I would bring you back. Aravis couldn't retrieve you himself because he knew that he would slaughter Raine at the sight of you and cause a war between realms."

Heavy tears rushed to my eyes at the information being poured into the room. My entire body felt weak as I replayed my first encounter with Aravis in my head. *When I first met Aravis, he told me that he sent for me.*

Everything I thought I knew about my life was crumbling right before me.

I turned back to Tessa in panic. I could see that she was doing everything she could to not fall to pieces in front of everyone, to hold herself together while sensing my emotions rising. Her lips parted as she shook her head. "I was so envious of knowing that you were secretly mother's favorite that I treated you terribly. I knew in my heart that she placed so much responsibility on you because she knew what you were capable of. Amira, I'm so sorry—"

I stopped her with a raise of my hand before she could finish. "Y-you knew? This whole time... you knew?"

I could feel the room shift as my hard gaze settled on Tessa. She swallowed, rubbing her palms against her thighs. "I figured it would be best if you were told by someone other than me. I didn't have the full story, and I wasn't sure if—"

"You are my fucking sister!"

My outburst pulled a reaction from everyone in the room as they either gasped or blanched. My vision turned red as I surveyed Tessa looking at me with wide, pitiful eyes. I turned in a full circle to look over the others.

"All of you knew?" I asked while slowly surveying everyone in the room who ducked their heads again at my question. Raya was the only one that shook her head in denial. Her teal eyes large with shock.

An ear-piercing scream left me as my arms stiffened at my side, palms facing the ground. Frost began to fall from my palms to the marble floors. Those closest to me jumped back.

"Everyone out. *That is an order*," Thane shouted while advancing on me. Silas and Xavier refused to move as the others quickly filtered from the room at Thane's command. I lifted my palms in his direction with the intention to cause pain—the same pain that was flowing through every inch of me. Someone had to share it with me to relieve the burden that was crushing every fiber of my soul.

Throwing his shadows in my direction to stop my attack, Thane demanded Xavier and Silas to leave again as they hesitated at the sight of me attempting to kill their friend.

Their High King.

After another moment's pause, they exited the room, and I thrust more ice in his direction. I didn't need a mirror to see the crazed look in my eyes as I did everything I could to pierce his perfectly tanned skin.

In a single blink, he was gone from in front of me. My arms

were slammed into my sides, and the harder I fought to release them, the tighter the hold became. I glanced down to see darkness wrapped around me. Thane continued to wrap his shadows around me until I couldn't move, and my palms tightly pressed against my thighs.

"You're going to listen to me. And after you listen to me... If you still want to kill me, then we can battle it out. Understand?"

He stared at me until I nodded my head in agreement.

Releasing his shadows, he instructed me to sit at the large round table in the center of the room. Slowly, I settled into the chair and arched a brow to insinuate that he start talking. He studied my face before turning to look out the large bay window into the night storm that surrounded us. A bolt of lightning skittered across the night sky as he ran his hand through his thick, dark locs.

"The day that Aravis called a meeting in the observatory and deemed it only for those from Obsidian," he started and took a slight pause to gather himself. "That's when he told us that you were his daughter." Turning around to face me, he leaned his back on the thick glass. "When he instructed me to retrieve you from Solaris, he told me that it was someone near and dear to his heart. I never questioned him about it because there's not much I wouldn't do for Aravis."

I fought hard to keep my breaths steady as I processed his words.

"Then why didn't he retrieve me himself from Solaris? I understand that he didn't want to start a war, but this doesn't make any sense," I rambled.

"Because Aravis refuses to use his dark magic anymore. And when he made that decision, he also handed the ability to travel to any realm over to me. By doing that, it only enhanced my magic to be even more powerful."

"Even more powerful than Aravis?"

"Yes."

"Even more powerful than... Raine?"

"Yes. Apparently, I'm the most powerful High King from any realm, but I refuse to claim the title because it belongs to Aravis. He should be king, not me. He deserves it not... not me."

"That still doesn't explain why he wasn't part of the group that came to save me," I countered.

"He didn't accompany us because Aravis knew that his love for you would get in the way of his own order to bring you here. And by him refusing to use his dark magic that would have made him useless against Raine while retrieving you."

I shook my head to push away the tears rushing to my eyes.

"From the moment Aravis told us who you were, I knew why Raine wanted you. He knew that being the mate of a High King's daughter would grant him a specific rank. But, the daughter of a high king that is half mortal, half immortal could open doors to things we've never even known before," he said before walking over to the chair opposite me and plopping down in it. "Every mean thing I said to you out there on that platform tonight was because I knew you possessed some sort of magic within your veins. That anxiety that consumes you isn't anxiety, Amira. It was your powers fighting to come through."

I lifted my hands and held them out in front of me to examine them. The flinch from Thane as I lifted them almost brought a smile to my lips.

"Whatever questions you have, now is the time to ask," he said while folding his hands on the table in front of him. I ground my teeth together, wondering if I could trust him. He might not have outright lied to me about who I was, but he kept a secret that I had deserved to know. But if he was offering to answer questions, I was going to take the opportunity to get answers.

"Was Atlas the wolf I saw in the forest back in Medlar?"

Thane's lips pressed into a thin line as he rolled his neck.

"Yes."

"Why did you lie to me when I said it was him?"

The rise and fall of Thane's chest told me how stressed he already was from the first question.

"Because I didn't know how to explain to you why he was in Medlar."

I raised a brow again, waiting for him to explain why Atlas was in Medlar before I ever stepped foot in an immortal realm. He threw his head back and blew out a deep breath before bringing his attention back to me.

"Your mother had reached out to Aravis for the first time since before you were born to inform him that she feared your true identity had been compromised. And she was right. Before Millie and Ellie died, they had informed Anya that Lorena was supposed to turn you over to Raine in exchange for a large amount of coin and free range in Solaris. But once she saw how..."

"Saw what, Thane?" I hissed, waiting for him to continue. His eyes narrowed as if he didn't want to complete his sentence. Digging his teeth into his bottom lip, he released it and continued. "Once she saw how beautiful you are, she wanted to take that for herself. And once she got that, she felt she could offer you to the highest bidder in exchange for your bloodline."

I winced at his last statement. I could feel my chest getting heavy at the thought of men rushing to take me for the sole purpose of breeding.

She was going to sell me like a piece of cattle.

"So, Aravis requested for me to beam Atlas to find you to ensure that you were okay. Along with Silas and a shapeshifter from another realm that we trust by his side. When he returned to me, the hurt in his eyes and whimpering let us know that something was extremely wrong, and you were in harm's way. From there Silas filled us in on what he saw. But by the time I... *we* returned to Medlar, it was too late. You were already gone."

My head was spinning while trying to store the information being fed to me. But I pocketed whatever information I could and continued with my questions.

"And where is Lorena now?"

Thane ran his tongue between his lips as he glanced back out the bay window. A loud clap of thunder caused me to look as well.

"We can't locate her."

My body sagged in the chair at the thought of her roaming freely throughout Medlar.

"Why did I feel such a connection to Atlas when I was in the forest?"

The memory of a pull toward the largest wolf flooded my mind while Thane remained rigid in his chair. His golden eyes flared. He stood suddenly from his seat.

"We're done here."

"I'm sorry, what?"

"You received your answers. I will see to it that you get the proper training needed to control your new...magic."

"Fuck you, Thane."

His shoulders tensed and his eyes darkened. I held my breath, waiting for him to close the distance between us. He never moved as his chest rose and fell rapidly. "I just had a bunch of information dropped on me to shatter my world and you tell me we're done here? You're so fucking selfish."

A fake laugh erupted between us as he leaned over the table, "Who the fuck do you think sent that trail of dust to you leading you back to the market? To your father?"

Every muscle in my body loosened at the words he threw across the table.

That sole question let me know he wasn't lying about anything he just told me. How would he know about that?

Standing from my seat, I raised my chin in his direction. "When I first met you, I wanted to kill you for the way you treated me. The mean things you said and glares you threw in my direction. But now.... now I'm just disappointed in you for not telling me the truth sooner. For not thinking that I could handle the information provided to me tonight. Instead, I had to find out like this."

Atlas came padding back into the library, nudging his head into the back of my thigh. I glanced back up at Thane from across the table. "You're going to teach me how to control my magic. You're going to teach me how to wield a sword. And you're going to help me save my family."

His honey-colored eyes flared and narrowed at my assertiveness.

"And when it comes to Raine, I'm the one that gets to sever his fucking head from his body," I seethed with a finger pointed at him. I could be wrong, but a sense of pride flashed across his face before he nodded his head in agreement.

"I will figure out a training schedule that I see fit for when the time is right."

My eyes turned to slits. "Let's go boy," I said to Atlas while patting the top of his head and walking out the door knowing that he would lead me to my room.

"Atlas get back here," Thane yelled from behind us. But to my satisfaction, Atlas only moved closer to me as we stalked our way through the halls of the palace.

Chapter Twenty

I tossed and turned until the sun rose over the mountains and cast golden beams through my window. Tessa didn't return to our room last night, and I didn't care. My brain couldn't form the words to explain how angry I was with her for keeping such a detrimental secret from me.

A storm raged in my mind while trying to process the amount of information that was thrown at me last night.

My father wasn't really my father.

Aravis was my real father.

I was half Fae.

Was I immortal?

Instead of fighting with my own thoughts, I snapped back to reality and changed out of my nightgown into proper training clothes.

If I was going to have to accept these new changes, then I was going to do it the right way. I refused to have powers that I couldn't control or use to my advantage when needed. I wasn't going to allow for everything to be dropped on top of me without digging myself out and climbing out of the current hole I'd plummeted into.

There wasn't a chance in hell that I was going to let Thane decide when I got started on my training.

It started *today*.

I padded down the halls that I had finally memorized with Atlas by my side until I reached the dining hall. Bursting through the doors, I was caught off guard and pulled from my rage when Thackery pranced up the stairs to greet me. I patted his head and stomped over to Thane who was forking eggs into his mouth. I avoided the sets of eyes that were landing on me as I marched up to the man that never raised his head. Reaching him, I snatched the fork from his hand and slammed it on the table, sending eggs flying.

"I want to train," I snapped, with my arms crossed over my chest.

Without glancing at me, he picked his fork back up and began stabbing the remaining eggs on his plate.

"*Now*," I added and clenched my jaw in annoyance.

Still never glancing at me, he pointed his fork in the direction of the food on the table. "Eat."

Shocked at his lone statement, I bent down to bring my face in front of his, "I said I want to—"

"And I said *eat*. If you want to train and learn to your full capacity, then eat and fuel yourself to train like a Vaternian."

Snapping my mouth shut, I couldn't argue with him. I was beyond hungry, and the smell of the delectable food laid out was reeling me in quickly. His golden eyes raised to meet mine with a tight-lipped, dry smile and a raise of his brow. Glaring at him, I walked to the open seat next to Xavier and piled food onto my plate, followed by a servant pouring a cup of coffee.

Devouring everything in front of me was as easy as breathing air. Whoever was responsible for cooking these meals was sent from The Heavens. Wiping my mouth, I set my napkin down on my plate and swiveled my head to stare at Thane who was already focused on me with an expressionless, handsome face. "Ready, Pixie?"

My upper lip curled at the nickname as I rose from my seat.

Standing from his, he began leading the way to the platform I had seen them train at before. "Don't go easy on him," Xavier shouted from the dining hall when we exited the room, bringing a smile to my face.

~

Apparently, it was everyone's off day for training because no one else followed behind us. *Meaning we would be alone.* And I would be a liar if I said I wasn't nervous to be out there alone with *him.*

Thane walked to the edge of the platform, setting his sword against the stone and taking off his shirt, laying it across the ledge. Despite my hate for him, I couldn't deny how divine he was. Truly, handsome wasn't even a word that did him justice. His golden tan skin glistened in the sun, illuminated every swirl of black ink engrained in his skin. The muscles in his back flexed as he turned his face upward toward the sun, inviting it in as if it could flow through his veins to get the day started. Squinting, I blinked a few times to make sure my vision was correct. I noticed multiple scars across his back. As if he could feel my gaze on his wounds, he swiftly turned around.

Clearing my throat, I walked over to where his sword was propped against the stone. Its dark blade thrived in the sunlight. I could see Thane eyeing me from the corner of his eye. Reaching out, I placed my fingertips on the hilt and screeched in pain, dropping to my knees while holding my hand.

An authentic chuckle erupted from Thane as he held out his hand, the sword flying to him as the hilt rested in his palm. He propped it on his shoulder and smiled down at me. "Sorry, Pixie. Only those chosen by The Obsidian Blade are allowed to wield it.

Hasn't anyone told you not to touch what doesn't belong to you anyway?"

I mumbled a few choice words under my breath and plopped backwards onto the ground to tighten the laces of my boots.

"I'm not going to go easy on you," he said while stretching his arms. "I'll train you in combat, and Anya will help with your new magic."

I reared back, shocked that he handed the magic training off to Anya. "Why not you for the magic portion?"

Thane ran his tongue across his bottom lip. "I've never seen ice magic. I could only do my best to bring whatever power you held from within. I would rather someone with knowledge of it to help you tame it."

"And if I don't want to be tamed?" I asked with an arch of my brow.

Thane fought to let it show, but a small smirk formed in the corner of his mouth before it vanished.

The morning passed quickly, and before I knew it, both of us were a sweaty mess under the blazing sun. The bun I had thrown my curls into was slowly faltering. Thane hadn't hit me full force, but he didn't lie about not holding back. The number of times he had thrown me to the ground and maneuvered his way on top of me to show how weak I truly was against Fae was insane.

But the last time was personal.

"At least fight back, Amira," he taunted in my ear as he held both of my arms above my head.

"I am fighting back, asshole." He chuckled at my response, which made a small smile tear at my lips as I thought about how Raine constantly told me to talk like a *"lady"*.

"Take your left leg and wrap it around mine," he instructed, and I followed. "Now take your other leg and use your knee to press into my side as hard as you can right below my ribcage." Without second guessing it, I did as I was told and felt him wince as I plunged my knee into the target area. I did it again, more forcefully, causing him to fall to my side. In the same movement I maneuvered myself on top of him, remembering him telling me that if I get a chance, take the shot.

Bringing my fist down to meet his face, the shock in his eyes caused me to freeze. "Why did you stop?" he gritted out as his eyes darkened.

"I- I... I can't hit you. I don't—" I stammered before he flipped me on my back again and grabbed my jaw with a calloused hand. "The enemy will never stop, Amira. Even as beautiful as you are, if their mission is to kill you, they will finish the job. *You never fucking stop.* Do you understand?"

He was clenching his jaw so tight I could see the tick of his muscles in his face. I nodded quickly. His eyes softened as if he could see the small amount of fear seeping through my gaze. Releasing my jaw, he sat up and pulled me to my feet, not letting go of my hands. "You may have everyone else fooled with your hard exterior, but I see you. I see who you really are. Who you're afraid to be on the inside and outside. What is hidden in the dark always comes to light, Amira."

My breathing hitched in my throat as he inched closer to me. The flecks of brown in his eyes made him even more unique, along with the tiny sliver of a scar through his left eyebrow. But as soon as I noticed those unique characteristics, he snatched his hands from mine. "Same time tomorrow," he announced. "Anya will be out here in a bit. I'll be sure to send some food and lots of water out in the meantime."

Before I could utter a word to him, he was already at the wooden door without a glance back in my direction. I ground my boot into the stone ground, watching a small bit of dust accumulate. With my hands on my hips and the sun beating down on me, I scoffed at the area where he was just standing in front of me while holding my hands in his.

How could he see me when I couldn't even see myself?

Chapter Twenty-One

I'd forever be grateful for Nova's kindness since I arrived in Obsidian. She graciously offered to take a walk around the town after my training with Anya that morning. Frustration of not knowing how to perfectly execute my newfound magic still flowed through me, but seeing the pure beauty of this realm had helped to put it at bay for the time being.

The town was surrounded by rolling hills and an accompanying river. Sunlight filtered between the shops and tents of the bustling streets, illuminating the cozy taverns where Fae sat with drinks in hand, laughing and conversating with each other. The swirls of inviting spices and scents from the busy market hummed with invitation, awakening each of my senses. With each step, we were greeted by smiling merchants shoving samples into our hands. My heart swelled when I experienced the inviting culture of Obsidian that's instilled in its people.

I was soaking up the laughter and chatter surrounding us while marveling at the delicious, freshly baked bread I'd been devouring for the last twenty minutes when Tessa blurted out a question about Merakai. "So why are you all doing this anyway? Seems like a lot of work."

She wasn't wrong in her statement. Multiple Fae were carrying cases of wine and alcohol to their destination. Decorations were being hung by women around their shops as they laughed with their friends, making it look more like a get-together than work. A smile bloomed on my face when I saw their children close by, playing tug-o-war for piles of candy.

"Merakai is where the night becomes longer than the day in Obsidian," Nova answered with a large smile. "Basically, we just use it as an excuse to drink more than we should and dance until our bodies can no longer stand upright."

We all shared a laugh together before Nova raised her hand and waved it, telling us that she was only joking. "It is to show an appreciation for our culture. To show appreciation for the people of Obsidian that refuse to let who we are be lost in history."

Raya became antsy next to me before speaking. "Sounds way better than Solstice..." she said before drifting off into silence while staring out at the water in the distance. Nova studied Raya, debating on asking her to elaborate on what Solstice entailed.

"It doesn't seem like there's much commotion happening with such an important celebration right around the corner," I chimed in as I didn't recall anyone back at the palace in a frantic mess. Nova explained to us that in Obsidian, they were not focused on the extraordinary things during Merakai. "The sole purpose of Merakai is to unite everyone and enjoy what joys life has to offer. Nothing more. Nothing less," she informed us while still brandishing the same smile.

We walked a little further before Tessa finally spoke, snapping out of her admiration for the town of Obsidian. "So, Amira, how does it feel to be turning twenty-five tomorrow during such a big event?"

I stopped cold in my tracks and glared at my sister for outing the secrecy of my birthday. I'd never liked to celebrate it and that certainly hadn't changed just because we were in a different realm, especially with everything I just learned about myself. I hissed under my breath as Nova and Raya, giddy with excitement, began to make plans to celebrate me.

"That's really not necessary, you two," I commented with pleading eyes as Tessa threw her arm around my shoulders. "We've been through a lot recently. Let us celebrate how we see fit for your birthday in a world that we didn't even know existed a bit ago," she teased from my side as I jokingly elbowed her in the ribs.

"Fine," I conceded. "Just nothing over-the-top. Please, you guys?" I begged as the three of them smirked at each other before we continued walking.

By the time we returned to the palace it was dusk. When we reached the top of the stairs while laughing and enjoying the sunset, a servant opened the large double doors to inform me that I was requested in the observatory.

And just like that, the carefree mindset I adopted while wandering around town was gone. The harsh reminders of my reality swept back in, and sadness drowned me at the thoughts of my mother and brother.

Saying goodbye to Tessa, Nova and Raya, I headed to the Observatory where I found Aravis and Thane seated at the round table in a quiet discussion. When Thane's eyes landed on me, he blinked a few times before standing to leave. "Sit down, Thanasis," Aravis snapped from his seat. Thane clenched his jaw before reclaiming his seat. His gaze remained on me, causing me to avert mine to anything but him.

"Come, have a seat, dear," Aravis called to me while pulling out the wooden chair next to him. His soft, kind tone always made it hard not to accept him, but then a reminder that he was my biological father ripped through me. Slowly, I shuffled to the open chair and sat down, not wanting to look at either of the men on both sides of me.

Silence steadily fell as the three of us refused to speak first. I peaked at Thane through my lashes and quickly shifted to look at

Aravis before I cast my focus back down on the wooden table where my hands were clasped in front of me.

"I'm sorry that I left abruptly," Aravis spoke, causing me to snap my head up.

I see it now.

My eyes. My mannerisms. My nose. All of them were pulled from Aravis and given to me.

Tears lined my eyes as his arm stretched out with his palm up, resting on the table. I stared at it a moment before I placed my hand in his and rested my forehead in my hand that remained on the table. The tears that I'd held at bay for so long came rushing out in waves when I felt a large hand on my back, and I didn't need to look up to know who it was.

"Your mother made me promise to never come back to Medlar. She can't stand the sight of me Amira, and rightfully so."

My head snapped up at his words while fresh tears streamed down my cheeks. Aravis' furrowed brow let me know he was concentrating to say the right words while speaking. His other hand was fiddling with the neckline of his tunic until he released a deep sigh and forced it to settle in his lap.

"When you were born, it was right here in Obsidian," Aravis continued before clearing his throat and looking out the large window behind Thane. "I asked for one more day with you, and your mother agreed."

His hand squeezed mine firmly. *Lovingly.* Bringing more tears to my eyes.

"When the time came to take you back to Medlar, I couldn't bear the thought of you not returning home with me. So, I turned to the only immortal woman that I fully trust and would lay my life down for," he explained before refocusing on me. "Anya."

My mouth dropped open as a thousand pieces of information came piecing themselves together in my head.

"Maybe I should go," Thane whispered from my side as I shook my head at his statement.

Glancing back to Aravis, his shoulders were slumped, his head bowed to avoid eye contact with either of us. He subtly rocked back and forth in his chair before speaking again and urging Thane to stay. Aravis stood from his chair. "No, I'm leaving. But I wanted Amira to know that I never stopped loving her. Never stopped calling her my daughter in my mind and in my heart. I kept you a secret for your safety. Unfortunately, somehow word got out about you and that word fell into the hands of Raine. But you can mark my words that he will pay for what he has done to you and your family."

As he turned to leave, I gripped his hand once more. "Why wouldn't my mother let you return to Medlar?"

I have to know. I have to know why my biological father wasn't allowed to see me. To know me. To let me know... anything about myself.

Fresh tears rolled down my face at the thought of what my life would have been like if I would have remained in Obsidian with Aravis instead of Medlar.

Was that ever an option?

"Please... please tell me. What could have been so bad that my mother wouldn't allow for you to see your only daughter?" I begged one last time when I could no longer handle the silence. I could hear Thane adjusting anxiously in his chair, and I forced myself not to look at him.

Aravis moved around to my side of the table, never releasing my hold. He expressed a forced, weak smile before kissing the top of my hand and running a palm down the side of my face while barely holding back tears of his own.

"That is for your mother to tell."

A thousand more questions for him flooded my mind but I couldn't bring myself to ask them. Instead, I watched as he released my hand and trudged toward the hallway. I forcefully bit my bottom lip to avoid the onslaught of emotions producing fresh tears.

His hand was pressed against the door when he looked back at me with a smile. "I want you to know that the man you've known as your father before now is a good man. A very good man, Amira."

He exited the room as I fully broke down and stood to look out the window while fresh tears fell from my eyes and down my face.

"I'll get out of your way in a moment. I'm sorry," I announced to Thane.

"Why are you sorry? And why do you feel that you need to leave?"

My brow shot up at his questions. I pivoted to face him and found him standing a few feet away from me.

"You're not a burden, Amira. I think you're still stuck on my unacceptable behavior when you first arrived here," he said while hesitantly taking another step toward me. "And the rest of my behavior after Aravis told us who you were was solely to push you into finding your magic."

I bit back another sob before I turned back around to face the outside world. My shoulders relaxed while I observed the sky that now held hues of purple as the sun faded into the distance.

"I don't want to celebrate my birthday," I blurted out and wanted to take the statement back immediately.

"Why?" Thane questioned in a silky, smooth voice that had my lips parting and my breath becoming shallow.

"I'm a nobody that everyone wants to make into a somebody of importance," I said while placing a single palm to the large window. "To be belittled my entire life and carry the burden of digging my family out of poverty, then have Raine try to make me damn near a slave, to coming here for you to treat me like shit for whatever reason I don't know..." I rambled before stopping myself.

A break of silence fell for so long that I bit on my lower lip to halt my emotions from flowing again.

"I'm sorry for how I treated you."

His words caused my spine to stiffen. "You already apologized. I shouldn't have brought it up."

"I said I'm sorry because it still kills me knowing how I treated you when I simply just couldn't control my emotions from—"

He cut himself off before finishing. I knew he moved closer because I could feel the heat from his body radiating near my own. The scent of him, pine and musk, heavily surrounded me.

"Because what, Thane?" I asked without turning around, afraid to find out just how close he was to me.

"Do you dance, Amira?"

Not again.

"No, I—"

"Perfect," he said before grabbing my hand, turning me around and leading me to the center platform of the room.

Before I could object any more, his hands were lightly placed on my waist as mine were placed on his biceps. We began to sway, moving slowly around the platform.

Thane flicked his wrist, and multiple sconces dimly lit the surrounding walls. I was buried deep in my own thoughts when a finger gently touched my chin and tilted my head toward the night sky. "Beautiful, isn't it?" Thane asked. "The constellations will forever hold my attention."

His hand traveled back to my waist as I focused on the stars through the glass ceiling above.

Thane flicked his wrist once more and soft music played throughout the observatory, once again forcing the tension from my body as I brought my focus back to the man in front of me. My heart hammered in my chest as my hands felt the muscles of his biceps where they laid. His golden eyes bore into mine while I did my best not to focus on his full lips that his tongue ran across, sending my mind into darkness as I wondered what those parts of him would feel like on my body.

"Will you just tell me why you acted the way that you did

when you brought me here? And then I won't bring it up anymore," I whispered into the space between us.

His grip on my waist tightened briefly as he clenched and unclenched that perfect jawline of his. "I know what I saw in you the first time I laid eyes on you, Amira. And it fucking terrified me to my core," he whispered huskily before finally breaking our gaze and looking off to the side. I reached my hand to his cheek, gently bringing his focus back to me. "And what did you see?" I asked. The music seemed to fade, my breathing the only thing I could hear as I awaited his answer.

His eyes searched my face for what felt like hours before he spoke again. "I don't want to break you, Amira."

His words sent goosebumps down my spine as my breathing increased.

"No one has been successful in doing that yet. What makes you think you'd be the one to make it happen?" I spoke with confidence until I glanced at his lips again while forcefully biting the corner of my own. "I can handle whatever you throw at me," I followed up. His expression never waivered. My throat turned dry as a deep rumble left his chest. He brushed a curl from my face and tucked it behind my ear while I refrained from leaning my head into his palm. Everything about this man turned me into a different person when he was near—a stark contrast from when we first met.

"You're provoking someone who thrives in the dark, Pixie. You've bargained with a witch, but you've never made a deal with the devil."

A spark shot up my spine and I forced myself to breath. He subtly pulled me closer to his firm chest, causing me to adjust my hand placement so they rested on his chest.

"You may have everyone else fooled with your hard exterior, but I see you. I see who you really are, Thanasis. What is hidden in the dark always comes to light," I said, using his own words on him which brought out a genuine smile on his handsome face. The small slash in his eyebrow flexed as he chuckled.

We continued to sway under the stars as he asked about my family, letting me know that he would get them back while gently insinuating that I needed to take a moment to recenter myself. "I know it's not easy with such a heavy burden on your conscience but try to enjoy Merakai before things get serious again."

I let his words soak in before I nodded my head in understanding.

"And let yourself be celebrated on your birthday, Amira. You're not a burden."

I rolled my lips inward as I fought the emotions begging to take flight.

I glanced down at my feet as I noticed myself gliding to the delightful sound of the music, in rhythm with Thane.

I was doing it on my own.

He talked to me, distracting me from dancing so it would come naturally. I glanced back up at him with a wide smile, noticing him focus on my lips as my lungs refused to work properly.

"Freckles," he murmured breathlessly, and I tilted my head while scrunching my brow in confusion. "You have very faint freckles," he continued with a gentle smile. My cheeks heated from the stated observation. He studied them for a moment as if they were constellations in the star-filled, night sky before running his thumb across them, sliding it down to run across my bottom lip.

The heat from his touch threatened to consume me as we focused on each other's lips, slowly closing the space between us as he dipped his head lower. His scent of pine and musk encapsulated me so heavily that my eyes closed as I imagined being forever wrapped in his embrace. His arms tightened around me, our lips lingering an inch apart.

"Amira, I—"

His words were cut short and so was our moment of solitude when Atlas burst through the doors and padded into the room. He'd been sleeping at the foot of my bed every evening, and this must have been his way of telling me it was time to call it an early night. A subtle laugh left me as he nudged his large head into the backs of my knees while Thane cursed under his breath.

"I think you've forgotten who your owner is," Thane hissed at Atlas who huffed in return.

"Well, goodnight," I said with a wave as I followed the large black wolf to the door, grateful that my breaths had regulated themselves.

"Pixie," Thane shouted, causing me to turn around at the horrid nickname. His eyes shone under the moonlight as he crossed his arms over his chest. "I don't hate you."

His voice turned my heart into melted butter while I looked at the godlike man that I almost kissed moments ago.

"I know," I said with a smirk. "But you'll have to prove it to me," I replied, turning to follow Atlas into the hall toward my room.

Chapter Twenty-Two

The next morning was a satisfying blur of laughs, cheerfulness and as always... an overabundance of delicious food.

Everyone was participating in playful arguments about who would win the "*games*" after breakfast. It was hard for Tessa and me to fully participate in the joy and cheerfulness of the others while the only thing on our mind was our mother and brother. Nova caught our attention from across the table and leaned in. "I know that there's a dark cloud hovering over your heads right now, but I promise the sun will break through soon," she said before stretching herself across the table and grabbing each of our hands. "You guys deserve one day of full, complete happiness."

Raya bumped my shoulder while sipping her coffee. "She's right, ya know. Might as well live it up before we plunge ourselves back into hell tomorrow."

Her words made me chuckle as I eyed Tessa, who was smiling as well. "Twenty-four hours of fun would probably help us more than hurt us at this point," she said with a shrug of her shoulders.

I nodded my head in agreement and leaned back in my seat

while holding my warm cup of coffee. "Alright, explain these games to me."

~

I was a sweaty, melting mound of flesh by the time the final game was set up. Raya was bent over with her hands on her knees, staring at me with a reddened face. "How the hell are you and your sister keeping up with us immortals? I'm dying over here," she said through labored breaths. We just finished climbing an eighteen-foot rock wall, followed up with a three-mile race to the finish line. So far, the women were behind by nine points.

Tessa was over by some flowers hurling up her breakfast, while Nova and Athena were trying to plan out our next win. Thane's sister had arrived that morning after breakfast, and I'd never seen Thane so excited throughout our entire stay in Obsidian. Unfortunately for him, Nova knocked him over to get to Athena first.

A servant standing in as a mediator whistled and waited for our silence. While he spoke, my eyes wandered over to Silas who was rubbing Tessa's back while she finished dry heaving, pausing intermittently to apologize to Silas before turning her head back to the bushes. I winced when I heard her cough and double over again.

"Your last game for the day will be the concord," the mediator announced, and my brow puckered in confusion. The mediator must have detected my confusion, along with Tessa's, because he smiled and clarified. "I believe mortals know this one as tug-o-war from adolescence," he followed up, causing my jaw to hang loose.

Against male Fae?!

"We might as well call it now," I said as I scrunched my face and stared at Thane who was shirtless with his hands on his hips, smirking at me in amusement.

"And as always," the mediator continued, "Magic is permitted for the last game."

Mine and Tessa's eyes almost bulged from their sockets as I stood up straight. *I didn't know how to use my magic yet.*

"Hope you've been practicing, Pixie," Thane shouted from across the open field. I narrowed my eyes and raised two middle fingers in his direction, drawing a laugh out of everyone, including Thane.

"Teams, please grab your designated sides of the rope," the mediator requested gleefully as I groaned.

"Alright, Athena, you're the strongest so you're the anchor in the back," Nova announced.

"On it," Athena remarked while looping the rope around her waist. Nova continued laying out the game plan while instructing Raya to stand in front of Athena.

Nova sauntered in front of Raya before nudging me, "Think you can handle line-lead, lady?"

My eyes blew wide again at her question. I shook my head in protest, and she gave a thumbs up in reply. "Fantastic," she said, like I had agreed with her, taking her place along the rope.

"I'm sitting this one out. Fuck that. I have nothing left in me and I already know where this is going," Tessa said while plopping on the ground near us. I glanced down to see her vomit smeared on her boots. My nose scrunched at the sight before turning back to face our opponents.

Of course, Thane was in the back. *He's the strongest out of everyone, why wouldn't he be in the back.* In front of him was Xavier followed up by Silas in the very front.

"Don't let them intimidate you," Anya called from the stone wall next to Tessa.

"Silas can't even win sparring sessions against Athena, don't sweat it," Aravis said, causing everyone to laugh as Silas told Aravis to shut up with an embarrassed grin.

The mediator held both hands out to his sides before making sure the flag in the middle of the rope was centered. My heart hammered from adrenaline, and I dug the heels of my boots into the soiled ground.

"Alright, first team to pull this flag across their line, wins this game," he announced. "This game is worth ten points; therefore, ladies, you have a chance to win."

I gently rubbed the stone of my necklace for good luck before gripping the tan rope firmly. I glanced at my friends behind me and prepared for the worst.

"Ready...Set...Go!"

The mediator placed two fingers between his lips and a piercing whistle traveled through the air. I was already being dragged across the grass as Nova cursed from behind me.

"Come on over ladies," Silas bellowed across from me as sweat poured down my forehead. We were sliding across the ground so quickly that I lost my footing, dropping to my knees. My gaze flicked upward to see Silas replaced by a woman of my stature with curly brown hair and eyes that matched mine. I blinked rapidly, trying to figure out what was happening.

"Don't fall for his shit, Amira!" Nova called from behind me.

Heavens above... Silas had transformed right in front of me. His plan of shapeshifting was meant to throw me off. And not only did he shapeshift...*He was me.*

Shaking my head to ignore the visual of my doppelganger in front of me, I got back on my feet. Furrowing my brow, I felt a small sense of satisfaction when his eyes blew wide at the realization that I'd caught on to his plan.

I was about to give up when I felt the burning of the rope slipping through my grasp, and I knew my mortal hands couldn't handle the pain. I tightened my grip in one last, faithful attempt when the ground began to shake. I glanced behind me and opened my mouth in awe. Athena had her foot so firmly planted into the ground it caused a crack that stopped right behind my right foot. She took another step back, and her foot broke the hardened soil again.

"Oh shit," I stammered as Raya screamed to pull.

I caught Thane's glare as he lifted a finger and curled it at me, motioning me to come towards him as he yanked the rope. I flew forward.

"Amira, use your magic!" Tessa shouted, and I saw Thane's shadows begin to seep from him.

Pulling from the sheer panic running through my veins, thin strands of ice shot out from my palms and across the rope, striking Silas's hands and forcing him to let go. The momentum of losing a player gave us leverage and we took advantage of the moment. Athena grunted and yanked the rope twice, causing Xavier to stumble forward.

"Sorry guys," Raya whispered.

A subtle bright light flashed before Xavier yelped and fell to his knees, pressing his palms to his eyes.

"*NOW!*" Nova cried out and the four of us pulled at the same time, dragging Thane across the ground where the flag was less than an inch to our line. His boots left tracks in the soil as he used every ounce of muscle to avoid their flag crossing our line. Sweat poured down his temple as his shadows wrapped around my waist and slithered up my neck. I could tell by their touch it was not meant to be painful—quite the opposite as I felt their teasing, feathery touch. I squeezed my eyes shut to block out the breathtaking sensation.

The warmth of his touch flowed through his shadows.

My eyes sprang back open, glaring daggers at Thane. "I'm not that easily breakable, Thanasis." His mouth dropped open, and I threw a single palm in his direction. Ice shot out onto the ground in front of his feet, causing him to lose balance and slide without being able to stop his movement. The sight of him dropping to his ass and making every effort to still pull us toward him made my chest fill with laughter.

"Hold on tight, brother," Athena howled. With one last tug, I watched as their red flag was dragged across our line to victory. We released the rope, watching each of them fall backwards in a pile on top of each other. Thane—who fell the hardest—groaned in pain on the ground as Silas and Xavier look bewildered in our direction while we boasted with laughter and cheers of victory.

Silas and Xavier helped their friend to his feet as they all rubbed different body parts that were in pain.

I glanced at the sidelines where Tessa and Anya were jumping up and down in an embrace. Aravis clapped, while Atlas and Thackery ran in circles around him.

"Wait…" I said, causing everyone to pause their celebrations. "What do we win?"

Nova and Athena smiled enthusiastically, rubbing their hands together like two mischievous teenagers. "The men have to pay for everything the rest of the night," Nova announced, and my smile widened with laughter.

The playful frowns on the faces of the losing team only sent us into further fits of laughter. Without a word, the three of them narrowed their eyes and started heading back toward the palace. I caught a glimpse of Thane before he was out of view and marveled at the ripples and grooves of his back muscles. As if he could sense my gaze on him, he swiftly turned around, winked, and vanished from sight through the trees.

"Pick your jaw up off the floor. You're embarrassing us, sister," Tessa said while hip checking me.

She was not wrong. The drool on my bottom lip agreed with her wholeheartedly.

Chapter Twenty-Three

After our victory in the games, the day consisted of eating more food and complete, content leisure. Typically, during my days in Obsidian, everyone was scattered throughout the palace or even throughout the realm. But today, everyone was piled on top of each other in the library, filling it with laughter and fun-filled banter.

The sun could be seen through the windows, threatening to vanish in the distance whenever I set down my fourth helping of a truffle cream cake that I couldn't stop eating. Nova cleared her throat before making a facial expression at Raya and Tessa. I groaned in protest with squinted eyes and threw my head back. It was too easy to read their interactions and know what they were up to. "Please don't—"

My protesting was cut short by the door bursting open and a terrible rendition of "Happy Birthday" sung by a chorus of servants and everyone else in the room. I blushed with warmth at the smiles on everyone's faces while they sang for *me*.

For *my* birthday. In a place that wasn't even my home.

Raya and Nova danced in circles while Tessa was laughing as hard as I was at the scene displayed before us. My attention landed on Silas who was now finishing up the song by standing on a chair with a mouth full of cake that was falling onto his shirt. Tears from laughter fell down my cheeks at the sight of him, subsiding when I noticed Thane and Xavier clinking their mugs together in the air with wide, toothy smiles. Thane's heavy stare held mine through the final lines of the song, and the warmth I felt before matured to an inferno. His wide smile was gone, but a subtle, teasing smirk now rested on his handsome face, making it hard to look away.

At the end of the song, my breath hitched as I watched Thane gently take the cake littered with candles from the servant and begin walking over to me. I sat up in my chair, preparing for him to throw it in my face, candles and all.

He knelt on one knee in front of me, with a beautiful smile on his tanned face, while looking from the candles to me. "Make it a good one, Pixie," he said in a voice woven in silk. I forced myself to clear the lust from my brain. Imagining him kneeling before me without a cake in his hand was not appropriate in a room full of people watching me. I thought about what I wanted most in life for a few seconds before leaning forward and blowing out the rainbow-colored candles. We met each other's gaze over the candles' smoke, the unusual warmth in his honey-colored eyes holding me in its confines. A rush of lust-filled emotions sent hundreds of butterfly wings fluttering within my belly as I watched him balance the cake in one hand and lick frosting from his thumb. Entranced, I wet my lips and watched as his eyes followed every movement of my tongue.

"Yep. I saw the spit fly on the right side of the cake, give me a piece from the left corner," Silas joked, earning a pointed look from Raya, wrenching me from the moment. Nova reached over, smacking him on the back of the head. The room filled with laughter once again. But while everyone was preparing to get their share of cake, Thane remained kneeling before me, as if we were the only two in the room.

"Thane?" I whispered so that only he could hear me below the laughter in the room. "Are you okay?" He blinked once, as if he were in a trance before brandishing a quick smile and a wink, standing to hand the cake over to Nova.

Once the cake was cut and served, we were all questioning if we would be able to stand to celebrate the night ahead of us. But naturally, the upbeat one in the room let us know we didn't have a choice in the matter.

"It's tiiiiiiiiiiiime," Nova sang in the most high-pitched squeal I'd ever heard in my life.

"For the sake of Erebus, Nova. Are you trying to make our ears bleed before we get to enjoy any music tonight?" Thane asked with a wince that made us all chuckle. Nova stuck out her tongue at her High King and friend before pointing at each of the women in the room. "Time to get dressed ladies!" she echoed while Anya groaned in protest. "I don't want to hear it, Anya. You promised."

Anya threw up her hands in truce while standing from the couch.

"Ten o'clock sharp on the front steps. I have something special planned to start the night," Thane announced, proceeding to round up the guys and head out of the library to prepare for the night's festivities.

We piled into Nova's room that was the size of the library, followed by multiple female servants shortly after. I curl into myself at the thought of being forced to wear certain dresses back in Solaris to appease Raine and prepared to endure it all over again. The unwelcomed memory forced me into sadness at the reminder of Millie and Ellie assisting me. Taking a deep breath, I centered myself and vowed not to get in my own head for the rest of the night.

"So, champagne or wine?" Nova inquired while plopping down on her bed. My ears perked up at her question, expecting to hear demands about my wardrobe.

"Um... aren't we required to wearing something specific? A dress perhaps?" I questioned in confusion.

Nova pops her head up, resting on her elbows. "Oh, Erebus no! I know what Thane's surprise is for tonight, and a dress would not be good for such an occasion."

I raised a brow at her statement, wondering what his surprise could be.

"We typically just wear black to celebrate Merakai. But other than that, you have freedom to dress as you please," she said with a smile.

Everyone requested their drink of choice from the kind servants taking orders before Nova and Anya dismissed them with instructions to have fun and enjoy the rest of the night off.

"The servants participate in the festivities?" Raya asked with wide eyes.

"Well of course! They deserve to be celebrated just as much as we do. We would let them have the entire day off, but they refuse to do so," Nova responded while waltzing over to her armoire. She pulled out black boots, black leather pants, and a black top with a plunging neckline that cropped above her navel. The attached hood had two holes in the top of it to accommodate her short horns, and the hem was lined with crystals.

Anya walked over to me. "What would you like to wear for the night ahead, Amira?"

It hadn't occurred to me that my clothes were back in my room. And even then, I was not sure that I would have anything to wear for such a special occasion.

"Uh...I...Um... I'm not sure actually," I said with a nervous smile, shrugging both shoulders up to my ears.

She pursed her lips. "Do you trust me?" I nodded my head multiple times.

"Of course I trust you."

Her smile widened in satisfaction, and she brought her hand up, flicking her wrist three times. A puff of green smoke flourished around me and disappeared in seconds. She tugged me over to the tall mirror in the corner of the room. The gasps in the room as I walked by caused me to blush and duck my head. When we reached the mirror, my mouth popped open, and I sucked in a breath.

The pants and corset formed into one piece of clothing that cinched at my waist. The flow of the legs gave me freedom, while the top comfortably accentuated my curves and breasts in all the right places. The crystals on the bodice intricately swirled throughout.

Anya placed both hands on my bare shoulders, maneuvering me to turn around and view the lace of the bodice which revealed pieces of my flesh throughout. The cut and flow of the garment hugged my bottom and hips into the perfect shape. *My shape.* Not forcing my body to be contorted unnaturally like the two unknown women had tried to back in Solaris.

I turned back around to see the stone in my necklace shimmer into a light color to match the diamonds encrusted into the bodice of my outfit, bringing a smile to my face. I remembered Millie placing the charm upon it to match what I wore so that I never had to take it off.

"How would you like your hair styled?" Nova asked from beside me.

I stared at the curls that I almost always threw into a bun atop my head.

"Down," Tessa suggested from across the room. "Your hair is gorgeous, and I think you should put it on display for once."

The smile on her face was so genuine that I wanted to run over and squeeze her. She clasped her hands in front of her as I eyed her clothing: a black top with a deep, plunging V-neck that accentuated her breasts and tight, navel-high pants with three buttons in the front. Her shirt ended slightly above her pants, showing just enough skin on her waist to drive a man crazy.

"Down it is," I relayed to Nova.

Chapter Twenty-Four

We met on the front steps, at Thane's requested time, to find horses the color of the night sky awaiting us. Descending the steps to get closer to the horses, I gasped at the sight before me.

"Are those...." I trailed off in awe of the animal staring back at me with large, round eyes.

"They're Pegasi. Quite rare in immortal realms even. Stunning nonetheless," Thane explained from behind us at the top of the stairs. "A good friend of mine was only able to loan us five, but I figured it was good enough for the night."

I snapped my mouth shut when I realized this was his surprise. We were going to ride them into town.

I was going to ride on a pegasus.

Aravis and Anya had already beamed themselves into town to get a head start on the night, so that left the rest of us to pair up on each pegasus.

Silas grabbed Tessa by the waist to claim her, and she quickly attempted to push him away before laughing at his "Prince Charming" imitation stance. Xavier held out his hand to Raya, who cautiously took it after eyeing the man that resembled the size of a Greek God. Watching her place her hand in his made me pray to the heavens above that he didn't crush it by accident.

I cast a hopeful smile at Nova when I noticed she was petting a pegasus by herself. I was about to claim her as my riding partner when Athena came running down the steps. "Room for one more?" she asked while bouncing over to Nova, placing a kiss on her cheek. Athena had flown off on a "quick journey" after the games that morning, promising Thane a million times that she would be back for the festival. The bright look of happiness in his eyes and the wide, toothy grin he displayed, showed how grateful he was that she followed through on her promise.

My heart skipped several beats as my chance of not being paired with Thane was snatched from under me. The hairs on the back of my neck stood as I felt a hard body pressed to my back.

"If I didn't know any better, I would think you were about to try to ditch me," Thane whispered into my ear before stepping beside me and offering me the palm of his hand. I stared at it for a moment before willingly placing my hand in his. The heat trailing up my arm from his touch must have been mutual because he flinched the moment I touched him with a subtle flare in his eyes. When I attempted to pull my hand back, he closed his around mine and stared into my eyes with a fierceness that I'd never seen in a man. I swallowed and looked down at the ground, doing everything I could to avoid his handsome face.

Slowly, he led me down the rest of the stairs to the side of the lead pegasus before wrapping his hands around my waist and lifting me onto its back. Moments later, he positioned himself behind me as I stiffened when I felt him firmly press against my back.

"I have wings to catch you, but I'd still feel safer knowing I can hold you in place," he said with a velvety smooth voice as he patted the animal on its ribs.

I glanced over at Tessa to see that Silas had placed her in the same position as me. He caught my gaze, which I quickly turned into a warning glare. In natural Silas fashion, he responded with a double raise and wiggle of his brows. I made a mental note to threaten him about any intentions he had with my sister when we landed.

"First stop, Verdanthia," Nova shouted from her position.

And before I could question what that was, Thane gave a single command to our pegasus, and we shot into the sky with a flap of its wings. The ascent into the night sky caused my stomach to do a flip as I threw my hand to my midsection, finding Thane's arm wrapped around it. His other hand was bracing us onto the pegasus with its reins.

We evened out in the sky and my muscles relaxed. "Smooth ride, isn't it?" Thane asked from behind me, his voice so deep that I could feel his chest rumble as he spoke. I chewed my bottom lip as I nodded my head. "Grab the reins to steady yourself," he instructed. I hesitantly stretched out an arm and quickly brought it back in when I glanced down at the treetops below us. I shook my head in protest while digging my fingers into his forearm that was still wrapped around me. His warm breath floated to my ear again, and I fought the shudder that trailed down my spine. "Go ahead, Pixie. I won't let you fall," he said gently before leaning closer and tightening his grip on my waist. "I've got you."

Those three words could be any woman's undoing, but those exact words coming from Thane stirred my soul as I relaxed into him. If my legs weren't sprawled across a pegasus, I would have been snapping my thighs shut at the sensations I felt from those words alone leaving his mouth.

Confidently, I reached both hands out to grab the reins, steadying myself as Thane took in a deep breath behind me and reminded me to take in the view. "As Fae, we're always beaming or flying ourselves somewhere with intent. We rarely remember to admire our surroundings when we're up here."

We flew in silence the rest of the way to Verdanthia.

When we landed, Thane reached up to help me off the beautiful beast.. His large hands wrapped around my waist, causing me to hold my breath until my feet were planted on the ground. Silence encapsulated us as I forbid myself from making eye contact with him while his hands remained wrapped around my waist. The heat from his body radiated between us and I could sense his stare above me. Slowly, I tilted my head, bringing my eyes to meet his golden ones for a fraction of a second. He opened his mouth to speak at the same time the pegasus nudged its head gently into my ribs, causing me to stumble. Thane steadied me once more with his hands on my waist. This time our eyes met in unison, and my lungs fought for air. I couldn't look away from the hazel hue of his eyes shining so brightly they were almost yellow under the moonlight.

"He wants your attention," Thane said with a nod in the direction of the pegasus.

I slowly turned my attention to the animal requesting my recognition. Reaching out my hand, Thane intercepted it, directing me toward the majestic animal's body instead of its head. "They don't allow anyone to touch their heads."

Inclining my head in understanding, I rubbed the body of the animal for a few moments and whispered a thank you before we followed the rest of our group down the hill to a bridge. Crossing it, I looked out over the dark waters of the new city and my heart skipped a few beats as I thought about my mother and brother stuck in Solaris.

"Anya would have seen if something happened to them. We will get them back, Amira. I promise. Tonight, be free. You never know when you'll get this chance again—if any of us will get this chance again," Thane whispered beside me.

His words held truth. I didn't know if I would ever experience anything like this again. I didn't even know if I would live to see anything like this again once we made our decision and met with Raine. I nodded my head as we wandered into the city, and my eyes bulged at the scenery before me.

The moment we crossed the bridge, and my feet met the smooth obsidian cobblestoned ground of the town, I was entranced. Perfectly set lighting along the roads and pathways illuminated the streets with a warm, amber glow, enhancing their beauty. My gaze drifted upward to the starry night sky casting an additional blanket of light over the velvety darkness of Verdanthia. I wanted to engrain all of it to my memory. The instant electric feeling mixed with the calmness in the air was something I never wanted to forget.

Despite the shadowy radiance of the buildings, multiple small taverns and shops were filled with smiling and laughing patrons while the night air hummed with the melodies of street musicians. Nova led us into the largest tavern noticeable on the cliff that oversaw the inky dark river that weaved throughout the town. Every set of female eyes found Thane, and a small hint of jealousy spread through my chest like wildfire. How could they not fawn over him? He was gorgeous without trying, and the power he exuded so effortlessly would shift a room the moment he entered.

The musicians in the corner blared an upbeat tune as I watched Fae glide across the floor dancing with one another, their drinks spilling from their cups as they swayed. Laughter filled the room, battling with the sound of music to see which could be the loudest. The scene brought a genuine smile to my face as I observed everyone enjoying the beginning of the night.

Unlike Solaris, not a single Fae had glared or turned their nose up at me and Tessa because we were human. Well... I guess I would be considered half human now.

Raya and Nova wandered over to the bar and came back with a drink for Tessa and me. "I know you try not to drink, but I figured I'd offer it since it's your birthday. No pressure if—"

I snatched the mug from Raya's hand and chugged half the contents, wiped my mouth, and stared at her before we burst into laughter. In the far corner, I could see Thane laughing with Silas and Xavier before catching my gaze. His laugh faded as he stared at me with what looked like lust-filled eyes. I turned around to see if there was someone behind me that he was eyeing instead, but no one was there. When I turned my attention back to him, he had already jumped back into conversation with his friends.

Hours of dancing, drinking, and laughter passed before I realized I needed water, or I was going to spend the night on the floor of this place. Anya brought pitchers of water to our group before announcing that her and Aravis were heading back to the palace. The group collectively begged them to stay but they chalked it up to being the elders of the group, kissing us all on the cheek before departing.

Finishing my water, plus two more, I plopped down in a wooden chair at a table where the men from our group were seated playing cards. Silas looked up from the cards in his hand and smirked. "Amira, just the person we were looking for," he said while casting a look in Nova's direction.

Me? Why would they be looking for me?

Panic ensued when I realized that he was referring to my birthday. I shook my head to stop her but it was too late. Nova tapped a utensil to her glass multiple times until the music dropped to a whisper.

"I know that many of you don't know our dear immortal friend, Amira. But today is her birthday and her first time experiencing Merakai," she announced with a wink in my direction. "Our favorite High King has requested something special in her honor to celebrate the night. So, if you wouldn't mind, please head to the balcony to witness the show."

I cowered into the wooden chair while covering my face when I heard the "happy birthdays," clapping, and whistling that ensued from the surrounding Fae. I had tried to glue myself to the seat while Fae proceeded outside to see what Nova was talking about when a pair of hands grabbed my shoulders and hoisted me up. My head popped up to see Silas standing above me with a contagious grin, nodding toward the balcony. He offered his arm, and I took it, letting him lead me outside.

Silas lead me over to the railing next to Tessa as the sky darkened even further, the clouds drifting to cover the moon. Looking out over the water, I was entranced by its shimmering hues of violet and sapphire. I saw hundreds of Fae stare into the night sky with hopeful eyes as I heard a deep, smooth voice on the opposite side of me.

"Happy twenty-fifth birthday, Amira."

I turned to see Thane standing next to me, his focus on the night sky above.

"I'm sure you've already been told by the dozens of Fae males staring at you, but you look beautiful tonight," he complimented me and sipped from his cup. When I was about to respond, I saw a flicker of light from the corner of my eye. I turned my head and saw dozens more join the small ball of light until there were hundreds. Quickly, those hundreds turned into thousands of small lights filling the still insanely darkened night sky.

Soft music began playing in the background as the small flickers of light started to move in unison with the rhythm of the instruments.

"What are they?" I whispered to Thane in pure amusement.

I heard a suppressed laugh come from him before he took another sip from his tankard, pausing deliberately before offering an answer.

"Pixies."

My mouth dropped open midway through me whipping my head in his direction. His gaze connected with mine as a broad smile slowly spread across his face. He inched closer to me until we were almost hip-to-hip. "Pixies are the backbone of Obsidian. They're the smartest and strongest willed little women you'll ever meet," he explained, turning his attention back to the bright balls of light floating in the air. "Their pixie dust works miracles, but they only use it on those deserving. And for that, Eryx doesn't care for them. Rumor has it they refused to bring his entire family back to life in his realm because of how vile they were."

I focused on the small Pixie floating toward me.

"But here in Obsidian, we know their kindness. Their love. The fight that they will give for those they believe are kindhearted and worthy," he continued as we watched one float directly in front of my face. I held my palm upright in front of me and held my breath as it gently landed in my hand with an inviting smile on its tiny heart-shaped face. Pixie dust fell from its wings and into my palm.

Thane had called me Pixie from the moment I arrived here. A lump formed in my throat as a wave of emotions gripped me. Even when I asked him to stop, he continued with the nickname.

Looking away and clearing my throat, I turned back to face Thane. "So, what I'm hearing is that you think I'm tiny and cute like them?"

He grunted in response, doing his best to hold back a smile while rolling his eyes. "I called you Pixie because I knew on the outside you were a hard shell that couldn't be cracked open. But beneath that shell, I knew who and what you were on the inside. You love hard. Work hard for what you want and believe in." A tear slid down my cheek. I raised a hand to wipe it away, but the Pixie in my palm fluttered her wings to reach it before I could and wiped it with her tiny hand. "But those same actions are never reciprocated back. Yet, you never break. You stand strong for those you love," Thane followed up.

The Pixie looked from Thane to me and cupped my cheek before flying back to the group with a warm smile.

"You called me Pixie to get a rise out of me instead of telling me what—"

"Don't act like you weren't shit talking too," Thane cut me off with a bump into my side with his arm. I glared up at him, but the smile he wore was contagious as we both ended up grinning at each other.

Fae had begun to break off into couples, dancing along with the pixies to the now upbeat music in the background. Thane held out his hand and I stared at it before I felt a nudge from Tessa next to me. "He's not as bad as he seemed when I first got here," she said loud enough for Thane to hear, and I dropped my head between my shoulders in embarrassment. "I mean look at that face and body. You can't really go wrong even if it is just for one night," she added before I cut her a glare so deep that it could cut glass. With a laugh, she threw up her hands in protest and stepped away with everyone else, leaving just the two of us at the railing.

"If you take it, that means you'll give us hope at starting over," Thane said, offering his hand once again. I glanced back up to the pixies flying above and looked further into the sky—looking for a sign, any sign, that I was not making a mistake if I placed my hand in his. As I gripped the railing in front of me, multiple people pointed to the sky above the pixies. Our gaze followed to see a single shooting star crossing the sky and I gasped at the sight.

My first shooting star on my birthday underneath the night sky filled with magic.

I turned to Thane who was still gazing at me with the same look in his eyes from when we first arrived in the tavern. I released my hand from the rail and placed it in his, feeling the warmth from his touch surge up my arm until it reached the center of my chest.

The flutter of my heart had me breathing rapidly as his other hand wrapped around my waist and we glided across the balcony with the other pool of Fae. The area quickly became a rush of enchantment and harmony as my head rested against his chest, feeling the rise and fall from his deep breaths. My eyes drifted close to enjoy and take in the night, the smell, and the sound of this moment in time when Thane pulled back, focusing on my face.

"I believe I still have one question left," Thane whispered from above me, and I froze in his grasp. I licked my lips as I recalled our moment in the hot springs when I first arrived in Obsidian. I asked my three questions, but he only asked two of his.

"Do you forgive me?"

I raised my head to study his features, my eyes resting on the slash in his eyebrow before bouncing to his lips and back to his eyes that transfixed me every time.

"For what?"

A flash of a smile flit across his full lips and then disappeared.

"It's the last time I'll ask, but I need to know for sure. Do you forgive me for how I treated you when you first arrived? For the things I said to you when I was trying to pull the magic from you that you were unaware of."

I rolled my lips inward before biting my bottom lip as I heard a groan in his throat. My eyes snapped up to see him staring at my lips. I tilted my head back to stare deeper into his eyes. "I do. But I just want to know your reason for treating me so horridly when I first arrived. Why did you—"

Before I could finish my question, his lips crashed into mine as I was lifted from the ground.

Time slowed down.

The electricity and heat that formed as our lips touched was ethereal. Our heartbeats surged in unison as we forgot we weren't alone. My fingers intwined in his hair as his hand gripped the back of my neck, raising to cradle the back of my head as our tongues clashed.

Breathless, he finally set me back on the ground, while tucking a loose curl behind my ear.

No words were exchanged as those golden eyes bore into mine. His tongue darted out to lick his lips from the remnants of our kiss before he grabbed me and resumed dancing.

His touch. His charm. His smell. His features.

It was that moment when I knew he would be the only one capable of breaking me in a world that had always tried and failed.

Chapter Twenty-Five

The night grew late as we continued to dance and share drinks and laughter. Aware that we were human, the tavern keeper provided Tessa and me with diluted drinks, and that tiny bit of kindness allowed me to enjoy Merakai without getting sick shortly into the night.

Multiple times, my mind raced as I wondered if anyone in our group saw the kiss Thane and I shared. Thankfully, no one had yet to address it which allowed for me to continue through the night as usual. Raya, Tessa, Nova and I danced in our own little circle until Xavier cut in, asking Raya to dance, shortly followed by Silas who shyly asked Tessa. I playfully glared at the men as Nova and I raised our cups in salute before continuing to dance. Moments later, I felt a hand on the small of my back.

"Don't you dare take the last friend I have available," Nova said while poking her finger into Thane's chest. I smacked my lips together to hold my laugh in knowing that she was much smaller than Thane, but he threw his hands up in defense. Just as he was about to back off, Athena threw her arms around Nova. "I'm back if I count for anything."

Thane glared at his sister who had wandered off after the Pixie show and now returned with disheveled hair and flushed cheeks. "And just where have you been?" Thane interrogated her with his hands balled into firm fists at his sides. She gave her brother a wink and puckered her lips to blow him a kiss. Her actions led to her brother scolding her about the Fae men of Obsidian. She cocked her head to the side while still attached to Nova's back.

"Funny you say that because aren't you a Fae male of Obsidian? The High King to be exact," she countered in a mocking tone. Everyone laughed, except Thane who grumbled a curse under his breath and grabbed my hand to pull me away. I shrugged an apology to Nova and Athena who were still laughing and continued to dance without me after they wiggled their brows at us.

Thane continued to lead the way, guiding us over the bridge we crossed when we arrived in Verdanthia before reaching the pegasus we arrived on. Confusion etched across my face when we reached them.

Was he sending me back to the palace?

Panic began to rise in my throat. Maybe the kiss was too much. We aren't exactly the kindest to each other after all. *The drinks definitely clouded my judgement.*

"Do you trust me, Amira?"

My eyes bounced upward to observe the man who was causing my world to spin in disarray. His dark hair, almost purple in the moonlight, starkly contrasted his bright golden eyes that were locked on me as he awaited an answer. After admiring how attractive he was for the hundredth time since we had met, I nodded.

A smile broke on his lips, and he grabbed me by the waist, hoisted me onto the back of the Pegasus, and mounted behind me.

"Where are we going?" I asked flustered.

"Back to the palace grounds."

So he was sending me back to the palace...

When we landed, I patted the pegasus on its back and snuggled my head into it. Not forgetting to thank it for its service. The animal let out a faint noise and flapped its wings into the night as Thane informed me it was returning home.

He walked me to the back of the palace, into the garden, and sat at a bench overlooking the garden pond in the back. He patted the seat directly next to him and raised his eyebrows. Sighing and accepting his invitation, I claimed a seat on the bench a foot or two away from him, earning me a quick narrowing of his eyes.

"What's wrong, Thane?" I inquired with squinted eyes of my own. "Was it the kiss? If it was a mistake I—"

"Do you think it was a mistake?" he asked coldly. His relaxed posture now rigid as he awaited my reply.

I swallowed, afraid to answer. I knew by the fire I felt inside me when his lips graced mine that it wasn't a mistake. A mere touch from him sent my senses into overdrive.

"I don't think so. But I've never—"

"Neither do I. And I would do it a thousand times over if I could," he said while leaning back on the bench, splaying his legs in front of him and arms across the back.

Stars above he was huge.

His arms almost took up the entire backside of the bench while his torso towered over it. And his legs looked like they were never-ending while spread out in front of him. I did my best to avoid my gaze drifting down to the space between his legs.

"What's your favorite flower?" he asked nonchalantly.

I racked my brain as I ran through the flowers I knew of in my head. I was embarrassingly stumped until only one definitive answer came to mind.

"The lotus flower," I answered, and he nodded a few times while looking out over the garden. "Preferably black," I added on.

My answer caused him to choke. As he worked to clear his

throat, he looked at me in bewilderment. "Have you—have you ever seen a black lotus flower... in person?" he inquired. I nodded and his eyes blew wide. "In Solaris?"

I gently smiled at him as he pieced things together in his head.

"I see. Story for another time I suppose."

He lifted a hand and waved it in front of him. A burst of air rippled through the space between us to the garden pond. A cloud of smoke dissipates before I stood and walked over to the water. I gasped and threw my hand over my mouth. "How?! I thought they were banned?"

He strode over from the bench until he was standing directly behind me.

"Banned in Solaris. But the black lotus *is* the flower of Obsidian."

I turned to face him in disbelief.

"In the harshest of places, the most beautiful things bloom," he whispered while running a thumb across my bottom lip and cupping my cheek. Impulse had me leaning my head into his large, warm palm. "I had to bring you back here to know if it was real."

My eyes snapped open from when I had closed them at the warmth and comfort of his hand on my cheek.

"I need to know if you felt what I felt back there. Anything at all."

My heart beat a steady drum as I remembered the feeling of our lips touching. His hands on me causing a fire to burn deep inside. I straightened my posture to study him. His eyes were wide, pleading for an answer. To see him so open and vulnerable before me compared to the man I first met had my knees weak.

"I felt it too," I whispered.

He stepped closer, wrapping an arm around my lower back where his hand now splayed, the other cupping the back of my head. I panted at the sensation of his warm breath brushing against my lips, our faces inches apart.

"Stay with me tonight," he said as my brow scrunched in confusion. "In my bed. Stay with me, Amira."

I struggled to understand if it was a request or a demand in his cool, calm tone.

His lust-filled eyes had me squeezing my thighs together, fighting to have some type of reservations with a male I barely knew. My mind raced as I remembered my promiscuity back in Medlar, but this didn't feel like that. *Not that I was ashamed of it.* But I knew that if I agreed, it wouldn't be like how it was back home. I knew that if I laid in Thane's bed it wouldn't end after one night.

A man like him would have a hold on me even when he grew bored and decided he was done.

"I know tomorrow we must return to reality. And I know what your priority is, as it is mine too. But for tonight, let us live the life we deserve," he said, his voice a silken hum to my ears. Gently placing my hands on his chest, I smirked, cocking a brow.

"Beg."

He jerked his head back at my answer, releasing me from his grasp. Cocking his head, he waited for an explanation.

"You heard me. You said you weren't interested in me when I first got here. If I remember correctly, you said you never would be. *So. Fucking. Beg,"* I clarified with my head held high.

His eyes went dark, matching the sky above us. "I beg for no one."

"I understand. And I aim to please no one. Have a good night *Thanasis,"* I said with a smile, turning on my heel to head toward the palace steps.

"Wait," his husky voice boomed from behind me, and a hand wrapped around my wrist. I cast my gaze to his calloused hand, his touch sending a comforting warmth through me that rested in my belly. Turning to fully face him again, I stumbled backwards when I noticed him on his knees. The eyes that were dark just a moment ago were now filled with an intensity that fire couldn't hold a flame to.

"What are you doing?" I asked, completely awestruck at his position.

"You said to beg. And if it's any consolation, I've never bent a knee for *anyone*," his words were clipped as his eyes flared with solemnity. "I'll beg if I have to, Amira. But you need to know something," he said on a hard swallow. "Once I let my guard down, I'll have zero self-control."

His words sent shivers down my spine and heat between my legs.

Studying him with his bright golden eyes peaking from under his thick, dark lashes filled with feral desire for me had my mouth running dry. I had a High King, the *most powerful* High King, on his knees in front of me. Pleading, *begging*, to have me for the night.

Just one night.

Slowly, he stood, grasping both of my hands in his. "If you give me a chance—this chance—to show you why I acted the way I did, Amira I—"

His words fell short as he looked away from me, sucking in his bottom lip and biting down. He focused back on me, staring as if I was a meal he couldn't wait to devour.

"I can't promise I won't break you. *Because I know you'll end up breaking me as well.*"

The fire that I forced to burn low inside of me fully ignited as I allowed myself the freedom of being lost in his golden eyes that grew darker by the second. I knew I'd regret my next words when he was bored with me, but I also knew I'd enjoy every second he gave me while it lasted.

"Break me, Thane."

What color was left in his eyes vanished and the darkness consumed them. His grip tightened on my hands and my breath got stuck in my throat. He dipped down, lifting me up by my waist and pulling me into him as I wrapped my legs around his large, muscular frame.

We stared at each other before our lips clashed, our tongues meeting each other's as he effortlessly walked across the garden and up the palace steps.

Our first kiss was filled with lust, but the lust disappeared in this moment. It was now replaced with a deep, unreadable emotion and *want*.

The desire that I felt to have this man take control of me was unbearable. The irritable pull that I had towards him grew stronger by the second. The way I craved his skin touching mine had my body ready to burst into flames.

Entranced in the moment, I hadn't realized that we had already made it inside of his room until he shut the door, locking it with a flick of his wrist. Walking over to the front of the bed, he broke our everlasting kiss and sat me down on the floor, turning me to have my back to him as he undid the corset. Once it fell to the floor, he spun me back around and forced me to sit on the edge of the bed.

"Tell me that you want this," he panted, running his hands through his dark locs.

I didn't answer with words because the emotions building in my body overrode my thoughts. Instead of speaking, I let my actions do the talking. Rising from the bed, I removed the straps of my dress, allowing it to fall to the floor. My breaths came in ragged bursts as I stood before him in nothing except the lace of my black underwear. I watched as he practically salivated at the image of me offering myself to him. My heart skipped a beat when my gaze flicked to his shadows peeking out from behind him.

I gave into temptation and my eyes dipped to the bulge in his pants that made me swallow hard. The clouds of desire moving into my head forced me to fall back down to the bed. Remembering exactly who I was, I began moving back until I was propped on my elbows, and I spread my legs wide for him.

"Fuck," he growled under his breath. I bit my lip at the same time that he raised his fist to his mouth and bit his bare knuckles.

In an instant he was crawling on top of me. The weight of him was pure bliss as it pressed down on me. I felt his hand snake between our bodies until it met the lining of my underwear. Slipping his fingers inside, I felt a tug and heard the satisfying sound of them ripping from my body. A gasp escaped me as I watched him bring the lace to his face, breathing in my scent as a shiver raced through him.

My eyes were hooded with lust as I gaped at him.

"I've smelled this scent from the moment I laid eyes on you in Solaris," he hissed while throwing the material to the side. "Do you know how long I've waited to taste you. To feel you writhe beneath me," he said while wrapping his hand around the side of my neck. "To have you moaning at *my* mercy."

On impulse, I tried to squeeze my thighs shut as he sat up, but both of his hands quickly settled on my knees, pushing them further apart. My breathing becomes sporadic when his eyes slowly trailed up my body and transfixed on my face.

"Don't try to run now, Pixie."

The sight of him unbuttoning his shirt above me already had me on the edge of whatever cliff I was desperately trying to hold on to. When he removed his top, the swirls of ink running across his tanned body had me in a euphoric state. Time lapsed as I watched him unbutton his pants, pushing them down his thighs and kicking them off with ease. I must have been biting my lip so hard for so long that I drew blood. The tang of metal was bitter on my tongue when I released my lip. He reached out a finger and swiped the small trickle of blood from my lip before thrusting it into his mouth and sucking it, releasing it with a distinctive popping sound. The smile he produced had me blinking in a daze.

I whimpered at the sight of him tasting my blood with a smile on his face and ran a hand down my own.

I was entirely fucked with whatever I'd gotten myself into.

His hand gently wrapped around my neck and slowly trailed between my breasts, where he stopped to admire them, licking his lips in the process. "The number of times I've dreamed of you begging for mercy while my hand was wrapped around your throat is astonishing." My heavily hooded eyes were filled with lust, and I peered at him through my lashes.

"Thane," I whispered, begging him to stop teasing me. His hand continued to move further down until it reached my navel, and he bent to hover his face above mine.

"There's no going back from this," he said in a low, gravelly voice.

His movements were fast, as two fingers slid down to my slit. My body tensed when I realized he could feel the pool of wetness I'd created from his touch and words alone. He brought his hand back up to hover between us, marveling at what was dripping from his hand and onto my chest. He stuck two fingers into his mouth, sucking until he got every last drop of me. A groan left him as he closed his eyes and dropped his head, removing his fingers. *Just like fucking honey,* he hummed, opening his eyes to find mine.

A subtle cry left me as he shifted his face between my legs, placing them over his shoulders. The sound of a satisfied groan escaped him before his tongue began its assault on my pussy. My hands tangled in his hair as I felt the flick of his tongue on my clit when he inserted his fingers back inside of me. The rhythmic swirl of his tongue sent me into overdrive, and I felt myself teetering on the edge of climax. I was about to announce how close I was when his fingers stilled inside of me, pulling another whimper from me.

"Don't you even think about coming until I'm inside of you," he snapped while bringing his head up to stare at me. Heat flooded through me when I noted the serious look on his face.

"Thane, I can't hold –"

Before I could finish speaking, he was already off the bed removing the rest of his clothing. I watched as his erection sprang free, causing a sharp intake of breath from me. I squirmed at the delicious sight of the man before me and the part of him that I knew was about to ruin me even further. His eyes were heavily hooded as he stood stroking himself above me. "I'm going to take you now. You okay with that, darling?"

His asking for permission had me panting in anticipation.

"I think so..." I answered as I grew impatient, unsure if I could take what he continued to stroke in his hand. But my answer caused him to pause, tilting his head in concern.

"You think so or you know so? This isn't one sided. Either we're both in agreement or—"

"I know so."

"I don't want to do anything you don't want to—"

"*Please, Thane*. I need this," I cut him off in desperation, realizing that I was now the one pleading for him to ruin me.

He stalked back to the edge of the bed, pushing my legs apart again, and confidently stared at my core. "Stars above... look at this," he said through labored breaths.

Panic and dread flooded me. "What? What's wrong? Something's wrong with me? Are Fae women different from mortals?"

A low chuckle escaped him as he ran both hands up and over my thighs, bringing them down to my core and running a finger down my slit. I shuddered at the feel of him right where I wanted him, again. "Not a single fucking thing is wrong with you. You're perfect."

The blush of my cheeks spread as he reclaimed his position on top of me, kissing me like he'd never get the chance again. I felt him align the tip of his cock with my entrance as our eyes snapped open at the same time. He pressed his forehead to mine, and I knew he was waiting for one more confirmation before he lost control. "I need this," I whispered again, and it was all he needed to give me what I was craving. Slowly, he forced the length of himself inside of me, and I cried out.

He caressed the side of my face while slightly pulling back and gently working himself back in. The pressure of his size was over-whelming, yet pleasurable, and impatience took over. I could read the concentration on his face, focusing on not hurting me.

"Fuck me, Thane. I'm not fragile. You won't break me," I said between labored breaths. His eyes searched mine before he sucked his teeth, clamped a hand over my mouth, and pushed himself inside of me, forcing me to take every last inch of him. I writhed below him in bliss and pleasurable pain as he pulled back, burying himself in me over and over while planting sweet kisses down my neck and trailing them to my collarbone.

The strokes he delivered were now filled with overbearing pleasure, the flame between us burning brighter with every deliv-ery. His head dipped down to take my nipple between his teeth, and I felt myself tightening around him, causing him to shudder.

"Fuck, Amira. If you get any tighter, this is going to end in the next thirty seconds," he said while releasing my breast from his mouth and clenching his teeth. Cockiness got the best of me.

"Looks like I won then, doesn't it? The immortal Fae can't handle the mortal pussy." I winked at him and his eyes flared. Something snapped within him, and he moved quickly, too quickly. He sat up and flipped me over onto my stomach with zero effort. A strangled cry left my lips. I flailed my limbs in every direction, fighting his actions, scared of what beast I just unleashed.

"Thane, I was just –"

A large hand grabbed a fistful of my curls, yanking my head back. "You asked for this."

His voice was clipped, harsh, yet filled with desire.

I felt pressure around my wrists, and I noticed his shadows wrapping around, connecting them to the posts of the bed. I yanked them hard to be released and they barely budged. Both of his rough hands grabbed my hips, pulling them upwards until my ass was in the air with my face buried in the sheets. I wiggled my ass, convinced I could get free when I felt him settle himself behind me. I took in a deep breath, preparing for him to continue what he had already started. My eyes widened when I felt the full thickness of him inside of me in one thrust and I cried out at the pleasure.

"Outside of this room, you'll always be in control. But here, in my bed. It's me," he announced while bringing his opposite hand around to splay it on my lower stomach. The hand wrapped in my curls pulled my head off the bed, turning it to the side to see him from the corners of my vision. Pressing his splayed hand firmly into my stomach, he released a satisfied groan. "I want to feel myself inside of you."

My eyes rolled to the back of my head as he fucked me into oblivion. Every thrust was filled with heat and pleasure, forcing me to audibly beg for any deity that would listen to me for mercy. I was fighting to catch my breath between thrusts when a smack to my ass startled me and I yelped. "You're begging for mercy from the merciless, Beautiful."

My lips part at his words, and another smack to my cheek is my final undoing. I feel myself preparing to topple over when a harsh shudder runs through me. His movements become sporadic at the same time and my brain short circuits while I tried to reason with him. "Thane, I'm not—"

"I take the required elixir. We're safe," he forced out on a grunt while increasing his speed. "I'm filling you with everything I have. Can you take that for me, Sweetheart?"

I stifled a moan into the sheets and felt his hand grab a fistful of my curls again, yanking my head up. "Don't do that. Don't deprive me of those sweet little moans you're trying to muffle. Let me hear the pleasure my cock brings you."

I tumbled over that same cliff I was teetering on before as he held me upright, an earthshattering orgasm rippling through me. The feeling was like no other as what felt like electricity raced up my spine and around my sides, settling in the center of my chest. I felt a searing hot pain at the base of my neck before the pressure built so high that we both moaned as we fought not to collapse. Confusion was a fleeting emotion as ice began to shoot from my palms, his shadows wrapping around my hands to halt them. His strokes became more sporadic as I felt him tremble while my body convulsed beneath him. I felt the heat from his cum dripping down my thighs in what felt like a never-ending release before his shadows freed me and he collapsed next to me, pulling my body into his.

"Thank you," he whispered from behind me.

I rustled around, turning to face him while his arm was still draped over my waist. "For what?" I asked, searching his face with skepticism while running a thumb over the scar of his brow. He removed my hand from his face, kissing each knuckle.

"For giving yourself to me," he clarified and pulled me tighter to his chest.

My heart skipped several beats as I processed his words. I'd been used and I'd used before.

But I'd never been thanked for my body. For giving myself to someone.

I nestled my head under his chin as his index finger drew swirls on my hip. Drowsiness rolled in while I tried to make out what he was drawing. But my body lost the fight against sleep, and I succumbed to the warmth of his body graciously pressed against mine and fell into slumber.

Chapter Twenty-Six

Through the cracks of the shades, the sun shone brightly throughout Thane's massive room. I brushed the loose strands of hair from my face and glanced down at the arm wrapped around my waist as my backside was firmly pressed to his front. I felt his chest rise and fall slow and steady against my back as he still slept.

Enjoying the warmth of his body, my heart squeezed at the thought of how annoyed he would be when he woke to still find me in his bed. Slowly, I peeled his arm from my torso, planning my silent escape. I was halfway free when his arm snapped back down and curled around my midsection, tighter than before.

"She's not going anywhere," a husky voice blared.

"What?" I asked, turning to face Thane. My eyes squinted when I saw he was still asleep.

"The curve of her ass fits perfectly against my cock."

My eyes bulged, and I scrambled to sit up against the weight of him, his eyes snapping open at my frantic movement. He reached a hand out for me as I scooted so far back I teetered off the side of the bed. He caught my leg, pulling me back toward him until I straddled his lap. His golden eyes searched my worried face.

"Could... could you hear me as I slept?" he asked through squinted eyes that mimicked mine. I swallowed hard while nodding my head.

His eyes grew soft at my answer, bringing a hand up to graze the side of my face.

"I want to know if I can hear you as well," his voice said in my mind again, startling me. *"Focus your mind on me and only me."*

With wide eyes and my mouth dropped open in shock, I smashed my lips together and clamped down the panic arising from what I was witnessing. I studied the man that should be placed in the heavens above as a God. Closing my eyes, I focused on the thought of him while knowing that it'd never work as a half mortal. My mind drifted back to the memories of last night, him between my legs, devouring me like I was his last meal on earth.

"I wouldn't mind having the same meal for breakfast," his voice carried through my mind, jerking me from the memory. My eyes burst open on a gasp, and I scrambled to get away from him.

His grip tightened around me, pressing me into his bare chest.

"What the fuck is going on, Thane?" I cried, my panicked voice causing him to loosen his grip on me. His hands unwrapped from around me, running down the sides of my ribs, sending shivers through me as the lust took over once again. My eyes fluttered back open to see our lips inches apart, but he forced himself to pull his face from mine. Picking me up and setting me atop the sheets, he ran a hand through his hair before wrapping me in the covers. And it was only then that I remembered we were both still naked.

"I guess now is as good as ever to let you know why I acted the way I did when I first met you," he mumbled. Casting a quick glance in my direction, he wet his lips before continuing. "I knew the moment that my eyes landed on you on that dais next to Raine that I would burn the world down for you, Amira.”

His declaration sent thousands of butterflies from their cocoons to fly freely throughout my belly. I adjusted myself on the bed, trying to clamp down the feeling.

“The moment I saw those,” he said while pointing at my eyes, “I knew that you would be my undoing. Every fiber of my body pulled toward you the moment I entered Solaris. I didn’t need Silas’ guidance to get to you. I knew exactly where you were, and *nothing* was going to stop me from getting to you.”

His breathing was steadily increasing as he spoke about Solaris. I reached out, placing a hand on his bare skin. Removing my hand from his shoulder, he placed it in his and squeezed tightly. “I wanted so badly to rip his wings and head from his body right there, but I promised Aravis I wouldn’t start a war.”

He turned his body to face me, evaluating my face for any signs of panic. I remained quiet, letting him speak and vent as much as he wanted.

“When we returned to Obsidian, I knew I was going to lose control over myself like I have heard so many others do,” he said with soft eyes searching mine. His statement caused confusion, and I cocked a brow waiting for him to explain. He scooted closer to me, searching for my other hand to take in his. “Atlas is attached at your hip because he knew the moment he saw you in the forest in Medlar.”

My mind trying to put the pieces together from what he was hinting at was becoming frustrating. “Knew what, Thane?” I whispered. I could see him swallow before he bit his lip and released a breath while throwing his head back.

“You’re my mate, Amira.”

Those four words sent the room into a spinning fit as I tried to remain focused. I’d heard those words before, and they turned out to be a lie.

“Everything that I felt last night, could never be explained in words. I thought it was better to show you…to make you feel what I feel for you. But I didn't know this," he said while tapping the side of his head, "Would happen after last night. That usually doesn't happen until after the bond has been accepted by both individuals. You have to believe me."

The consistent ringing in my ears was making it hard to focus on the man speaking to me.

"If you don't feel the same toward me then…" his voice broke. "Then you can reject me. But I know, Amira. I know you felt what I felt last night—the burning sensation of fate flowing between our connection. It was more than just pleasure between us, and I know that."

My breaths were few and far between as I searched for the right words to deliver.

He stared at me, awaiting my input. His words replayed in my head about Atlas sensing our fate when we crossed paths in Medlar. My eyes snapped back up to meet his. "Is that why I felt such a strong pull in Atlas' direction when I saw him in the woods?"

Thane let out a light chuckle before nodding his head and brandishing a small smile. "Most likely."

I threw myself back onto the pillows behind me, pressing my palms into my eyes. I knew that sleeping with Thane would ruin me, but not this type of way. Despite his hostility toward me in the beginning, I'd always been attracted to him. *Felt a subtle pull to him that turned into much more over time.*

But… *mates?*

I popped my head back up. "I need to know what a mate exactly is, Thane."

He nodded his head in understanding and threw himself down next to me. Resting his hand on my stomach sent more butterflies with wildly flapping winks into that familiar area of my lower belly.

"Fated mates are two beings that are destined to be together, coming together at some point in their lives through destiny. The mate bond creates an irresistible connection between the two of them. It's a bond as deep as the soul runs," he said in one long breath. "If the woman accepts what fate offers that is."

His last sentence had me swiftly twisting my neck in his direction. "I have a choice?" I asked while searching his impossible bone structure. His attractiveness got harder and harder to ignore the more I was around him.

Propping himself up on one elbow, he moved his splayed hand to rest against my cheek while cupping my jaw. "I have no idea how things work anywhere else in this world. But here, within Obsidian, within my home, you will always have a choice, Amira. Always."

His words brought tears to my eyes, and I stared into his as they rolled down my cheeks and dropped to the sheets. Concern sketched across his face at the sight of my tears, sending him into a panic as he sat up, wiping them away and cupping my face with both hands. "I-I'm sorry if you find last night to be a mistake. I am so –"

"Do you think it was a mistake?" I asked, cutting him off. He huffed a laugh, smoothing my hair back from my face.

"I'd sell everything I have to be able to claim you as my mate. And I'd offer my soul to Erebus to relive last night every night for the rest of immortality."

My thighs squeezed shut at the fire in his words.

"It's not something you need to accept right now. Your priority right now is saving your family. *And we will.* I know that it's a lot to take in, especially when you weren't raised in a realm like this. I don't expect you to agree to a seat on a throne overnight."

My breathing ceased at once. *Seat on a throne?*

Forgetting that he could read my mind if I projected it or left it open to him, he winced. "I'm the High King of Obsidian. You would ultimately be the High Queen. The first mortal High Queen... to be honest," he said with hope shining in his eyes.

I opened and closed my mouth at his explanation. I was a nobody in a realm like this. There was no way I could help rule a realm that was filled with Fae and who knows what other immortal kind that live here.

"Thane... I am not deserving of a crown. I'm not even worthy of a throne. I'm a nobody," I whispered with my gaze on the sheets. He stiffened next to me. I peeked up at him through my lashes and his eyes flared with anger. He pulled me closer to him in one swift motion, and took a breath before speaking, but was cut short by a frantic knock at his door.

"I have no idea who you brought home last night, and I won't ask. But there's something you need to read. I'm sliding it under the door," Xavier said from the other side and a piece of parchment slid across the marble floor.

Thane surveyed my face, wanting to say so much in such a short time but settled for a kiss to my forehead before jumping out of bed, throwing on his undergarments.

"Reading it now. Meet you downstairs," he called to Xavier while picking up the piece of paper and opening it. His shoulders dropped while he skimmed over it, bringing his gaze from the paper to meet mine. I sat up on my knees with the sheets still wrapped around me. My heart hammered away in my chest, waiting for him to speak. I jumped and threw my hand over my mouth when he sent a heel into the door behind him.

"It's a letter from Raine demanding an immediate meeting in Bavaria."

Chapter Twenty-Seven

The moments following the summons were frantic as both of us dressed for the immediate request. The others were forcing themselves back to reality from relaxing throughout the palace, nursing their own hangovers.

The only difference was that my hangover was from lust.

I threw on my clothes to face the dreadful day ahead, but I couldn't stop my mind from wandering back to last night. The memory of Thane's hands on me sent goosebumps across my body. His flesh pressed against mine still sent heat to my core as panic of the meeting we were about to attend fought to take control.

The battle of worrying about the well-being of my mother and brother while trying to comprehend being fated mates with Thane was causing my brain to go haywire. Sitting on the edge of my own bed with my head in my hands, the door flew open, and I was met with wide eyes from Tessa. The silence between the two of us was a communication we'd been able to hold since childhood.

She knew. She knew why I didn't come back to my room last night.

And in an instant, a realization snapped into place. *Tessa wasn't in our room when I came in this morning.* I drew my head back at the realization as she subtly shook her head. I nodded. A mutual agreement to ignore the activities of last night. *For now.*

She continued into the room, shutting the door behind her. "Nova let me know about the letter. I'm coming with. I'm not much help, but I refuse to let you handle this alone."

Her words sent warmth straight to my heart. Our gazes connected once again as silence filled the room.

"I'm scared," we both said in synchrony. The two of us let out a low chuckle before Tessa pressed her palms to her eyes and began rambling. "How the fuck are we going to resolve this? I'm the older sister and I'm the least likely to be able to help. At least you're half Fae. You have... powers or magic. Are they the same thing? I don't know. I have nothing to offer."

I stood from the bed, stalking over to her and grabbing both her hands in mine. "You don't need magic to fight for your family, Tessa." Her eyes studied my face like she hadn't known me since the day I entered this world. She nodded, straightening her spine. "Then we get our fucking family back."

Once both of us were dressed and lacing our boots, Raya joined us in the room. "I don't know what my brother has up his sleeve, but we've got this," she said with a tight-lipped smile. The three of us hugged in a tight, warm embrace before heading out to the sparring platform to meet everyone else.

Walking up the few stone steps to the platform, the sun was a subtle kiss to my skin, and I drank it in. My eyes snapped open when I heard his voice.

"Good morning, Beautiful," Thane said with a voice as smooth as silk. I tripped on the last step, having forgot that we could communicate through our minds now.

"You okay?" Raya asked while catching my elbow to steady me.

"Too much wine last night," I joked, bringing a laugh from her and Tessa.

I cleared my throat before I replied to Thane more easily than I thought it would be. *"Maybe let me get my footing right before scaring the shit out of me this early in the morning?"*

Hearing him chuckle in my head sent the anxiety in my bones out the window. It was like warm vanilla on a Sunday morning. *"Apologies, Pixie. I forgot this is all new to you. You can always sever it by declining me as your mate."*

My eyes snapped to his just in time to see him wink at me before speaking to everyone.

"Before we leave," he started and cast another quick glance in my direction. "I'm not sure what Raine's plan is, but I can assure you that it's nothing that will be in our favor. His mind is set on receiving Amira and Raya as collateral, but we don't hand over our own."

Our own.

I looked over at Raya who was fighting the tears that were attempting to flow.

"Whatever he throws at us, we will handle it. We don't need magic to hand them their asses."

"That's a fact," Xavier said with a deep laugh as Silas bumped into his shoulder with a smile.

"Whatever happens, don't let Raine know that you now possess magic. And don't make him aware that you know who you truly are. We won't be able to communicate via our channel while we're there because it's considered magic," Thane instructed me while staring with his lips set in a thin line.

We huddled closely together, preparing to be transported to the meeting. Anya and Aravis walked up with forced smiles on their faces and good morning greetings. Aravis reaches out to subtly tap my cheek. And in the blink of an eye, we were thrown into another realm.

Once we landed in Bavaria, the smell of sand and water

greeted me like last time. To our surprise, Raine and Eryx were already waiting for us with fire in their eyes. Without light conversation, Raine began to bolt toward us and Eryx grabbed his shirt to restrain him.

"You went to the reaper to ban me from Medlar?" Raine spewed with lips peeled back. The multiple black cords that I didn't miss seeing were snaked up his arms and rested under his chin. I glanced at Thane whose brows were furrowed in confusion.

"Don't act like you're confused you bastard. Apple doesn't fall far from the tree, does it?" Raine hissed. I'm unsure why, but Thane lunged forward with so much force that Anya had to step in front of him, accompanied by Xavier and Silas having to hold him back. "My men nor I can enter Medlar anymore. Immortals have never been *banned* from a mortal realm."

Thane was still seething at Raine when Aravis stepped forward. "It was I that paid a visit to the Reaper."

Thane stopped tussling, and the area fell silent as all attention was placed on Aravis. He stood tall before addressing the matter. "Your ways have gone on long enough, Raine. You want to ruin peace between realms for what reason? To feed your ego? To weasel your way into ruling multiple realms?"

Raine grunted before eyeing Aravis up and down. "You think you're so high and mighty in Obsidian. You are not above *taking* someone's mate from them. And if I want to go to Medlar to search for anyone that can help me get her back, I have that right."

An audible roar could be heard from Thane at the mention of me being Raine's mate. Xavier pressed a palm to his chest to keep him grounded while eyeing him suspiciously.

"Where is the proof of this mating bond?" Aravis asked with his hands behind his back. "Nevertheless, a mate is not a slave. A bond can be denounced by either party at any time. That is the rule across all realms."

Raine groaned in protest while running a hand through his

thick, white hair. A devilish smile crossed his face when he eyed me from head to toe. "To you and your people I'm a villain, but to her... I'm a God. Or it least that's what she called me when I'd drag her soul from her."

I could see a visible shudder in Thane's shoulders. "Yet, we've already established that you never slept with her. So, do you think because you gave her a few mediocre orgasms that you're viewed as a mate?"

I swallowed, my face turning a deep shade of red. Having my sex life aired in front of multiple people was not something I ever wished to do—especially not in front of my biological father.

"Her lies are growing by the moment. Her acceptance of our bond has already happened," Raine said with his head held high. I shook my head in protest at his lie.

"Then share your binding with us," Anya urged from beside Thane. My eyes blew wide at her statement. *There's a way to show the bond?*

Raine blanched at Anya's request. "Under Fae law you must return my mate until—"

"Someone always adds a lie to a story to make it go in their favor now don't they Raine?" Thane added with anger-laced words. "We come from the dark. We are the dark. We're who those with light fear when they realize their time is up. And your time is almost up through your lies and deceit. You cannot force your way into power."

Raine slowly peeled his top lip back while shifting his gaze to me. "Keep my sorry excuse for a sister. But I'll take what belongs to me with my bare hands if I must."

Those words were Thane's destruction as he threw Xavier and Silas to the ground with a simple outward flex of his arms. Everyone yelled in protest, but it was too late as Thane had already advanced, his hand around Raine's throat as Eryx pressed a dagger to Thane's heart. My blood ran cold at the sight of the metal to Thane's chest. I rushed toward him, but Tessa and Raya both grounded me.

"Touch her. Go ahead. Make my entire existence worth it," Thane spewed as spit flew from his mouth. Raine's eyes blew wide as he fought to draw in a breath, his feet barely touching the ground. "*TOUCH. HER.*" Thane's voice boomed so loudly that the surrounding rocks shifted. He dropped his hand from Raine's throat while licking his lips with a crazed look in his eyes. "If you ever lay a hand on any of my people, I'll rip your soul from your body," he seethed while Xavier and Silas pulled him back forcefully.

Regaining his footing and changing his expression from the panicked one he wore moments before, Raine released a menacing laugh as he stepped back. Running a hand down his front, smoothing out his clothing, he tilted his head to the side. "What soul?"

His eyes turned to the milky white I'd seen in my nightmares since my time in Solaris.

"Selling your soul to the Reaper for wings and the kiss of death is laughable," Thane said while allowing Xavier and Silas to bring him back toward the group.

A sinister smile crossed over Raine's face before his eyes settled on Raya. "Oddly enough, my own parents didn't laugh when they experienced that exact kiss from me."

Raya's grip on my arm loosened, as I caught her mid fall. Landing on her knees, she palmed the sand below us while releasing an ear-piercing scream. The echoes of Raine's laughter carried as my mouth remained agape at his confession.

"You'll forever live in my shadow. A useless, overly kind soul that would have been the downfall to our people," he said to Raya as he spat at the ground. "And Ezra wasn't far behind."

How could he speak of his parents and siblings with such ice in his tone?

Raya choked back tears. "Ezra... you knew. You know how he

vanished. It was you." She leapt to her feet and sprinted toward her brother as Silas dipped in, grabbing her by the waist and hoisting her into the air. He whispered into her ear as she went limp, weeping at the information dumped about her family in a careless fashion. "You searched for days with me to find the three of them and you knew the whole time," she wailed from Silas' arms.

Raine rolled his eyes at his sister. "All trash has to be disposed of for the greater good. But, speaking of trash, bring the boy," he instructed Eryx with a snap of his fingers.

My heart plummeted when I realized he was speaking of Alix.

A portal opened behind them and two guards stepped out holding Alix's limp body. Tessa and I cried out for our baby brother as we dropped next to him. The sight of his severely battered and bruised body sent uncontrollable trembling through my body as tears began to blur my vision. Sobs threatened to rack my body as I noticed his blue lips. My gaze bounced to Tessa who had turned ashen as she stared down at Alix.

"Figured this would be a perfect warning. Instead of having you choose who dies, I made the decision for you. Next, I'll send your mother's limbs piece by piece until you come back to me. *Your fucking mate*," Raine seethed from behind me. The urge to freeze his body where he stood flowed through me. I clamped down the shudder that ran through me and pressed my palms into the sand.

I glared at Raine with the heat of a thousand suns.

"Let me see my mother," I demanded. I refused to make any more requests from a man this heartless. He shrugged his shoulders before snapping and another guard brought out my mother in chains, sobbing uncontrollably. "I told them to take me. Not my baby, not my son," she wept on her knees while staring at her children.

My gaze cut to Aravis whose stare wouldn't leave the sight of my mother. "Let her go. Take me," Aravis said. Raine chuckled at his command while Aravis slowly dropped to his knees, holding his hands up. "Please. Have mercy on a grieving mother, and take me," Aravis bellowed. My mother's eyes snapped to Aravis and I couldn't pinpoint the emotion that flashed through them.

Raine tilted his head back and forth as if a realization had settled upon him.

"I think I made the right choice on who to keep alive. Let's go," Raine said with a twirl of his finger, instructing his men that it was time to leave. The guard roughly grabbed my mother by her hair, forcing her to stand.

"Do not do this, Raine," Aravis begged from the ground, causing Raine to whip back around.

"When people talk too much without substance it takes up too much of my time. Time that I don't have," Raine replied, and his eyes snapped to Thane. "That whore belongs to me. And I'll get her one way or another. You may be the most powerful High King, but the power of the Reaper flows through *my* veins. Your days of power are numbered," he fumed before focusing back on me, pointing a single finger in my direction. "I gave you a chance to return to your rightful place in Solaris and you didn't take it. Now the game will be played on my terms. *And it starts today.*"

His lips turned upward in a thin, scornful smile. His bright white teeth flashing as it widened.

And as if he hadn't already made my world crumble, he turned on his heel to return to his realm, his men dragging my weeping mother behind them, leaving me with nothing but grief and loss.

Chapter Twenty-Eight

We landed back in Obsidian with hope and despair as my baby brother laid limp on the stone ground. Tessa hovered over him as her tears fell atop his chest.

"Aravis," I pleaded in a whisper, hoping that by the grace of the heavens above he could fix this.

His hand rested on my upper back, "The raising of the dead can only be done once with my magic. And I—I used that on your father when we were in Medlar." My eyes bulged and fear began to surge through me at the thought of losing my sibling. I searched the platform for Anya, but when I found her, she had a look of pure dread as she shook her head.

"I can only revive those from my own coven. I'm so sorry, Amira."

My heart shattered into a million pieces as Thane came running out of the palace with the healer that resided there. They dropped down next to him, checking for his pulse as mine quickened to an unhealthy range. Silas gently pulled Tessa from the ground to give the healer room to work.

"It's very faint, but there's a pulse," he chimed hesitantly from the ground. I let out a lone sob and I could hear the others release the breaths they were holding. "I can give him an elixir, and it will mildly stabilize him. It will wear off in forty-eight hours give or take. And then..." his words trailed off without looking up as he retrieved the bottle from his bag.

"And then he will be dead," Tessa stated, her voice devoid of emotion as her tears continuing to fall. The healer nodded his head to let us know that she was correct before continuing. "There is... one other option."

I noted Thane stiffen at his statement, as if he knew what option the healer was about to propose.

"You could pay a visit to Knull," he suggested. Thane cursed under his breath, his hands on his hips as he paced. I studied him and his reaction before facing the healer again.

"Then I'll leave today. How do I find him?" I asked, desperate to save my brother. The healer finally removed his gaze from my brother to look up at me.

"There are only two people that know where he is located," he informed me and his eyes flicked over to Thane, who was giving a hard glare in the healer's direction.

I paced over to Thane. "I have to go, Thane. Just tell me where—"

"It's not that easy, Amira," he said, cutting me off. "Knull lives in hiding deep within The Glades due to being banished from *all* realms."

I reared my head back at his statement.

"How do you get banished from all realms?" I asked him in a hushed voice. He looked off to the side before answering, matching my tone.

"My parents spared Knull's life when everyone called for his death. But for whatever reason, they strongly believed that every-thing he did was for the greater good. They gave him sanctuary where no one could ever find him."

That information still didn't tell me what he did to get banned from all realms, but that was the least of my worries at the moment. Forgetting how good Thane was at reading my expressions, he barged into my head. *"His dark magic was so strong that even immortals feared him. So strong that he could bring anyone back from the dead. But... it is said if he brings you back, part of the darkness resides within you."*

I flinched, blinking an ungodly number of times while processing his information as he added on another piece: *"And even though he has the power to revive, he's very selective on who he grants the luxury to."*

"Fuck," I mumbled under my breath. My mind roamed with every possible outcome if I did or didn't take the chance of going to The Glades.

"We have to try," I whispered to Thane again with pleading eyes. He searched the faces of those surrounding us and back to Alix laying on the ground. He licked his lips, nodding his head. *"It was never a question on if we were going,"* he communicated before addressing the others. My heart sputtered, spiking with another surge of emotion at his decision.

He was never considering *not* going to help my brother. *He was evaluating how we were going to make it happen.*

"We will leave to seek Knull's help within the hour. The two of us will need assistance," Thane stated as Xavier and Nova immediately stepped up to accompany us. I took note of Raya's wide, worry-filled eyes, as Xavier volunteered, quickly masking it when she caught sight of me watching her reaction. She glanced to my siblings, indicating that she would stay here to watch over them. Everyone else begged Thane to accompany us on the journey. "The rest of you are needed here in case Raine or his army figures out a way to break through our wards. Obsidian will need you," Thane commanded. They agreed reluctantly before multiple servants came out to assist carrying Alix into a room to rest.

Tessa and I rushed to his side, assisting the servants who insisted they could handle it. "Thank you for your help, but I cannot stand by while others carry my brother to comfort," I expressed kindly. The servants nodded in understanding as Tessa and I helped carry my brother inside.

Laying him in a room with ample sunlight and space, the servants left my sister and I alone with him. I brushed his hair from his forehead with my hand as my body trembled, threatening to release the rising, heavy emotions.

"We must save him. We're his older sisters. His protectors. I'll never forgive myself if—"

I cut Tessa off, turning to grab her shoulders. "Don't speak it into existence. I will get what is needed and Alix will be back to his antics in no time," I declared, pulling a small, pitiful laugh from her.

"I feel useless staying here," Tessa uttered, casting her gaze to the floor before walking over and searching for Alix's hand to hold. I walked up behind her, placing my hands on her shoulders.

"Don't. He needs you more than ever right now. I'm sure he would appreciate any shit talking you could give him," I reassured her, pulling a genuine smile from the both of us.

"Fucker just had to make this about him," she said with a much louder chuckle and sniffle. The two of us gasped when Alix's finger lifted in her hand. Our wide eyes connected before I hugged her and kissed Alix on the forehead. I let her know I was going to meet everyone in the observatory to discuss plans and I'd fill her in before I left, knowing she didn't want to leave his side.

I had one foot out the door when I heard her voice. "Amira?"

I turned to face her with raised brows.

"I know you'll make him pay for this, but I want him to suffer," she said regarding Raine. I ground my teeth together, nodding my head in agreement, and shut the door behind me.

He will wish he never knew me when I was done.

Chapter Twenty-Nine

I made my way to the Observatory where I could already hear bickering echoing throughout the halls. My pace quickened when more voices were added into the mix. I turned the corner to find the door already open and everyone huddled over the long table with a large map sprawled across it.

"All this will do is lead Raine back to the Reaper to conjure another deal to be granted access to Medlar," Aravis argued across from Thane, pulling a groan from him.

"He's probably already working on that, but we have to do things in this order, or her brother will die. And do you want to explain that to Amira? Because I don't," Thane snapped before anyone realized I was already in the room.

Silas cleared his throat, casting his eyes in my direction to announce my arrival.

"All I'm saying is that the Reaper cannot be trusted to make any type of bargain. I took a chance, I—," Aravis stopped himself before glancing around the room. "I gave a piece of my soul for that agreement to keep Raine out of Medlar."

The room fell silent before it broke out in pure chaos at his admission.

Questions were thrown at Aravis from every angle about his decision until Anya slammed her mug onto the table and held Aravis' stare. "Did you lose your mind on the way there?"

Aravis cast a pitiful look in her direction.

"Don't you dare give me that look. You won't receive any sympathy from me. That was a stupid decision and we both know it. Or did you forget who you are?" she hissed at him. Aravis winced and scratched the back of his neck before straightening his shoulders, looking away from Anya.

"What's done is done," Aravis shouted, silencing the uproar. He waved a hand for me to join them at the table. "Thane, tell us what we will do to execute the plan. If you say this is the only way, then I trust your judgement."

I stood next to Thane and looked over the intricate map lying on the table. Realms and landmarks were noted throughout that I'd never even heard of. Medlar was such a miniscule part of the map and that made a small huff escape from my mouth. How foolish I was to think we were the only ones to exist in this world.

All eyes fell on me before Thane began to discuss the plan.

"We're going to travel through The Glades while we still have the full moon upon us," Thane announced as the other men cursed under their breath. "The full moon suppresses the malevolent magic of The Glades. It's our only option if we want to get to Knull in time. We can't travel through without a full moon, and this one started on the third night of Merakai. That gives us roughly two more days."

I searched over the map for the location that Thane mentioned.

"If you're searching for The Glades, you won't find it. It's a forbidden area for good reason," Nova said with a pained expression and turned to face Thane. "I will accompany you. You can't travel through there alone."

"As will I," Xavier said, receiving a nod from Thane.

"The rest of you must remain here. Our wards may be the

strongest of any realm, but I put nothing past Raine and The Reaper now. I would feel better knowing that my best are here to protect Obsidian if needed," Thane explained. Everyone around the table nodded in understanding but still looked disappointed that they could not accompany us. "Once we return, we will handle infiltrating Solaris and bringing your mother home," he finished while settling his gaze on me. "Assuming that your brother is the top priority in this matter?"

My ribs felt as though they were caving in on themselves. Having to choose between my mother and brother was a battle in itself. But if my mother ever found out I chose her life over one of my siblings', she would kill me herself.

I confirmed that my brother came first. Thane studied me for a moment before announcing that we would be leaving in one hour, tacking on the command to pack lightly, as we all separated to prepare for the journey ahead.

"Can I speak to you for a moment?" Thane asked while grabbing my wrist and guiding me to a different room of the palace. Once we were inside, he closed the door behind him and locked it. My brow furrowed, trying to figure out what was on his mind. He ran his hands through his thick, dark hair before placing his hands on his hips and glancing down at me. "I don't think you've been trained enough to travel through The Glades, Amira," he said on a loosed breath.

I shook my head fervently. "Don't, Thane. Do not do this. That is my brother upstairs dying," I retaliated. I would not send them to get help for my own brother without me. "I'm not just a human anymore. I'm not weak," I blurted out, pleading my case.

Thane's eyes blow wide before they glower as he strides over to me in two large steps. "You were never weak, Amira. Get that notion out of your fucking head," he hissed with fire in his eyes as he searched mine. He turned around and paced back toward the door before stopping in his tracks.

"He fucking reached for you," he said with his hands folded

on top of his head. He whipped back around to face me. My face scrunched in confusion until I realized he was talking about Raine. "He brought up moments of touching you. Intimate moments. The look he has in his eyes for you makes me sick," he snarled, his lips peeled back.

I took a few steps toward him and timidly placed my palm on his cheek. "Thane... that was the past. I wasn't aware of who he was. What he was even. I was stupid at that time and—"

Thane growled and pulled his face from my hand. "You give yourself no credit. Stop taking the blame for everything. For everyone." He picked up the wooden chair next to him, throwing it against the stone wall, shattering it.

I gasped and stepped away from him, swallowing at the mere sight of his anger overpowering him. Anger that was boiling over just because of Raine's words in Bavaria.

"He was waiting to drain you dry because he knew how special you were. Everyone knew how special you were except *you*. I've known since the moment I saw you in those fucking chains," he proclaimed before banging his fists on top of the wooden table, breaking it in half.

"Thane stop," I whispered. But he continued to destroy whatever furniture was in his path. Whatever object he could release his wrath upon was destroyed in seconds.

"He doesn't even care about you. He just wants your bloodline. To fathom that someone like that almost had you for eternity makes me physically sick to think about. And now he has your brother upstairs hanging by a thread," he said, picking up another chair and throwing it. "I should have killed him on that dais. This is *my* fault."

I rushed over to him when he grabbed a smaller table and placed my hands on top of his. "None of this is your fault. Raine would have found a way to do all of this regardless. You were making a rational choice not to start a war between realms." I searched his eyes, hoping to see some sort of sign that I was getting through to him. "You made the smart choice. You showed him who was a true High King."

His golden eyes that had begun to darken were now softening, returning to their original hue.

I peeled both of his hands from the table and pulled him closer to me. "Raine doesn't have me. I'm here. *I am right here*," I said while grabbing his face and tilting his head down to meet my gaze. "I can accompany you through The Glades. I promise I will be okay. I've had a great combat trainer," I said with a small smirk, pulling a throaty chuckle from him. His eyes turned a deep gold as he studied my face, tucking a lone curl behind my ear.

"There's one other thing I think that you should know," he said, his voice a mixture of velvet and steel.

I swallowed hard, waiting for him to tell me something dreadful, something that would make this mess even worse. He ran his tongue across his bottom lip and my knees threatened to buckle at the visual.

"I'll burn everything and anyone in my path before I let him or anyone else take you from me."

Chapter Thirty

The hour before we left was a rush as servants helped me into comfortable clothing for the trip and pack a bag that wouldn't weigh me down. I said my goodbye to Tessa who refused to leave Alix's side, even as he slept. The servants had put another bed in his room so that she could always watch over him per her request. The thought filled my heart with warmth as I leaned down to kiss Alix on the forehead. "I won't let you down," I whispered before waving one last goodbye and closing their door.

I rested the back of my head against the wood while still holding onto the doorknob. A thousand thoughts ran rampant in my mind before I let go of the cool metal and traveled through the halls.

I stepped out onto the sparring platform to see Thane by himself, sitting on the stone ledge. "I have something for you, Pixie," he said. The nickname now being one that brought a smile to my face. I treaded over to him, throwing my bag to the ground. My eyes drifted to his side where his usual dark blade rested, and saw it accompanied by a silver one. "Turn around," he demanded, and I complied. He strapped the sword to the middle of my back, an exact replica of how his usually rested.

"What's this for?" I asked while reaching back, feeling the sheath resting against my back.

"You can't go into the grove unarmed. And we've had more than enough training with a blade. It's just in case," he said before strapping his own to his back, and I couldn't help but marvel at the way its obsidian blade glistened in the sunlight. I was smart enough to know—now that I'd unsuccessfully tried—that no one could touch it except Thane. And after watching Silas determinedly try to pick it up, and having burns on his hands, I wouldn't be trying again.

After he checked to make sure I had at least two daggers strapped to my waist, Thane reached down and picked up my bag. He didn't even look at me as he threw it on his back.

"Nope, hand it over," I said with my hand held out. His expression was priceless as I raised a brow waiting for my bag to be returned to me. "I said I can handle myself. That means my bag as well. I appreciate the gesture, but I can handle it."

A wide grin spread across his handsome, tan face before he reluctantly handed it back to me with a grunt.

Nova and Xavier ascended the steps to the platform at the same time, saving me from whatever lecture I was about to receive from Thane.

"Not being able to fly there sucks," Xavier said with a grimace.

"I second that," Nova chimed in. "I get we have to stay discreet for Knull's protection, but we can't even use a portal or beam there?"

Thane shook his head. "My parents made all beaming and portals impenetrable to where he's located. Our feet are our means of travel this time. Too many things for a horse to get tangled in on the forest grounds. And the dark magic that resides within it startles them anyway."

The three of us moaned and groaned while Thane rolled his eyes and laughed. I took a moment to admire his true form that he now allowed to shine through every so often. He still had his grumpy and brooding moments, but hearing him laugh brought a jolt of satisfaction through me.

I can hear your thoughts, Pixie. Might want to clamp down on letting everything through the channel.

His voice in my head startled me, causing Nova and Xavier to look at me in confusion. I released a fake laugh before asking how long it would take us to get there.

"It takes a full day to get there, so we will make a stop for lodging along the way," Thane explained. "It's not safe for us to camp overnight within The Glades with just the four of us."

I was rustling through my bag to ensure I hadn't forgotten any essentials and glanced up to see the others doing the same except for Thane. "You're not worried that you forgot something?" I questioned him while closing my sack.

He stuck out his bottom lip and shook his head. "I've been doing this longer than you, Pixie." I rolled my eyes at his cockiness and stood, throwing my bag on my back.

In unison, Nova, Xavier, and I made one more complaint about walking until Thane pursed his lips, ignoring us, and we accepted our fate.

"Let's do this and get back to your brother," Xavier affirmed with a smile and slap to my shoulder. The weight of his hand brought my shoulder down. He mumbled an apology while Nova laughed heartily.

It was going to be a *long* trip.

~

The sun had begun to set above the trees as we continued our hike. The uneven terrain had my thighs on fire, but I'd be damned if I announced that to the others.

The air within Shadow Grove felt heavy as I focused on my breathing while I glanced around to see the three of them walking at a steady pace as if they were taking a quick stroll to the market. We'd been walking for hours, and they were not even breaking a slight sweat.

Fucking Fae *stamina.*

Then I snapped upright, remembering I was half Fae. Where was my stamina and additional perks at? *"Feel free to kick in any second now,"* I whispered to myself, my annoyance at an all-time high.

"How are you doing back there, Pixie?" Thane asked from up ahead as Nova and I trailed behind.

I wanted to express how petrified I was of my surroundings, but choked back my retort. The Glades were nothing short of terrifying. The moment I stepped foot on the grounds I got an unsettling feeling that we were under constant surveillance. The twisted trees surrounding us were filled with leaves the color of night and a flock of ravens eerily watched us from the trees.

"All good back here," I answered, masking the pain from my burning thighs as Nova glanced over at me with a sympathetic look. She pointed at her back, offering to carry me the rest of the way. I shook my head and mouthed a thank you for the offer.

The others would never let me live that one down.

I brought my hand to my nose to take a break from the subtle smell of decay mixed in with the damp, earthy scent of the forest. I was too fearful of their answers to ask if anyone else thought there were decaying bodies in the ground. I glanced back up at the trees and blanched, noticing their branches mimicking frail skeletal hands reaching out for help.

"We should be there before sundown. Only two more hours or so," Xavier announced, and my mind wanted to explode.

Two more hours of this?

I was about to announce my defeat when rustling came from the left side of the forest.

Nova tightly grabbed my arm, holding a finger to her lips indicating for me to remain silent. The hairs on the back of my neck stood as my eyes roamed the uninviting forest surrounding me. I heard more rustling as Thane quickly unsheathed the jet-black blade from his back and took his stance, Xavier doing the same with his daggers.

I noted Thane making gestures at Nova to remove me from the situation and I shook my head in rebellion. His golden eyes flared at my refusal as I grabbed my blade from its sheath and tapped into our channel. *"I got this."*

"You have not trained enough for this, Amira," Thane hissed.

"Fuck training," I hissed back. *"For the record, you're insanely handsome when you're protective."*

Thane squinted his eyes and tilted his head when I winked at him, questioning my sanity in such a serious situation. Nova surveyed me to confirm my decision, and I nodded. At the same time, a hairless figure sprinted across our path, leaving black soot in its trail. A second one quickly moved from behind the trees, revealing its gruesome dark grey leathery face.

"What the fuck is that?" Xavier whispered to Thane who shook his head, indicating that he had no idea.

The creature's limbs were unnaturally long as it dropped down to all fours and produced a terrifying smile showcasing its sharp, uneven double rows of teeth. Its large eyes were a pure black abyss as they roamed over us. I jumped at the sound of an unknown man's voice.

"Women," the deep, raspy voice said.

A man stepped from the darkness, moving in front of the creature as two more of them came into view. "It's been so long since we have had fresh meat in The Glades," another man said while stepping out into view. Thane and Xavier remained quiet as Nova and I stood shoulder to shoulder, her daggers resting in both hands. My grip tightened on the hilt of my blade as I prepared for whatever they were about to throw at us.

"Hand over the women and you can keep going to your destination," the tall, grey-haired man said. My nose scrunched at the sight of him. His long, stringy hair was plastered to his head, his teeth a decaying black and grey.

Xavier huffed before audibly growling. "I think it's in your best interest to call off your beasts and move along."

The men exchanged a mocking glance and laughed before one of them threw a command to the creature on all fours. It creeped from the shadows, its movements unusual as it slowly stalked in front of the men.

I gripped the handle of my sword, preparing for it to come in our direction.

Its limbs were much longer than the rest of its body as it crouched down, snapping its crooked, sharp rows of teeth at us. The harsh gnashing sound that accompanied the movement made my skin crawl. A bead of sweat trickled down my spine as I tightened my grip on my sword. The creature's mouth hung open, drool falling to the ground as if it was preparing for a meal that it may never get again.

Its large body swayed back and forth as it remained crouched, its sunken black eyes widening at the sight of us. Without warning, it straightened its legs and began sprinting toward us at lightning speed. Black soot trailed its path as the stench of decay grew the closer it got, making me gag. I raised my sword in defense, but was caught off guard when what looked like dark smoke rose before the creature, halting it in its tracks. Looking over, I saw Thane's shadows rushing out from him, wrapping around the creature and squeezing so tightly that the cracking of its bones echoed between the trees. I cringed as the creature writhed under the hold of Thane's shadows until it stopped moving and he released it with a thud to the soiled ground.

A third man stepped from the shadows of the trees and spat onto the ground. His thumbs rested in his pockets while he surveyed the now dead creature and then us. "You'll pay for that," he claimed before raising two fingers, whistling and flicking them in our direction, instructing the rest of the creatures to finish what the first one hadn't had the chance to.

Nova and I prepared to fight but were caught off guard when we were manhandled from behind. My sword clanged to the ground as my wrists were twisted until I couldn't bear the pain. I was wrestled to the ground, air rushing out of my lungs as my body connected with the hardened soil. The man flipped me over and straddled me. My vision realigned and the points of his ears let me know they were Fae as well.

I turned my head to see Nova being straddled by another Fae. She wrenched both of her arms free and pressed her thumbs into the eyes of the man threatening to harm her. His scream was music to my ears as the ice in my veins formed. Pressing my hands to the chest of the man who had pinned me to the ground, I forced my power from my palms. Shock overtook me as splinters of ice pierced his chest where my palms laid.

The shock on his face mimicked mine when I noticed my right hand laid directly next to his heart, missing it by barely an inch. He stood, breaking the ice from my grasp and stumbling backwards—his clothes now soaked in his own blood.

I scrambled to my feet to help Nova but remained frozen in place when I located her. Standing before the man that was straddling her, she tilted her head back and forth while the man stopped before her without moving. Streams of blood fell from his eyes where Nova had pressed her thumbs mercilessly. Slowly, one of his hands moved below his chin and the other rests on the back of his head.

I took a step forward and stopped when his arms made a sudden violent movement. His head made a quick twisting motion before a sickening crack and pop reverberated through the air.

My eyes bulged as the man went limp, his lifeless body falling to the ground.

Nova shuddered and turned toward me. My mouth hung open while rushing over to her, unable to speak as we shared a look. A loud thud broke us out of the moment, and we shifted, preparing to help Xavier and Thane when we were stunned at the sight before us. Roughly eight large creatures were lifelessly displayed around them as they stood back-to-back with their weapons raised.

"Did... did you just slay all of them in less than a minute?" I stammered when Thane's eyes connected with mine, flames blazing in each one. He began walking in our direction with vexation etched across his face.

"I-I'm sorry I did that, I panicked and—" I stammered, thinking that he was upset with my use of power. But Thane walked right past me, grabbing the male that was on top of me by his hair and forced him to his knees. I stared at his chest that was slowly healing from the wounds. My focus drifted over to Xavier who took his dagger to the throat of the male that attacked Nova and sliced so deep that his head fell to the side, hanging by a thread as blood gushed from the stump of his neck.

"Thane don't lose your composure," Nova said in a calm, soothing voice from my side. I could tell she was doing her best to bring Thane back from whatever darkness he had traveled to in his mind.

He glanced up at us with eyes as dark as coal and my breath stuck in my throat. A dark shadow cast over him as I saw his chest rising and falling with each breath he took. He was filled with rage, and no one could bring him down.

"Get over here," Thane commanded while staring at me and I shuffled toward him, scared of the repercussions if I didn't.

I shuffled forward until I was in front of the man who squirmed under Thane's grip. "Hold his head back," he instructed me. Stepping behind the man, I placed my hands that were slick with sweat on each side of his head and looked at Thane in confusion.

"Open your fucking mouth," he spat at the man on his knees. The male refused and Thane's head began to tremble with how hard he was clenching his teeth.

"Release his head."

I did as I was told just in time for Thane to deliver a punch to the man's jaw. He spat out blood onto the dirt and I swallowed when I saw a lone tooth in the dark red liquid. I took a step back when he looked back up, spitting in Thane's face while maniacally laughing.

"This is going to be good," Xavier said from behind us. I glanced back to see that he and Nova had already slayed the additional men that were begging for mercy on the forest floor and were now focused back on us.

"Hold his fucking head back."

Thane's voice blared in my head, and I scrambled to place my hands back on each side of the man's head, pulling it back to expose his throat. My eyes bulged when Thane held his sword above the man with lips peeled back. "You put your hands on her," he observed. Thane's shadows revealed themselves at his feet and snaked up the man's body, forcing their way into his mouth and holding it open.

The man did his best to squirm and jerk in my grasp, but the additional shadows held him in place. My breath hitched when Thane began to force the sword down the man's throat. I fought down the bile threatening to escape me as he gagged while Thane's shadows tightened around him.

"Open your fucking eyes and look at her before I let you heal and do it all over again."

His words made my spine stiffen. *He was that angry over another man threatening me.*

The gurgles of the man were harsh as blood filled his mouth, pooling around his lips and down his chin. I could see the blade moving down his throat and I cringed as my pulse quickened imagining the pain he was enduring. When the blade was down to the hilt, Thane slammed his fist into the top of the handle, knocking the Fae's teeth loose.

Unable to scream, he shook uncontrollably as the sword was quickly withdrawn and I let go of his head, allowing him to fall. "Any man that threatens your life will have his ended by *my hand*," he growled, staring into my wide eyes before raising the obsidian blade once more. And in one swipe, the man's head was severed from his body and rolled to the tip of my boots.

Thane cleaned his blade off on the headless body's clothing before sheathing it and pointing ahead. "That way. We're closer to the inn than I thought."

I stood speechless, frozen in time, while staring into the eyes of the severed head below me. The shock on his face perfectly mirrored what I felt, but I was too numb to portray it. I was stuck in my stupor until Nova walked over to me, grabbing my hand and pulling me in the right direction.

I glanced back at the bloodshed behind us, stumbling at the sight of the slain bodies of both Fae and beasts. I quickly regained my footing, and knew, in that moment, that it was only the beginning of the blood that would need to be spilled.

Chapter Thirty-One

The remainder of the trek to the inn was a colorless blur. The need for Nova to hold my hand, guiding me on the path to our destination was almost a requirement. My brain couldn't comprehend the actions of Thane with the Fae that had attacked me.

Flashbacks of his darkened aura and midnight black eyes played in my mind as Thane knocked in a specific sequence on the wooden door of the inn. A small window slid open, showing a pair of eyes before it closed shut and the door swung open. An older, large gentlemen greeted us with outstretched arms.

"Thanasis! How are you? It's been so long!"

They greeted each other, exchanging pleasantries and introducing me last. "This is Amira, she's a guest of Obsidian," Thane said with a sheepish grin, placing his hand on my arm before dropping it. The older man eyed me suspiciously.

"Mortal? A human mortal? Sorry, no rooms available here," he said while shaking his head. My mouth dropped open at his statement while I stared at everyone, bewildered, before they burst out laughing. "I'm only messing, come along this way kiddo," he said while slinging an arm around my shoulders. "Everyone is welcomed by the Yubari."

We stopped in an open area where a few others were eating by an open fire. "Food is to the right. Coffee should be coming out soon, and blankets are to the left. Put some grub in your belly before a good night's sleep why don't ya?" he said while eyeing the blood stains on our clothes. "We can get those cleaned up for ya too. Just leave them outside your doors tonight; have 'em ready before ya wake."

He patted Xavier and Thane on the back, offering a gentle smile to Nova and me, before going back the way we came.

"He said everyone is welcomed by the Yubari. What does that mean?" I questioned while watching the man smile and make small talk with others on his way out.

"The Yubari is a tribe mixed with different kinds of immortals," Nova informed me.

My eyes roamed around the room, noticing the differences between individuals that I hadn't recognized before. Multiple guests mingling around the room had pointy ears and were clearly Fae. A lady sat with her young child, both with ears shaped like mine but longer than usual canines. The child noticed me staring and cowered into its mother. I offered a subtle wave, making her smile and giggle.

A male closer to the fire appeared human until he moved in his seat and his eyes shifted upwards to speak with a companion. He glanced in our direction, landing on Nova, offering a quick bow of his head. His deep, glowing red eyes elicited a gasp from me, and I cast my gaze downward.

"They are a tribe of peace. Regardless of their origin or immortal nature, they are one in the same," Xavier reassured me when he noticed my startlement. I shifted my gaze back to the male who was laughing uncontrollably with a beautiful Fae woman, her hand resting on his knee.

The four of us stuffed ourselves with a deliciously thick soup and warm bread before finding our assigned rooms. Standing in the small hallway, Xavier surveyed the square paper that was handed to him. "Looks like all they had left was three rooms. One with two beds and the others a sing-"

"I'll go with Nova," I interrupted, cutting off Xavier.

"Girl time," Nova sing-songed while bumping her hip into mine.

Thane growled before violently pushing open the door across from our room and stalking inside, shutting the door behind him without a word.

Xavier surveyed the closed door before turning back to us. "He gets more and more irritable every decade." We laughed and said goodnight, understanding that Xavier would wake us in time for breakfast before we continued our journey to Knull in the morning.

Nova and I bathed, throwing on the nightgowns and robes loaned to us by the inn before setting our soiled clothes outside the door as instructed. In unison, we fell face first into our beds and let out deep sighs. Our conversations consisted of everything from questions about Obsidian to how things worked in the mortal realm before silence fell between us.

"Can I ask you something?" I mustered while playing with a lone curl on my head.

Nova shifted to her side, propping her head up with her hand. "Of course."

I mimicked her position, and every fiber of my being wished to ask her what happened back in The Grove. A flashback of the Fae male snapping his own neck caused me to swallow down the bile rising in my throat. Refocusing, and not wanting to ruin the moment, I convinced myself that she would tell me in time and moved on with my original question.

"What the hell was up with Thane back there with those Fae that attacked us?"

Nova inhaled and let out a long breath before arching a brow.

"His eyes... they turned completely dark, and his shadows..." I drifted off in thought for a moment. "His shadows usually have a purple aura to them but in that moment, they were only black. What happened?"

Nova sat upright and studied me for a moment. "I think it might have something to do with protecting those he *really* cares for," she said with a smirk and waggle of her brow. I shook my head in protest before she shook her index finger at me. "Don't do that. You're the one that started this conversation."

I threw myself back on the pillows with outstretched arms. "Nova, you're making something out of—"

"Don't even try it. I see the way he looks at you," she cut in with a serious tone that had me going rigid. "And what the hell was up with you so quickly claiming to room with me?"

I stuttered incoherently, finally shutting up when I realized that Nova wasn't falling for any of the bullshit I was trying, and failing, to deliver.

"You and I both know that you should be in a specific room across the hall getting a release that we both deserve," she pointed with a giggle, and I launched a pillow at her. "Look, Thane may have his moments of being an ass, but he's fighting demons to control himself around you, Amira."

Her words sent chills up my spine.

She leapt from her bed, grabbing both of my arms and pulling me to a standing position. Effortlessly, she pushed me toward the door. "What are you doing?" I asked while trying to find my footing, but I was no match for her strength.

"Doing what you should have already done," she replied while opening the door and throwing me into the hall. My hands moved quickly to retie my robe that had fallen open. "Your mortal lives are too short to live in denial," she said with a wink and nod toward Thane's door, shutting ours with a parting wave.

I ran back to our door and knocked. "Nova open this damn door right now. Or I'll—"

"Exactly what are you going to do, Pixie?" a deep voice said from behind me that I was far too familiar with. I stood up straight and turned around to see a shirtless Thane with his pants hanging low on his hips. The delicious deep v-cut of his hips had lust filling my brain quicker than common sense. He cleared his throat while leaning against his doorframe. I gathered my composure and held my head high.

"Sleep in the hallway, I guess."

I bit my bottom lip in subtle panic before making eye contact with Thane again. A quick huff of a laugh came from him before he stepped aside, holding his door open for me and nodding for me to head inside. I threw my head back and let out a puff of air while walking over to him, pressing my index finger into his firm chest. "No funny business," I said, and he threw his hands up to portray his innocence.

I could hear the lock of the door set into place as I stopped in front of the small window overlooking the clearing. I turned around to the sound of soft thuds hitting the ground. "What are you doing?" I asked in confusion while watching him lay an extra blanket across the ground.

"Getting ready to go to sleep. What does it look like?"

My heart squeezed tight at the thought of him sleeping on the floor.

"Get in bed, Pixie," he instructed me while dropping to the ground.

I removed my robe and climbed into the large bed, sinking into the pillows and thick cover. After a long, silent moment of me staring at the ceiling, I came to my senses.

"Thane," I whispered, only to be met with a long silence. Convinced that he was already asleep, I rolled over to my side.

"Yes, Amira?"

My heart thumped in my chest at the sound of his voice in the dark. I cleared my throat and squeezed my eyes shut. "Get in the bed. We've already slept together so why are we acting like immature adults?"

And why am I acting like I didn't enjoy it in the first place? It's not like he kicked me out the very next morning or went back to treating me like an asshole. Things have been... different ever since.

Thane let out a huff. "For the same reason you're still acting like you're not attracted to me. Like you regret that night and don't want it to happen again."

My eyelids blinked rapidly at his statement. "Just get in the damn bed, Thane."

A deep, husky laugh came from him as he stood and shimmied under the covers. We both remained silent until I rolled onto my side to face him. "What came over you back there?"

I could feel the moment his body stiffened at my question. After a moment, he turned his head and studied my face. I held a breath when his eyes dropped to my lips and he adjusted himself.

"I meant what I said."

I furrowed my brow at his statement, causing him to growl. My stomach rolled at the sound.

"Amira, fate has chosen you for me and me for you. Until you decline the bond, the attraction I have for you is unwavering. The... what I feel..."

His words were clipped as he ground his teeth together. He raised his hand and the sconces on the walls turned off, sending the room into darkness. The moonlight through the small window was all I had to see Thane's face, his honey-colored eyes still focused on mine.

"Tell me that you don't want me. Tell me that what you felt that night was only lust. Say those things out loud and that pull toward each other will be gone," he said quietly. I could hear the nervousness on his tongue and my heart rate increased.

I licked my lips as I considered his offer. His hands were tucked behind his head, and with the blanket down by his hips, I could see every chiseled muscle on his godlike frame. "I can't do that," I whispered as the warmth of him traveled across the sheets.

He finally turned on his side, placing a hand on my cheek. "I won't do anything you don't want me to do. Nor will I force you to make a decision about us."

I ran my tongue across my bottom lip and his eyes followed. Raising his thumb to my lips and mimicking the movement of my tongue had my thighs squeezing together with all their might. "Can I make one request before you close those beautiful eyes of yours?"

My breaths were shallow at his question, forbidding me to speak, so I nodded my head.

"Let me taste you," he pleaded while trailing his hand down to my breast and squeezing, earning him a moan. My eyes popped open to see his full of lust and desire. The magnetic pull between us intensified as I climbed on top of him. Surprise swept across his face before he pulled me down so our lips collided like a wave falling and finding its place back in the ocean. Our tongues glided across each other as I took in his scent that reeled me in. His hands tangled in my hair, and I could feel them form into fists around the curls. Gently yanking my head back, he sat up, removing the straps of my nightgown and drank me in while revealing my bare breasts. His lips grazed one of my nipples before taking it into his mouth.

I dropped my head into his shoulder to stifle the moan produced by his action as he released one nipple to give the other attention. My nails dug into his shoulders, bringing a hum of approval from him. I heard a pop as he removed his mouth from my breast and gazed up at me. "It is impossible to control myself around you," he said as his eyes darkened to a deep gold. I pushed my index finger into his mouth, allowing him to suck it while a heated ache began to build between my thighs. I took it out and sensually wrapped my tongue around my finger, licking it clean before mimicking his popping sound when I removed it from my mouth.

"Then don't," I said breathlessly.

Those words were his cue to do as he pleased with me. And before I could understand what happened, my back was on the bed, his body hovering over mine. The lines and swirls of black ink on his torso were a work of art that I allowed my hands to run over. My eyes flicked up to his, and the world stopped as a smile spread across his face.

"Thane," I whispered huskily. His eyes fell heavily lidded at the sound of his name.

Slowly, he lifted each of my legs onto his shoulders. And without a word, I could feel his warm, wet tongue trail up my slit. A shudder snaked its way up my spine. My hands found his hair as his tongue worked its magic around my clit and the instant buildup was electric. A hand disappears from around my thigh, and I felt two fingers slide into me. I did my best to stifle a deep moan, reaching behind me to grab a pillow but felt it instantly ripped away from my grasp.

"Let them hear how I please you," he said while staring from between my legs, my arousal dripping from his lips as his tongue jutted out to lap it up before he drops back down to my core. His tongue continued its assault as his fingers curled perfectly to rub the spot that sent me to another realm.

"Thane, I'm going to—"

"I know," he said confidently, and it sent me spiraling out of control. My back bowed off the bed as he removed his fingers from inside of me and plunged them into my mouth. The shock from his action was quick as I sucked my own arousal from his fingers while my orgasm ripped through me. My thighs clamped shut around his head as I shook uncontrollably, and my screams were barely muffled by his two fingers in my mouth. I dropped back onto the pillows, breathing as if all oxygen had been sucked from the room.

A satisfied chuckle left him as he crawled back up and under the covers next to me. I immediately reached down to please him and reciprocate what was just given to me. Brushing over his firm cock only increases my lust filled mood, but his hand wrapped around mine, halting any further movement.

"What are you doing?" his husky voice filled with confusion as he pulled my hand away from him and hurt washed over me. "Trust me, there's nothing more I want than to be pleased by you. But you need to learn that it's okay to be pleased and *only* pleased. Go to sleep, Amira. Before the urge to taste you overcomes me again," he ordered before wrapping an arm around my waist and pulling me into his chest.

Our lips were an inch apart as his index fingers trails to my hip once again, writing a word that I tried to decipher through a fogged mind.

"Thane..." I forced his name out while trying to stifle a yawn.

He tucked a stray curl behind my ear and kissed my forehead. His action caused me to forget what I was going to say, forcing my eyelids to fall shut and nuzzle my head down into his chest.

"If only you knew," I heard him whisper before squeezing me tighter, and we drifted into a heavy sleep.

Chapter Thirty-Two

I woke to the smell of bacon and coffee in a bed without Thane.

Forcing myself to sit up with the thick white sheets wrapped around my body, memories of last night flooded my mind, bringing a smile to my face. The door opened to a sight that I could get used to every morning, and I pressed my teeth into my bottom lip. Thane was holding a large tray in one hand and a single rose between his perfect teeth as he shut the door behind him.

"I wasn't sure what you would want to eat, so I grabbed a little of everything," he informed me while setting the rose on the pillow next to me, flashing a toothy smile. I eye the red rose, at a loss for words.

"Ah, forgot," he said and flicked his wrist. The rose shimmered and turned black before my eyes. I picked it up with a smile and my heart threatened to combust at the same time.

"Thank you," I said, still wondering how he could change so much from the time I met him. And unfortunately, that sparked a memory of how I let Raine in so easily. The smile dropped from my face, and I could see Thane was about to question my thoughts when Xavier burst through the door and startled when he saw me in Thane's bed.

"Holy... I uh—" he said while running a hand through his hair before he grinned and tilted his head back and forth. "I mean I was wondering how long the tension was going to build but I wasn't expecting—"

Thane growled before marching over to Xavier. "Have you never heard of knocking you idiot?"

"Heard of it? Yes. Done it? Nope."

Xavier leaned around Thane to wiggle his eyebrows at me and I had to roll my lips inward to stifle my laugh.

"What do you need Xavier?" Thane hissed through clenched teeth.

"Right. Sorry. Heard there's a storm rolling in. We might want to get moving sooner rather than later."

Thane agreed, threatening him to keep what he saw a secret and dismissed him with a door to the face.

"Are they going to begin to treat me differently now?" I asked, worried about what might change with this group I'd grown to call my friends. Thane looked taken aback by my question.

"Why would they treat you differently?"

I shifted in the bed to grab a piece of bacon and took a bite. "That's two High Kings I've fooled around with now. I don't want to be the common whore of multiple realms."

Thane stared at me with an unhinged jaw before bursting out in a laughter so heavy that he bent at the waist. "Amira, darling. No one is going to think that. In Obsidian everyone is well uh... well everyone has... we've slept around. Trust me. No one is going to think any different of you," he said, offering a genuine smile. "Not to mention, the first one was a fluke," he added on, speaking of Raine, and winked, causing me to blush.

The two different sides of him kept me on my toes. One moment he was a cold as ice and the next he was someone I could lay next to forever.

"When your belly is full, let's get dressed and make our way to Knull before we're stuck in that bad weather Xavier mentioned," he claimed while opening the door and grabbing our cleaned clothes from the hall. "We have a brother that needs healing."

~

Saying goodbye to everyone at the inn made me somber, leaving their kindness and the warmth that came with it when I stepped outside. Xavier was right about the storm brewing; the sky overhead was exceptionally dark with hues of purple and pink swirling within. My attention was pulled upwards as the small number of leaves left on the tree branches swayed in the wind, and the temperature had dropped drastically. I could only send up a hope and a prayer that we made it to our destination before the predicted storm hit.

My feet were already tired from the uneven soil a couple of hours in, but I kept my mouth shut with complaints. The water I brought with me only had a few sips left, and I silently cursed myself for not rationing better. I looked down once I felt the change of the ground beneath my boots after walking countless miles. What was dirt and leaves before was now gravel.

"We're here," Thane said from my side. "We must be here. But everything looks so different."

I surveyed the area around us and saw stone steps leading up the side of an extremely tall hill. I winced and dropped down into a squat. "The heavens truly hate me," I said out loud, preparing to climb. "There's no way these legs can handle that."

"And why is that?" A voice presented itself from behind us, causing all of us to jump. Xavier and Thane already had their weapons drawn.

"Let me do the talking," Thane instructed me before focusing on the figure draped in a large gray cloak.

"I am—" Thane began before the figure interrupted him.

"I know who you are, Thanasis. You may have grown up, but you still have the same face as when you were crawling," the figure said. Thin, boney hands reached up and pulled the hood back, revealing a Fae male with no hair and an extremely long white beard. His eyebrows were so bushy that I could barely see his glistening blue eyes. Thane released a chuckle before sheathing his sword and introducing everyone.

Knull offered greetings but his gaze lingered on me before inquiring about our visit.

"And how can I help you all?"

Thane scratched the back of his neck. "Well, long story—"

"Then perhaps we should have some tea while you explain," Knull said, lifting his hand and waving it at the area around us. In the blink of an eye, the surrounding area shifted.

"I knew I wasn't crazy; I just didn't take into consideration you probably glamoured your home to keep us out," Thane announced with a wry smile.

Knull nodded his head while leading us into the dark cabin where the stone steps once were. "I've had a few unruly ones come through here and I didn't want to take any chances. But when I heard your voice," he said, turning around with a smile and holding the door open for us.

The four of us filed into the large, cozy cabin. A pot of tea was sitting on the wooden table and Knull pulled down five cups from his cupboard. "Now tell me why you've come for me after all these years," he inquired, placing the cups at the table and began to pour the fragrant tea. Knull listened intently while Thane informed him about Alix and what we needed from him in order to keep him alive. When Thane was done explaining, Knull looked around the table at us. "Does he always do all the talking?" he asked with a smile and lighthearted chuckle before taking another sip from his cup.

"He likes to hear himself talk," Xavier said and laughed at his own joke. Thane shot him a glare while Nova agreed with Xavier.

I took a long, hard look at the older Fae and wondered why he was depicted as being so terrifying when he didn't seem to be that way.

"And you," Knull said with a tilt of his head. "You haven't spoken a single word. What else is going on?" he asked while standing from his seat and walking over to a cabinet that contained a barrage of glass bottles and jars.

I glanced over at Thane with a sardonic raise of my brow. It was his silent instructions to allow him to lead that had led to my own silence.

"Go ahead," he tapped into my head.

"Well, my... my mother is stuck in Solaris. Against her will, actually. Until they hand me over to Raine who is—"

"A pathetic excuse for a High King," Knull finished for me while mixing liquids. He snuck a peek over his shoulder at me. "I'm assuming they all know who and what you are as well?" he asked. I went rigid and set my cup down on the table while I surveyed the others who carried the same shock at his statement.

"What do you mean?" Thane questioned with both of his hands gripping the table, preparing for the worst.

Is he powerful enough to fight Knull's magic if needed?

"My dearest, Amira. You didn't know about us, but a handful of us knew about you," he said while grinding leaves together in a bowl. "You all can let your guards down; I am no threat to the half-blood."

I loosed a breath and could sense the rest of the table do the same.

"How did you know?" I asked, letting curiosity get the best of me. He released a suppressed laugh, mixing the leaves and liquid together. "I knew that you existed, just not who you were. But the moment I laid my aged eyes on you, your aura and spirit spoke for itself."

I swallowed as my heart pounded in my chest. I didn't *feel* any different since I found out about who I was.

"You speak of Raine requesting you to be handed over in return for your mother, but I can assure you there is no other of your kind in any realm," he continued before pouring his concoction into a clear bottle and pressing a cork into it. "Many will do what is deemed necessary to have their grasp on you for their own sake, waiting for you to realize your full potential to help elevate themselves for a type of power they could never fathom of possessing on their own."

He glided back over to the table, placing the vial down and sliding it over to me. I stared at it before making eye contact with him. "Thank you. For trusting us and helping my brother," I said with tear filled eyes.

He stared back at me and took a deep breath, dropping back down into his chair. "The strongest weapon you need will become available once the blood of a certain witch is spilled," he informed us with a distant gaze. "The destiny and salvation of your realm depends on you, Amira. Do not give up on yourself so easily."

His divination was a blow to my gut. My mouth ran dry trying to understand the advice that was just thrown at me and the sheer confidence in his words.

"From what I gather, you are short on time to save your brother," he said with a weakened smile.

Breaking everyone from their own stupor, Thane clears his throat. "Yes, the elixir that was given to him will only last for so long. We have to try our best to travel overnight through The Glades to get this back to him."

Knull waved a thin hand in the air. "No need. No one can beam or portal here, but I can summon one to come and go."

Elation overcame me at his offer, and Nova let out a squeal of appreciation that widened the smile on Knull's face. He brought three fingers in front of him from each hand and circled them in opposite directions until a dark swirl of smoke formed, creating a portal in his home.

"Make sure your brother drinks every last drop. It will still take a bit of time for him to recover, but he will pull through." I nodded my head in understanding and thanked him as the four of us rose from the table, thanking him again for his hospitality and help. Nova and Xavier were the first to walk through the portal and I moved forward to enter next.

"Amira," Knull called from behind. I turned around to face him as he pulled his hood back over his head. "Don't fight the fire burning within you. Surrender to it," his low, haunting voice offered with confidence.

His long slender fingers rose, offering a wave goodbye and my heart skipped several beats. A fleeting, knowing smile snaked across his slender face.

His facial expression hadn't changed since we arrived. *Until that moment.* Chills slithered down my spine as I registered his words. I raised my own hand to bid farewell with my brow etched in confusion. Thane's hand grasped mine and we stepped through the portal back to Obsidian.

Chapter Thirty-Three

We landed back in Obsidian with the elixir that had hope blooming in my chest for my brother's recovery. Silas, Raya, Aravis and Anya rushed to our side to ensure we were unharmed and hopeful that we received what was needed. After a long embrace with Raya and quickly informing them about Knull's cure, , we made our way through the palace until we reached the room where Alix lay silently, still battered and bruised from Raine's wrath.

"We'll give your family privacy," Thane whispered from behind me as I stood in the doorway clutching the clear vial near my chest. I thanked everyone before grasping Raya's hand, asking her to stay. The rest of our circle disappeared down the halls out of sight and we stepped into the room where Tessa sat staring at me with widened eyes. She bounded across the room until she was in front of me, gripping my shoulders.

"What happened? Are you guys okay?" she rushed out while scanning every inch of me. I let a small laugh release, and I assured her that we were okay. She requested details, but I held up the small glass cylinder instead, bringing another wide-eyed reaction as she studied the swirling green liquid.

"Let's take care of our brat of a brother first," I said with a lazy smile. Tessa nodded her head in agreement while flashing a smile at Raya as we walked over to the bed. I uncorked the vial carefully and nodded at my sister, indicating for her to open our brother's mouth. She lifted his head slightly and I poured every drop until there was nothing left. And then we were left hanging by a thread of anticipation.

"Knull said it will take some time for him to fully heal, but he was confident that it would work as needed," I whispered while waiting for a sign that it was working.

My prayers were answered when I saw the minor cuts on his flesh slowly healing and fading into his brown skin. "It's working," Tessa gasped from the other side of the bed. We sat and watched as the elixir slowly ran its course on our brother. My heart swelled when I saw Raya staring at Alix silently as if she was his blood as well.

We spent a few hours together at Alix's side while I explained the journey to Knull and the escapades that came with it. Wrapping my head around my own stories, I left the two of them behind while I stepped away to catch a breath. Releasing the doorknob, I found Thane sitting against the wall right outside of Alix's door.

"How is he?" he asked with a concerned expression while standing. I smiled and filled him in on Alix's recovery after administering the elixir. Thane ran a relieved hand through his hair and down the side of his face while releasing a long breath.

I studied the man that never hesitated to take a risk traveling through The Glades to help my family. "Thank you," I murmured, and his gaze focused on me. "For everything. For letting us stay here and for taking me to Knull."

"You say that as if you expect anything less," he responded while folding his arms across his chest and leaning his shoulder into the stone wall.

I raised my brows and mimicked his action with my arms,

leaning into the wall with my shoulder as well. Tilting my head, I responded, "I'm sorry, did we so quickly forget how you treated me when we first met?"

Thane blanched at my reply, biting his lower lip and scratching the back of his neck. "What exactly will it take for you to forget about all of that?" he asked with a sheepish smile that could bring any woman to her knees.

I raised my chin with a devilish grin. "What are you offering?"

Thane eyed me from head to toe, sending a wave of heat to my core and causing me to blank on my witty responses. He offered me his hand. "I have an idea. Do you trust me?"

His question had my mind calculating exactly how many people I trusted in this world, including Fae. And I was not sure what emotion settled within when I realized he was one of them. I smiled and placed my hand in his, resulting in him yanking me forward until I clashed into his hard chest. A deep smile bloomed on his face before we were surrounded by his magic and beamed away.

We landed underneath a large weeping willow tree and my eyes widened with surprise when I focused on the leaves. Each one was a bright, shimmering purple that illuminated the area. "Where are we?" I whispered in awe while wandering over and raising a hand to gently feel a tiny purple leaf above my head. I felt him draw near before I heard his voice behind me again. "We're on the outskirts of Obsidian. This place is a secret keepsake of mine," he said on a quiet breath. "My father, he—"

His cut off sentence sent chills up my arms. Slowly, I turned to face him. I didn't know why, but my hands reached out to rub both of his upper arms in comfort while forcing a small smile of my own to encourage him to continue speaking. His tongue ran across his bottom lip before he sucked it in and clenched his jaw. "My father created this tree out of his own rare magic. My mother's favorite color was purple, and he wanted somewhere for them to go whenever they got in a disagreement. A place to clear their mind in silence and come back together as a team to continue ruling over Obsidian."

The distant look in his eyes had me catching my breath. "You don't speak of your parents. Are they—"

"Dead? Yes."

His answer was so quick and clipped that it startled me.

"I know that you noticed the scars on my back," he commented, and I choked on air at how blunt he was. "I'm hoping that if I give a piece of myself to you, then you will take that as my peace offering. To never question my feelings toward you again. And understand how sorry I am for putting you through hell and back. What do you say?"

I couldn't look away from his eyes that carried a heavy weight of emotion as he stared at me, waiting for an answer. I brought my palm to his cheek and nodded.

"Deal."

His eyes lit up at my answer and he blew out a long, drawn breath.

"Here goes nothing," he murmured while holding out a hand toward the deep brown bench near the tree trunk. I sat down on a shaky breath, wondering what story he was about to tell me to get me to completely forgive him. He got comfortable next to me, and it pained me that there was such ample room between us, but I gave him his space. Without looking at me, he stared off into the distance.

"Centuries ago, my family went to the realm of Unetica with the intentions to bring peace across all realms. When they arrived, it was too late to know that it was an ambush waiting for them," he said while resting his back against the bench. "I watched from a distance as they pushed my parents to their knees with swords drawn. And before I could formulate a proper plan, I beamed my sister back to Obsidian knowing that she hadn't yet learned how to transport and wouldn't be able to return."

I forced myself to take a breath when he paused to run his

hands down his thighs. "Then I surrendered myself to their army. I offered myself to them, knowing how powerful I was at a young age. I knew they would want me. I begged them to take me in exchange for the life of my parents and the people of Obsidian. I knew deep in my heart that once my parents were dead, they would infiltrate our home."

His words fell silent, and I shifted myself a few inches closer to him. "Did they accept your offer?" I asked hesitantly. Thane nodded his head, his eyes filled with vulnerability as his hands molded into clenched fists. "They did. I watched as my parents screamed and begged for them to ignore me and my offer. I watched as my mother vomited on the ground when they gave me the same number of lashes for the soldiers that were murdered when my parents fought back against their ambush."

I stared at him, wide-eyed and filled with horror. "The scars on your back," I whispered in mournful understanding. Thane's jaw clenched so tightly that I feared it would break. I reached a hand out to bring him back from the darkness he was returning to.

"Thane..."

He raised a gentle hand, indicating for me to let him finish.

"I served them for five decades, doing whatever magic they asked of me. Working as a slave to them to ensure they wouldn't harm the people of Obsidian or come for my parents. I was content in knowing that my family was safe at home in our realm," he continued and released a deep sigh. "Until a day came when my parents requested to renegotiate the terms of my imprisonment. The High King of Unetica agreed to a discussion, and my parents met in their courtyard."

Thane fell silent again as he brought his fist up to his mouth, biting so hard that a trickle of blood streamed down his wrist. I quickly moved so close to him that our thighs touched and grabbed his fist in my hand. His usually golden eyes were black with rage, but this time I wasn't scared of him. Instead, my heart filled with his pain as I firmly pulled his fist from his mouth and placed it in my lap. "It's okay, you don't have to finish. I forgive you. You don't have—"

"The entire realm came to the courtyard to witness another foul meeting. Each one of them was as evil and twisted as their High King. I watched, chained to the ground as they laughed and chanted while their King sent his dark magic straight through my parent's hearts."

His words were a knife to my heart as tears welled in my eyes.

"Whatever deep rooted magic was embedded in my blood came to life in that moment and I broke the chains that were meant to dampen my powers," he hissed. I swallowed at the rage he was fighting to tamper down.

"And what did you do next?"

A deep, unnerving laugh escaped him before he threw his head back against the bench and slowly turned to face me. "I murdered every single one of them."

His confession turned my blood cold.

"The entire realm's blood is on my hands, and I don't regret it for one second. And I would do it again for those I love," he confessed, his voice a husky velvet sound to my ears. The darkness of his eyes spread to the edges until the whites of his eyes disappeared. "Every time I look at Raine—every time I think about him—he reminds me of the High King of Unetica."

Thane's breaths were elevated and labored as he provided that detail while baring his teeth. "I had to force myself to not rip Raya to shreds knowing that she is his blood. I had to come to my senses to understand she is nothing like him."

I recoiled when he mentioned Raya. His words angering me for a moment before I understood where he was coming from.

"Why are you telling me all of this?" I questioned through silent tears. He could have stopped after telling me where his scars came from, but he continued. His darkened eyes eased back to gold as he brought a palm to the side of my neck. "Because I need you to know the access you have to me. There's nothing in any world, any realm that I wouldn't do for you, Amira. And I'm sorry I ever gave you the notion to believe otherwise."

His words chipped away the last pieces of any defensive shield I had in place over my heart. The vulnerability in his tone ignited a fire in me that I couldn't put out if my life depended on it. And before I could stop myself, the magnetic pull between us intensified. I leapt into his lap and his grip on my waist tightened with lust as our deep, labored breaths synchronized.

"I'm scared, Thane. I don't know anything about a mate, and I'm scared to—"

His thumb ran across my bottom lip, halting my words.

"Take as much time as you need, Pixie. If you're going to be mine forever, I want it to be of your own free will. And until then, I'll take whatever pieces of you that you're willing to give me," he said with eyes filled with hunger. Eyes that I could see myself getting lost in for the rest of my life. My hips unintentionally rocked back and forth on his lap. A rush of desire washed over me when Thane pressed his teeth into his lip and I could tell he was fighting to clamp down the emotions threatening to consume him as well. He raised a hand, cupping the back of my head and forcing our lips to come together in a blazing heat of passion.

Our hands flew to each other's clothing, frantically working to undress each other before we were both successfully naked and Thane placed me back on his lap. The intensity of the pull between us brought our lips back together as two worlds collided.

After a moment, I raised myself until I felt his length pressing against my entrance. Our eyes met between heavy breaths, and I shuddered when his hands on my hips slowly pulled me back down. My head fell back as the length of him pushed into me and I was unsure how I'd take him in this position.

"Don't do that," he whispered on a suppressed groan.

"Do what?" I croaked, forcing myself to speak through the intensity of trying to settle myself in his lap. Attempting to take every inch of him in this position had me fighting demons I didn't know I possessed.

"Don't act like you can't take me," he said as one arm wrapped around my waist and the other got lost in my hair. "You were fucking made for me."

His words barely had time to register before he forced me down until he fully rested inside of me. I produced a moan that released every ounce of air from my lungs, and I let my head fall on his shoulder. The fingertips he ran down my spine made me shiver as my hips rocked rhythmically and I heard his breath hitch at the steady movement.

I raised my head and placed my forehead against his. A wide grin bloomed across his face, "Try not to break me, beautiful."

A playful laugh released from me before I did an assault of my own, bouncing until I felt myself tighten around my favorite part of him. But my plan backfired when my eyes began to flutter shut letting me know I was quickly reaching the edge of my climax. Thane forced me to lean back, bringing his mouth to my nipple and sucking hard. "Thane," I cried out. He moved his head to my other breast and flicked his tongue at my hardened nipple.

"Tell me you don't feel that between us," he said while raising his hips from the bench and I felt every inch of him thrust inside of me. "Tell me that every time I'm inside of you, you don't feel like I was made for you. Molded for you," he said on another thrust, and I felt myself about to topple over the edge when I felt his shadows wrap around my throat. "You can only deny your heart's desires for so long before it bursts, Amira. And I'll be right here to hear you speak the words to snap our bond into place."

His last statement had me teetering on the edge of destruction when his thrusts quickened. My brain was trying to decide between replaying his words in my mind or coming uncontrollably before it settled on the latter option.

Our gazes connected, followed by our mouths, as we fell over the edge together, our tongues dancing in unison. I convulsed in his arms with his mouth catching every moan I released at the feel of him unraveling beneath me. His body jerked and he moved his mouth to my neck, biting and sucking in a moment of ecstasy as I felt him release inside of me.

We remained in the same position for what felt like eternity while we worked to catch our breaths.

Slowly, Thane lifted me from him with a sharp intake of breath and a hiss. He stood, putting his clothes on before rushing to get mine together and dressing me. "You don't have to do that," I whispered while standing to let him clasp my pants.

His golden eyes connected with mine. "I know."

He plucked me from the ground and spun us to sit back on the bench while he cradled me in his lap. His large hand playing with a strand of my curls had my core tightening with an aching heat again.

"Thane..." I said, snapping us back to reality. "I've decided I'm going to give myself over in exchange for my mother."

I could feel his hard body stiffen while he held me. My pulse quickened when he brought his face down to search my eyes. "You're not a quitter, Amira." I swallowed at his affirmation.

"Then what do we do?" I questioned. I was out of answers on how to get my mother back and end Raine at the same time.

Thane sat me back upright on the bench. "We call one last meeting as if we're going to hand you and Raya over," he said in a serious tone. "And we fight."

His plan froze me in place.

"We convince them to meet somewhere other than Bavaria. Strike at Raine's ego. Claim that he's terrified his power isn't strong enough against us to meet somewhere where magic is allowed. His pride won't allow for him to back down."

I shook my head at the plan. I refused to have the blood of the people that had helped me on my hands. Thane placed both of his hands on the sides of my face. "You always solve everyone else's problems, let me solve yours," he begged with sincerity. "I've got you, Amira."

Those four little words spun my world upside down. Tears fell like an open river as they played over and over in my head freely. His thumbs reached up to swipe them away as I nodded my head.

It's been so long since I've had someone carry the weight of my burdens with me.

Chapter Thirty-Four

Spending the night in Thane's bed was a blessing and a curse.

A blessing because feeling safe and secure in his arms put me in a deep and comfortable sleep. A curse because that deep sleep made me want to waste away in bed for the rest of my life.

Unfortunately, this morning we were both awakened by a pounding at his door. "Thane, you need to come down here quickly," Nova chimed from the other side. "You too, Amira."

The sound of my name made me blush. Did the others know now too?

Thane's arm around my waist tightened and released before we both jumped out of bed to find appropriate clothing and raced down the halls to the library where everyone was huddled around Anya. Aravis connected a worried look with mine before sadness washed over them. "I'm afraid we're too late to get the upper hand," he said while resting a hand on a nearby table.

I heard the pounding of my heart in my ears as Thane pushed through to look at the ball of magic floating between Anya's hands. I squeezed in next to him to see Raine and his army marching through the fields of Medlar. My breathing became sporadic as Aravis' words played in my head.

We're too late.

"I received a message this morning that the Reaper has rescinded our agreement of Raine being banned from Medlar," Aravis spoke.

Thane spun around to face him with a deep scowl. "How is that even possible?"

Aravis shook his head with a hand raised to his brow. "He is the Reaper. He can do what he wants. He answers to no one in the Under World."

Thane cursed under his breath, resisting the urge to lash out. "Did he say what the collateral was to void your agreement?"

Aravis' eyes wandered to Raya who stiffened under his gaze while he admitted to paying a visit to the Under World after receiving the message that morning.

"He has promised the soul of an heir. His sister."

Anger consumed me as I felt the cold shoot from the tips of my fingers and slam into the tiled floor beneath me, cracking it. Nova's hands rested on my shoulders, "It's okay."

"There's one more issue," Anya said quietly. Thane glared at her, waiting for another blow to be delivered. "I can no longer feel the enchantment I placed on your home in Medlar."

The remaining oxygen in my lungs was sucked out as my knees went weak. The room spun and Nova caught me before I hit the floor.

"Close it," Thane snapped at Anya who disbursed the globe between her hands. "I'm done playing by his rules. We leave now. Gather your weapons," he commanded from where he stood. The room was silent as Silas bounced on his toes in anticipation.

"If you don't want to defend my mate's family, you have a right to do so. But just know that you will no longer have a home in Obsidian when I return."

His words had me blinking at lightning speed as I could hear a pin drop in the room.

He called me his mate. They all know now.

"Calm down, Amira. We knew the moment we brought you here. We could smell Thane's arousal from a mile away," Silas said, earning him a slap to the back of the head from Nova.

"Y-you knew this whole time?" I asked, astonished at his disclosure. Everyone in the room nodded their heads.

"It's why he was such a brooding asshole from the start," Xavier announced with a chuckle. Raya stared at me in shock before explaining she had an inkling but wasn't fully sure.

"Would everyone please shut up. She hasn't accepted the bond and it's not priority right now. Her family and realm are," Thane boomed from the center of the room, commanding attention.

"You're crazy for not claiming that," a familiar voice whispered from behind me and I whipped around to see Tessa. My arms flew around her, and she squeezes me back. "I was listening from the doorway," she said and shrugged her shoulders.

"If anyone wishes to remain here and not fight, now is your time to speak. You will not be harmed," Thane notified everyone in the room. A sob formed in my throat when no one spoke or moved. This room was filled with Fae who had become family that I would lay my life down for as I wholeheartedly knew they would do for me.

Thane inclined his head with pride before instructing everyone to meet on the training deck in thirty minutes.

"There's one more bit of information from my visit to the Reaper this morning," Aravis chimed once more. Almost everyone ran their hands over their face in frustration. "In exchange for backing out of our agreement, the Reaper gave me information that we have one weapon that may help us exponentially... but it'll take the blood of a certain witch to summon it."

The words were so similar to Knull's that I choked. I stared at the floor while running through my mind on who they were talking about when the realization dawned on me.

"Lorena," I said through the channel to Thane who looked at me with a flare of alarm and understanding.

The room disbursed after everyone exchanged confused look about Aravis' last bit of information.

I turned back around to face my sister. "Tessa there's no way for you—"

"I already know I'm no match for Fae," she said with a smile. "But my little sister is."

Tears formed in her eyes as she grabbed both of my hands. "Amira, you have to come back to us. It's not an option."

I bowed my head while holding back tears of my own. "You have my word."

We embraced for a long moment before separating for me to prepare for our departure. Before I left the library, Thane grabbed my wrist to catch my attention. "You're not fully trained on controlling your magic," he pointed out with a concerned expression.

"Are you saying I cannot go?" I asked him with anger-laced words.

Thane shook his head. "I just wanted to make sure you're confident in holding your own in case things take a turn." His eyes searched my face for confirmation. And I could see the worry in his eyes that something would happen to me. "Your choice. It's always your choice, Amira."

My lips pursed before the corners tipped upwards.

"No matter what happens to me, promise me that you'll save my family," I said while stepping toward him.

Thane went rigid, his mouth popping open. "Amira, I can't do that. You will always be my first priority."

I shook my head while stepping closer to him. "Promise me."

His face turned to a pained expression, and I could see he was preparing to refuse my request again.

"If it were Athena, wouldn't you want everyone that was in this room to promise you the same?" I questioned and pressed my palms to his chest. "Promise me right here, right now. Or I will never forgive you for choosing me over them."

His hands wrapped around my wrists, his eyes turning a slightly darker hue while he calculated my ultimatum.

"You have my word," he muttered before closing his eyes and looking away. I took in a deep breath and released it. "He's going to take everything from me," I said on a shaky breath. Thane's eyes darted back to mine before they hardened.

"Over my dead body," he growled.

Chapter Thirty-Five

Tessa was quickly braiding my hair into a long plait in our room when the door cracked open. Seeing Raya's white hair startled me, reminding me of Raine in that moment. I flashed an inviting smile, and she stepped in with a piece of clothing in her hand. Walking to stand next to Tessa in the mirror, she placed the deep purple garment on the dresser.

"I'll be by your side in Medlar, but I felt that you needed a bit more protection out there. I hope you don't mind the alterations," she said timidly.

I grabbed the piece of thick clothing and my shoulders dropped forward in shock. I turned my head to see Raya with wary eyes. "You cut the dress you gifted me into a vest?" I asked in awe.

Raya nodded with a deep grin. "And with a little help from Anya, there's additional coverage with a leather underlay."

I ran my hand across the fabric that was much thicker than the dress once was. The harsh memory of it saving my life on the dais back in Solaris flooded me and my fingers clutched the garment tighter.

"Oh, I almost forgot. She put some type of enchantment on it where it will change color if you place your hand over your heart. Apparently, it will know your mood," she added on. The three of us furrowed our brows, trying to decipher how magic like that worked. "Dark magic is a whole different world," Raya said, pulling a laugh from each of us.

It was quiet for a moment as Tessa finished off my braid. I stood from the chair and threw my arms around Raya, squeezing her so tightly that if she wasn't Fae, I would have broken her ribs. When I let go, I was stunned to see Tessa step forward and mimic my actions. My wide eyes connected with Raya's before she reciprocated the hug and squeezed Tessa back.

"Thank you," Tessa said. "For being the protector my sister needed when I couldn't be there."

Raya swallowed and nodded with a genuine smile. "She was the sister I needed in a dark time as well." I forced myself to fiddle with the vest on the dresser to avoid my emotions taking over the moment. Tessa cleared her throat while stepping back a few steps.

"Both of you have to come back. Just... I can't handle being separated again. Please just—" her words broke as she cleared her throat once more. "Just promise to walk back through these doors again."

Since I had entered this world, Tessa had always been the one to hold it together. But in that moment, I could read on her face how terrified she was of losing everything just like me. The three of us held each other in an embrace before I gathered what was needed, donning the vest Raya gifted to me with leather pants and boots, and headed to the sparring platform. I stopped along the way to place a kiss atop Alix's head and check his progress.

"Don't worry about him while you're gone. I'll take care of him *when* he wakes," Tessa assured me.

My shoulders relaxed at her reassurance. "I know."

Within the hall, Thackery bound up to Raya and dug his claws into her clothing, climbing up to her shoulder. She did her best to fight the black cat off of her, but he shoved his head against hers, and reluctantly, she scratched behind his ears with a pat to his back before placing him on the ground. "I don't know what your obsession with me is, buddy," she said while turning her nose upwards. The cat purred and stared as we continued toward the platform.

Everyone was waiting for us when we reached the center of the platform. Instinctively, I stopped at Thane's side and noticed Atlas seated next to him. My brows shot up as my concern darted to Thane. "He refused to leave your side knowing where we were going. He's bonded to me, so he feels our fate," Thane explained, and my emotions were riding higher than moments before. I walked around Thane to hug the giant wolf who buried his head into my body.

"I'm unsure of Raine's plans when we reach Medlar, therefore we will need as much power as we can bring. Additional Vaternians will be on guard at all times throughout all of Obsidian to ensure safety if our wards should falter," Thane said before finding Tessa. "You and Alix will be safe here, I assure you."

Tessa dipped her head and thanked Thane.

Xavier strode over to me and began sliding multiple daggers into specific placeholders of my vest that I hadn't noticed. "High King's orders. Better safe than sorry," he said with a wink before wandering over to Raya and asking if she had what she needed. She held up the palms of her hands while wiggling her fingers with a smile, earning a chuckle from Xavier who shook his head.

My eyes roamed the platform before it dawned on me that Athena was nowhere to be found.

"Where is Athena?" I whispered to Nova who was on the other side of me. She leaned her head into mine, "Thane forbade her from coming with us." My eyes snapped to hers as she licked her lips with a wince. "You and her in one place would send every Fae with bad intentions into a feral rampage."

My mind raced as I remembered that I never asked what

magic Athena held. I remembered her strength, but outside of that, I didn't know why Thane was so protective of her.

"We won't be able to beam or fly directly there because they'll see us coming. We can beam a few miles out from Medlar and make our way there by foot," Anya announced, pulling me from my thoughts. All of us hugged Tessa goodbye, Silas taking longer than everyone else, and watched her head back into the palace with a servant before we huddled together.

The warm sensation of Anya's magic wrapping around us no longer felt foreign as I prepared to return home for the first time in what felt like an eternity.

~

We dropped into Medlar, and it felt like a fever dream to be back in a mortal realm. Everything felt different from the realms I'd resided in over the past few months. The air wasn't as pure, and as I took in my surroundings, the colors weren't as vibrant.

"Well, we're definitely in a mortal realm," Silas mumbled from behind me. And I could sense Nova's hand connecting with the back of his head before it even happened. I laughed at the action but agreed with Silas.

"He is right though. And it's not like our king does much to help Medlar," I said remembering how our new king could care less about the citizens of Medlar.

We fell into stride with Aravis and Thane towards my home and I ended up side by side with Nova. Her silence was deafening, and I wanted to know what was running through her mind. "What are you thinking about?" I asked her with a bump of my shoulder. She cast a side glance at me with her lips pulled up in a pursed smile.

"How our time is limited in this world. Some more than others," she said with her smile slightly faltering.

She's talking about me.

I could see in her expression that she was terrified of me fighting if we needed to. And if I was honest, I was scared as well. I understood that I was half Fae, but what qualities did that give me? If I got impaled, would I heal rapidly or die? Would I live forever or have the same lifespan of a mortal?

Nova linked her arm with mine as we continued to walk. "And with us immortals, we're like a moth to a flame with danger —not knowing our life is about to end because we believe that we're irrevocably invincible."

I chewed on my bottom lip as I processed her words. "Aren't you though?"

"Aren't we what?" Nova replied.

"Aren't all Fae and immortals invincible within reason?"

Nova moves her head from side to side. "More or less. There are ways to end the life of an immortal. Obviously if we lose our head, we can't regenerate that. But there are worse ways."

My eyes squinted at her explanation as I surveyed her chewing on her bottom lip.

"There are other ways. If one's mate dies, the other won't survive for long after. The bond and their heart simply cannot handle the pain of the loss. A bond makes two beings become one," she said with a slump in her shoulders. I could feel her pain travel between us.

"Have you witnessed… that?" I asked hesitantly. Slowly, Nova nodded in answer.

"My brother."

My heart broke in half when I heard the hurt in her voice.

The group stopped abruptly as Aravis and Thane came to a halt. We moved close together as Thane motioned for us to come to him. "We make no deals or agreements, and we take no prisoners. If we spill blood, we deal with the consequences later."

The others were unphased by his words, but all eyes landed on Raya with caution. "If you're worried about me feeling some type of way about my brother's blood on your hands it's unnecessary.

I'll kill him first if I get the opportunity," she said nonchalantly while picking at her nail.

"Your brother is mine," Thane said and Raya snapped her head up.

"Guess it's a race then," she responded with a cocked brow and nodded her head in my direction. "You have competition with this one as well."

Thane stiffened at her statement, peeling his lips back as his eyes widened and settled into a hardened glare. His next words were a blow to my soul. "Priority is Amira. If things get so heavy that we can't handle it, whoever is closest to her beams her out of here and back to Obsidian."

You promised me, I hissed straight into his head. His tongue ran across his bottom lip as he ignored me.

"That's an order," he finished. I heard agreement from the circle, and I ground my teeth together. We divided back up and resumed walking as I fell into stride with Thane.

"You promised me," I seethed. He grabbed my arm, pulling me to the side and ordered the others to continue ahead. Aravis cast a glare in Thane's direction to tread lightly while Atlas tossed a threat with a low growl. Thane loosened his grip before he dropped his head down to my eye level.

"Do you have any idea what it's like to live a hundred lives without your other half?" he hissed back. "Do you know what it's like to constantly feel incomplete?"

I stared at him dumbfoundedly. His lips rolled inward when I didn't respond, and his large hands found my biceps. "Constantly having a fucking pull to a mortal realm and unsure why is *crippling*, Amira. And then I found you. Yet I realized we would most likely never have the bond sealed because our two realms cannot get along because one is immortal and one is not. And I—"

His teeth clenched together, and I could see the muscles of his jaw tick.

"Tell me that you don't feel more than lust for me, and I'll retract my order. Tell me that you decline our bond, and I will retract it," he said, and the blood drained from my face. His dark brow cocked, waiting for a reply.

"Say it, damnit," he spat with fire in his eyes.

I forced myself to swallow past the dryness in my throat. I wanted to lie to both of us and denounce my feelings for him. The thought of lying and declining the bond made my stomach roll.

"I can't do that. I won't," I breathed.

Thane nodded his head with a husky, low laugh. Standing up straight, he grabbed my jaw, lifting my head to connect our gazes. "I know, Pixie. Just waiting for you to realize everything I'm ready to give you." He planted a drawn-out kiss to my forehead and forced us to move in the direction of the group as butterflies threatened to burst from my stomach, through my throat and out my mouth. I was fighting against fire to stop the feelings I had for Thane from forming.

I didn't want a knight in shining armor. I didn't need one.

"My armor isn't shiny," his words floated into my head, and I startled, noticing that I accidentally sent my thought down our channel. *"It has cracks and scratches and is the furthest thing from shiny. But it works just as good to protect those I love."*

Those four letters had me tripping over my own feet as Thane caught my arm. I stared up at him as he stared straight ahead at the gravel road leading to my home in Medlar. We moved so quickly that I didn't have time to process his admission.

We traveled up the gravel road to my home and what I saw had my stomach in knots. Thane reached out to stop me but I quickly dodged his grasp and raced up the steps of my home to the bloodied, limp body on the porch. I dropped to my knees next to Knox while I surveyed the large open wound in his side. The others surrounded us as he spat up blood.

"No, no, no! Knox, what happened?" I asked while grabbing his hand and Aravis stood above him surveying the damage.

Knox let out multiple wet coughs, and I wiped the blood from his mouth. "I came to look for you when I saw so many unknown men marching through. When I got here, a man with long white hair showed up demanding to speak with your father," he stopped midway to cough and I glanced at Aravis to see what could be done. Aravis subtly shook his head to let me know Knox couldn't be saved and my stomach plummeted.

"Your father opened the door and I remember seeing a long blade flash toward him so I—"

"You stepped in front of him and took the blow," I finished for him while wiping the sweat from his brow. Knox let out a whisper of a laugh.

"Does that finally grant me a date with you?"

His question squeezed my heart so hard I was afraid it would stop. I nodded my head reverently as a tear fell from my eye and onto his chest. "Yes, Knox. I'll take you up on that date. Just tell me when and where."

A deep smile spread across his face, and I felt a tight squeeze on my hand before I saw him slowly slip away from this world. I said his name repeatedly, hoping he held on, but I knew he was gone when his brown eyes glossed over and stared upwards. I dry heaved as Thane pulled me upright. My pain cut deeply when Silas gently moved his hand over Knox's eyes, closing his eyelids.

My father.

As I was about to let them know we must find him, I heard a laugh I hadn't heard in a long time and my blood ran cold.

Thane's grasp tightened as everyone turned toward the sound of laughter, ready to wield their magic. I turned to join them, and my breaths were instantly uneven and shallow. My eyes darted around the surrounding area, silently begging for this to be an illusion. Every muscle in my body was so tense that they could snap at any moment when my eyes finally focused on her for the first time since she created the bargain that started everything.

My body shook as I took in the sight before me, the sight of the woman that changed the course of my entire life and left me fighting to put the pieces back together.

"Do not act on impulse," Thane demanded. His words floated through my head that was already hazy and filled with thick, impulsive clouds of rage.

Tremors flowed down my arms as her laugh echoed louder, piercing my ears. She called for the name of an unknown man in the distance. My tremors increased as I saw a large figure dragging my father from beyond the trees. Sweat trickled down my spine, and the impulsiveness won. I lunged forward at the sight of him, but Thane's strength outmatched mine as he firmly wrapped an arm around my thrashing form.

My father fought to remain standing but was thrown to his knees in front of us.

The panic I felt moments ago dissipated as anger and fury took over every inch of my body. My gaze connected with my father's, and I stood tall, refusing to let him see any trace of worry on my face.

I clenched my teeth, pressing my nails into the palms of my hands while averting my gaze.

And for the first time in a long time, I stared directly into the eyes of Lorena.

Chapter Thirty-Six

Lorena's howling persisted and I studied the changes in her appearance since the last time I had seen her. The lines etched into her pale skin had deepened. Her blue eyes were sunken but still held that same eerie look as before. A shiver crept up my spine when her voice shrieked with annoyance, bringing me back to the moment.

"How many lives will need to suffer before you just give yourself over, child?" she questioned with a shove to my father's back. I could see the bruising on each side of his face, and I felt the bile rise in my throat.

"Dad..." I croaked, my body feeling weak, and I leaned into Thane for balance.

"Sweetheart do not hand yourself over. I know everything, always have," my father rushed out. Warmth bloomed within as I realized my father had always known I wasn't his biological daughter, yet he loved me as his very own. "You're special and that's all they –"

His words were cut short when a figure revealed itself in the distance, and long white hair came into sight. My breath caught as I heard a groan from Raya. A slow clap came from Raine as he surveyed us on the porch of my childhood home, claiming a spot at Lorena's side. I glanced over where her arm was now re-attached from where it once was ripped away by Raine's fury.

Yet here they stand together in unison.

"Wow. Brought the whole calvary for a mere mortal," he said mockingly while halting his demeaning clapping. A sneer spread across his pale face when he spotted Thane so close to me and moved to locking his gaze onto me. "It seems the High King of Obsidian finally got bored with his toy and is ready to hand you back to your rightful owner."

My hands tingled with the urge to send ice straight to his heart.

"Don't display your power. It will only make them fight harder for you. Save it for if you desperately need to use it," Thane instructed me.

"You do not own her, Raine. Release her father and let's discuss this like adults," Aravis said from the stairs he was now descending, and everyone else followed suit. Raine tilted his head to the side and eyed Aravis suspiciously.

"I-I'm confused. It seems her father is already free," Raine said with a sinister smile.

The ice in my veins was fighting to come through as I saw the pain spread across my father's face while he remained kneeling on the ground. "I love you, Amira. I always have and you will always be my daughter," he professed and my heart swelled with every type of emotion I could conjure.

Raine made an exasperated noise before raising a boot to the side of my father's face. Atlas leapt toward them at Thane's command, a blur of motion that was halted almost as soon as it had begun. His large body was thrown backwards with a loud whimper, eliciting a gasp from me. I moved to run to his side, but Thane tightened his grip on me, assuring me through our channel that Atlas was okay.

"Perks of having a witch as an ally. They know how to create things like forcefields to keep unwanted mutts out," Raine announced while sneering at Atlas who padded back to us looking defeated. I broke from Thane's grasp and got halfway down the stairs before I was stopped by Aravis. "You cannot save him. Do not sacrifice yourself to suffer alongside him," he said in a hushed tone. He casually cast a glance at Anya who I could tell was calculating how to break the barrier as Silas and Xavier stepped in front of her.

"Get away from him. He has nothing to do with any of this. It's me you want."

The laugh produced by Lorena and Raine made me sick to my stomach. Lorena abruptly stopped laughing, squinting her ice blue eyes. She clicked her tongue and pointed a long, slender finger in my direction. "She knows," Lorena hissed and Raine's eyes blew wide. "She knows she's a half-blood. She's playing us for fools. She didn't flinch at the mention of her real father."

Panic flooded me as my friends moved closer, surrounding protectively while pushing Raya to the middle as well.

Raine's eyes flared at my friends' actions and grabbed my father by the collar. "I'll spare his life for yours and my sister's. Just put your hand in mine, Amira," he negotiated while holding a pale hand out in my direction.

My heart raced at the thought of another bargain. The time ticked by slowly as I weighed my options in my head.

I moved down a step before a firm arm wrapped around my waist. *"Don't even think about it,"* I heard Thane in my head.

"He has my father," I snapped back. Thane tightened his hold on me.

"And do you think your father will live a happy life knowing his daughter is held captive to be bred because she saved his life?"

The truth held within his words brought heavy tears to my eyes that threatened to fall. I held them at bay, refusing to let Raine see the fear he ignited within me.

When I didn't reach for Raine's hand, he curled it into a fist and I was instantly met with the cloudy white eyes I had grown accustomed to in Solaris. I shook my head pleadingly, knowing his next move would be anything but merciful.

"Raine please," I begged while holding his stare.

He nodded, taking a step back from my father. "I will save the bloodshed for your mother."

My mind was confused between relief and panic at the thought of one parent surviving and one dying at the hand of Raine. But before I could breathe a sigh of relief, Lorena stepped forward with her lip curled until it unraveled into a contemptuous smile. Thane stepped forward and my mouth fell agape when my father subtly shook his head, instructing Thane to stop. He halted, reaching back for me and fear surged when I realized my father knew there was no outcome where we both lived. Thane pushed me directly behind him and I peered over his shoulder to see my father smile.

"But I have no such conviction," Lorena proclaimed and cast her hand in my father's direction. A strangled scream fell from my lips as I watched the veins in my father's body turn purple, his eyes bulging from his head as blood dripped from his mouth. Anya and Aravis cast their magic toward Lorena, but it bounced off the barrier.

My scream turned feral as I watched him fall to the side, his eyes rolled back.

"I've got you, Amira. Don't break now. Your people need you. Your family needs you," Thane pleaded, but my scream drowned him out. My tears broke the dam, and my breaths were few and far between. *"Do not let him break you,"* Thane hissed and released me, as if he knew those six words would bring me to my senses. Mustering everything I had left, I gathered myself, wiping the tears from my face and averting my eyes from my father's limp body.

"You may be a half-blood, but you come from dirt," Lorena spat from beside Raine.

My jaw clenched as my mind drifted back to the memory of Raya and me in Solaris—the first time I saw a lotus flower floating in the fountain and Raya spoke of her mother. *"My mother used to tell me that like the lotus flower that is born out of mud, we too must honor the darkest parts of ourselves and the most painful of our life's experiences, because they're what allow us to birth our most beautiful selves."*

This very moment was the most painful experience of my life. If I broke now, my father would die in vain. And that alone would be a dishonor. I brushed my palm over my necklace and drew a dagger from my vest, pressing a palm to my heart. I stared ahead as my vest changed from a deep purple to black. The stone of my necklace shimmering for a moment as the charm from Millie worked its magic. An odd sense of comfort and vigor washed over me when my gaze settled back on Lorena.

"Her blood gets drawn from my hand and no one else's," I said sternly. I wouldn't rest until I saw the life drain from her eyes.

The sounds of swords and daggers being unsheathed around me broke me from my thoughts and I glanced at Thane. "No one else dies because of me. *No one,*" I proclaimed, and he nodded with a clenched jaw.

A wicked cackle came from behind me, making the hairs on my neck stand.

The witch who I now called friend was terrifying as her jet-black hair floated in the air. The inky black smoke falling from her fingertips had Lorena cursing under her breath with fear and panic in her eyes. Silas and Xavier stepped aside, allowing Anya to move down the front steps, only stopping when she stood feet away from the invisible, magic barrier.

My palms turned sweaty at the sight before me. Anya's usual bright green eyes were now darkened, and she smiled so sinisterly it sent chills up my spine when she focused on Lorena. "Your magic is weak, just like its vessel," she said before turning her hands in a clockwise motion. Her usual soft-spoken voice had now turned venomous with a strong thread of power laced throughout.

I squinted my eyes and watched as she turned her hands once more before a shattering sound exploded around us. I threw my hands up over my ears which rang painfully, an echo of that initial blast.

"A fucking warning next time would be nice," Silas murmured under his breath.

Re-orienting myself, I pivoted to face Lorena and Raine, my mouth refusing to close at the sight. I vividly saw the magic of Lorena's forcefield shattered and crackling in the air surrounding the two of them before completely dispersing between us.

Without conversation.

Without hesitation.

Two realms clashed in the blink of an eye.

Chapter Thirty-Seven

Forces and magic collided as I was thrown into a battle of immortals before I reminded myself that I too was half Fae. I shoved the daggers back into my vest and drew the sword strapped to my back. The soldiers of Solaris came in droves as I saw my friends battling to protect my family. To protect a realm that was foreign to them from falling under Raine's rule.

To protect me.

My sword sliced through the air toward a male that was doing his best to injure me.

"The girl remains alive. I want her and my sister *alive*," Raine commanded while standing on the sideline with Lorena.

I was disoriented when the other side of my blade wedged between the ribs of the male advancing on me. Blood drained from my face when I realized I'd never killed someone before, and the alarm threatened to overpower me.

"Keep fighting, Amira. If not his life, the life of someone you love," Thane commanded through our channel. And I flicked my eyes to the side to see him fighting right beside me, his eyes on me while he strangled a soldier with his shadows.

I was frozen in place as I shifted my gaze to see Aravis and

Anya fighting back-to-back against ten soldiers. Their technique was flawless as they slew them with little to no effort. Raya and Xavier held their own against other soldiers, putting my anxiety at ease that I knew Raya could survive this.

The clashing of weapons rang loud as I heard Silas taunting men as him and Nova battled to end the lives of those threatening us.

My mind raced back to the present and I snapped out of the anxious stupor, re-sheathing the blood-soaked sword and retrieving the two daggers I originally held from my vest. A male charged at me with a dagger of his own, but I dropped down and make a deep slice to his Achilles tendon and watched as he toppled over. Standing up, I drove the second blade into a soldier's underjaw who had his arms open wide to brace me for capture. The bloodshed on my hands quickly became a visual engrained in my mind.

But revenge for the heartbreak and pain caused by them was a gratifying reward.

I stumbled forward with a blow to my back and turned to see a soldier standing with a long dagger still pointed in my direction, the tip of the blade bent.

The vest.

Atlas flew across the yard in the blink of an eye, ripping the soldier's head halfway from his shoulders and moving on to his next victim. A devilish grin bloomed across my face before I resumed my assault with the two daggers in hand. The grunts and groans of the opposing men falling around us was sweet music to my ears as I was flooded with the reminder of the pain and suffering they'd caused.

Unfortunately for us, we underestimated what we would be facing upon returning to Medlar as we witnessed many more soldiers from Solaris arriving via the portal Raine acquired.

Too many soldiers.

Our small group could no longer hold our ground as a large

arm wrapped around my neck, tightening and pulling me back as a dark powder was blown through the air. My arms and legs flailed to be released while I watched my friends cough and stumble when it reached their lungs. Hysteria threatened to consume me at the sight of Silas and Xavier collapsing to their knees, their faces red as they gasped for air.

The arm around my neck cut off what little oxygen I had left as the person dragged me to Raine. Dark thoughts of me failing my family, my realm, and Obsidian ran through my mind when I was thrown to the ground. I gasped and wheezed, fighting to catch my breath on all fours. When I regained my composure, I raised my head to look at the face of the bastard that manhandled me. My head spun when I saw Eryx standing above me with a look of satisfaction. His smug look fell flat while he made another attempt to read my mind.

A menacing laugh escaped me when I read the look of defeat on his face. "The new look still catches me off guard," I said, pointedly focusing on his missing eye before his foot connected to my stomach.

"Enough, you fool," Raine spat from my side and gripped my braid at the nape of my neck. My instinct was to unleash my power, but I remembered Thane's command to not let him know what I was capable of. And it was in that moment that I noticed my friends were no longer fighting.

"That damper you feel on your magic is a variant of Cryo. Curtesy of your favorite witch," Raine announced with a tilt of his head toward Lorena. "Finely crushed into a thin dust to be inhaled just enough for you to yield for the time being."

I squirmed and writhed within his hold as he jerked me to my feet and pulled a dagger from his hip.

"Kneel for her life," he demanded while pointing the dagger toward Thane. "Test me if you want Thanasis, but I will spill her blood right here. I will make her suffer, healing her to be bred and do it all over again once I have my heir."

His soulless words made me sick to my stomach.

The defeat in Thane's eyes killed all hope I tightly grasped as he treaded forward and dropped to his knees while never looking away from me. I shook my head violently. *"What are you doing? Get the fuck up."*

"I'm sorry," he said, and my hysteria kicked into overdrive.

"You made a promise. You promised me." I lost control of my emotions as fear dug its way in. He was invincible. He could not die like this. He could not die at all. I wouldn't survive.

"And I told you that it will always be you first," he replied, and I was met with a cold, hard wall against our channel. My mind began to spiral out of control when he cut of the communication between us.

Raine tossed me over to Eryx who placed me in the same hold, his arm tight around my throat as I thrashed to be released.

Raine approached Thane while the others were held down by the other soldiers. His black ropes wrapped around Thane as I reached out to speak to him through our channel and was still met with nothing but a dark void. My body fell limp when I couldn't reach him and watched in horror as Raine's hold tightened on him. Thane's shadows rose and dispersed into puffs of air, falling victim to the Cyro in his system. My eyes searched for Atlas who laid limply on his side next to the others. His big brown eyes wide with angst as he focused on Thane.

"The strongest High King kneels to save a half-blood whore. Never thought I'd see the day," Raine said before taking a fist to Thane's jaw. His blood sprayed across the cold, hard ground and my stomach caved in.

"Bring my sister to her knees as well," Raine commanded.

I threw myself forward as a soldier wrapped a rope around Raya's throat, tightening it and pulling her to the ground. Her hands pulled and scratched at the tether, but it didn't budge.

"Stop!" I screamed in terror. My stomach twisted in knots as

my gaze bounced between Raya and Thane. "*I am right here.* You got what you wanted. Let them go."

Raine didn't even acknowledge my begging as his ropes began to seep into Thane's mouth, making an exit through his nose and ears as I watched the light begin to drain from his eyes.

"I will go willingly, just please release them. *Take me, you want me,*" I cried out again as Raine turned back to survey me with brightened, white eyes. I heard the others begging for mercy in the distance. The sound of Silas and Xavier's cries as they watched their brother suffer, struggling helplessly against their captors, almost broke me.

Raine finally turned to face me, and his smile was so menacing that my breaths ceased. "I claimed you as mine and you repay me by threatening to leave me for him," he seethed. "You will watch what happens to anyone that threatens to claim you as theirs. *You* belong to me. *Your body* belongs to me. *Your life...* is mine to own."

His demeaning remarks ignite me with unexplainable wrath as heat consumed me. My skin was consumed with a burning sensation, and I wanted to claw at my clothing as I sneered in his direction. "You have me and my mother. What more do you want?" I yelled as he turned his back to me before whipping back around.

"*I want it all,*" he claimed, giving his back to me once more.

Raine raised his hands, his back arching to the point of resistance. The voices around me became dimmed and warped as my focus never left Thane. I watched in horror as his body stiffened, tears falling down my face.

No. He is immortal. Visbane or not, he is the strongest of them all.

I felt Eryx's breath at my ear as I dry heaved at the scene before me, falling limp in his hold. "I can't wait to use her again before sending her off to the reaper. The way she squirms beneath me every time is the satisfaction that I crave."

I froze in place. Every inch of me stiffened when I realized he was speaking about Raya.

The visual of his words played in my mind as shards of ice began to creep from my palms from the rage that now controlled me. And the cool, yet warm sensation flooding through my veins was too much to bear. I screamed in fury.

"That's the exact scream you did the last time you watched on when lives your cared for were slain before you," he chastised from behind me.

Memories of Millie and Ellie ran through my mind as sobs racked my body. The way they cared for me. The way they looked out for me.

The way they never betrayed me.

Raine bent down to grab Thane by the hair and pulled his head back, showcasing his throat as the tip of his blade pressed to the hallow of his throat.

"Raine," I bellowed once more.

He bared his teeth before standing upright and marching up to me, meeting the flesh of my cheek with the back of his hand. "I cannot wait to break every single one of your little friends until their bones are ash. And I'll make sure you're watching, by my side, on the throne where you fucking belong."

His hand darted out to summon and my eyes blew wide with dread when I saw Nova floating toward us. "Raine stop. I will—"

"You will do whatever I ask of you regardless," he hissed.

He placed Nova facedown onto the ground, pressing his boot to her back as hard as he could until her wings sprang outward. His large hands gripped a black wing in each, never removing his boot from her back. I shook at the visual and heard the others scream in protest. Nova slightly raised her head with tightened lips and our gazes connected. A single tear fell from her face as her body was pressed further into the dirt.

"Do not let them win," she protested through an agonizing scream.

I reached my hand out toward her as Raine groaned and began to rip her wings from her body. Another piercing cry released from her that I couldn't bear. Uncontrollably, shards of ice shot from my palms at the sound of her pain, narrowly missing Raine's head. His shock caused him to release her wings and the tightness in my chest loosened a fraction.

Time stood still as everyone realized what I'd done.

I produced two more sharp shards of ice in each palm and slammed them into Eryx's thighs, causing him to shuffle backwards.

Thane. I have to get to Thane.

But the air around me had become increasingly still. A quiet release filled my head as I felt a snap where our channel of communication once was. My mind suddenly floated through a dark void as deep as the ocean.

My heart pounded so heavily in my chest as I teetered on my feet, disoriented as I turned to find him. And in an instant, my world was turned upside down when I heard a thud. Pivoting once more in the direction of the sound, I saw Thane's motionless body on the ground.

My heart stopped beating as the heat I'd felt over time became an inferno.

The rage I felt before was now a wildfire of emotion and all rationality escaped me. The sharp breaths and pounding of my heart surged until it poured from me in licks of flames that sprayed from my palms toward Raine. He fell back from Nova and writhed on the ground in pain.

The flames continued to pour from me, spreading to any soldier in reach, burning them alive as my friends watched on, stunned and in awe.

I was blinded by the venom of my own flames as my palms splayed outward, consumed by a scorching emotion that demanded release until it was met with a cool, metal feeling extinguishing the blaze in the palm of my hand.

Thane's blade.

Gripping it, I turned and plunged the obsidian blade through Eryx's torso. My brain urged me to finish the task, but my heart pulled me to Thane's limp body and my friends in need.

Outstretching my free hand, I sent a single shard of ice through the heart of the soldier holding the rope wrapped around Raya's neck. She fell to all fours, removing the rope and gasping for air.

"This is my home. My people. *My family,*" I said while glancing over the found family that I'd come to love as my own. "And no one, will take them from me."

My anger rose further as I saw Eryx stumbling over to Raine as blood poured from his torso. I moved toward them and stumbled backwards in anger when I saw them surrounded by a puff of smoke and beamed away by two soldiers.

Every inch of me burned at the thought of them escaping. My breathing becomes ragged and fast. My lungs felt like they would be incinerated at any moment. My hands clenched so tightly around Thane's blade that my knuckles turned visibly white with rage.

As if I'd known my powers my entire life, I instinctively raised the blade to the sky. My lips curled back, baring my teeth as I glanced over the soldiers of Solaris who still had my friends in their grasp. The stillness that had taken over my body terrified me and I knew in my heart that it was the calm before a storm that I couldn't control.

I looked upwards as a swirl of fire and ice formed above and opened into a heated blast of fury. The surrounding air turned cool before it was filled with a harsh wave of heat, becoming an instant wildfire.

Satisfaction ran over me in waves as I watched the remaining soldiers fall to ash. I blinked at the control of my power. As if my flames knew my intentions, my friends were left untouched.

My legs refused to move as my people stood and rushed to Nova and Thane.

Nova fanned them away, stating that she was fine as the small tears Raine made in her wings were already healing. But the air turned thin when every gaze locked on Thane whose eyes were wide and staring up at the now bright blue sky infused with smoke. His pale skin was a heavy contrast to its usual tanned pigment.

I forced myself to swallow while whatever remaining breath in my lungs was sucked from me, my legs buckling beneath me. I dropped to my knees, releasing the blade from my grasp and crawled to him with heavy streams of tears blurring my vision.

I placed my hand over his heart and my voice broke when it was met without a single beat.

Chapter Thirty-Eight

Sobs took over as I surveyed Thane's lifeless body in my arms.

I could feel the presence of everyone else around us, but I couldn't bring my eyes to focus on anyone but him.

"Help him," I screamed with so much force my throat burned. I searched for Aravis and Anya. "Please. Please, you two have the power to—"

"We do not have the kind of power to revive a High King," Anya said through whimpers of her own. My eyes darted to Aravis who shook his head with wide eyes, disbelief consuming him.

"Fuck. Fucking hell... please," I heard Silas say from behind followed by the cries of Nova and Raya. I could hear Xavier pleading with Aravis to fix the terror that had unfolded while Atlas whimpered at Thane's side.

Thane's body was too heavy to pull into my lap as I wrapped an arm under his head and placed my hand back atop his heart. *Thane please,* I whispered into a void that used to be the channel we could communicate on.

Reality slapped me in the face, and I was forced to understand that he was gone when there was nothing on the other end. I threw my head back and screamed into the sky before dropping my forehead back down to meet his.

"I will not live this life without you. I refuse to continue this fucking battle without you. Wake the fuck up Thane," I yelled out loud. I didn't care who heard me anymore.

"I get it now Thane... I get it. Please come back to me..." I whispered. "I want the bond. I want it. I cannot do this without the man fate gave me. *I love you.*"

The silence behind me was crushing as the three words fell from my lips.

"*I said I fucking love you. Come back to me.*"

The searing hot pain that pierced my chest forced me to cry out as I released Thane and dropped next to him in agony. Nova and Raya rolled me over onto my back as I clutched the middle of my chest, the same pain blooming at the base of my neck. They attempted to sit me up, but the affliction was unbearable as I dropped back down into a fetal position, and I heard Aravis instruct them to back away from me.

I inched closer to Thane and involuntarily placed my hand back on his heart. The heat overpowered me when I felt a subtle thud under my palm and my eyes burst open.

"Is his chest rising?" Xavier asked with hope flooding his voice a few feet away.

"I believe their bond is snapping into place," Aravis announced while forcing them to back up.

I cried out in pain once more as the intense pain burst one more time in the middle of my chest and at the nape of my neck. A large gasp of air was heard next to me, and I sat up in time to see Thane open his golden eyes. Our bodies were covered in sweat and blood, but it didn't stop our embrace as I climbed into his lap.

I could hear the explosion of relief from the others as Thane and I were trapped in our own little bubble.

"You accepted the bond," Thane whispered huskily.

"You were dead and I...my heart. I never want to witness that feeling again. I never got to tell you how I feel."

A smile bloomed on his beautiful face. "Which is what exactly, Pixie?"

The hoarseness of his voice had me cupping his face with my hands. The electricity floating through me when his gaze never left mine was ethereal.

"I love you, Thane," I said confidently. "I'm yours."

Not caring who was watching, the kiss we shared turned the world back on its axis. But we were quickly pulled from our own little world when Atlas forced his head between ours and licked both of us uncontrollably. And then we were met with an abundance of questions thrown at us.

"What the fuck just happened?" Silas asked with his hands on his head.

"Amira accepting the mating bond made the two of them so powerful that it poured life back into Thanasis. The strength of their type of bond was too much even for Raine's power of death," Aravis explained in astonishment.

My hand fell to the center of my chest where I still felt the warmth. I slightly pulled my vest down to peer inside. A symbol was engraved between my breasts in black ink and my eyes snapped up to meet Thane who was holding a hand to his chest in the same area. Reaching down, I pulled the hem of his shirt up to see the same exact symbol engraved in him.

"*Soul bond*," he whispered with a lopsided smile.

My hand flew to the back of my neck and Thane's brow furrowed. Anya dropped next to me and pushed my braid out of the way to release a gasp. "She has a—"

"A binding signet mixed with..." Aravis concluded, refraining from finishing before a chuckle escaped him. "Mixed with a mark of immortality."

I ran my hand over the warm area on the back of my neck

again. Thane's eyes were wide as he rubbed the same area on his neck and blew out a breath. Panic arose as his hands fly to my shoulders, "Nothing to worry about. It's just been a long time since that has happened between mates."

I shook my head in confusion, waiting for an explanation.

"A binding signet means that you get to share this brooding bastards' powers as well," Xavier said while slapping a hand on Silas' back. "Good luck during sparring."

Thane snorted and a smile bloomed across my face when I surveyed the man that was now my mate.

"And the mark of immortality means that you're now immortal. I'm not sure what that implies with you being half Fae and half human," Anya said while studying my neck before backing away.

A surge of attraction shot through me, and Thane's eyes darkened. The look in his eyes was the same as a wolf that had been hunting for hours and finally found its meal. The feeling was mutual when I was tempted to rip off every piece of clothing that separated us regardless of who was watching.

"Are you guys seeing what I'm seeing?" Nova asked with a tilt of her head. Our gazes drifted to where she was focusing, and my mouth fell agape.

In the distance, Lorena was crawling in an attempt to vanish into the forest.

Chapter Thirty-Nine

Even at a distance, burns noticeably covered Lorena's body, preventing her from walking.

"They left her here and she's burned so badly that she can't will herself to use her magic to leave," Anya said while holding in a satisfied laugh. "You must have burned her with that blast, but it wasn't strong enough to end her unfortunately."

A small glimmer of happiness bloomed inside of me knowing that she was alive. I pulled the Obsidian blade from the ground and stood.

"Did she just pick up my sword?" Thane asked in confusion.

Silas snickered while Xavier attempted to explain. "Brother there's quite a bit you missed while you uh... were gone from us."

I reached Lorena before the others and plunged the sword through her thigh, ensuring she was pinned to the solid soil. Her wail of pain had me taking in a relieved breath before squatting down to meet her ugly, pale face. Her pale blue eyes were set ablaze when she recognized who caused her agony.

"You ripped everything away from me. And now it's my turn," I professed, removing the sword and flipping her over. She attempted to crawl backwards, but I forced the sword into the right side of her chest pinning her down again. The deep red blood that spurted from her lips brought a smile to my face.

"Y-your mother is still in Solaris. I can take you to her," she offered in an attempt for me to spare her life. My breaths become shallow as I considered her offer. Then I remembered how I got here in the first place.

A bargain.

Gripping the hilt of the sword, I pressed down and watched her seethe as I hovered my face over hers. I heard the footsteps of the others gathering around us as I took a moment to study the writhing old hag below me.

"Whatever I want in this world. I'll get it myself from here," I snarled in return.

Wrapping both of my hands around her throat while standing above her, I watched as her eyes grew wide with fear. I forced both of my powers to erupt and watched as my hands began to burn the flesh from her throat while she begged for her life.

"I begged for mercy from you once and was shunned. You deserve the same fate," I responded with venom lacing my words. Pressing my palm to her temple, I forced a long spike of ice through her skull to the other side.

Her ice blue eyes filled with the darkness of her pupil as I watched the life drain from her body. Standing and studying the woman that now lay dead, I wondered if she even had a soul to take.

I snapped back to reality when Silas barged in front of me. "Sorry, this one is definitely needed for the collection," he said before digging his thumb into Lorena's eye and removing it from the socket. He studied it in the air before walking over to Xavier and handing it off.

The action made me gag as my face scrunched up. Xavier opened the satchel strapped across his chest and threw the eyeball inside, as if their actions were a common occurrence. I squinted my eyes and shook my head at the two of them while Thane held in a laugh.

A thought clicked in my head when I remembered that witches didn't simply die so easily.

Turning back to find Anya, I rolled my lips inward when I noted her expression. She stood behind me like a proud mother of her kin when I asked what to do to ensure she never returned. Stepping forward, she bloomed a wide smile and took my hand in her palm, turning it upward and pressing her index finger in the center. "Your answer is right here, my High Queen," she said with satisfaction.

My flames.

Thane removed his blade from Lorena's chest and sheathed it before making his way next to me. Wrapping an arm around my waist and raising my arm until my hand was over her body, he pressed a kiss to the side of my head. "This is your time. Your time for revenge. It begins here," he said.

My gaze turned to him. A deep, heavy feeling sinks its claws into my chest as I shut my eyes. "We failed."

Thane squinted and pulled his face back to look at me. "We didn't fail. This war has just begun."

"War?" I questioned on a shaky breath.

"In war you fight for what you believe. And the people of Solaris deserve to be free. This world deserves to be free of those like Raine. His ruling ends now. It's time we paid Solaris a visit and bring your mother home. I'm done waiting and playing by the rules."

I was at a loss for words as I stared at him.

"Obsidian wants a committed High King. And now they've got one," he added with a hardened expression. I quickly peered at Aravis who portrayed a heavy amount of fulfillment when Thane acknowledged being a High King.

Hope found its way back in as I turned to focus back on the woman that started everything.

My body adjusted to the feeling of the flames forming in my veins, and I acknowledged the fire within me. Shortly after, bright flames flowed from my palm and set the frail body ablaze. The anger from her words and actions played in my mind and my other hand raised to send another burst, reducing her to ashes instantly.

I spun around to see everyone watching on with looks of approval and triumph.

"I'm sorry you have all suffered and had to fight because of me," I apologized with my head hung low.

"This war was brewing before you ever came into our lives," Nova said, causing me to raise my head. The looks on the others' faces agreed with her statement.

"Raine has slowly been working to infiltrate the mortal realms. Starting with your new king," Xavier spoke, sending a shiver down my spine.

His words added fuel to the fire as I looked at my surroundings.

The homes of other civilians of Medlar came into view as some peeked through their windows and doors, most likely horrified at the scenes that just played out before them. They were so blissfully unaware that immortals were now among them.

"I'm ready for whatever war is needed to bring peace to all realms."

A faint chuckle came from Thane. "We need to pay someone a visit first."

My brow furrowed at his statement, and I raised a brow, waiting for him to inform me of who we needed to meet with. He released a deep breath, crossing his arms over his chest.

"The Reaper."

<h1 style="text-align:center">Epilogue</h1>

We returned to Obsidian after giving my father a proper burial behind our cabin under his favorite tree. Anya was kind enough to mend Knox as best she could to not portray the assault he received. I couldn't bear to be the one to deliver him to his family. I'd be forever thankful for Silas who shapeshifted into a mortal from Medlar, delivering his body to his family.

My legs threatened to give out beneath me when I saw Tessa and Alix stand from the ledge of the sparring platform at my arrival. The three of us raced to each other and held an embrace much longer than necessary. I gripped Alix's face in my hands and pressed my forehead to his, acknowledging that this moment was real. My brother was alive and breathing before me.

"Lorena is dead?" Tessa asked.

I nodded my head in answer, dreading the additional information that I had to provide next. "Yes, and so is—"

"Our father," Alix finished the sentence for me.

I pulled my head back in shock. How did they know?

"Anya promised to leave this with us so we would be with you at all times. We didn't want you to know for fear of you altering your actions if you knew we were watching," Tessa explained while holding up a clear crystal orb that now mirrored us standing on the platform. I gave a playful side glare to Anya who smiled and shrugged her shoulder.

"She's a scary girl to decline a request from," Anya said with a nod toward Tessa.

"Thank you for burying him under his favorite place," Alix said, and the three of us embraced once more.

We made our way into the palace where we were met by servants demanding to take care of us. We bathed and changed into clean clothes before settling down in the dining area as servants insisted we be seated and serve us.

As we began to devour the delicious food served before us, Thane and Aravis began to discuss a plan to infiltrate Solaris. It hadn't even been twenty-four hours, and we were already discussing the plans to retrieve my mother before Raine made a move.

Tessa cleared her throat and placed her glass of wine onto the table. "So, I think we figured out the weapon that The Reaper and Knull were talking about," she exclaimed, gaining the attention of everyone who was now silent and leaning toward her. "While you were gone, Thackery um... well he—"

An exasperated breath came from Silas, earning him a glare from everyone, causing him to wince.

"Thackery made some... changes."

Laughter erupted around the table, including myself as I refocused on Tessa.

"What, does he hump everything walking now or something?" Silas inquired on a hoarse laugh. Tessa threw a glare in his direction and Raya demanded he shut up as a rumbling caused the table to shake. The servants exchanged looks and exited out the side door of the dining hall. We exchanged glances with each other while Tessa and Alix gave an excited expression.

The double wooden doors burst open, and everyone rose

from the table. A deep gasp came from Raya while she gripped the table with both hands to steady herself.

"I believe we have a realm or two to save," the tall, muscular man boasted while descending the few steps from the entryway. A wide, toothy smile spread across his handsome face.

The power exuding from him was strong, close to the feeling of Thane's.

Heads turned from the male to Raya and back. Tears fell from her face as she fought to gather her strength to remain standing while small, subtle sobs left her. The male noted her tears and his smile faltered slightly as he reached her, pulling her into an embrace and raising her off the floor.

My head spun while trying to figure out who this random male was in the palace and where Thackery was. "While I'm glad this is some sort of a reunion... we were just discussing a key point of an urgent matter. Raya who is this? And Tessa where is Thackery?"

The unknown male released a deep laugh after placing Raya back on the ground and addressing me. "That was a name given to me."

Confusion contorted everyone's faces and I spoke for us when no one else would. "We don't know your name. I'm speaking of the black cat that is... well he belongs to Anya."

The male locked eyes with Anya who was standing in a stupor before a small smile appeared on his face. He returned his attention back to Raya who raised a hand to the male's cheek and moved it to his shoulder, checking to ensure that he was real. The veins in his forearms began to glow and the men at the table started to reach for the weapons when Raya held up a hand.

Raya's voice was a barely audible whisper.

"Ezra..."

My breath got stuck in my throat, and I began to choke as pieces of information were puzzled together.

"Welp... um. There's the change Thackery had while you were

gone. Happened right when you ended Lorena," Tessa said while continuing to eat her food. My eyes averted to Alix who was sucking in his cheeks to hold in a laugh.

I placed my focus back on the male that everyone was now staring at in astonishment. He waved at everyone around the table to show that he meant no harm to anyone before returning his attention back on Raya.

"Hello, sister."

Acknowledgments

I won't talk your ears off like I did my first book. But everyone that has helped me along this journey, I love and cherish you more than you will ever know. I appreciate every single last one of you.

Thank you from the bottom of my heart!

About the Author

O'Junea Brown is an emerging author of Romantasy. This is her second published novel with many more to come. She was born and raised in the suburbs of Chicago, Illinois.

She loves her books, comics, video games, sports (go Cubs!), and anything fitness related. O'Junea has a bit too much dark humor and somewhat of a sailor's mouth, but her husband loves her the way that she is and that's all that matters.

Her baby boy Phoenix and dog Khloe are her only babies.

Follow her on Instagram and Tik Tok at @ojunea.brown

www.ingramcontent.com/pod-product-compliance
Lightning Source LLC
Chambersburg PA
CBHW030118010826

48973CB00002B/324